I0665634

SHADOW
DEVOTED

Book One of the
Shadow Divided Trilogy

By Peter Sartucci

SHADOW

DEVOTED

Book One of the Shadow Divided Trilogy

Second Edition

This is a work of fiction. All characters and events portrayed in this book are fictional, and any resemblance to real persons or incidents is purely coincidental.

Copyright 2015 by Peter E. Sartucci

All rights reserved, including the right to reproduce this book or portions thereof in any form.

ISBN: 978-1-7335745-2-5

Edited by Kier Salmon

Cover art copyright by Claire Peacey, used by permission.

Map image copyright by Rob Chansky, used by permission.

Solar system graphic by Gregory Sartucci, used by permission.

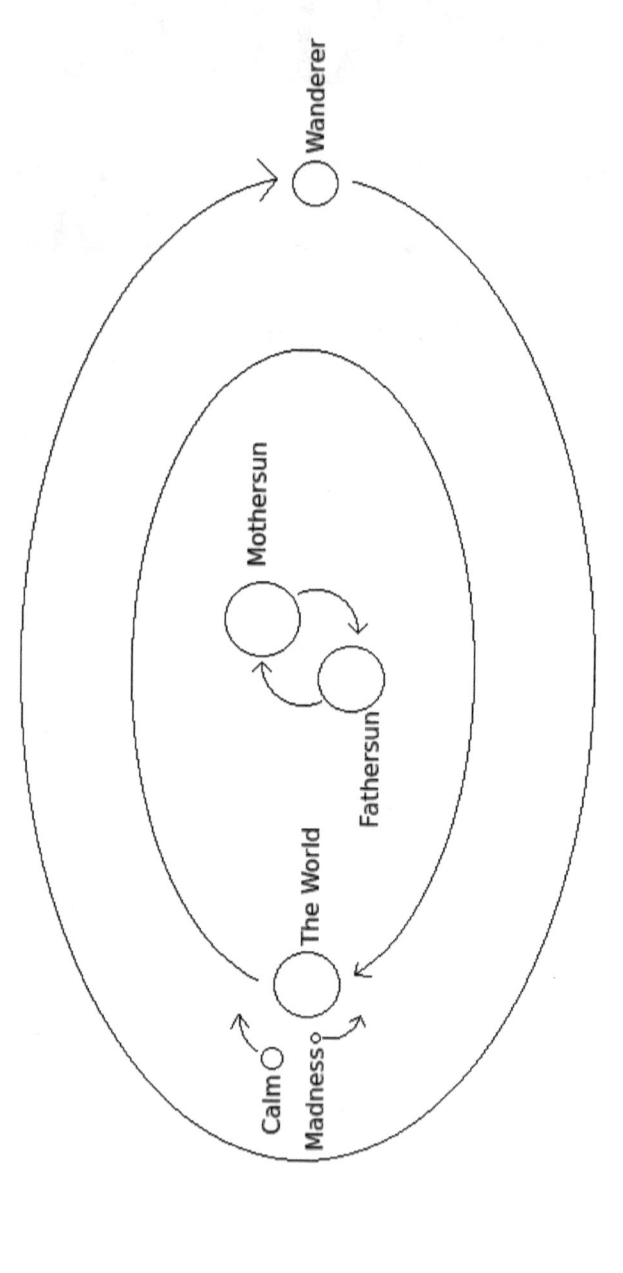

ACKNOWLEDGEMENTS

No author writes in a vacuum, we all receive help and support from countless others. I want to share a few of those names here.

To the members of my writer's group, Northern Colorado Writers Workshop, especially our late founder Ed Bryant and including Eneasz Brodski, Vivian Cathe, Rob Chansky, Marie Desjardin, Rick Friesen, Ron Hosler, Kathee Jones, Dave Kilman, Ronnie Seagren, and Pat Smyth, my grateful thanks for many hours of combing over chapters and marshalling criticism. I am a much better writer thanks to all of you.

To my First Readers, including Markus Bauer, Steve Brady, Scott Palter, and Kier Salmon. Whew! Without you this text would have been a much bigger mess.

To Kier Salmon, editor extraordinary, for imposing necessary consistency and catching bloopers that nobody else noticed. Oops! Thanks tremendously, Kier!

To Stephen M. Stirling, for encouragement when I really needed it.

To Kevin Anderson, Dave Farland, Eric Flint, and James Artemis Owen, for organizing and running 'Super Stars Writing Seminars', which taught me about the business of being a writer. If you share my writerly ambitions, you need to get yourself to Colorado Springs for the first weekend of February and join your Tribe!

To my friend Brandon Slaten, for quiet support and encouragement over years and years. There were many times when I would have given up, if not for your unwavering confidence. Thank you.

All the dumb mistakes are solely mine.

DEDICATION

To my wife Elizabeth, who tolerated endless late-night typing and weekends spent in painful plotting instead of yard work, while I labored under the lash of my muse; all my heart's love.

TABLE OF CONTENTS

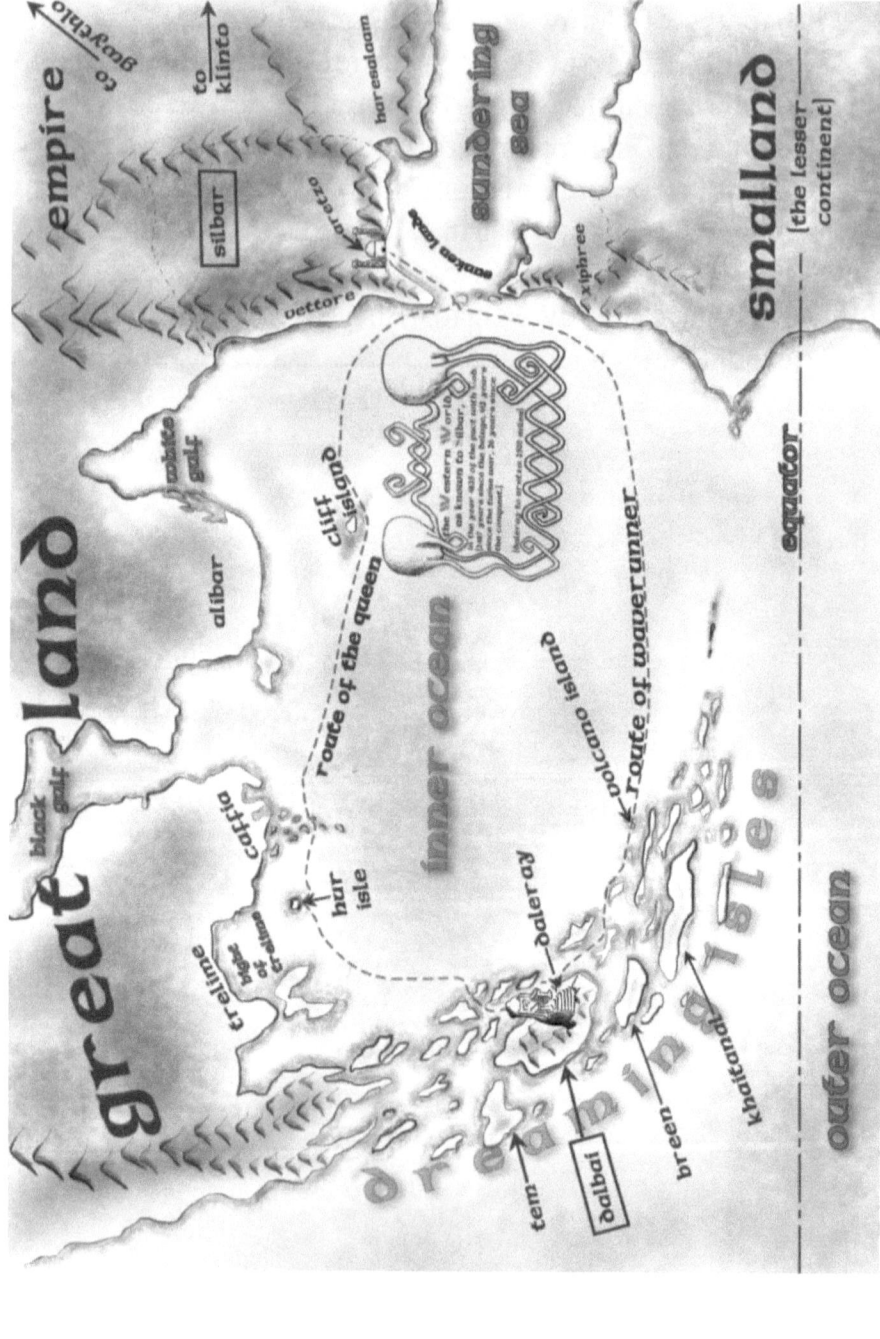

PREFACE

Before we met Callia, my brother and I were sure we knew all we needed to know about love and loyalty.

But we didn't. By all the angels and demons, we didn't.

Chapter 1: Aretzo - Kirin

Thirty-sixth day of Summer

My blood brother always gives me the dirty tasks.

That's all right. I'm good at them, better than anyone, even Penghar. When the realm needs a haunt or a shade put down, or a mage who's got too full of himself has to be humbled, I, Kirin DiUmbra, can handle it. And if it's tough, if blades come out and I get cut, Terrell's got my back — while my Shadow has the rest of me.

But when the job's done, I want to go home again, to my adopted family, and forget for a while that I've got a living Shadow inside me. Forget that I'm every mage's worst nightmare. Forget how easily I kill. Forget the souls of my dead.

I'd been home for three hours, enough to hug everybody and do some stretching and hit the trapeze again. Swooping through the air, leaping, flying with the family I love, it was heaven! I was about to dare a somersault when the voice I least wanted to hear floated into the Sulfur Serpent's Attic.

"Sir Kirin DiUmbra. Your presence is required."

I killed the momentum of my trapeze. My brother-in-law Sevan already hung upside-down from his own trapeze ready to catch me. He turned his head and scowled at the interruption. His wife nursed their youngest while various cousins and uncles and aunts and nephews and nieces stood around to cheer us on. They all turned and mirrored the scowl.

Penghar stood with one foot on the Attic floor and the other still on the stairs. In another man it might have been hesitation, with him it was probably disdain. He stared around the high-arched rafters, the worn plank floor, the rows of dormers with oiled-paper windows, the disapproving stares, and gave back one of his own. He did haughty really well.

The quiet radiance from his angelic sword didn't soften it a bit.

I dropped off my trapeze, bounced once in the net and landed on my feet in front of him.

"Baron Sir Penghar DuVerhys DiLione." I gave him his rank and all three names and a fancy bow too, loaded with enough excess courtesy so he'd know I was pissed. "What in the Nine Hells is this about?"

I'd put him at a disadvantage, so he stepped up onto the Attic floor to take back his height over me. I almost let my Shadow rise to my eyes, I was that annoyed. But that would just have tempted him to be an even bigger prick than usual.

"Your Lord requires you to attend upon him," Pen answered stiffly. "A knight of the Old Order such as you shouldn't require any more explanation than that."

He looked down his nose at me with his usual dubious gaze. Unlike his brown skin, round ears, and straight brown hair, which he shared with everyone else in the room, I am a light golden-brown like toasted wheat, with curly hair and beard blacker than night and the pointed ears of the Klinto side of the Imperial line. From the waist up, I look exactly like the Tormentor's Imps painted inside the Mother Temple. There are plenty of pious folk in Silbar who still spew bile at me over that. Terrell has told me I should be glad that Pen's disapproval is usually silent.

Glad. Hah.

I quelled my irritation, tamped my Shadow down and reached through the back of my mind. Simple as talking, I called across the miles to Terrell to demand, *What's this about

– and why didn't you just call out to me?* Only to find his mind closed to me. We had talked mentally only the day before yesterday when I reported my most recent success to him.

I didn't know whether to be annoyed or worried. Behind me, I heard Sevan dismount from his trapeze. His heels thumped the floor hard.

"Fine," I told Pen sourly. "I'll wash up and change."

I turned on my heel and walked away without waiting for his answer. Sevan followed me into the little washroom crammed into a dormer at the back of the Attic. The door had barely closed behind him when he burst out with, "Kirin, this isn't right! That damn prince can't take you away from us again so soon!"

I peeled off my tights, tossed them to him as I stepped onto the tiled patch of floor that passed for a wash-space, and dumped a bucket from the rain-barrel over my head. I said nothing while I rapidly scrubbed down with a battered chunk of sea-sponge and Sevan glowered at me. After a second bucket his face was as red as mahogany. I pulled the plug that let the water drain into a downspout and hung up the bucket.

"You could refuse him," he urged as he handed a towel to me. "You could!"

"I could," I agreed as I dried off.

Sevan gave me a long look. "But you won't. You'll go wherever, whenever, he asks you to go."

"Yes." I clawed my ink-black hair into an imitation of neatness. It would dry and curl as soon as I stepped outside.

"And you never explain why." There was hurt in his voice now.

"Because he *asks*," I said. "Prince Terrell has never once given me an order."

Silence fell between us as I finished with the towel. Silence was the price of safety for Sevan and my whole adopted family, so I endured it like a poor man endures a bad tooth.

Sevan handed me a clean pair of hose and I pulled them on while his anger ebbed. Marli, Sevan's daughter and my seven-year-old niece, slipped through the door with a perfunctory knock to bring me my best tunic and my boots. When I had put them on, she pinned my badge in place, produced my Knight's-ring and solemnly held it out.

"Uncle," she said to me as I took it. "Will you be home for supper?"

I slipped the ring on, held my fist up so that the gold and amethyst gleamed in a ray of light from the open dormer window. "I don't know. Tell your grandmother not to hold it for me."

Sevan closed his eyes and his shoulders slumped in resignation. "I'll wait up for you," he offered quietly.

"Thank you. No later than the ninth bell, all right? Your wife needs sleep too, and we both know she won't get it if you're not in the bed." I held out my hand.

He accepted my peace offering and shook hands while he nodded. "See you when you get back."

"Count on it."

Sevan's brother Attir waited in the huge high-ceilinged Attic with my belt and sword. Sevan took it from him and belted it about my waist as if defying Pen. Then I knew a familiar sorrow as my family drew back from the stranger I had become again. The acrobat, him they knew and loved. The knight . . . they didn't know him.

They didn't really know me.

I met Pen's eyes. "Let's go."

We slogged through summer's heat across the Old City and the bazaar. Most people got out of our way – no surprise, we were the two deadliest people in all of Silbar. We did step around the little kids playing ball-and-stick. We also paused for a limping old woman with a muttered "Goodwoman" from Pen and a "Grandmater" from me. But otherwise, everyone else yielded to us. Rank has its privileges, which I still wasn't quite used to.

Temples rang the second bell past noon as we strode through the Middle Court. We waded through throngs of earnest clerks and squabbling petitioners surging like tides between the granite halls of Treasury and Justice. The last echo fell silent as we flashed our rings to the stiff guards at the Inner Court gate. Behind them the many-storied palace sprawled across the lower slopes of the Hill of Sight.

All the while I wondered what was so cursed important and why Terrell didn't share it with me mind-to-mind. We had certainly talked that way plenty of times before, and I wouldn't have had to walk through stinking streets that had not known rain in three tendays.

I wouldn't have had to leave my family. Again.

When I got to Terrell's frescoed office, Pen stepped aside. Terrell immediately dragged me out the back door and up to the top of the Hill! Yes, up every damned one of those five hundred steps, he silent as a mute despite my questions. Though by the time we got to the sacred space at the top he panted so hard that I quit badgering him. He doesn't get enough exercise living in that damned pile of marble and intrigue.

Me, I hardly panted at all.

When we were high above the city and Terrell had caught his breath, he finally turned to me and burst out with it.

"Kirin, I'm getting married!"

I squinted at him through hot double sunshine, Mothersun and Fathersun both overhead. My liege lord Terrell DuRillin DiGwythlo, king of Silbar in all but title, and ruler of twenty million souls. Probably the second or third most powerful man in our world – who had shared our mother's womb with me. He looked nervous as a cat on a hot slate roof.

Yeah, a new betrothal would sure explain that. His first one hadn't gone so well.

I answered him with a thought. A surly one.

So this is why your mind has been so closed today – you were plotting with that pack of parasites in the Diplomatic Court while I was gone!

An aggravating little nod was his only answer as he gazed out over the city below us. The domes and spires of temples loomed over blocks of anonymous tenements and family courts and the walled gardens of the wealthy, all spilled down the long slope to the harbor and the shining bay beyond. I knew his damaged blue eyes couldn't actually see most of it. He had gotten that hurt saving me from the lip of Hell, a guilt that still made me squirm – today, with resentment. My squint turned into a frown and I pointedly 'thought' at him some more.

Is that really why you dragged me up these cursed steps? Just to tell me in private that you're getting hitched?

Meanwhile I bowed. Any watcher from below, like Pen, would see only me submitting to my Lord's 'orders.' I know how to put on a show.

By the Nine Hells, my whole life these days is one big show.

Terrell flushed slightly under his brown skin and ran his fingers through that startling yellow hair of his. That's always a sure sign he's really worried. My annoyance faded and I studied him more closely. His skin is a bit pale for a Silbari, not quite the walnut-color of most, but his eyes and hair are his real legacies of our Imperial Father's blood.

Me, I wasn't so lucky. Or maybe I am. Nobody would believe we're twins based on the way we look. That's probably saved our lives.

His Light was leaking out through his skin, another sign of his agitation and a reminder that I'd been away from him too long. That searing purity fills him like Shadow fills me. He wouldn't be in pain from it yet, but if something wasn't done –

Terrell. Give me your hand.

He did, extending his own in a lordly gesture that we both knew was meant for anyone watching. Though oddly enough, my Shadow sensed no mage-spells spying on us. Maybe the damned mages have gotten smarter, or cautious. I went to one knee and touched my palm to his, as callused from sword and reins as my own. For a moment we both knew again that burning intimacy as more than our minds met. I struggled to hold my sense of self apart even as my Shadow drank Light from him like a worshiper at a chalice – and my ghosts faded and disappeared for a while.

He sighed in relief, squeezed my hand back in silent gratitude before he let go and got himself back under control.

"It has taken me years to negotiate this alliance," he told me earnestly. "It was extremely difficult to find someone acceptable to the Temple and also to Osrick. But I've done it."

I snorted as I stood again. "You mean our loving half-brother didn't try to deny you a legitimate heir? That bastard would rather cut your nuts off. I mean, he thinks he had me killed; enough said, right?" Our half-brother Osrick is Emperor of Gwythlo and Silbar and Klinto and most of our continent too. There's nothing quite like having a bloody-handed tyrant in the family to fill you up with joy.

Terrell grimaced. "Yes, Osrick is — difficult, and a challenge to bargain with. I dangled the possibility of Imperial expansion done inexpensively through marriage, and he went for it. Conquest has failed him; he's got all those daughters coming along, time to try something else."

I winced a little. "Yeah, I heard about his army's latest battle-balls-up in the far East. Another defeat like that and, hell — I'll bet you gold to dung that there'll be a rebellion that'll split the whole damn Empire."

"Until Osrick drowns it in blood." Terrell's face grew bleak. "By all the Angels and Seraphs, Kirin, I swear to you it won't be Silbar that bleeds."

His promise lay between us, pregnant with the future. He never makes a promise unless he is ready to do whatever it takes to keep it. By silent consent, we both turned the conversation away.

"There aren't any words for how glad I am that I don't have to deal with him," I admitted. "Thanks for keeping me out of it."

He nodded minutely, a silent acknowledgement of what we both knew but dared not say aloud. If Osrick knew I still lived, he would descend on Silbar with every army at his command and slay and slay until I was dead at his feet, and Terrell beside me. And the Empire would shatter behind him; a quarter of the world might die before the slaughter stopped. It was no comfort at all to know the son-of-a bitch wouldn't survive a day longer than us.

I shook off my dark mood and turned to something cheerful.

"So, does this bride have a name?"

"Callia," Terrell told me shyly.

"Only the one?"

"Callia Abn Serziza."

"Aha! She's from Dalbai! The heir?"

"No, Callia's the second daughter of the Royal House; it's her sister Alliet who'll be Queen after their mother."

His coup still impressed me. Dalbai is the biggest of the Dreaming Isles, more than half the size of Silbar itself, and we cover more than a thousand miles from our northern border to the southernmost point at Cape Woe. And unlike Silbar, Dalbai is not mostly desert. But –

"Hold. I remember now. Didn't you tell me they had a war with Khaitanial while I was up north?"

He nodded. "Yes. It ended a season ago in a 'negotiated peace,' meaning neither side got what they wanted. Dalbai lost both their Crown Prince and their King in a nasty sea battle, but Khaitanial's fleet was mauled so badly that they withdrew and sued for peace."

"Ballsy of them. Way I remember it, you said they started the fight!"

He turned his palms up and shrugged. "Yes, and got their heads handed to them. But it cost Dalbai dear, and Khaitanial has six new warships under construction. Dalbai needs an ally and we need a solid trade partner in the Isles."

"And you need to be married." I said it gently, because it was true, and nothing can hurt like the truth. "Concubines are a lousy substitute. Congratulations."

He touched the silver circlet on his head, the deceptively simple crown of Silbar. One circle of plain silver with two smaller linked ones standing up from the front, and in their overlap, the thumb-sized pure amethyst that, sometimes, connects the wearer to our God. Most Silbaris feel only awe at the sight. Seven years ago, I had held its blood-warm weight in my bare hands, lighter than thistledown and heavy enough to tear the World beneath me. It is no dead piece of metal, but a live connection to the spirit that inhabits the powerful Node under our feet, a fountain of raw power welling up from deep inside our world. Touching it was much like finding the rope you had grabbed was really the tail of an elephant and it was about to crush you for your insolence. The memory still terrified me. But because of that simple Crown, he is rightfully the King of Silbar even though Osrick won't let him use the title.

He took a deep breath and let it out slowly. "I didn't really understand before I accepted the Crown, or it accepted me, but the ruler of Silbar is less free than most folk can imagine. Between the Temple Hierarchy and the Palace Staff, I am chained by tradition and protocol even in my bedroom. I can call for a woman any time my lust wants one, but I'll never be allowed to learn her real name or grow close to her. As soon as I do, the priestesses send her away, and no pleas or threats will bring her back. Dona Seraphina and the rest of the Hierarchy lecture me about love and commitment, but the only woman they'll ever let me really know will be the one I marry."

He paused a moment, then looked directly at me as his mind spoke inside mine. *You were married, and you've let me know enough about what you had —*

I almost shut him out then as an old scab tore and flooded my mind with memories. But I owed him too much for that, so I let him see it again, all the joy and the sorrow of that brief year. I only chopped off the memory when death came between Maia and me.

Yes, I thought back. *If I could ever find such happiness again, I'd grab it with both hands and never let go.*

The few times I thought — wrongly — that I *had* found it again festered bitterly at the back of my mind. The companion echo came back from him; his betrothal to Duke DiMerio's daughter Alixia had ended in a disaster from which I had barely saved him. We both still hurt to remember it.

"I understand now that I will have to build happiness," Terrell said simply. "But I think I can. Silbar will join with Dalbai in an alliance bound and sealed by marriage, if Callia is truly willing. Only I need someone I trust to help me find that out, before I —"

"Whoa!" I interrupted as I flung my hands up between us. "Are you asking what I think you're asking?"

Be my eyes, be my ears, he pleaded silently. *Let me see her face, hear her voice, touch her hand, get to know her through you, before she ever reaches this shore. Kirin, please, I am at the edge of a step from which I can't step back. After Alixia I need to *know* this will work.*

I swallowed a hard lump in my throat. Seven years I'd shared minds with him. Longer if you count the years before our Talents fully bloomed when we dreamed each other's lives and didn't know what it meant. But always I had kept him at a distance. I showed him only what I wished and denied him the rest. To deliberately share so much —

I stalled. "Why Dalbai? Couldn't you find a nice princess closer to home?"

"Because Dalbai is the key to Silbari control of the Inner Ocean. My warships control the eastern end directly, the White Gulf and the Straits, but the west —"

"The Dreaming Isles," I interrupted. "'The two-thousand-mile long archipelago that separates Inner Ocean from Outer Ocean.' See, I do remember the things you tell me."

"Yes, that we cannot control, at least not at any expense we can afford. The logistics are impossible. Our ships would spend more time sailing to and from our ports for provisions than they would spend actually patrolling. However, with a strong allied port right in the Isles, the whole balance of power changes. If I can project Silbari power all the way across the Inner Ocean, I can impose a Pax Silbari on the wars and piracy that sap everyone's wealth. Trade will expand fourfold or more, benefitting everybody —"

"I get it, Terrell, I do, you've preached at me about your politics a hundred times. But *can* you even marry a Dalbai princess? Aren't we related to their royal house even closer than we were to the DiMerios?"

"No, we're only second half-cousins. Callia's great-grandmother was a younger half-sister to our great-grandfather King Tollir XII. The consanguinity is small enough to be acceptable to the Hierarchy. Plenty of peasants marry closer than that."

"Dalbai is what, twenty-five hundred miles away? Can your mind even reach mine across that distance?"

I finally realized why he had dragged me up here when he sat on the carved stone throne set on the highest point of the Hill of Sight. Eyes closed, he summoned a power that will only serve the Crowned King. The crown on his head flared an eye-searing purple as the Hill awoke under us and a purple glow surrounded him in my eyes. Strong as a bell I heard him in my head.

I can if I use this.

Ancient magic leaked through his mental 'voice' like lamplight around a door. In forty centuries we Silbaris have learned a thing or two about harnessing our world's Power.

The wight that lives inside the Node awoke too, and the damned creature *looked* at me. Even the Shadow that lives inside me cowered before that. Thank the One God that it didn't talk to me.

So what he wanted was possible. That didn't mean I had to like it, or agree. I'd given him my fealty as a Knight and as his Left Hand. I did *not* owe him a seat inside my head.

But he hadn't given me an order. This was a plea, one that let the pain of his heart's need argue for him. Clever brother, anything else would have put my back up. Now I could feel his wistful, hungry yearning all the way down to my toes. Alexia and her cursed brother Cathghar had hurt him badly; he was scarred down deep where he lived. But still willing to try, if I would help him.

Well, damn.

"Terrell. This is a bad idea," I told him as he let the Hill fall back to sleep and opened his clouded eyes once more. "I'm sure to screw it up. But if you really want me to, I'll do it."

His smile then had all the warmth of both Suns. "I'll take the risk. Thank you, Kirin."

~ ~ ~

Chapter 2: Daleray Palace - Callia

Thirty-ninth day of Summer

Callia Abn Serziza threw up her hands. "I just said that wrong again, didn't I?" She slapped a silk pillow on the comfortable divan in frustration.

Dona Catalona DuVego Abnell, her imported language teacher, nodded. "Remember that in Silbari many words have different genders than they do in Dalbai. 'Bridge' is masculine, not feminine, and 'island' is feminine, not masculine."

"Which is all backward!" Callia jumped to her feet and paced in anxiety. Her iridescent trill-birds on their stand in the corner left off their mutual preening and fluffed up in alarm. "I'll sound like some ignorant provincial. They'll call me the barbarian Island Queen! Or barbarian Island Princess. I don't understand why the Gwythlo Emperor is so petty about Prince Terrell using his hereditary title; they are brothers! Half-brothers anyway. And a Kingdom ought to have a King even when he's the vassal of an Emperor."

"Please, your Highness," demurred the diminutive priestess as she shifted uncomfortably on her stool. "Your title will be 'queen', and no one will call you anything derogatory."

"Not to my face, no," Callia grumbled. "Just behind my back. I can hear the whispers and giggles now. 'She doesn't know how to dress! She can barely talk!'" Her voice mimicked one of the Dalbai court's more notorious gossips.

Dona Catalona failed to conceal a smile, tapped her lap-lectern with a finger and said, "You've really made quite excellent progress, your Highness. One can hardly tell you only began to learn Silbari twenty days ago."

Callia sighed. "And I spent three years learning Temish so I could marry Prince Carchem." She picked up the black-bordered miniature painted by the court's best artist and gazed sadly at the handsome young face. "I'd even started to rather like him, he was so cute while he courted me, and rather clever, for a man. Wrote superb poetry, too." She set it back down next to the larger pair for her father and brother, and conscientiously lit a scented candle in memory of the three men. "Then he had to go get himself killed by the Khaitanials like Father and Mikkal." She drooped a little at the thought and plopped down on a different set of cushions. "Oh why, why couldn't we have won that horrible battle without all three of them getting killed?"

"That is something no mere mortal can answer, Princess," Dona Catalona answered delicately as she fingered her ebony and ivory prayer beads.

Callia glanced up from her incipient brooding and said, with a slight touch of mischief, "What is that phrase you Silbaris like to use? Something about one of the heavenly pantheon and dice."

The priestess pursed her lips and answered in a voice devoid of tone. "I believe you refer to Seraph Ifni, patroness of gamblers and traders and the commoner sorts of soldiers. Her domain is the realm of Chance, and her symbol is a pair of dice. The customary phrase is 'Let Ifni roll her dice', generally spoken just before the speaker tries an act typical of the young, male, and foolish. They are the famous 'last words' of several characters in tragic ballads."

Callia leaned back on the cushions, intrigued. "So she's really a deity for young Silbari men?"

"No, she's a Minor Seraph, one of the lesser faces of the One God," Catalona corrected with barely a hint of frost, or maybe it was impatience at being diverted from the language lesson in a way that she couldn't dismiss. "Her charge is twofold; the serious student of the Writ will understand her as the embodiment of uncertainty and unknowability."

Dona Catalona could rattle on for hours about the Silbari Holy Writ, in the tongue of Dalbai as easily as in Silbari. Callia found both interest and entertainment in the stories. She composed herself for a nice long break from language lessons. Unfortunately the Silbari priestess was also clever. She switched languages at several points of her disquisition and Callia had to work to keep up. Eventually she found a chance to break from theological exposition back to the point of today's preparations.

"All right, Dona, I can cope with Silbar's religion. It's nice to know it puts women in charge of the important matters, I like that. Mother does too, I think she is happier about that than even the trade agreements Silbar has offered us. But this prince of yours that Mother wants me to marry is only half Silbari, isn't he? The other half is those pale people from the north of the Continent, the Gwythlos. Do I have to learn their holy things too?"

"No, Princess!" The priestess looked like she would have shouted it if she were not so bound by decorum. "Prince Terrell hews to his mother's ways. If it weren't for that yellow hair and his blue eyes, you'd scarcely know he's a halfblood."

Dona Catalona looked as though the last word tasted faintly off, like spoiled coconut milk. Callia thought about the lengthy messages that had flown back and forth between her mother and the Silbari ruler by message-construct for the last hundred days. She hugged a pillow.

"Hmm. I saw a Gwythlo mercenary once, his hair was red like a flower and under the sunburn he was pale as milk. A lot like a fish-belly. Is Prince Terrell's skin paler than mine?"

Catalona pursed her lips thoughtfully. "Slightly. The peoples of the Isles and of Silbar are quite similar, all more-or-less the color of a walnut. His Highness is a shade lighter."

"And is it really true that he has *yellow* hair? That's not just a metaphor?" That seemed delightfully bizarre to Callia. She wondered what it would be like to touch it, and idly stroked her own waist-long raven locks.

"Yes, yellow as a lemon, and it is very curly too."

"Is he tall?" She hoped he would be, as she'd become the tallest girl in her family and felt gawky with it. Alliet had called her 'Stork' for a few months when Callia had passed her sister's height a year ago.

"Not particularly, perhaps two or three fingers taller than you, your highness. You will not loom over him, or he over you."

Callia considered. "That could be nice. I think I will like it. He sent me a personal letter with a nice poem and a silver-and-jet image. If it is a true likeness then at least his features are regular and he does not seem to have any blemishes on his face. He's not a warrior though, is he?"

"Not a distinguished one," the priestess agreed. "Possibly by prudent choice. As you noted, his older brother His Imperial Majesty Osrick is known to be quite jealous and might take any display of prowess in arms on the part of His Highness as a personal challenge. But Prince Terrell is a very good horseman and quite energetic. He's only twenty-five years old, less than six years older than you."

"That's good," Callia decided. "I would prefer a young husband, not someone likely to leave me a widow half my life." She wondered for a moment how to phrase her next question, decided to just be blunt. "Rumors say the Silbari court provides the King with concubines. Will I still have to put up with those after my wedding?"

"Emphatically not, Highness," Dona Catalona replied evenly. "It is vital tradition that the King cleave only to his wife. There have been enough troubles with bastard offspring in the past that the Temple now goes to considerable lengths to guard against their conception. That is why he has three carefully-chosen concubines. Prince Terrell has no such bastards and will not be allowed to create any, if we can prevent it. On your marriage-day all of his concubines will be pensioned off and retired to private life. Usually most of them marry within a year, since they are regarded as prize wives. Some choose monastic orders instead and a very few have pursued other choices, as their pensions are quite generous. In any case, from your wedding day on you will have your husband's attentions solely to yourself."

Callia's aunt, Princess Gadet, hugely pregnant with her fifth child, entered the room with two maids in tow just in time to hear that last. She sniffed. "You may wish you had a couple concubines around to relieve his demands on you once you get pregnant, Callie. I get downright sick of your Uncle Yare wanting to bed me when I'm full of child, or for tendays after each birth. Though it is pleasant to have him around the rest of the time, I admit I am quite fond of 'the clouds and the rain'. But pardon my interruption; I wonder if you have seen my ivory fan? These stupid cows that your mother assigned me can't seem to find it anywhere."

"I believe you left it on the breakfast table this morning, Aunt," Callia pointed out, suppressing a stab of annoyance at the way Gadet tended to blame the long-suffering servants for everything. "It's probably still there." She knew for a fact that it was, since her mother had given orders that the servants were not to pick up after Gadet unless the princess specifically asked. But she didn't think it wise to mention that.

"Excellent! Thank you, dear. I'll be *so* glad when summer ends and this beastly heat goes away." Gadet padded out again, looking like a ship under sail. Her two maids followed with carefully blank expressions.

Callia thought about Gadet's words and reflected on the different attitudes of the Court's women towards their men. Some, like Gadet, seemed to regard men as a necessary evil, but most women seemed to quite enjoy them. The poets spoke fondly and often of love and its sibling, lust, that 'drew bees to flowers' and brought 'the clouds and the rain'.

"And Mother liked Father to be close all the time, so I probably will too," Callia finished the chain of thought aloud, and shivered a little inside in anticipation. She had had basic preparation for becoming a married woman but remained a virgin. She thought she would not mind shedding that status. Carchem had been awfully cute, and this Prince Terrell seemed to be very handsome. "Dona Catalona, is this prince – considerate – to his concubines?"

"The reports say so," the priestess sidestepped the issue. "He is also gracious to his petitioners, close with his friends, and treats his servants well. He rarely displays any temper. He may be the most equitable, or perhaps controlled, King that Silbar has had in centuries. Perhaps in response to his half-brother's, hmmm, less controlled displays."

Callia had heard stories about Emperor Osrick. "Did the Emperor really murder his brother? The other one, I mean, Terrell's twin."

"Beyond question," Catalona answered flatly. "It wasn't his hand that did the deed, Tagir the Traitor cast the spell that sank the babe's ship, but he did it at Crown Prince Osrick's command. They confessed it in Emperor Brion's court before all the assembled nobles. I've spoken to a Priestess who was there."

A vengeful smile crept over the Silbari priestess's face. "Osrick is a confessed fratricide, as well as the murderer of the babe's nurse and a crew of twenty. That is why he had to take oath before all the Imperial court that Prince Terrell would have Silbar for his own. It was that act of contrition and redemption that let Osrick succeed to the Imperium on their father's death, no matter how much he chokes on it." The smile faded. "Though the Emperor has been dangerously petty ever since."

Callia remembered how Father had remarked a few years ago that he wouldn't give the Gwythlo Empire ten more years before Osrick wrecked it with his temper tantrums; that time was almost half gone. She thought her mother would not have agreed to this marriage at all if Dalbai did not need a powerful ally so desperately.

But we do, she thought, *and I can make it happen. It is my duty. Prince Terrell does not seem like a bad choice for a husband. And I would like to have children, more than just the three Mother had. I see how much Gadet enjoys her four and how happy she is to be pregnant again. I want seven of them! A young King could give me that. And he might be exciting, too.*

But that distant threat still loomed out there in the future. If the Empire dissolved, there would be war, maybe several wars. Silbar was powerful, but not all-powerful.

In five years, she speculated, *who knows? I might end up Empress if Osrick gets himself assassinated.*

Though Mother thought it more likely the Empire would be gone and chaos take its place. Silbar had mountains to defend it and already ruled the Sundering Sea. With Dalbai shipbuilding skill and Silbari wealth, her Mother had told her, their alliance could rule three oceans as well.

But only if we mingle our bloodlines with theirs. Nothing less will endure that storm. There isn't a safer choice for my hoped-for children than that.

She sighed and told herself, '*Let Ifni roll her dice.' It is already decided anyway; soon there will be ships on the way to collect me and my dowry. Our Royal Shipyard launched the* Queen of the Seas *two days ago and has already laid the keel of another that will be her twin. The Scroll of Events will unroll regardless of what I want. All I can do is make the best of it.*

She suppressed a stab of resentment. She had never really expected life to be otherwise. A princess learned early just how little control she had over her fate. But it would have been nice if life had been a little more like a romantic ballad . . .

~ ~ ~

Chapter 3: Aretzo - Kirin

Thirty-sixth day of Summer

"Thank you, Kirin," Terrell said to me, and I knew I was committed now.

Terrell and I walked down the five hundred steps side by side, back to the Palace, without another word. The guards at the Hill Door rapped their ceremonial (but perfectly sharp) spears on the pavement as we entered and the courtiers surrounded and fawned over us. Silbar's aristocracy doesn't know I'm Terrell's lost twin, thought dead for so long. They just think I'm some bastard halfbreed acrobat from the Sump jumped into a Knighthood by royal whim.

But they all know why I'm his Left Hand. They've all seen my Shadow.

"Sir DiUmbra has agreed to accept my commission," Terrell told them as he continued his stately walk right through the pack without a pause. His royal fingers speared out and identified the handful that had actual work to do. "Milord Exchequer, Milord Admiral, Milord Archmage, and Milord Secretary, please arrange the necessary."

He's always polite and rarely even uses harsh language, but they all scurry to do his bidding as if he lopped off heads regularly. Given the way Osrick behaves, I guess that's no surprise. No, I'm being cynical again. Terrell's a man they're glad to serve.

Most of the time I am too.

Pen reattached himself to his usual place at Terrell's right hand. I stood still and resisted the temptation to sigh in relief as the rest of the pack followed Terrell away. Then I looked at Terrell's Secretary and newest rising star, Gellir DuTallisen DiMaratini, one of the Old Hundred families that had served Silbar for generations. He had typical brown hair above his brown eyes and brown skin, and round ears, the lucky man. Barely half a year younger than us, ambitious and capable, he also boasted a wicked sense of humor that both Terrell and I treasured. Even though he's a Baron's son, I liked Gellir better than any other denizen of the Diplomatic Court. But I tried not to let it show; my approval would do him no favors.

Gellir had a twinkle in his eyes as he addressed me, all suitably formal, but after he got the honorifics out of the way he dropped into the casual speech of equals. Lord Snowdon the Exchequer looked like he'd bitten his lip at the presumption and Archmage Cervisi twitched.

"The latest message construct arrived this morning with Dalbai's formal acceptance. We have sixty days to send a ship to fetch Princess Callia, sixty more to get back, and another twenty to prepare for the wedding. Milord Admiral DiRovigo tells me he can have your escort ready to sail in four days."

The Admiral grunted a noise that passed for assent.

Gellir continued "His Highness has tasked me to supervise the arrangements, though of course Duchess DiCerrai and Dona Seraphina will handle the actual decisions about the wedding. I'll just do whatever they tell me to!" His grin flashed.

I winced a little at that. A few years ago Duke DiCerrai-Swansea, the younger son of one of my Imperial Father's sisters, had jumped to the conclusion that I had to be his bastard son, a rumor which Terrell still subtly encouraged. I wouldn't have minded if it had been true. I admired the man — one of the few Gwythlos I could say that about — and genuinely liked his eldest son and heir Alain. I did favors for the family now and then to keep up the illusion, though the lie shamed me in ways I couldn't admit to anyone but Terrell. That Duchess DiCerrai, who was by birth our mother's cousin and our nearest living female relative, seemed to honestly like me too, only made it all hurt more.

Gellir nodded in misunderstanding. "Don't worry, I'll handle the groom's side of the actual ceremony, and your cues will be very simple."

"Wait. I'm expected to *participate* in this show?" I couldn't keep the horror out of my voice.

All four of them nodded. "Of course," Gellir answered with a faintly surprised air. "Socially, His Highness simply must have his Right and Left Hands at his side for the wedding ceremony, and the politics most certainly require it. All the aristocracy will be there and representatives of every realm in or near the Empire. He has to show a glimpse of the mailed fist to them even as he surrenders his heart to his bride. What better way to do that than to have the two individuals who are popularly regarded as emissaries of Light and Dark both standing by at his bidding?"

I kneaded my forehead with both hands and said "Gah!" even as I sent a barbed thought after my twin. *You sneaky bastard!*

His thought came back too swiftly; he'd been ready for me. *It's an old Silbari tradition, Kirin, and I of all people can't very well defy tradition. Don't worry, you'll do fine. You only have ten words to say.*

I repeated "Gah!" for both him and Gellir, shook my head and said "Okay, we can argue about that later. I have four days to get ready to go, right?"

"And they'll be rather busy days at that," Urhys Snowdon the Kingdom Exchequer sniffed in his Gwythlo-accented Silbari. He waved fish-belly pale hands at me, mottled with ink stains, and nodded his blond head. His eyes wandered with disapproval over my clothes. I'd finally gotten my good tunic and hose worn enough to be comfortable. "I've commissioned new ambassadorial garb by His Highness' command, which includes a wedding set that will have to be tailored to you. All funded by the Treasury." He looked like that gave him heartburn. "In addition, you'll be supplied with gifts for the Dalbai court. And an expenses budget, quite a generous one, I might add." I could practically see him mourn for the hole the wedding would put in the Treasury.

"So I get to hand out gifts? That could be fun," I teased him, though I knew he had a nose for fraud and chicanery that had saved the Treasury millions of gold royals. Terrell had told me Snowdon's hard work was critical to the realm's solvency every year when it came time to pay Osrick the bribe, excuse me, tribute.

"This alliance is Silbar's biggest gift to Dalbai," Admiral DiRovigo growled. Snowdon's opposite in appearance, walnut-skinned and brown-haired, brown-eyed, he was as short and broad as a bale of cotton. Put him in a loincloth and drop him in any farm field in Silbar and he'd look right at home. Except for the peg leg, perhaps, or the absent left hand. I'd heard that he'd barely survived the Conquest when my Imperial grandfather took Silbar into his Empire by sword and traitorous magery. Then DiRovigo had been a second officer who led the rescue of a thousand sailors while ships burned around and under him during the final assault. Now he sent a new generation out into the seas of the World with Silbar's silver-and-purple flag flying below the Empire's red banner. If that galled his soul he never spoke of it in Terrell's hearing, or mine. That was probably wise, though if he knew the plans my brother had shared with me, he'd dance with joy. He needed to live another decade to see it all come together, but until then we didn't dare tell him. Sometimes I felt bad about that.

DiRovigo continued in a gravelly voice. "The dowry they've pledged to send is worth forty thousand pounds of our silver, maybe fifty thousand. The Queen of Dalbai will give us their fastest, and newest, warship. She's bigger than anything we've ever built and has a sail plan like nothing our admiralty's ever seen. If she isn't worth at least three of ours in a fight, I'll eat my hat. We'll gain advantage over every fleet east of Cape Woe the moment we look her over. And she's a personal possession of the bride, so the Emperor can't try to steal the ship away from us." His face lit in what I bet was the closest thing to a smile that he'd shown in decades. "Two years for our shipwrights to learn from her and we'll turn the whole Sundering Sea into Silbar's harbor. Five more years and our Navy will rule every wave from the Perfumed Coast and the Gates of Xir to Khaitanial and the Black Gulf."

"And Osrick's Navy will just love that," I said drily. "The Klinto slavers will be ecstatic too." Not that I had the slightest pity for those murderous bastards. "Wait, do the Klintos even know about this marriage yet?"

"Right now nobody in Silbar 'knows' but His Highness and the five of us,' Gellir answered cheerfully. "The Temple's Circle only approved it three days ago and the Hierarch signed the approval the day before yesterday. His Highness only signed the final commitment a few hours ago. We won't make the official announcement until tomorrow and the word probably won't reach Klinto for two days more, even by message construct. I think all four of us have been careful of stray words. As careful as we could be, anyway."

Urk. Two can keep a secret, if one of them is dead, but four? Or eight, or twenty-four, depending on how you counted the priestesses? No way.

"Salim's Tail!" I blurted as the realization hit. "Everyone who stands to lose from this alliance will be out to scuttle the marriage before I get there! By the Nine Hells, right up to the moment of the wedding!"

"Yes, this will draw the world's attention to our Dalbai embassy in general and you in particular, Sir DiUmbra," said

Aytin D'Ivor Cervisi, Archmage of Silbar. Dark as DiRovigo but thin and willowy compared to the Admiral's squat immovability, Cervisi could never quite hide how much I made his skin crawl. Like any high-skilled Mage he wore layers of spells that enfolded him closer than his mage robes, and heavier than his silver chain of office. Usually they rippled around him for yards in every direction, unless I came near. Right now Aytin had most of his aura drawn in as tight as a corpse-wrapping so as not to lose any of his jealously hoarded Power to me. "I'm still taking thought for whom we can send along to provide sorcerous protection, but, ah, your reputation will lend considerable weight to any shelter that the Mage Guild can offer. So long as you don't mind working with us?"

He put just a slight emphasis on the 'with.' His spells flickered and pulsed in worry and I had to tamp my Shadow down to make sure it didn't go for them.

I passed up the temptation to rub my forehead again in favor of wishing I could pound it against a wall. A hard stone one with a rough finish.

"Of course I don't mind, Archmage," I lied; I'd rather sleep with snakes. In a lower tone I added "Just don't stick me with some thumb-fingered apprentices who can't light a candle without setting their own hair on fire."

"Gentlemen," interrupted Penghar's baritone voice, "I beg your pardons but I require Sir DiUmbra's attention for a while. Privately."

It says much that I was actually glad to see him this time. I managed halfway-polite nods and farewells and yes-I'll-see-you-laters to the other four.

Pen waited stolidly while they moved off into the palace, and then said "Will you walk with me for a few minutes, Sir DiUmbra?"

"Pen, I'm too rattled for good manners right now, but damn *yes* I'll walk with you as long as it's away from here."

I let him lead me back out onto the Hill of Sight and the guards rapped their spears again. We two had the right to go anywhere in the Palace at will, the only two men in all Silbar to whom Terrell had given that privilege. I eyed the long stair and added, "Just not up five hundred steps again, damnit!"

He actually chuckled. "I wonder whether Terrell would be annoyed or amused if I did that? He sent me back to give you time to settle down and get used to this mission."

Instead of the long flight he followed a level path eastward around the curve of the Hill's steep slope. The paved walk led through acres of wildflowers – trees won't grow on the Hill of Sight – to a fancy pergola perched on the wall that surrounds the giant cone. Hundreds of years ago the toe of the slope had been cut away and then walled up thirty feet high, with the leftover dirt spread out to make a giant crescent around the Hill's north side. We looked down into and over the vast cemetery that occupies that crescent and spreads like a stony skirt around half of the Hill. Through the blue glow of the wall-wards I gazed unseeing over the mausoleums of the nobles. Maia's plot lay much farther around, by the edge of the Poor Field. I went there once a year in the dark after Remembrance Day to torment myself over what I'd lost, but today was not that day. My ghosts stirred in the back of my mind and I ruthlessly quelled them.

Pen sat easily on a backless bench and shifted his sword Irreneetha so she wouldn't catch on the stone. The move was so natural he probably wasn't even aware of it anymore. I couldn't sit still. The excess Light that my Shadow had drunk from Terrell made me restless. So I paced instead, in and out of the pergola's doubled shadow. Both suns were high overhead. White Mothersun still led but red Fathersun trailed ever closer to her as he waxed toward Passing. In a little more than sixty days they would trade places and begin the long slide toward the end of autumn as warm Mother waned and cool Father led us toward winter.

"Angels and Demons, Pen!" I burst out. "Why didn't he have you do this?" I could have asked Terrell himself the same question with a thought, but I could tell he'd begun an audience with a mob of petitioners. He hated to be disturbed while he tried to give people his undivided attention; he always said they deserved no less from their King. (Pardon me, their Prince, mustn't let Osrick think we're uppity disobedient subjects, oh no!) Even if the petitioners were more boring than a carpenter's auger.

Pen contemplated me as I paced to and fro. My Shadow leaked out, I could feel it trail in viscous wraiths behind me, but I didn't care. Pen knows what I am, or thinks he does.

"I thought I was the logical choice," he admitted. "But he chose you instead, and after a little more thought I realized he needed something from this ambassador that I can't give him."

Pen doesn't know the truth about me, exactly, but he must suspect by now that I'm not just an acrobat born of the gutters. Not originally. The secret Terrell and I daren't speak aloud lay heavily between Pen and me in that moment. I stopped in front of a mosaic that covered one wall of the pergola, and then twitched as I realized what it was. Tales of twins who can speak mind-to-mind have haunted Silbar for centuries. The one before me showed Princes Azerin and Zablok, who tore the Kingdom apart and left a rip across the heart of the Valley that now forms a fifty-mile lake.

I could become such a legend.

It would be so easy. If I gave free reign to what lives inside me, I could leave a trail of horror across my country that would put all of Silbar's tortured past to shame. But I have enough problems being thought a soldier's by-blow, even a soldier who's now a Duke. And if Osrick ever suspected that I wasn't dead, well. All the Shadows in the world couldn't save me from his army of fears.

Quietly Pen went on. "Terrell needs so much, Kirin, and is allowed so little choice. And I cannot help him in this, for I've never been and will never be a husband." His hand caressed Irrenetha's hilt and I shuddered as, just for a moment, the angel inside the sword manifested in the air between us. An instant later She vanished, but the image of Her face still burned into my mind.

I have never known what to say to Her. After seven years I can barely face those eyes that see through all disguise right into my soul. I often wonder why She doesn't burn me to ashes. She *must* see the nightmare that lives under my heart, hateful and hungry and afraid of little else in this world but Her and her ilk. She cuts stone like butter, spells like air. I'm sure I would be no challenge for Her. But then, I'm never alone, and my fear makes my Shadow stronger.

"You're more married than I ever was." I gestured blindly and rags of Shadow peeled from my fingers as they fled Irreneetha's too-close presence to bury themselves in my chest. Her Light agitates and hurts it. Strange; it never reacts like that to Terrell's Light.

Pen's eyes followed those black rags. Once that sight would have made him draw and threaten me with live steel, now he only blinked thoughtfully. "No," he said. "This bee will know no flowers. I gave myself to Her before my own lust could develop, and now no human woman's touch can move me. But they move Terrell, and they move you. You understand, in the way that I cannot. You can help him."

He paused, looked at me hard and his voice got stern. "If you're truly willing."

"'Truly willing'? You –!" I rounded on him, furious over how I was being manipulated and wanting to hurt him, with words at least. "You expect me to pimp for him? Seduce this princess and see if she's good enough in bed for a king? You want me to do what you can't, you limp-rod holier-than-thou asshole!?"

"No! That would be a betrayal!" He frowned at me as if he thought I was actually capable of it.

"Betrayal!" The word was more bitter than a mug of wormwood. "All these years, all I've given up for him and you still think that of me?"

For a moment we glared at each other, his hand on his sword and my hands clenched into fists so tight they hurt. The old urge to punch his perfect teeth in welled up in me and the suns were suddenly cold as my Shadow unfurled about me.

We faced each other, Darkness and Light between us like blade and shield, and a ravenous ache shot from my head to my heels and back. I could kill him, sword or no sword. I didn't even need to touch him. The sick lust for his blood-power surged through me as Gerlach's ghost awoke. Urged me to just reach out and take –

"It pushes at you, doesn't it?" Pen said softly. He let go of his sword hilt and held out empty hands to me. "Tries to rule you as well as ride you. Don't give in to it, Kirin."

Empty hands, in the face of me with my Shadow uncloaked. He didn't understand at all, and still his courage stole my anger away and shamed me down to my boots. Irreneetha chimed a single note soft as a baby's sigh and strong as a typhoon. She must know what a ghost-ridden monster I really am . . .

"*Damn* you," I groaned, "For testing me like this. Do you think I'll never fail?"

I swayed dizzily as I wrestled with the treacherous thing inside me. Finger by finger I unclenched my fists even as my blood still shouted for a fight. I stumbled into the pergola's shade, clutched my Shadow about me, and trembled as my blood-song gradually grew quiet again. My victims are but ghosts, they have no power, I told myself.

Except to suggest . . .

In a calm voice Pen went on, "I expect you to exercise the judgment and good sense that I have learned you are capable of, Kirin. And thus find out what he needs to know. Is she willing to become his wife in deed as well as name, take her place in the pageant of time and give Silbar another generation of kings? To give him sons and daughters and teach them to fulfill their duty and to love their father's homeland? To walk the path two hundred Queens have followed before her?"

"It's not fair," I grumbled. "You're supposed to be the arrogant prick, not the one who talks sense. I don't know what to do when you jabber like a wise man. That's supposed to be my role in this play, damn you. You're stealing my act!"

He grinned then. "I don't know how to follow an acrobat's script. And it's past time you left behind your net, your trapeze, and your tightrope. You're a true knight now who acts on the stage of kings, not a youth in a show. Time to get used to new cues."

"Terrell put you up to saying that?"

"No. Hard as you may find it to believe, I do occasionally have thoughts of my own." He waited.

I pressed my face to the cool stone, quelled the unruly Shadow within me. Its outer rags sank back through my skin and gathered once more under my heart. Quiet, until the next time. There's always a next time when you carry your dead inside you.

"Alright already," I sighed. "I'll quit whining. I already said I'd do it. I'll probably screw it up, but I will do it. And after the wedding's over, when we leave the stage, I will trip you so you fall flat on your face."

He arched one perfect eyebrow at me. "Thanks for the warning. I'll watch for it."

"Ha," I said blackly. "Now excuse me, Sir Penghar, but I have to go find Lord Snowdon's tailors. The thumb-fingered sons-of-sows'll probably stick me with pins and choke me with measuring strings. I hope their shop's nearby."

"They're already here. I'll show you to the room. His Highness ordered them summoned just before you two started up the five hundred steps."

"Terrell – what? He already knew I'd accept? Son of a bitch!" I growled, and then felt ashamed.

Even though I never knew her, I really shouldn't talk about my mother like that.

~ ~ ~

Chapter 4: Aretzo - Kirin, Zartos

Thirty-sixth day of Summer

Both suns were low in the west by the time I finally returned to my room in the Sulphur Serpent Inn. Sevan Sule DiUmbra, brother to my dead Maia, and his brother Attir and cousin Habbir in the DiUmbra Acrobatic Troupe, came from their own rooms and gathered around me.

"How soon is *he*," Sevan didn't like to refer to Terrell by title or name if he could avoid it, "Gonna send you away again?" He rocked his baby son in his big strong arms even as he stared at me with mingled anger and worry.

"In four days," I answered shortly as I peeled out of my worn formal tunic. Attir handed me a cloth he'd wetted from the water pitcher on my wash stand and I gratefully mopped my face and chest. "I'll travel by ship."

"You've barely been back half a day," Habbir chimed in as he hung up my tunic for me. "It's not right. He shouldn't take you away from us again so soon."

I pulled off my knight's ring, held it up where they all could see it. The gold and amethyst winked in the suns' light that slanted through my open shutters. We were four stories above the courtyard here and I could see the distant Bright Mountains. Both suns poised above their toothed ridges.

"I swore an oath. I took his salt and his silver. Willingly, nobody made me do it. When he calls, I have to answer." I dropped the ring into a drawer and shut it firmly, for a few days.

I didn't add *You were all happy enough to have the money still come in while I was away*. It would have been unfair, since they'd have me back full time in the troupe in the beat of a bird's wing and wouldn't care if doing without my Knight's salary meant the family ate meat once a season instead of thrice a tenday, so long as I was with them. In some pocket of my heart, I felt the same even as I knew it could never be so again.

I know who I am now. I've known for seven long years.

"Enough, don't badger the poor man," Sevan's wife Carlai scolded them as she collected her youngest son out of her husband's arms. Her dancer's body hadn't lost much tone from bearing her third child and nursing only added to her impressive gifts. "You've got four days to work him back into passable shape, so stop pestering him over what he can't change and get to it."

"Whoa now, it's not like I didn't work plenty hard on my last mission," I protested. "See?" I posed and flexed for her and sneered at my elder brother-in-law as I grasped at the frayed edge of the rough camaraderie we'd shared for so long.

"Ha," Sevan sneered back and prodded my belly muscles impersonally. "Only a little flabby, I'll grant. Four days *might* be enough, if we work you without mercy."

"Then put aside the chatter," a new voice interrupted. "You four go help get the Attic ready for practice. Kirin will be along soon as I'm done with him."

Sevan's father, Sevan-the-elder, the leader of the Troupe now that his own father was under the cemetery turf, strode in. He had his four-year-old grandson piggyback. He set the boy down and shooed him out of my room with the others, then firmly shut the door behind them. Then he took his turn to study me with a critical eye.

I'm sure he saw the forced happiness leak out of my face.

35

"Magister," I said formally as I entitled him as the leader of the Troupe. I put my palms together to bow my head over them. "I'm glad to see you again. It was a long season to be away. I'm sorry I had to leave without warning you beforehand, and sorrier still that today I ran out to see the prince before you got back from the Guild House."

He dismissed that with a gesture. "Nothing to be sorry about. You're here now, son-in-law. Have you forgotten how to call me Papa?"

"No – Papa – but . . ." I trailed off and struggled to find the right words. "I'm not – I'm no longer – I . . ."

"Let me see if I can make it easier for you, Kirin." He reached out and gently took my head in his big strong hands as he had done when I was a child who needed instruction, pulled me close and leaned his forehead against mine. He whispered, "You have grown, husband-of-my-daughter. It has been years since you were the head-over-heels-in-love bridegroom that made me so proud, even though my own father raged at you so unjustly. Longer since you were that scared little boy my brother found in the gutters and brought home. You are still a joy to watch on the ropes and the bar, and when you dance I can still see my Maia dance with you."

He let my head go as I choked in a breath. My chest went tight and my eyes burned. If he knew of the monsters I carry inside me, would he still love me? I want to believe the answer is yes.

"But you are no longer merely an acrobat, even a very good one," he sighed. "And I have nothing I can teach you about your new path."

I clenched my hands, then folded them into a cup and filled it with Shadow where he could see. "You never called me Demon, or even Imp, Papa. And you always defended me, even during the hard times. I am so very grateful for that."

"Because I knew you were not Darkness' slave, but its master." He fearlessly dipped one thick index finger right into my Shadow and prodded my hand beneath. "You have been given a mighty Talent, one that I do not understand, perhaps cannot understand. So be it. Now you have mastered it, at least to journeyman status. And that means I must let you, who I have loved as one of my own sons, go as you will, where you will, when you will. Blessed be the Name of the One. I am not yet so great a fool that I cannot see the will of my God when it is writ man-tall before me!"

I opened my hands and let the Shadow drain back inside me. "I have no idea what will happen, Papa. On this trip, or after it."

He smiled at me kindly. "None of us ever do, Kirin. We can only do what we can do, and then a little more. Now, your brothers and cousins await. Get yourself upstairs and to work."

~ ~ ~

In a wealthy part of Aretzo, Dameon Zurtos of Xiphree, hidden beneath nondescript robe and hood, used a magic key to enter a brass-studded door in a high wall. Ensorcelled silver flashed in the moonlight, and then brass gleamed once more as the door closed.

He knew that Kirin DiUmbra had climbed over that wall a year ago, desperate to rescue his brother Sevan from the carefully-cultivated madness of Cathghar D'Ivor DiMerio. Zurtos jaw set as he remembered the days of effort he had spent on slowly leading the arrogant young Cathghar into the temptation of the blood-path. The burnt ruins inside the garden were witness to his failure. Not only had DiUmbra saved his brother-in-law and seven other almost-victims, but he had killed the royal betrothal that should have lead to Terrell's murder and a Silbari civil war that would have profited Xiphree greatly.

Instead, nothing! brooded Zurtos as he strode through the overgrown shrubbery.

Two others waited in the unkempt garden where jasmine perfumed the air and a nightjar sang atop a palm tree. The walls of the charred DiMerio mansion loomed above. A black cat stalking a mouse through the rubble froze into stillness at the intrusion, but Zurtos ignored it. A sliver of the Moon of Madness crept across the sky.

"He has decided," the messenger whispered to Zurtos and the other after making a hurried little bow. "The alliance will happen exactly as you feared."

"A disaster for our interests," grunted Zurtos. He kicked a crumbled bit of wall with an elegant black leather boot and dislodged more stucco.

The short woman swathed in veil and hooded robe shifted slightly on the rim of an empty fountain. No hint of skin could be seen but her voice was Silbari-accented. Zurtos knew perfectly well who she really was and thought her disguise a threadbare sham, one that he was done supporting.

"Yet we still have those in play who will do our bidding, if led carefully," she declared. "And that means there is still a chance to salvage victory."

The mage nodded and white teeth showed in a vulpine smile. "For if this marriage fails!"

"We have limited opportunities, Zurtos," the woman warned. "And *he* is not vulnerable to any spell either of us can cast."

"You need not remind me, *Dona Meltha*," he growled, discarding her pretense with visible annoyance. "I know it too well already. But he'll be 'vulnerable' to a knife under the ribs, I'll wager. My man can manage the thrust, we just need to know when and where to strike. When is he likely to walk alone? Where will he go over the next few days?"

The messenger looked from one to the other, discommoded by the mage's abrupt revelation, but at a calming gesture from the woman he spoke of a tailor shop and a set of clothes.

Zurtos smiled. "Perfect. Two days, plenty of time. But clearing this one piece from the board, satisfying as it will be, won't prevent this alliance. More will have to die, and not just here in Silbar."

"Take the most dangerous piece first, and the rest will be easier," insisted Dona Meltha. "There is time to reach Dalbai before this escort can arrive, if other allies can be brought into play. The Prince has disappointingly great faith in his pet Shadow. Curing that fault is as important as scuttling the alliance."

Zurtos favored her with a sour look and jerked a thumb at the ruin. "Did you learn nothing from your last blunder?"

"You mean *our* blunder, for which I paid in blood, never forget! While you escaped entirely because of my protection."

Zurtos waved that away. "That was then, this is now. You set priorities unwisely, which means you conceal some of your goals from me again."

"As do you!" she retorted. "Neither of us has complete freedom of action. But our needs run together in this."

"Truth." Zurtos conceded. "Very well, the halfbreed knight first. And then the Princess? I'll need a fast ship to reach Dalbai in time."

"You will have one," Meltha promised.

"Good. Do we know what force they will send, who will ward it? And what preparations are being made in Dalbai? Your Prince is no fool; he will have more than one string to his bow."

The messenger nodded. "I will find out," he promised.

"Do so, but remember," added the seated woman. "We can afford no mistakes, not when we deal with *him*." Loathing dripped from the last word. "You must not be caught."

"I will not forget," the messenger replied with a bow to her. "I shall be careful."

The mage grunted. "See that you are, else all our lives are forfeit."

The three parted and each left the garden by a different route.

~ ~ ~

Meanwhile the black cat resumed her stalk, pounced, and carried off her meal. The nightjar sang on alone in the ruined DiMerio garden, as Aretzo's multitudes slept and Madness slowly waxed.

And in another part of the city, hours later, the black cat leaped onto a garden wall where spells ran thick and deadly. Recognized, the cat was allowed to pass through without harm. Soon a window opened and the cat slipped inside. Hands whiter than moonlight offered a dish of milk and then some welcome petting.

"Come, my little darling, share with me what you've seen tonight," the woman with the pale hands purred.

~ ~ ~

Mage Dameon Zurtos of Xiphree made his way back through nighttime Aretzo to the private rooms he'd taken in the Old City. He had years of practice disguising himself as a minor Silbari mage, moving unnoticed through the dark streets with a little magelight that was enough to warn footpads away from him. Though Aretzo seemed increasingly bereft of such vermin these days. It was disappointing to see Xiphree's great enemy growing more competent.

His slave Jos admitted him to the warded rooms where a single candle flickered.

"Did your efforts bear fruit, Master?" Jos asked hopefully.

Zurtos shook his head moodily. "Some possibilities, but I've learned of added danger too. This young halfbreed Prince threatens to make an alliance that will put Xiphree at an even worse disadvantage than we face now. It must not be allowed."

"Does that mean we will leave soon?"

"Soon, yes, but first the wretched witch demands I carry out her vengeance on the one who defeated my hopes last time." Zurtos scowled.

Jos' dark face grew puzzled. "But Master, is that not a good thing for you?"

Zurtos snorted. "You mean, is it personally gratifying to slay an enemy who has frustrated me before? Of course it is, though doing so at her behest steals much of the savor. I am more annoyed that she makes this a priority over the true danger, the marriage alliance. But I have a season yet before that danger comes ripe, so, I can indulge her and myself at the same time."

"Shall I sharpen a knife, Master?"

"Perhaps . . . not yet. This enemy is very dangerous, possibly more so than any you have yet faced, and you are valuable to me."

Jos looked both disappointed and proud. Zurtos glanced at the covered cage in the room's darkest corner.

"Has my new pet fed today?"

Jos shook his head. "No, master, I had planned to feed it in the early morning to help it sleep through tomorrow."

"Good. Bring it with us. We're going for a little walk."

"Understood, Master." Jos' teeth gleamed in the darkness.

Two hours later they were on the Serpentine beneath the towering walls of the Sulfur Serpent Inn. The tavern had closed and the kitchen workers were dumping the garbage into a pig pen next to the back door. Zurtos had cast a concealment spell over the two of them but those were chancy things best not tested much. He waited patiently in the building's shadow until the last worker had trudged off to bed.

Almost all of the windows on the outside wall were dark. Candles were expensive and most city dwellers went to bed with the suns. When the building had been quiet for a while he spelled a gate open and led Jos through the adjacent stables and around to a side door opening into the courtyard between the two buildings. There were at least half-a-dozen watching spells on the inn, some of them mobile, but most of them were the close-in type that could be fooled if you kept your distance and were good at counter spells.

Zurtos grinned without revealing his teeth. He knew he was *very* good at a dozen magic specialties, counter spells not the least of them.

A fountain burbled quietly but he ignored it, sticking to the shadow of the stables' door as he craned his neck to study the inner wall of the inn. He was guessing, but if half what he'd learned about the Shadowmaster was true . . .

And there it was. A black hole in the building's wards centered on a fourth floor window. The shutters stood wide open in the summer heat. DiUmbra's room, unprotected, by magic at least. Zurtos suspected that the darkness within housed something more than air. But that was acceptable, so long as it also housed a sleeping Shadowmaster.

The stables held only the quiet breathing of horses and the snores of stable boys in the loft. Zurtos uncovered the cage Jos had carried. The creature within hissed and struck at him uselessly, as the wicker bars were ensorcelled to resist its claws and teeth. Zurtos quickly cast the small spell that would slave it to his will and it calmed. He gingerly opened the cage and lifted it out. The thing might still snap out of reflex and those fangs carried enough poison to kill him in seconds. Jos ducked back out of the stable by prearrangement and scuttled away with the empty cage and cover. Zurtos gave him time enough to get back to the Serpentine, gentling the creature with spells even as he wove his mind into its own.

It was ready. He stepped to the stable door and flung it into the sky.

Bat wings snapped wide, caught air, and it ascended. It scented pigeons and tried to turn aside but his will held it on course. After a few moments it stopped fighting him and spiraled higher. Then he urged it into a long dive straight for DiUmbra's window.

~ ~ ~

I awoke. There was something in my room. What in the Nine Hells? I never latched the door – it didn't have a lock – but nobody in my family would invade my room without waking me first. And both ends of the corridor outside were barred against strangers at night so the family could sleep soundly. So what had woken me?

A scratching sound came from the window, only two feet away from my head. Something moved against the moonlight there. I drew on my Shadow to see in the dark, and barely kept from gasping. A bat-winged snake-like wyvern pushed its way through the hanging cords of the string curtain. It shook its leathery wings to free them from the tangle, and opened jaws. Poison gleamed on the white fangs. It turned toward me and the long neck uncoiled to strike.

I jackknifed out of my bed. Since it's a pad laid on the flagstone floor, this just dumped me face first on the cool stone. The light blanket tangled my legs and for a very long second I thrashed, butt in the air and way too close to the wyvern. The string curtain saved me by tangling the creature's wings again when it tried to turn toward me. I managed to get to my feet and blunder against the opposite wall with a crash, pulling the blanket free of my legs.

The damn creature hissed and lunged at me again. Its neck was long enough to reach halfway across my room just by stretching.

I flipped the blanket over the horrible head, fangs and all, and grabbed it around the neck.

It promptly twisted and tried to bite through the thin fabric. The poison could kill me just as readily from a scratch as a bite, it would simply be slower. And more painful.

For a moment it threatened to break free, and then my hands got a good grip just behind the head. I squeezed.

It tried to jerk backwards out of my grasp, nearly dragging me off balance, but I braced myself and pulled. The leather wings battered the stone window frame, still tangled in the string curtain, and the body fell inside. It hissed like the monster it was and threshed in my grip. A moment more and it would get its clawed feet into the game too. Then this would get a lot more painful for me.

I gasped and struggled. I could kill it instantly with my Shadow — at the cost of having the wyvern's soul haunt me. No thanks, I had enough monsters in my mind. I denied the hungry Shadow.

Instead I broke the snaky neck.

It wasn't easy. The creature was every bit as flexible as a real snake and made more of muscle than bones. But neck bones are fragile and the throat on those things is just warded by rings of cartilage, not bone. Cartilage can be crushed. I'm an acrobat as well as a knight; my hands are stronger than some blacksmiths. The throat gave way in my terror-strengthened grip, the neck bones snapped, and the beast died.

The body collapsed in a leathery heap, and for a moment I shook the wyvern like a dog with a rat. I really wanted to be sure it was dead before I let go. So for good measure I twisted my shaking hands in opposite directions until I'd turned the head backward on its own neck.

The fight hadn't been silent. My door suddenly crashed open and Sevan was there holding up a rushlight, his belt knife in his free hand. As buck naked as me in the hot summer night. I drew my shadow back inside me so that he could see. He held up the rushlight and squinted.

"Sounded like you might need help,' he ventured, staring at the sagging leather wings. "Guess I was wrong." He started to lower the knife.

"Stab it!" I demanded, just managing not to shriek like a little girl. "Make sure it's dead!"

He obliged me. Three times, so I guess he was as shaken as me.

"What in the Nine Hells is a wyvern doing in Aretzo?" He demanded, forcing stillness on his hands as he carefully wiped his blade. I would be needing a new blanket.

"The jungle sides of the Ash Needles are lousy with them, and the City wall wards can't keep out anything that flies high enough." I poked the beast's body with a toe, glad that it didn't respond. "Once it got into the city, it must have started hunting for prey. Everybody with two coppers to rub together pays for spells on their windows to keep vermin out."

"Everybody except you," he nodded, following my logic. "But half the tenements in the Sump are too poor for even that. How did it get this far without trying to snack on somebody else?"

I shrugged, found my hose and pulled them on. "I don't know. Maybe it came in over the north wall and was drawn to the Serpent's height. We are taller than every building around us."

Sevan shifted the rush light before it burned his fingers, poked the dead wyvern once more and snorted. "What do you want to do with the body?"

His father harrumphed from my door, where he and four of the cousins were all peering in. "Wrap it up – carefully! – and in the morning we'll take it to the apothecary. He'll pay for the poison sacks to make medicines."

I nodded at my father-in-law's suggestion. "Then the body to the curio master in the Bazaar." Wyverns weren't common; he'd find someone who would want a dead one.

Sevan-the-Elder gave me a long look. "We can talk about the rest of it in the morning. For now, everybody go back to bed." He glanced at his eldest son's nakedness and twitched a grin, then shooed everyone else away.

Sevan went back to his room next door and I heard Carlai's voice. I closed my door, wrapped the beast thoroughly in my ruined blanket, and closed my shutters. Being too warm seemed better than sleeping with them open. Before I did, I carefully looked around the courtyard. Not a trace of out-of-place magic anywhere. The beast was a little more ambiguous. Wyverns have their own magic so it's tricky to tell if some mage has monkeyed with one. I'd never studied one up close like this before. If there had been any subtle spells on it, their rags were lost in the fading dregs of the wyvern's own aura.

It probably flew in from the jungle, I told myself as I lay down again. Moths and pigeons had flown through my window more than once. This was just a bigger nuisance. I told myself there was no need to see nefarious action behind every piece of bad luck. I almost believed it, too. The problem was, any of a hundred enemies could have launched it at my window. Maybe I'd better get a net to use for a curtain.

I could hear Sevan grunting while Carlai gave him something to forget the danger we'd been in. Second time tonight. She was going to be pregnant again if they kept this up. The old memory of my dead Maia came back and I quietly mourned. I no longer kept myself celibate in memory of her, but I wasn't currently bedding anyone. Knights don't lack for amorous opportunity, but I wanted another love like Maia.

Eventually I fell back asleep.

~ ~ ~

Zurtos cursed silently in five languages as he returned to his rental room. At least he'd managed to withdraw his controlling spells when DiUmbra began twisting the wyvern's neck, so he'd suffered no ill effects from its death. Even the best mage in Aretzo would not be able to link the creature to him. Hopefully the Shadowmaster couldn't either.

He sighed. It had been a gamble. Though the beast had been pricy, he could afford its loss easily enough.

"Jos," he told his slave. "Sharpen your knife."

~ ~ ~

Chapter 5: Aretzo - Seraphina

Thirty-seventh day of Summer

Dona Seraphina DuVigo Abnellambra, Chaplain of the Royal Household, Confessor and Healer to His Highness Terrell the First, and Seventh-ranked priestess of the faith that had dominated Silbar for over three thousand years, paused for breath halfway up the broad flight of steps that led into the Mother Temple of Aretzo. She was too old to climb ridiculously long flights of stairs anymore.

She glanced over her shoulder at the Hill of Sight that loomed behind the sprawl of the King's Palace, and suppressed a shudder. Five hundred steps. Seven years ago she could still do that, with lots of pauses, but today it didn't bear thinking about. The thirty-two white marble slabs under her feet were exhausting enough and she was only halfway up. She resolutely kept her eyes away from the distant bump of God's Footstool that dominated the horizon even though its base lay a hundred and fifty miles north. Scaling the thirty thousand feet of *that* height was beyond conceivable even had she been young.

"Do you need to rest, Dona?" Hainin, her youngest grandson, inquired.

The strapping youth stood over six feet tall and carried her stool and folded writing desk on his back while he balanced a shade parasol over her without perceptible effort. This was his third year as a Dedicant Scribe. He had early showed promise as a mage but his Talent had been slow to develop. She'd kept him under her eye since he turned fifteen while she waited to see what The One might bring forth in the boy, and prayed it wouldn't be a major Mage-gift. His father had been troublesome enough; she didn't need a second such man in the family. But so far it looked like whatever Talent he might possess would remain trivial. Meanwhile he had developed a fine hand for calligraphy and an excellent set of filing and secretarial skills, in addition to the customary martial training. He'd probably make some Priestess' daughter a good husband in a few more years, once the heat of his youth had been tamed. Perhaps one of his even-generation DuVigo cousins. It was time to reinforce the bloodline with a little judicious back cross, and any daughters he threw off would have an excellent chance to inherit strong Talents. He was certainly handsome enough that no mother of future priestesses should feel too put-upon by marrying him.

Not that either of their opinions would matter. Their bloodlines were all that did.

"No, Hainin, I'm fine." She resumed her determined march upward and strode through the right-most of the three giant doors into the chalcedony and travertine building.

The main hallway that opened into the Sanctuary straight ahead was as thronged as always. Folk parted at the sight of the seven-tiered silver-trimmed yellow parasol in Hainin's strong hands and the matching seven stars on her wimple that marked a Septissima of the Hierarchy. There were only two ranks above her own, since the sixteen Septissimas of the Temple' Inner Circle operated as a committee, officially 'advising' the Hierarch who wore the Eight Stars. Who was ranked in turn (theoretically) by the far off Seeress that lived in isolated splendor in the most holy monastery located on the knee of God's Footstool.

Seraphina rarely thought about *that* woman, if she could help it. It had been half of her own lifetime since this same Seeress had shaken the Temple from its proud golden crown to its deepest foundations with a prophecy of terror. Followed by the very real terror of the Gwythlo Conquest and loss of Silbar's independence. The longer that woman stayed silent, the better.

The work of my generation was to hold Silbar together through the storm, she thought as she turned right into a corridor that led to rows of Temple offices. *And we have done so! Twenty-five years of relative peace now. It is not life as we once knew it, but it is life. Should I be grateful or appalled at what we have come to accept?*

Her route down a corridor to the next stairway was relatively unimpeded except for the long line backed up from the Recorder's office, where impatient parents waited to register their squalling offspring. Each overheated, petulant infant was just old enough to provide the required lock of hair, which would be plucked and filed with their name. Crying babies, eh, Seraphina was glad that stage of life was behind her. The one-starred postulant who guarded the inside stairs recognized her and waved her through.

This time it was thirty-eight steps, thankfully with a landing in the middle.

She made it up those too, though she had to lean on Hainin more than she liked by the time they reached the second level. This hallway was much less busy, as only Priestesses were allowed up those stairs (and their retinues, of course). She paused for breath, and then tackled the third and final stair to the hallway of her destination, this time waved through by a knowing old scribe who sat behind a desk at its foot.

Someday Hainin might hold that position for his wife or one of his sisters, Seraphina thought hopefully as she paused to pant on the second landing. More tartly she wondered: *Why do the eldest among us have to climb so many stairs? You'd think we would have arranged this building more conveniently!*

The third level was more quietly sumptuous than the lower levels, with better frescoes and statuary. It also had fewer doors, the office spaces being larger. Seraphina trudged a hundred feet down the hall to a large door which Hainin opened for her. Its hinges squealed loudly, clearly an intended affect since the Holy Mission could certainly afford a little oil.

"Wait down the corridor, I'll send someone for you when we're done," she told Hainin before she swept through. He nodded obediently and closed the door behind her.

Inside an anteroom was brightly lit by mage lamps and skylights. And also stuffed with cabinets and shelves and desks to house three male secretaries and a middle-aged priestess-supervisor. They all stood up and bowed. The woman was about to speak when an interior door opened and another female voice overrode her.

"Dona Seraphina DuVigo Abnellambra! Welcome to the Holy Mission. Come in, Sister, come in!"

The short dumpy fifty-seven-year-old woman who bustled out of the inner sanctum wore the same seven stars on her own wimple. Seraphina didn't underestimate her for an instant. Dona Celestina Marati DiBelluno, Superior of the Holy Mission, assigned positions to over six thousand priestesses of the Faith, all in places located beyond Silbar's borders, and received their reports in return. She knew more about what happened in the wider world than any other of the Inner Circle.

"Celestina," Seraphina replied warmly to the woman. "I apologize for not sending you advance notice of my visit." Though Seraphina had made sure Celestina would be here, which her own informers had probably reported.

"No need, any member of the Inner Circle is always welcome here. Come, sit, sit!" She led Seraphina inside the inner office to a luxurious chair, ushered her into it, and sent for refreshments before she firmly shut the door to the anteroom. It was, Seraphina noticed, a heavy door unlikely to pass most sounds, and it closed tightly and without a squeak.

It would be possible to actually have a private conversation in this room.

Celestina seated herself on an identical chair set at a slight angle to the other with a small carved teak table in between. "It's been much too long since I last saw your face outside a Conclave. To what do I owe the pleasure of your visit?"

"Wedding plans," Seraphina replied. "Specifically, His Majesty's wedding plans." The Temple Hierarchy didn't consider themselves bound by mad Emperor Osrick's jealousies within their own walls, and only lightly bound by practicality outside them.

Celestina smiled. "So he has actually won his desired Dalbai Princess. I'm impressed. Her mother agreed surprisingly quickly!"

"Yes." Seraphina didn't bother to mention the arduous diplomatic negotiations of the past few tendays. "But I am given to understand that the girl speaks no Silbari."

"The reports I received indicated that was the case, true," Celestina nodded. "However half a season ago I took the liberty to assign one member of our mission there to tutor both Crown Princess Alliet and Princess Callia in our language. By now the tutor should have begun her duties. They were both likely to find it useful and the Holy Mission had a gifted young Dona available."

Seraphina permitted a small smile to appear on her aged face. "You anticipated our needs very neatly. May I ask why you didn't mention this at Conclave?"

"I expected you to make this visit and wanted to impress you with my foresight, of course!" Celestina smiled. "I did mention it in passing to Fenecia. I take it she didn't get around to mentioning it to you either. Perhaps she's been distracted? But then, haven't we all!"

Seraphina did not allow herself to frown. The Temple's Hierarch, Fenecia Crasset Demorian, had championed her own candidate for the Royal marriage, not excessively but right up to the limits of what was seemly. So had ten of the other Septissimas, including Celestina, offering a plethora of candidates guaranteed to defeat each other. In a way, that had made Seraphina's work easier when it came time for the actual negotiating; there was a solid majority against every internal candidate. Still the lobbying had been feverish right up to the end and the majority hadn't coalesced behind Prince Terrell's choice until three days ago. It had been the most exhausting Conclave she could remember. Her own personal preference had never had a chance, of course.

"Thank you, Celestina. It was gracious of you to prepare the way for His Majesty's choice even though she was not your own."

Celestina made a self-deprecating gesture that fooled neither of them, and remarked wryly "I had small hope for my niece from the beginning. I saw it would be necessary to cancel out most or all of the personal candidates before we could achieve a majority on anyone. So my loss was also everybody's gain, though I suspect most of the Circle doesn't see it that way!" If she was angry about it she did a superb job of concealing the fact.

"Still, you have made the coming task noticeably easier, and for that you have my gratitude." Seraphina hoped she had put enough sincerity in that line.

"And mine," said a voice from the door, which had opened silently as they spoke.

Celestina and Seraphina both stood and bowed.

"Hierarch," Celestina acknowledged. "I'm honored by your presence."

"Fenecia," Seraphina grumped. "You used to knock before you wore the Eight Stars."

"It's one of the petty pleasures that go with them, Seraphina," answered the Hierarch of the Faith. "The One witness there's little enough of fun in my duties these days."

"I do hope you two aren't about to regale me with reminiscences about your days together at seminary," Celestina said drily. "I get rather tired of being reminded that I'm the youngest in the Circle."

"Hardly." Fenecia snorted, a rude and lingering habit. "Officially my schedule says I'm here to pester you personally about the new overseas assignments, but I really just want to shove off my paperwork for an hour or two and gossip with you and Seraphina about the latest news. I don't get nearly enough informal time anymore." She turned to her aide. "Meltha, have a nice lunch for three sent here, then go fob off everyone clamoring for my attention until the second bell, there's a dear."

Meltha bowed and closed the door while the Hierarch settled her ample bulk into a third chair and the other two resumed their seats. "Good work on educating the Dalbai girl, Cel. Let's hope she's fond of popping out babies. As randy as our Prince has proven, she'll need to be."

Celestina gestured modest acceptance that was spoiled by her self-satisfied smirk, and then asked, "You mentioned 'latest news'? I haven't heard anything since I started my work this morning."

Seraphina added her own inquiring look. Fenecia frowned and dropped her voice.

"Duke Veglic DuCellini DiMosil died today."

Seraphina and Celestina were both shocked. "How?"

"Of a fall, superficially, but my initial report from his estate's resident Priestess suspects a brain hemorrhage or stroke. He was walking down the main stair of his mansion with his eldest daughter and new granddaughter when he dropped like a puppet with cut strings."

"Seraphs ward his soul," Seraphina murmured, her hand automatically tracing the Sign of the One in the air. Her mind raced over the political implications. DiMosil had been probably the most respected member of the Twenty, the slate of reserve candidates for the Crown should the current wearer die. He'd been one of the few survivors in his family of the Usurper's purge seven years ago.

Celestina's hand moved in the same blessing pattern while she said, "But he was so young! Two years younger than me!"

"Two decades younger than me," Seraphina grumbled. "Did he have a history of health problems?"

"Yes, two small ones that he'd taken great pains to cover up," Fenecia said. "Looks like that was a bad idea. There will be an Inquest of course, couldn't very well not be when one of the Twenty dies."

"I hope you're sending either Dona Carina or Dona Susana to investigate," Seraphina said with an intent expression. The two autopsy priestesses had the best reputations for probity and honesty in all of Aretzo.

"Credit me with basic political sense. I sent both. If I have to drop the DiMosil lineage from the Twenty I want as much hard evidence to support my decision as I can get."

"Do you have to?" Celestina asked. "Drop them, that is. They aren't completely without male heirs – there's still his nephew Burlen. Who is also your cousin."

Seraphina and Fenecia shook their heads simultaneously.

"Triply disqualified," the Hierarch said. "Burlen Crasset DiMosil's also Mage White of the Council of Colors. After the Usurper debacle, no high mage will be trusted on the

Throne for generations. He was fool enough to get caught up in Cathghar DiMerio's stupid 'Young Rebels' bunch, too, though he did turn against them in the end. And he's a follower of Sath on top of everything else."

"A man who loves men, eh? I'd forgotten or never knew that." Celestina shook her head, obviously trying to be conciliating. "Still, he might sire a son to carry on the lineage. Other Sath worshippers have."

"I didn't say 'disqualified' just because my nephew likes to stick his prick in abnormal places," Fenecia grumped, her stress showing again in her crude words. "He's a political 'hot rock' and if I don't disqualify him I'll never hear the end of the uproar."

"Especially if the Throne ignores you and picks him anyway," muttered Seraphina, reminding them both that the wight inside the Hill had its own standards, and wasn't bound by the Temple or the State, but only by the King.

Fenecia nodded sourly before continuing, "There are far too many traditionalists, in the Trade Guilds and the whole curs— ah, in the city, who distrust all Mages in general and any member of the Council of Colors in particular. They won't be content with him just declaring that he's a placeholder for his family and won't stand for the Throne if our Prince dies. They'll want him barred outright." She scowled at the sky outside the nearest window.

"I wonder if he wouldn't be happier that way," Celestina speculated.

"Plus he blames DiUmbra for Cathghar's death," sighed Fenecia. "So working with the Shadowmaster would be bound to get stressful."

"There's an understatement," Seraphina murmured.

"That acid tongue of Burlen's doesn't help." Fenecia shook her head. "I have to disqualify him. Which means there is no official DiMosil candidate for the first time in six hundred years."

"And with old Habbir DiLonigo dying three days ago, their clan is down to two candidates," Celestina observed. "That means you will have two new families moving into the Twenty inside a week. That's going to cause some waves."

Fenecia grimaced. "Tell me about it. You would not believe the heap of petitions already stacked on my desk. At least two dozen different nominations, each claiming to have purer bloodlines than any other. And talk about self-serving? Gellir DuTallisen DiMaratini nominated his own father! Though at least his lineage is about as clean as it gets. Aieee, I get a headache just looking at the pile. Ten more will probably jump on when the DiMosil news gets around. Pfffft! And people think the DiMerio succession is messy!"

Seraphina gave her a pitiless sniff. "You wanted the job, Fenecia, so don't whine about it to me. Pick a tradition to judge them by, or draw lots, or throw darts at a wall for all I care."

"Just, please, Hierarch," Celestina piped up. "Whatever selection criteria you choose, be sure you stick to it. Uncertainty causes more problems than a mediocre choice, and the Crown can be counted on to weed out the secretly unfit."

"It shouldn't matter anyway," Fenecia grumbled. "As soon as His-and-Her Majesty pop out a couple boys everybody else takes two steps back."

"But if Prince Terrell falls over dead between now and then, Emperor Osrick will be on our doorstep in a tenday," Seraphina pointed out acidly. "And he won't be here for tea and cakes! This dynasty is young and shaky. I'd really like to see it settled and secure before I lay my bones in my grave. I promised Terrell's mother that I would and she'll probably haunt me if I don't. Not one of the Twenty could keep the

Emperor at bay. Not even Duke Cerrai if it was his own son on the Throne! If we want Silbar to survive and stay free, it's Terrell or nothing."

"I know, I know, you can stop preaching," Fenecia waved a hand irritably. "In the short run though, I have to say 'yes' to two families and 'no' to all the others. Who will all try to make me pay for it. I hate choices like that."

"I for one am very glad it's you choosing," Celestina declared. "Everybody knows you can't be bullied and won't be bought. That'll rein in the nobility's worst excesses."

Seraphina nodded. "Play to your strength, Fenecia. Choose a traditional method and apply it publicly, then go with the results no matter who complains or how loud. They'll get over it."

The Hierarch sighed. "Yes, in a decade or two. Maybe less. I wonder how fast the little Dalbai princess can breed us a couple of heirs?"

"The usual time, I'm sure. I wouldn't try to rush her!" Celestina grinned, then grimaced. "We certainly don't want her producing twin boys, do we?"

"A point. Though first she has to get here. How much problem do you think there'll be with that?"

"You mean military problems?" Celestina shook her head. "Not my expertise. Her own country needs this alliance worse than Silbar does, so I expect matters will go smoothly there. As for the trip across the Inner Ocean past hostile states and pirates and goodness knows, ask the Admiralty."

"I wouldn't worry too much about the trip," Seraphina interrupted. "I'm quite sure His Majesty will send DiUmbra to squire her back."

"Ewww." Celestina made a distasteful face. "Not the man I'd want to represent Silbar before the world."

Fenecia was more direct. "Can he be trusted with something so diplomatic and sensitive? I'd fear giving his demon an opportunity like this. The damage he – or it – could do boggles my mind."

She didn't mention his peasant background or bastard status, but Seraphina was sure she was thinking about those as well.

"Good question." Seraphina turned her palms up in a shrug. "Only Her Serenity can know for sure, unless one of you has suddenly developed the gift of prophecy. In any case, I'm certainly not going to refer the question to *her*, and I hope you won't either, Hierarch. I still haven't recovered from the last answer to come down the Mountain. Unless The One God has seen fit to confide in his Majesty."

They all chewed on that for a few seconds. The rumors had been about for years that the Light that dwelled in Terrell sometimes gave him God-sent visions. The Temple had a Seeress who got them daily, and as soon as she spoke them aloud they became inescapable. A thousand years of that had taught the Hierarchy to be very careful what questions they asked.

"I won't risk it," the Hierarch decided. "It's the King's business, we'll stay out of it. Other than praying, of course, and the things that fall clearly within our duties. Such as preparing for the wedding."

The other two relaxed.

Celestina seized the chance to change the subject. "So what might either of you be willing to tell me about the rumors that Dalbai will send an extraordinary dowry with their Princess?"

Fenecia waved a hand at Seraphina. "Go ahead. The Palace will be releasing word tomorrow anyway."

Seraphina nodded. "They will send a new ship as bride-gift, and trained shipbuilders to advise our Silbari yards on how to build more. The speed and power of their new design is much better than anything we have, or the Klintos for that matter."

All three women smiled in grim delight at the anticipated consternation of Silbar's old enemy, the more so as being yoked with it into the Gwythlo's Empire these past twenty-five years had left chafe marks on Silbar's national soul.

Celestina's smile had the sharpest edge. No few Temple missionaries had been murdered by Klinto Slavers over the centuries. "That is very good news. I take it that the King is planning new ships soon, which will mean new postings for priestesses to the Fleet Branch."

"And new missions to the Archipelago," Fenecia pointed out. "There's a promising crop of young seminarians coming along. I'll be expecting you to fit a tenth of them into mission roles."

"Excellent! I've more requests than women to fill them." Celestina tried not to look too gloating. The Holy Mission usually got half that allowance. "But it is stifling in here and I don't believe either of you have seen what I've done with my terrace this year. That knock on the door means our lunch is here, so let's get a breath of air with it."

Shortly they were ensconced on a third floor balcony that overlooked the inner gardens where the tops of tall palm trees and spiky dark green cypresses punctuated masses of flower-decked bushes and trees. The bigger growths were easily taller than the building, though the golden dome of the Sanctuary and its lacy minarets towered much higher still beyond the gardens. Hummingbirds flashed like airborne jewels among the wisteria that twined the gallery's railing and draped from the overhung roof. The birds mobbed pots of Dream-of-Gold Roses in full blossom.

"Beautiful," Fenecia murmured as she chomped a delicate roll of sliced vegetables and spiced meats. The platter that the kitchen had delivered could have fed ten instead of three.

"Yes," Seraphina agreed as she nibbled one herself. "Exquisite color choices, magnificently handled."

"Indeed." Celestina glowed with pardonable pride. "The purple of Royalty and the yellow of the Faith, grown together in harmony to create greater beauty than either could alone. A fine metaphor for Throne and Temple, or for what both should be."

"And too often in these shaken days, are not," Fenecia opined sourly.

Celestina smiled once more and let her ambition show. "But perhaps now steps can be taken to deal with that problem. Steps in which I may be of assistance?"

The two older women crossed gazes. "I told you she's sharp," Seraphina muttered.

"Not surprised," Fenecia nodded without taking her eyes off the Missionary superior. "I'll talk to you about a thorny not-so-little problem, Cel. But first a minor matter. You know Melita of the Fleet Ministry quite well, don't you?"

"Our years at seminary overlapped, as well as being cousins of course. I consult with her regularly since many of my missionaries travel by Navy ship at one time or another. I would even say we are friends."

"Better and better." Fenecia scooped up a third roll. "I want to put someone where they'll be useful to me, but Melita gets almighty prickly when I lean on her. I want results, not a fight." The Hierarch waved a hand at Seraphina, who fixed the third woman with a suggestive stare.

"As it happens," the Royal Chaplain said, "I have a granddaughter whose fondest hope is a chaplain position aboard a ship. And what could be more fitting than the new one the Dalbais will send? Of course, she'll have to ride out there and back with the Ambassadorial party sent to fetch it."

Celestina's smile expanded to a grin as she nodded. "Yes, I do believe something can be worked out."

~ ~ ~

Chapter 6: Aretzo -Hainin

Thirty-seventh day of Summer

Hainin, Dona Seraphina's grandson, had found a seat in an alcove off the third floor corridor, a place nicely screened by potted palms and statuary where he could quietly practice his spellcasting. He kept an eye on the sparse traffic and saw the Hierarch sweep by on her way to the Holy Office. He was ready when her secretary came back, the Hierarch's own umbrella bearer at her elbow.

Hainin caught Meltha's attention with a small hand-movement. She stopped and told the umbrella bearer to go wait at the stairs, then when he was gone she stepped into the alcove.

He swept her into a passionate kiss. Her warm response belied her normal solemn appearance and she pressed herself against him eagerly. Her yielding body under the Priestess robes awoke his own fire and in a moment he needed to adjust his suddenly-tight uniform. She ground her hips against him and the need became urgent.

Too soon she broke the clinch and held him at arm's length. He tried to pull her back.

"Not now," she told him in a whisper, glancing over her shoulder. "Someone might see us."

"The umbrella bearer?" He whispered back, ready to kill the man at her merest whim if it would win him another such kiss. His senses swam with her scent and touch.

"He wouldn't dare, I caught him stealing wine and could have him dismissed in disgrace." She sniffed in self-satisfaction. "Don't worry about him. But anyone could walk by and see us!"

"I put a spell on the opening to hide us," he boasted softly. "Nobody will pay attention. Even you wouldn't have seen me if I hadn't opened it to your sight."

"Your magic's getting better," she praised him, then more calculatingly asked, "Does your grandmother know yet?"

"No, and I'm making sure she doesn't find out." He smirked. "I bet I could qualify for the Fifth Rank, but I've made sure she thinks I can't pass the test for Second." He tugged gently on her arms again. "Could we meet somewhere tonight? Maybe —"

She resisted him. "Impossible. I've got a meeting to attend and then a yard of correspondence to finish for her. I'll be lucky to get four hours of sleep." Then she relented and ran a finger down his face from brow to chin. As he shivered she added, "But after this coming Holyday I have time free from my duties."

"So long," he moaned softly.

Meltha grinned like the Temptress Herself. "You'll just have to wait. It won't be easy for me either."

She pulled herself free, blew him a kiss, and hurried back down the corridor.

Hainin flopped down on a stone bench and stifled a groan. If he had dared he'd have taken her right here and now, but she was a five-starred priestess despite her youth and could stop his heart or fry his nerves with a touch. Somehow that made her all the more desirable.

"Six days," he groaned to himself. "How will I survive?"

~ ~ ~

Chapter 7: Aretzo – Kirin; Zartos

Thirty-ninth day of Summer

Three mornings after Terrell talked me into this crazy scheme, I left home to visit the damn tailors. My new clothes were supposed to be ready to try on today. Tonight the tailors would make any changes needed; tomorrow I'd board a ship for Dalbai with a trunk full of expensive cloth and a heavy promise.

I glanced both ways from the worn front steps of the Sulfur Serpent Inn. The brick building occupies a whole city block at the west corner of Sulfur Street and the Serpentine, the twisty street cut along the high-water mark after half the Old City got drowned a thousand years ago. The main door opens at the bottom of the scale-carved, round-bellied tower that rears over the intersection to give the Inn its name. The DiUmbra Troupe has dwelt in the top floor and rehearsed in the Attic for most of two centuries.

For me, it had been home and heart for eighteen years. But how much longer?

I didn't want to think about the question, so I stepped out into traffic and dodged past a heavy six-horse dray bound for the docks at the harbor end of Sulfur Street. With long practice I forbade my Shadow to eat the ward spells plastered over the cargo. The tailor shop was most of the way across the city and I didn't want to take all day, so I broke into a jog.

Up Sulfur Street through Oldgate and into the Bazaar, then weave through the maze of tents and alleys to the broad Processional. Then across it and into the New City, that was only half a thousand years old. I avoided the streets that led to the mansions of Cliffside, then cut past the famous hospital next to the Mother Temple and over to Southgate. I arrived barely winded.

Which was lucky, because at that moment somebody tried to kill me.

The knife came from behind, aimed for my right kidney. The assassin had that diamond hard focus on his task that marks a man who is truly dedicated to his art. Luckily for me, he was also foreign. He had disguised himself in typical Aretzo working man's garb and loafed in plain sight like an ordinary man in no hurry to get where he should be bound, unnoticeable among hundreds who did likewise. But he smelled of an exotic oil that no working man would wear, and the hair peeking out under his cap was blacker than a Silbari's hair should be. The combination caught my attention as I walked past. Then I heard the whisper of steel blade against leather sheath. The gust of fishy onion breath he exhaled as he stabbed wouldn't have arrived in time to warn me, but by then I'd already dodged.

I sidestepped, slammed my hand down on his own as the blade whisked past instead of into me, and twisted. He was a runty little snake, strong but skinny. My hands were corded muscle thicker than his arms. I broke two bones in his knife hand.

He dropped the blade and screamed "Zeb eat you!"

Then he did something smart. He head-butted my face.

I turned my own head aside barely in time. The top of his skull rammed into the side of my face and damn near dislocated my jaw. White pain owned my eyes for a moment. My grip weakened just enough that he jerked his broken hand free – that must have hurt – and dodged back.

Then he did something even smarter. He ran.

I had to shake off the pain-blindness before I could chase him. By the time I did, he'd disappeared into the crowds. All I had was his knife, a footprint, and an over vivid imagination to show me what might have happened if I'd been even a little slower. For a couple moments I just trembled and gasped.

Carefully watching for anyone else out to kill me, I picked up his knife and glanced over it. The cheapest possible blade, the kind that would dull its edge when it cut butter. But it would hold a point long enough to kill. Probably made by an apprentice smith and could have come from any of a hundred forges right here in Aretzo. Oddly, it had no trace of magic about it at all. That was unusual. Few Master smiths would take a completely Untalented apprentice unless he was family.

I studied the footprint he'd left in a mud patch at the edge of the paved road and memorized the irregular shape. He wore buskins made from a single piece of leather cut and folded and laced around foot and ankle, just like fifty thousand other men in Aretzo. His clothes hadn't caught my eye, if not for that glimpse of black hair and whiff of imported oil, he'd have had me.

I thought about the damn wyvern, and growled. One is just the thing itself, and twice might be coincidence. But the odds of that wyvern having blundered into my window on its own were dropping like a stone. If I was right, this was the second time somebody had tried to kill me.

I looked around again. Nobody in the crowded street let on that they'd even noticed the violence. There was a shudder inside me that badly wanted out, so I stepped into the little entry-alcove of the shop and let it. When the shakes were over I went inside to get fitted.

While two tailors draped me with this and that and told me to stand still, I called out to my brother and told him what had just happened in his city.

So soon? I thought we'd have at least a tenday before anyone tipped their hand, he whispered inside my head.

Unless your City Watch can catch him, it doesn't look like anybody's hand got tipped at all, I answered, a little testy over the way I'd barely escaped a nasty death. *Should I even waste my time to tell those worthless drones?*

Yes. They'll ask around, and somebody might recognize the assassin's description.

Especially the broken hand. I wonder if he'll dare go to a Temple to get it fixed?

A good place to start the questions. Please Kirin, I know it's a nuisance for you, but tell the Watch. I can't very well do it.

All right. Had to be a foreign hire, he spoke Silbari with an odd accent and cursed by Zeb. That's no god or demon that I know.

Might be Xiphree, their language is close to ours and they have a set of short-named demons beholden to that twelve-horned monster they worship.

Could be. He smelled odd. I think he coated his hair with vanilla oil. The fish and scallions on his breath weren't enough to hide it. A new thought struck me then. *He didn't follow me from home, he was already here.*

That worries me even more than the attempt itself. We didn't make any announcements about your new clothes. Whoever he worked for knew enough to send an assassin to the right shop. That implies inside knowledge, a connection inside the Treasury. But it's been less than four days since I committed myself to the alliance and barely three since anyone but me knew you'd be the one to fetch Callia back here.

I tried to picture Exchequer Snowdon arranging an assassination, and failed. He had too much zeal for hunting tax crooks through his ledgers. The man lived for numbers. Hired knife work just wasn't his style. But a hundred clerks worked for him in that sweltering hall and they were bound to gossip. I was probably somewhere high on the list of favorite topics to gossip about, and Terrell's wedding would top it.

Yeah, two days for the word to spread and a day to arrange the assassin — hundreds must know by now. You got any better idea who's behind this?

Too many ideas. They start with anyone who backed another candidate for my bride, and then go on through all the nations with an interest at stake. It could even be leftover vengeance from one of your previous missions for me. The list of possible suspects is very large.

I was afraid of that. I could think of five or six past possibilities without trying. It's hard *not* to make enemies when you're the King's Left Hand. I heaved a sigh that made the tailors glance nervously at my face while they worked. *So I get to wait for the next one, and hope he's as sloppy as the first?*

It looks that way. He touched my mind gently, a resonance like a muffled bell and a scent of cinnamon. *I'm sorry. I thought this wouldn't start until you reached Dalbai. Be careful.*

Of course.

I broke our mind link and finished with the tailors. At a Watch post I spewed what I'd seen and done into the ears of an earnest scribe who was overawed by my knight's ring. Then I headed back home while I tried to watch and listen to every damn man in the crowds around me. An impossible feat.

Fortunately for me, my Shadow doesn't sleep, else I wouldn't have got any that night. I did make sure to replace my string curtain with a net. A strong one.

~ ~ ~

The robed woman muttered angrily as she Healed the broken hand. "You put us all at risk, coming to me this way!"

"I can't take Jos elsewhere," Zurtos retorted. "I will need him. Tomorrow they depart, if you still want me to take *him* out then our opportunity grows narrower by the hour. Should I attack his home tonight? He might be invulnerable to my spells, but that building is not."

"Don't talk foolishness, it is watched every instant by those whose attention we dare not draw. You can't challenge those ward spells from inside another building, you will have to be close to it and thus visible. You might succeed – doubtful, but possible – but you would not escape. And unless you plan to suicide, and know how to kill your own ghost as well, you would spill what you know under the Question and all would be lost."

"Curse your whole Hierarchy," Zurtos growled in frustration. "You think me ruthless and despicable? Look in a mirror!"

"We both know what we are," she answered testily as she finished with the man. "And why we work together. There, that will not be comfortable but it will serve normally, he'll simply have to endure the pain for a few days." The skinny man shuddered as she withdrew her numbing touch, but made no sound.

"Jos?" Zurtos asked, and his servant nodded. "My thanks, abominable Priestess. Let's hope the next idea works better."

"Simply keep trying," she advised. "Sooner or later you will kill the monster."

Zurtos's lips drew back from his teeth. "You can be assured of that. I already owe him one blood debt and today he nearly cost me a second. I'll not risk a third. He is a task I now reserve for myself."

~ ~ ~

Chapter 8: Aretzo ~ Kirin

Fortieth day of Summer

"You won't forget us, will you, Uncle?" Little Marli asked anxiously as I hugged her goodbye the next day. Seabirds screamed and sailors cursed as the ship behind me loaded final items and crew. And waited for its most important passenger; me.

"Of course not, who could forget such a wonderful niece?" I kissed her on the forehead and set her down. Carlai hugged me next, only a little encumbered by her baby, and then Sevan wrapped me in his powerful arms.

"Come back to us," he whispered in my ear. "Come back to your family."

"You can bet on it," I answered as I squeezed his own ribs in return. "I'll probably be back before the end of autumn; you'll barely have time to miss me."

I traded hugs with the rest and then boarded *Waverunner* as they all disconsolately filed back to dry land. Most of the Troupe had showed up to bid me farewell. I was both touched and grieved.

A midshipman responded to my jeweled Knight's ring and showed me to my berth. The cabin was small with just enough room between two bunks to move in and out. My fancy new clothes were already aboard in a trunk. I stuffed my duffel under the bunk next to it and set myself to learn my way around the ship.

An hour later I leaned on *Waverunner's* stern rail and waited while crewmen swarmed the dock in a final frenzy of activity. Within another hour the tide would change and I'd set out for Dalbai with three warships, four crews and four captains.

"I don't know if you've heard yet, Sir DiUmbra," Captain D'Auson told me as we watched the last loads come aboard. "The Dalbais have named their new ship *Queen of the Seas*." He had little else to do but gossip because he wasn't in command of the hull under us; Captain Velis ruled *Waverunner*. "I've been assigned to sail the *Queen* and our future Queen back, so I've brought enough men to crew a fourth ship."

"And an extra company of marines stacked like cordwood below," I joked as I shook my head. All three of our ships – *Defiance*, *Waverunner*, and *Stormrider* – were packed with soldiers and sailors. Even I, Terrell's Left Hand and official Ambassador for this trip, with a gold chain of office and a rank just as shiny, had to share a cabin.

With D'Auson, as it happened. Terrell had stuffed my head with everything he knew about the officers he sent with me. It made me want to sneeze, but I put up with it. Most of them were from well-born families with long traditions of service in Silbar's Navy. And nervous as a cat in heat over this mission. I could hardly hold it against them, since they were all sure they'd get blamed if disaster struck. Not that they actually had much to worry about. Terrell's not Osrick, so their heads were safe enough. They'd probably only end up demoted to command a sloop. Or if he was really upset, a garbage scow.

I found D'Auson easier to get along with than the others. That may have been because he had so little to do until we arrived, and because he wasn't arrogant. His family was very minor nobility and he only a third son with no prospects for inheritance. He'd enlisted in the Navy as a twelve-year-old midshipman just before the Gwythlo Empire's conquest of Silbar. This piece of bad timing got followed by the good luck to survive the naval battle outside Aretzo's harbor gates. He told me his ship had made it inside just before the Harbor Wizards raised the barrier.

"Happiest sight I'd yet seen when those chains came up out of the water behind us," he reminisced. "The Klinto galleon that chased us tried to ram through and ripped her bow open for her trouble. Then the spell on the chains made every nail in her jump right out of her boards. She went all to pieces in the middle of the channel. Her crew clung to any scrap that would float and screamed for quarter."

I looked across the mile-wide expanse of Aretzo's harbor to the seawall and the row of six octagonal guardian towers that flanked the New and Old Trade Gates and the Navy Gate. All three Gates were open, their chains lowered to rest on the harbor floor while ships busily passed in and out. I watched the blue wraiths of message constructs dart back and forth across the harbor as ships queued up to enter and leave. The port was busy today. Two ships jockeyed to enter by the Old Trade Gate even as a huge Fehdaran galleon wallowed its way out through the New Trade Gate, tugged by tow spells. A banner on one tower warned that the tide was on the ebb and departing ships had better take advantage of it. There was no visible sign at all of the bitter war fought here twenty-five years ago.

"What did you do next?" I asked.

"We spilled all sails and dropped anchor just thrice our length inside. There wasn't enough room to move another cable length, what with half the fleet jammed into the anchorage and ten times as many merchantmen too. Most of our catapults were smashed or dismounted and the foremast leaned like a drunk, but we were still afloat. Though we had forty holes in our hull, only two were below our waterline. An hour later we even had the fires out. But a dozen more Navy ships barely stayed ahead of their own leaks and three were outright sinking. The harbor was in the biggest mess you can imagine."

"Must have been a total balls-up."

He nodded. "It was defeat, and no excuses. The Imperial Navy outnumbered us, outfought us, and damn near sank most of us. We had hours of backbreaking work just to get our own *Seafalcon* back in order. And then they told us to anchor broadside to the Navy Gate and be ready to hit any ship that broke through! Most of the other ships' crews were ferried to the Wall to help stand off the attacks that we all thought would come. We didn't know that the land battle at Black Pass had been lost too, King Dolor was dead and the Empire was already on the march into Silbar over land. If our new Queen hadn't made peace and married young Emperor Brion before the land forces got to our Valley cities – arrr."

He talked about my mother and father now, little though he knew it. My thoughts sheered away from that with old practice. From the way he continued he didn't notice my twitch.

"It took two whole seasons to get the fleet seaworthy. I didn't ship out again until next midsummer."

"Mmmm." I nodded. "Sounds like a hell of a start to your career. Glad I wasn't around yet."

He glanced at my face. "Right, I forgot how young you are, no older than his Highness."

I shrugged. "A few tendays less, I suppose." I had actually been born two minutes before Terrell, according to Dona Seraphina, who'd midwifed both of us, but even she didn't know that the baby that had passed through her hands had grown up to become me. I hoped. "My mother's long dead so I can't very well ask her."

D'Auson's look grew probing. "Gossip says the Duke of Cerrai is your father, milord."

"I could hardly know, could I? Any more than he can be sure – no Mage or Priestess can cast a spell to reveal paternity. Motherhood's a fact, fatherhood's an opinion. Anyone can tell by one look at me that I'm another child of the Conquest. I grew up in the Sump like a thousand other bastard brats left behind when the Empire marched off to conquer someone else. And what does it matter? I've made my own way in the world."

He nodded again, his gaze still appraising. "That you certainly have, Sir DiUmbra. Left Hand of his Highness, famous mage killer, and now Special Ambassador to Dalbai."

"Just for this trip." I shuddered. "Speeches, formality, high court manners — gah. None of it comes naturally to me, Captain. I'd a thousand times rather have physical work to do."

"You may get your wish." He nodded to the fighting deck below us, where sailors oiled and checked the ship's catapults. "Any day now word of this marriage alliance will reach Khaitanial. Silbar and Dalbai joined together will put them at a hopeless disadvantage. I suspect they won't just sit on their hands."

"You think they'll attack us?" I'd never been in a shipboard fight before. I wondered what it would be like.

"I think they'll take some action. It could be warnings, threats, trickery, extortion, sabotage, attack, or any combination, there's no way to know. Khaitanials aren't known for subtlety, but that doesn't mean the dogs can't learn a new trick. And they may not be alone, either."

"You think they've got new allies against Dalbai?" My mind raced as I tried to guess who he might suspect. Unfortunately there are more than forty states and over a thousand islands in the Archipelago. Dalbai is merely the biggest.

"Not allies, quite. I just doubt the rest of the archipelago is very happy about Silbar and Dalbai potentially providing Emperor Osrick with a foot inside their door."

"Ah." I stared across the harbor. "That could be a problem."

A rumble from the land pulled my attention back that way. Two big carriages backed onto the dock. Their horses tossed heads in protest as the drivers each used Talents to persuade them. Step by step, the drivers alternately cursed each other and sent whispers into the big animals' ears, until they stopped alongside *Waverunner*. Both carriages began to spew men in robes and boxes that glowed with blue wards.

"At last," D'Auson grumbled. "I'd started to wonder if we would get any mages at all for this voyage."

Archmage Cervisi strode up the gangplank and kept his balance rather well as he stepped down onto the deck and made directly toward me. Captain Velis finished some orders to one of his officers and strode over to join us. D'Auson stood up straight; I did the same, more slowly.

The Archmage inclined his head to me and said "Ambassador Sir DiUmbra, Captain Morgin D'Ille Velis, Captain Wittin Raish D'Auson, please accept my apologies for this late arrival. I've persuaded one of the Council of Colors to serve as lead Mage for the voyage and four other ranked mages to accompany him. With the mages already assigned to *Stormrider* and *Defiance* that will give you nine mages for the squadron."

"Nine mages?" Velis growled. He was built much like the Admiral but about half again as tall, and looked like he could catch a catapult ball in his bare hands and fling it back. "I'm pleased to have the firepower, but *Waverunner's* only got one cabin to spare for ship's mages. With three bunks."

"The rest will go on the other ships," Cervisi soothed.

"Better," Velis grunted. "So who do I get? He'd better be a damn good battlemage as well as a Storm-grade air worker."

"I'm better than good," announced a voice from the gangplank. "I'm the best."

And Burlen Crasset DiMosil, Mage White, stepped off the ship's rail and floated down to the deck.

Appalled, I rounded on Cervisi. "You couldn't get Mage Red or Green instead? Pox and damnation, they both owe me favors!" By the Moons, I'd rather have had anybody but the White.

Cervisi looked at me in mute appeal and spread his hands. "Neither could come. The Red's amenable but he's also in the middle of a sixty-day-long rebuild of the Navy Gate's wards and can't leave it half done. And you know how easily Green gets seasick. White's the best I can get. No other of the Council of Colors is willing to, ah, work so close beneath your eye, Sir DiUmbra."

Then the White opened his mouth again and said "Aren't you glad to see me, demon lord? This could be your perfect chance to kill me! Wouldn't that please your King in Hell?"

"I'm not –!" I growled, then got my tongue under control and stuck my thumbs in my sword belt to keep my hands from his throat. "Keep your damned lies to yourself."

He looked infuriatingly cheerful as he made a formal half bow to Velis. "Captain. I've brought along a few special treats that I hope will come as a deadly surprise to anyone foolish enough to attack a ship with me aboard. Do you mind if I oversee their safe storage before we leave? They'll have to go as far away from Ambassador DiUmbra as possible so he won't waste them. Accidentally, of course."

I tamped down on my Shadow. "You're still the same arsehole you've always been, DiMosil, even promoted to White. Don't push me or it won't be the Captain who regrets it."

Before he could say another word a different voice piped up from the gangplank. A pleasant soprano with more sting than a scorpion.

"Mage DiMosil the White and Left Hand Sir DiUmbra, feuding like children, I see."

I looked and found Dona Seelie DuVigo D'Isernia, Quartissima, at the rail with her hands on hips and her lips pursed. Four silver stars winked from her wimple and her shy little husband balanced precariously on the gangplank behind her with his arms full of sacks. Dona Seraphina's eldest granddaughter favored us impartially with a younger version of the stern look for which her grandmother was famous.

"Why are you here?" I blurted. Even White looked at a loss for words.

"I am the Temple's appointed Priestess for the new ship. I'll assist *Waverunner's* own Dona Millente until then. And, no doubt, try to moderate you two several times a day." Her lip curled slightly under her falcon's beak of a nose. "May Our Serene Lady help me."

White looked at me, visibly thinking up some snide comment that he'd deliver any moment in a damned cheerful voice. Captain Velis looked at me doubtfully, every rumor he'd ever heard about me probably on his mind. I gritted my teeth and bit down on a dozen swear words.

"We all have the same mission from the Prince," I ground out. "Shall we get to it?"

That was the only thing that could have silenced them. We all got to work.

Soon the squadron was ready to leave. To my relief DiMosil didn't have another chance to snipe at me before it did. D'Auson and I loafed on the port side of the command deck and watched. *Stormrider* and *Defiance* would follow us out through the Navy Gate. The Harbor Wizards raised a banner from the Gate to signal *Waverunner* to slip her moorings.

"Ship's Mage," Captain Velis bellowed. "Prepare to receive *Waverunner.*"

"Ready, Captain," DiMosil replied with an unctuous bow from his station on a dais on the fighting deck, set right below the steering wheel that crowned the higher command deck. His two subordinate wizards, both Master-class themselves, also bowed and stood by. The White raised his hands and spells began to build. I tamped down on my hungry Shadow; he was barely twenty feet away from me and it would be embarrassing if I broke his spells at a crucial moment. Though I didn't at all mind if he worried about it.

Through the soles of my boots I felt *Waverunner's* sleeping wards awaken.

"Cast off!" Velis ordered. Dockhands released the mooring ropes and tossed them up to our sailors, who coiled and stowed them speedily.

White moved his right hand forward. Ponderous forces gripped *Waverunner* and she began to slide out of her berth stern first into the Navy's part of the Harbor. When the ship's bow cleared the pier his left hand made a slow circle.

"Helm two points to starboard," Velis ordered as he watched the mage and the ship and the surrounding piers and waters. *Waverunner's* bow slowly swung to the left and aimed towards the Navy Gate. Velis told the helmsman, "Straighten her out, Mister Aymis. Mister Sains, hands to the rigging, stand by to make all plain sail." Sains, the ship's Bosun, nodded and repeated the order with a leather-lunged bellow.

From the towers of the Navy Gate, twin blue tow spells floated snake-like across the water towards us. To my eyes they always looked like giant transparent leeches stretched out for prey, and I slapped down my too-active imagination and blamed the idea on my Shadow. Deep inside me, one of my ghosts sent back a sensation suspiciously like a giggle. I ignored the bastard.

The White made a gesture with both hands and spells fanned out from *Waverunner's* bow to clasp the tow spells sent out from the Gate. The ethereal cables tightened and our ship began to move faster. *Waverunner* cut through the flat harbor waters like a knife. He made small twitches of his fingers to correct the tension on the spells and keep her aimed for the center of the Gate.

The Gate's blunt octagonal towers loomed up on either side of us, sea-washed granite painted white by birdlime and barnacles. Green seaweeds writhed in the water and clouds of gulls screamed. I had a quick glimpse of wizards at work in the glass-windowed rooms at the top, caught the stench of burnt sulfur as they adjusted the spells that towed us. Then we were out of Aretzo's harbor and the tow spells fell away. Silbar Bay spread before us.

"Captain, the ship is yours," DiMosil reported.

"Ship received, Mage. Now, Mister Sains."

"Make all plain sail!" Sains bellowed.

Canvas bloomed and in moments *Waverunner* began to heel as she gained speed. I noticed that the White quietly set the ship's wards to watchful mode, which was probably too cautious when still in sight of Aretzo, but I wasn't about to complain. Behind us *Stormrider* began her own passage through the Navy Gate.

The Fehdaran galleon wallowed ahead and visibly struggled with her sails.

"Inexperienced commander," D'Auson commented to me as he pointed at her. "He should be past Long Reef and well into the bay by now but he's mismanaged her sails and practically becalmed her. If he's not careful he'll wreck her on the reef."

"Can we get past him?" I wondered aloud as we approached. We moved far faster than the floundering ship.

"Easily, there's five hundred feet of open water between him and the reef. See the channel markers?"

"Which set?" I asked as I scanned the water. It had been a couple years since I'd been on a ship headed out of Aretzo.

"What do you mean, 'which set?'" D'Auson stared at me, perplexed. "There's only one row of three markers, to mark Long Reef. Once we're past it the sailing is clear all the way to Broken Point."

"But I see two rows," I disagreed. "Three left and three right, with a spell on each float."

D'Auson stared ahead for a moment, then demanded "Quickly, which row has the larger floats?"

"The right, I mean starboard, the row closest to the galleon, maybe two hundred feet left of her. The other row's around three hundred feet farther to her left – ah, port. That one has just blocks of wood for floats, though the spells on them look stronger than the others." I began to get that acid bite in my gut that means trouble.

DiMosil the White turned his head and stared up at me for an instant, which proved he could listen. A shocked look covered his face, then he faced the bow again and frantically began to cast a spell. When he launched it the two rows of markers that I could see all flared red in my sight. We were lined up almost perfectly between them and the first marker was less than the ship's own length away on our right.

"Captain!" White yelled as he pointed ahead and left. "Those port channel markers are fake!"

"Hard starboard!" Velis shouted. "Helm, get us starboard of that first buoy!"

Waverunner heeled as her rudder came about, everybody grabbed for a hold as the deck tilted. Her bowsprit turned slowly, too slowly, we would still pass left of the first marker by at least forty feet.

"Too late!" D'Auson swore under his breath and tightened his grip on the rail. "We'll hit!"

"Hell no!" Snarled DiMosil. He made a gesture and the ship's wards came fully awake. He brought both hands together to his left and shoved them down and away as if he pushed against an invisible lever.

A giant dimple opened in the sea and revealed a yards-long fang of rock poised to puncture *Waverunner's* port side. The displaced water slammed against our hull and the whole ship creaked, shook, and slid away from the hidden reef. *Waverunner* rose and fell in the waves like a drunk. Our masts whipped through the air as we rocked and I was amazed none of the sailors up there was thrown overboard. One did shriek and several swore.

I tore my gaze away from the near threat and looked to the right. The galleon had put out more sail and now she turned much faster than the wind alone could manage. Her own wards were up and a suspiciously strong spell built on her command deck. The caster looked directly at us.

"Beware the Fehdaran!" I shouted.

White heard me and, wonder of wonders, acted. He raised *Waverunner's* shields just before an arrow of fire shot from the galleon to us. It hit our shields only a few feet from the vulnerable edge of the sails. I could see *Waverunner's* magical defenses flex under the assault. A sailor yowled in panic as flame splashed inches away from him. Then DiMosil and his assistants gestured in unison and the fire fell backwards to drop harmlessly into the sea. The shield was shriveled, nearly broken by the strain; there had been a brutal power in that firebolt.

I snatched Shadow into my hand and shaped it into a dart, flung it hard as I could at the enemy mage. He dodged but lost precious moments before he could cast his next attack. I grabbed for more Shadow to keep him busy until our mages could rebuild their shield.

Captain Velis shouted orders as *Waverunner* swayed and came upright again. Sailors heaved on ropes and our own sails turned to catch the wind. The deck tilted again as we swerved back to our course on the safe side of the real markers. And the galleon still turned, her sails full and bowsprit like a spear.

D'Auson yelled, "She'll ram us!"

"Not on my watch," White snarled. "Arlein, hold the Wards! Rellir, distract that treacherous pig! Trice, dice, now!"

Another divot appeared in the waves right next to the galleon's bow. A wave came out of nowhere and slapped her opposite side. The Fehdaran ship staggered sideways into the hole and her timbers groaned as she was literally sucked to our right, her bow wrenched along twice as fast as her own movement. White had added still more Power to the enemy mage's own turning spell and now the galleon's bow pointed behind us. The tip of her bowsprit just scraped our stern rail as she passed. I could have jumped to her foredeck.

Meanwhile a spray of fire darts burst from Rellir's hands and soared towards the galleon. Most were knocked down by her own wards but half a dozen got through and pocked her foredeck and sails with burning holes. One almost made it to the command deck. Even as they flew I filled my right hand with Shadow again and hurled it at the enemy Mage. This time I killed his next spell before it left his hands. I could see his shock and fury. I followed that with one for the helmsman on the galleon's command deck. As their ship rolled hard enough to fling a couple sailors overboard, my Shadow hit him in the face and he went down. The galleon's wheel spun with him and she turned even more sharply. She spilled the wind from her pierced sails as she almost capsized. By the time someone grabbed the wheel and righted the Fehdaran ship, *Waverunner* had left her behind. The gap widened steadily.

"She's still charging ahead," D'Auson remarked. "She'll hit –"

And with a shock that we could feel from *Waverunner's* deck, the galleon rammed the reef. Her last few sailors were flung from her rigging. One screamed all the way down until he struck the deck. Her maintop mast snapped off and fell. Her deck heeled toward us as her bow rode up onto the reef and her hull ripped open. The mage lost his footing and fell to the deck, saved from going over the side by a quick grab by the helmsman. The men working to clear the pierced sail had also been thrown flat, by the time they got back to their feet their ship was visibly down at the stern as water flooded into her bow. Someone started a rush for the galleon's boats while others just leaped overboard.

"Pox and damnation!" snarled Velis. "What is that dung-for-brains captain doing?"

I pointed to the Mage just as he regained his feet in time to see us sail away. He made a bitter gesture barely visible under the blue glow of his spells as distance widened between us, then flung another spell. Our mages deflected it into the water and for a moment the sea steamed.

"I don't see anybody but that Mage to give commands," I told Velis. "I bet he ran the whole scheme. The spell that hid the real markers to lure us in, the fire attack, the ramming attempt. You can bet gold to dung that it all came from him. And despite what your eyes may tell you, he doesn't look Fehdaran. He's dark skinned like a southerner, not northern-pale, and his hair is straight and black, not fair and curly like a Fehdaran. He's got a lot of layered spells, I think at least one is for disguise."

"He's probably a Xiphree by the taste of his magery," Rellir announced.

D'Auson scowled. "There is no chance that a Xiphree mage would be hired to captain a Fehdaran ship, or even be let on board. This smells wrong. Could he have stolen that ship and crew? Just to try to sink us?"

"He'd have done better to steal a ship armed with more than a couple of sternchasers," I answered. "But maybe he was in a hurry."

"Flagman, signal to *Defiance* to heave to and pick up survivors, especially that mage!" Velis ordered. "And make sure her own mages know to be damn careful with him."

Then the Xiphree mage made a gesture, and the whole galleon burst into flames. Sailors screamed as their flesh ignited.

"Monster!" I hissed as I clenched my fists. "He'll kill the sailors so they can't talk."

Only the mage and the helmsman weren't affected. He was another dark skinned black-haired Xiphree with a suspiciously familiar build. That one kicked a burning sailor away as he unrolled a carpet behind the mage. He favored his right hand.

"That's the assassin who tried to kill me yesterday!" I accused. "The mage must be his master, he's gonna –" I grabbed Shadow again.

The enemy Mage stepped onto the carpet and it rose into the air, rigid as a board, while his accomplice huddled beside him. Around them things that had been men crisped in the flames.

I shaped Shadow into a black javelin even as Captain Velis yelled. "Ships Mage! Take that bastard down!"

I flung my shadow-spear. The range was long and it widened by the second, but I might have made it.

Only White launched his own attack an instant later, a sizzling bolt that caught up to my javelin and tried to pass it too close. Both vanished as my Shadow ate the bolt but lost its shape and fell short. I swore but before I could shape a second spear the enemy Mage and his henchman glided off. Faster than a ship could sail they flew toward the jungle-clad islands at the far side of Silbar Bay. Out of my reach. He probably had a boat hidden where our deep-draft ships couldn't go.

White swore viciously and launched a second bolt. It must have been at the far edge of his own range when it hit the flying mage – and was deflected into the sea.

"Are there any survivors on that ship?" Captain Velis asked as fire and water battled over the foundered galleon. We were far enough away that the sparks didn't threaten *Waverunner. Stormrider* swung wide around the wreck.

"None that I can see. The cold-hearted bastard!" Arlein answered, his hands busy with a scryspell. He turned the scry aside, his face twisted in horror at what he'd seen through it, and started to focus it on the fleeing mage.

"He must've had that fire spell all ready to kill his pawns," I said. "I'd bet he had another one for us if they had gotten through our shields. I don't know what else he's done, but everybody should stay the hell away from that wreck until the Colors can get out here to go over it. Captain, please warn our other ships. DiMosil –"

"Already on it," he interrupted as his hands shaped a message construct. He threw it into the air and it sped towards the city. "My colleagues on the Council of Colors will know the details in moments. We're close enough that their early warning watchspell will have tripped, so they're already alerted. Rellir, alert the Harbormaster too, if all the fire and smoke hasn't tipped him off. Arlein, can you track that pig-humping murderer or his trick carpet?"

"No, Magister, his block is too good." He let his scryspell collapse. "All I got is a general sensation, we can *see* more than that. Even if I had some of his hair or a thread from the carpet I probably couldn't narrow it down enough to matter."

"May Salim flay the swine. He's too clever by half!" The White bowed to Velis. "Captain, I had to strain *Waverunner's* wards badly for all that water work. I'll need to dip into the ship's silver stock to get them back to full power."

"Granted." Velis nodded. "See the Chief Purser. And do it quick as you can, I don't want us vulnerable any longer than we have to be."

White looked at me. "Nicely done, demon lord. Your pawn got safely away and you look like a hero for blocking his last-ditch attacks. You're cleverer than I thought."

I sputtered as he walked away. "You – you poison-tongued viper! I didn't – you – you bloody arsehole!" I barely managed to restrain my Shadow from lunging for him, and that would have been disastrous. Velis and D'Auson gave me long thoughtful looks while the other two mages found work to do and the squadron forged on.

The ship's carpenter went below to check on our hull and make sure Waverunner hadn't started leaking from all that rough handling. For lack of something better to do I followed him, figuring it would be useful to learn more about how a ship worked.

He started on the orlop deck, below the artillery deck and above the hold, where those waves had hit hardest. It was a maze of passageways and rooms, most of the specialist functions of the ship were here, at or below the waterline; carpentry itself, sail repair, the Priestess' office and infirmary, the galley, and the Purser – ship's treasurer. The passageways were poorly lit and winding with branches everywhere. I followed the carpenter until I heard a voice down one side branch and turned aside to listen. It was Mage Arlein carrying a small magelight, loitering outside the Purser's door. I drew my Shadow around me so that he wouldn't see me, as I didn't care to get in an argument with any mage right now. But for some reason I stayed to listen.

White had just stepped out of the Purser's office, a half ingot of fresh silver in hand. He said, "What is it, Arlein?"

The shorter mage glanced around the seemingly-empty corridor, didn't see me hidden in Shadow, then said quietly, "Burlen, why did you make that terrible accusation against the Ambassador? You frightened me half to death, practically accusing the King's Left Hand of treason. He has the right of High Justice, he could have killed you for that!"

White's lips drew back in a silent snarl. "I wish he'd try! I said it because I believe it."

Arlein shook his head. "I know you're the rising star of the Council, but you mustn't just spout off like that! You shouldn't say such things without proof."

"Oh, I've got proof, at least proof that satisfies me."

"I don't understand. How can you possibly have any such thing? We didn't get a scrap from that murderer. We can't even prove his nationality, never mind his alliances."

"I got something better, at least for me. A thorough taste of his magic. I recognized it, Arlein. I've met the man's work before."

"What! Where?"

"When Cathghar died." White's face twisted in memory. "The same taste was on that infernal device Cath was trying to dismantle when that bastard DiUmbra murdered him. All over that triple-damned mechanism. I tell you, that same pig-raping Xiphree had a major hand in making it, I'm as sure of that as I am of anything."

Arlein gave him a long look. "Burlen, how does that make DiUmbra any kind of ally to this mass murderer?"

"Can't you see it?" DiMosil clenched his fists in frustration. "I suspected Cath was being influenced somehow, but I let it go, he told me he could take care of himself and I, fool that I was, believed him. I knew he had a weakness for the quick shortcut, and still I let myself believe he wouldn't ever get tripped up by it. How could I have been so stupid! Someone smart and subtle was seducing Cath away from me all the time, with hints and crazy promises of power. It must have been that Xiphree bastard! And DiUmbra didn't care! He stood by, and let Cath get suckered *on purpose*! He did nothing until his own damn family got caught up in the mess! Then, only then did he jump in with both feet and stop it — too late for Cath!"

White rubbed his eyes fiercely. "He set Cath up for that fall as sure as the Suns rise in the east. He let the Xiphree *use* him—"

"Burlen, stop!" Arlein waved his hands in protest. "You're weaving a whole tapestry out of a single thread. All you really know is that this murdering mage had some hand in the same artifact your lover was working on. There are a dozen possible explanations for that, and most of them don't require believing that the King's Left Hand is playing some deep double game."

White shook him off. "I know. I'm not blind, and my brain works just fine. But sometimes the improbable *is* the truth. We're talking about a man who carries a demon inside him! The evil explanation is a lot more probable when one of *those* is involved."

Arlein rubbed his jaw in nervous worry. "I — I don't want to argue that point with you, neither one of us is a Priestess. Just, think carefully about this. You could be wrong; odds are that you *are* wrong, and how will you feel if that gets proven? The Captain's already wondering about you after your outburst. Don't turn this voyage into a black mark on your record because of a suspicion. You could be Archmage someday, you've gift enough to rise that high. But you won't even keep your seat on the Council if you make reckless accusations like that one. Be patient, be calm, be polite, and wait to see what develops. If your suspicions are correct, and that's a very big if, something will slip eventually."

White tossed his head in acknowledgement. "I am calm. I can be patient. But damned if I'm going to be polite any more than I have to be. DiUmbra, or his demon, killed the man I loved, and I'm not just going to forget that."

"Nobody's asking you to," I said, stepping out of my Shadow. "But if you have to be an idiot about something that I had no choice in, at least remember your duty first. You should have told me about this connection between Cathghar and the Xiphree mage right away."

Arlein startled like a rabbit, then got his surprise under control.

DiMosil simply glared at me, and through gritted teeth said, "I included it in the message I sent to the Council. They have the remnants of his mechanism and his notes. If I'm right they'll be able to prove the link, as long as something of that ship survives to compare effects. And I am right."

"Good work," I grudgingly told him. "Now if you'd just take your head out of your ass about me, you might be a whole lot more useful on this trip."

The look he gave me would've scorched steel.

"My Lord Ambassador," he ground out with a barely polite bow, then he turned and stalked off towards the stern companionway. Arlein gave me an awkward bow and hurried along behind him.

I shook my head and went to find the carpenter again. Three attempts on my life, the latest attacking a whole ship.

Somebody very much wanted me dead, and my Ship's Mage might share that goal.

This was going to be a very long voyage.

~ ~ ~

Chapter 9: Aretzo - Terrell

Fortieth day of Summer

Terrell glanced up from his absorption with the wight that lived inside the Hill of Sight just in time to see Penghar top the five hundred steps.

Pen stepped to the edge of the hill and scanned the sea beyond the city. Despite the climb he barely breathed hard, and Terrell knew a moment of envy for that. His own legs were sore; he'd done the climb for four days in a row now.

"Three Mages from the Council of Colors are at the wreck," Pen reported. "They're being very cautious so it will probably be tomorrow before they have any real news for us." He used the familiar form of address the two of them had maintained when they were private, ever since their boyhood together.

"Three assassination attempts in three days," Terrell muttered. "I've truly set the cat among the pigeons, haven't I?"

"Or thrown meat to the sharks," Pen agreed. "Some of which may have been lurking in secret ever since that Young Rebels affair. But we won't learn much if I jog the Colors' elbows while they work, so. Time to wait." He fell silent and gazed at the sea while he shaded his eyes against the suns. He added "I watched the squadron set sail, but I can't see them from here. Have they left the Bay yet?"

"I'll find out."

Terrell paused before his mind looked through the vast gulf of air for the distant spark that carried his hopes. His physical eyes had never completely recovered from the terrible effort he'd spent to drag Kirin back out of Hell at the end of that Storm Pass Road mess. He'd grown used to relying on magic to make up the loss, and the constructs layered over the Hill did ever so much more than any spell cast by a simple human mage could do.

I should have dared to use this Node more often, he thought privately as he gathered his strength before he reached out once again. Out through the veils of the World, he searched for that scarred, shadowed mind that waited so close and yet so far away from his own. Meanwhile he touched one finger to his crown, not because he needed it to find Kirin but because Pen would be comforted to believe that Silbar's God-enchanted crown played a role in any magic his liege did.

Then he *looked.*

The World stretched and contracted around him. The palace and city flowed away as the bay shrank and the Sundering Sea rushed towards him. Distance collapsed and he briefly saw three proud ships, sails bellied and hulls rocking as they scudded south. Then his control slipped, the World snapped back to the ordered relationships that everyone knew, the Power furled itself, and he was left with only misted eyesight again. He let the melancholy ache persist for a moment before he spoke.

"*Waverunner* passed Broken Point mere minutes ago," he told Pen. "*Defiance* and *Stormrider* close behind. They make speed for Cape Woe."

"Good." Pen nodded shortly and crossed his arms. "Thank you."

They both stared south. Stray clouds stalked the coast and built toward the thunderheads that would drop needed rain later this afternoon. Orchards and vineyards sprawled over the hills south and west of Aretzo, gray olive trees on the drier slopes and vivid oranges, figs, lemons and pomegranates in the sheltered spots. Long lines of staked grapevines curved around hillsides like lumpy green beads on strings. East across Silbar Bay the near end of the Ash Needles reared jagged cones in a line that ran dawnward out of sight. Their seaside slopes were streaked green with jungle while their rain-starved inland faces withered under the Suns. To the south and southeast the Sundering Sea glinted silver between cloud shadows where it covered the sunken lands. Westward the towering spine of the Bright Mountains walled away the Inner Ocean. The peaks dwindled as they marched southwest over the curve of the world.

But he already knew that the ancient spells on the stone seat would let him see much farther than just this little part of Silbar. He'd practiced several times in the past few days. Three hundred miles south lay the final mountain above Cape Woe and the junction of Sundering Sea and Inner Ocean. He'd managed to see that today. He couldn't yet reach across the twice-a-thousand miles west to Dalbai, the Jewel of the Dreaming Isles, but he had hopes. Legend claimed the Hill could do remarkable things if the King could only persuade the wight within it to do his will.

And I will persuade it. Kirin will be there, ready to help me meet her.

"So far still to go," Terrell whispered. "The next hundred days already seem like years."

"You sent three of our fastest ships armed with everything they could possibly need," Pen pointed out reasonably. "Silbar hasn't dispatched such a well-defended squadron since the Conquest. Nobody should be able to move against it before they reach Dalbai."

"I know, Pen. But then they have to come back, through whatever our enemies have assembled to stop them. And it will be very difficult for us to help them at this remove."

They stared south a while longer, then Pen spoke as if he had to force the words out. "He's quite capable, I have to admit."

My dearest friend. If only you could know Kirin's heart the way I do, you'd understand. Aloud, he simply said, "I know that too. That's why I've put him at risk like this. I gamble with his life on the table and the Kingdom's future at stake. It shames me, but needs must."

Pen frowned. "It is a knight's honor to do his lord's will," he began.

"He's never fit the mold that makes a Knight," Terrell interrupted, trying to make his best friend see without revealing the dangerous truth. "I wonder if I was wrong to try to squeeze him into it. He does it because he loves me, in his awkward prickly way, and loves Silbar even more. But I don't think he's had more than a dozen truly happy days since I elevated him out of the gutters. I hope that's not eating away at his soul."

"Such as he's got," Pen added lightly, but his eyes narrowed.

Not this again. "He has one, Pen, never doubt it. You've seen the proof yourself. And Irreneetha knows."

"Ye-es-ss." Pen drew his sword a few inches out of her sheath. The blade glowed a soft warm white with hints of deep purple fire. "But what is it that she knows? She's never said, yet she watches him when he's near. And he's afraid of her, as any evil creature should be."

Terrell made himself take a deep breath before he answered. "Pen, Kirin's not evil. He's proven that a dozen times over the years."

"But he carries evil under his heart."

Terrell blinked. "What do you mean?"

"The Holy Writ says that's what a living Shadow *is*. Evil. How long can even a saint carry one before he's eaten up by it? And he's no saint, Terrell."

Is anyone? Terrell shook his head and slapped his royal right hand against the stone seat. "I trust him, Pen. More than I dare explain to you, much as I love you, for there are some burdens I won't demand you carry. Be content with that."

There followed a long pause while Pen pushed Irreneetha back into her sheath, clasped his hands behind him and stared out to sea. Finally he stirred again.

"So. Your Highness." Pen turned to face him and made a half bow. "Do you need to sit here and stare after the ships a while longer? I can tell the Chamberlain to stall the next batch of petitioners for an hour or two."

Terrell sighed. Pen knew how to deliver a rebuke that sounded respectful. He'd become more like Kirin in the past seven years than either of them would admit.

"No." Terrell rose from the stone seat and stretched. "Let's get a couple hours of exercise after I hear today's petitions and before I have to get ready for that dinner with the Trade Council. We got some riding in this morning and sword work yesterday, so I think it should be wrestling this afternoon."

"You want me to throw you around the palestra floor?"

Terrell grinned. "It might be me who throws you this time. I've learned a new trick from Kirin."

Pen rolled his eyes. "Well, we both need the exercise. And it'll get you in the right frame of mind to deal with a bunch of merchants."

Terrell shook his head. "No, the merchants are simple to deal with. They just want to make money, and they will always try to find a compromise that lets them get on with it.

They and I understand each other quite well. Negotiations with the Temple and the Mage Guild are what get tricky, because their desires aren't nearly so clear-cut. Sometimes they can be very indirect indeed."

~ ~ ~

Chapter 10: Aretzo – Zurtos

Fortieth day of Summer

That night three figures met again in the abandoned DiMerio garden in Aretzo. The same black cat paused in her hunt, and overhead the nightjar still sang, but the tone below was uglier this time.

"You failed," the veiled woman accused Zurtos. "You knew from Cathghar's debacle what *he* could do, and still you failed."

"I had too little to work with," the Xiphree Mage answered testily. "And too little time to arrange it. I would have waited until their return trip, if the decision had been up to me. But you insisted, and we reaped the fruits of your damnable impatience. Now the Colors hunt me. Have you any idea how hard it was to slip back into this accursed city while sought by them? And if they find me, your schemes fall to ruin and our interests go with them."

"They don't have enough evidence of your identity to find you," the messenger assured him. "I was able to overhear their report to His Highness today. All they salvaged from the wreck was a few threads of your carpet and a swatch of bloody hair where your servant hit his head."

"Which means they can find him, eventually, and then they'll have found me." The Xiphree glared at the woman. "I'll have to flee immediately. Years of preparation wasted because of your foolish impatience."

"Don't expect sympathy," she retorted. "And don't waste your breath on whining. I promised you a fast ship, which is why I've invited a certain 'sailor' here."

A gesture made, a tall man who waited under a palm tree stepped forward and bowed, then folded back the hood and front of his shapeless robe. His ears were plain in the moons' light, pointed at the top, and his garb beneath the dull cloth was military but not Silbari.

The newcomer did not speak, but the Xiphree chuckled and addressed him insolently.

"So. Captain Beliat of Klinto's Second Fleet, I recognize you."

"As I do you, Mage Dameon Zurtos of Xiphree," Beliat nodded, unperturbed. "Your actions are well known to the Klinto Comandante, both those against Silbar and against us."

Zurtos chuckled. "I serve my God and my King first and no other after, Klinto. That is your only warning. So. It's to be ships against ships, eh? And you expect my King to bring Xiphree's fleet to dance attendance on yours at the gavotte?"

"That will give us enough. But you must move immediately. The farther from Silbar's reach we engage, the better the chance of success."

"Agreed!" Zurtos replied. "Only where will this 'engagement' take place? The Inner Ocean is large and our enemy will move fast."

"Not fast enough," the woman said. "They must come toward us; you need merely wait anywhere on their path. Their locations will be known to you every step of the way. Simply track this."

A small pouch was held out and received. The Xiphree felt its thickness and the crackle of parchment within, gave a low whistle and chuckled again. "You know that nothing of *his* will work, of course. So instead you give me – who?"

"Names are attached to each packet. Some may not return on the new ship, but at least one should. Follow them all, and when you see a gathering in the same place you will know what to close upon."

"Expensive, but cheaper than failure. Yet I think more is required, and this effort has become annoyingly personal now for both of us." Zurtos exaggerated his bow to the edge of insult, and then turned to the Klinto. "It seems we are to work together. You can start by smuggling two men and a carpet out of this city tonight. Then we must discuss possibilities, including the speed of your ship."

Beliat gestured toward the brass-studded door out of the garden. "Then let's be about it." He bowed precisely to the veiled woman and said, "May we never meet again."

"The feeling is mutual. As will be your success, or failure," the figure answered.

All four left the garden by three different routes. The cat played with a mouse, let it go for a while and then pounced for the kill.

~ ~ ~

Hours later a small fast sloop left the Old Trade Gate on the last of the ebb tide. It flew the Imperial pennant over the black-and-gold Klinto flag and the banner of a minor trading house, but the crew was unusually fit and strong, and more numerous than most merchant houses could afford.

The midranked Mage who managed the Gate on this midnight-to-morning shift made careful note in the daily log book, then forgot about it. There were three ships ready to enter with the rising tide and that would start in half an hour. He had to get the Gate spells refueled and ready and he was already miserable from colitis. Maybe he should listen to his Temple Priestess and give up eating pistachios.

~ ~ ~

Chapter 11: Daleray Palace - Callia

Forty-Third day of Summer

Princess Callia entered the salon used for her language lessons and asked her teacher, "Did you hear? Prince Terrell said in his latest message that he's sent three ships and some lordling to escort me to my new home. They'll be here before the end of Summer. Who is this 'Left Hand' person?" She'd wondered about that mysterious reference the moment her mother read the message aloud.

Dona Catalona looked like she fought the temptation to frown outright. "His name is Sir Kirin DiUmbra."

Callia sat on a divan and folded her legs under her, waited a moment, then realized the priestess wasn't going to supply a third name. "He only has two names? I thought all Silbaris used three names; personal, mother's line, father's line. Isn't two names alone a Gwythlo style? But DiUmbra sounds like a Silbari name."

Dona Catalona lost the fight. The frown that followed impressed Callia, who had seen some magnificent ones. The priestess cleared her throat and said, "Understand please, Highness, I don't know the man personally."

"But you know plenty of gossip about him, don't you." Callia smiled at her winningly. "Come, Dona, tell me what you know. This is my future, I need to understand what I'm getting into. Your Temple sent you here to help me; so help me."

Dona Catalona nodded. "Sir DiUmbra presently uses only two names. By ordinary rank he is merely a knight, and was raised into that by His Highness' fiat. He was not born to the aristocracy, in fact —" her voice went low "— he has no proven lineage at all."

She delivered that last as if it were the most shocking fact in a realm of shocking facts about the man. Callia knew the Silbari priestesses kept records of the lineages of every soul in their care from the lowliest village peasant to the enormous extended lineage of the Royal House. They kept *that* in gold-bound books in the Mother Temple and it supposedly included a hundred thousand relations out to the twentieth degree. For the first time she realized that she must already be in those books, since her great-grandmother had been a Silbari princess. This marriage would mean she and her children would become prominent in those records, her own line woven into the center of the tapestry of Silbar's people.

Do I want that? She examined the idea uneasily. *To be recorded in books is a powerful thing. To be mother to a dynasty still more. If it is to happen to me, I'll need allies to make sure it isn't used against me or my children. Allies within their Temple.* Her attention returned to Catalona.

"The DiUmbra family is a clan of acrobats with an honorable if penurious lineage," the Dona continued. "Devout enough but like many of their caste somewhat slipshod in their observances, ahem! They apparently adopted him as an orphan babe found in, ah, the gutters of Aretzo. Quite irregularly, it wasn't even recorded until *years* later, but alas, that sort of carelessness wasn't unknown in the decade that followed Gwythlo's Conquest of Silbar. So he has neither mother lineage nor father lineage in his name, only the personal name he was known by as a child – Kirin means Black Eyes in Old Silbari – and his adoptive father's surname. In a sense, he is as nameless as a Haunt."

Callia remembered stories about the lesser demons called Haunts that walked the world in the guise of men, nameless and destructive. "That sounds like a bard's tale. If I hadn't heard it from you, I'd suspect it entirely made up."

"Indeed." The priestess twisted her mouth as if she'd bitten into a ripe fruit and found foulness inside. "But it is all quite true. The Hierarchy investigated him thoroughly when he was elevated, and he is indeed an unrecorded orphan. The Duke of Cerrai has quietly let it be known that he acknowledges Sir Kirin as his illegitimate offspring, and no less a personage than Dona Seraphina DuVigo Abnellambra, Septissima, has opined that it is likely. But of course, at this remove in time and with his mother long dead, it is unlikely that there will ever be certainty."

"He's an acknowledged bastard?" Callia tasted the words, unsure what she thought about them. "We have a few of those in Dalbai, I think Uncle Yare has two. Father truly loved Mother, anyone could tell who saw them together, so he never made any bastards. If any of my other uncles or cousins have one, they've kept quiet about it. I can't imagine a bastard would be admitted at court without plenty of talk."

"His Highness Prince Terrell has walked a narrow line between a sincere and heartfelt respect for tradition that does his ancestors proud, and a willingness to adopt some alarming innovations." The priestess spoke the last word like an epithet. "Of which Sir DiUmbra is among the *most* alarming."

This grew more fascinating by the moment. The last several minutes of it had been delivered in Dona Catalona's native Silbari tongue. Callia labored to squeeze meaning out of the foreign words. "Innovations? This has to do with the new forms of spellcasting that have spread out of Aretzo, right? But that started before I was born! How does Sir Kirin fit into it?"

"He has held the post of Prince Terrell's Left Hand for several years now. 'Hand' is the title traditionally given to the King of Silbar's enforcers of Law, and our kings have had as many as two dozen or as few as one. At present his Highness has only two. The Right Hand is Baron Sir Penghar Verhys DiLione, a distinguished nobleman and bearer of a Holy Sword."

"The handsome one," Callia interjected dreamily. Ballads about the deeds of the literally unobtainable Sir Penghar had made the rounds of the bards in the Dreaming Isles. A chaste knight soulbound to his holy sword was safe for even a Princess to dream about.

"Indeed." Dona Catalona's mouth quirked. "I've seen him and can testify that he most emphatically is that. Sir DiUmbra is, um, somewhat plainer though not ugly. He has an unfortunate tendency to frown, which does his otherwise-regular visage no favors."

"Is that why he's known as the Left Hand?" Callia wondered. "That sounds cruel."

"No. He is called the Left Hand because his prime duty is to regulate the behavior of Silbar's Mages." The priestess paused. "A function he seems to accomplish with the help of a demon inside him."

Callia stared. "What?"

"It's not a rumor." Dona Catalona shifted on her seat as if the wood had suddenly grown splinters. "It's a logical inference from many recorded observations. He doesn't even hide it, especially when he's sent by His Highness to put down a rebellious Mage or a Shade. He has a living Shadow within him, and when he lets it out it devours spells and Power and even life itself like the darkest creatures of Scripture. He has been witnessed to command Shades. So far, always to send them back into the Pit from whence they came, but who knows what else he might do with them?"

The last words were delivered with the sort of passion that the priestess typically reserved for her beloved Holy Writ. Living Shadows didn't plague Dalbai as much as they reputedly did Silbar. Or maybe, Callia reflected, the Silbaris just had better stories about them. But they certainly weren't a subject that anyone took lightly.

Callia stared at Catalona, mind stumbling through the implications. "I thought – only women can banish Shades. We can heal, we command flesh, life and death. Men can only manipulate the Four Elements; Earth, Air, Fire and Water. They generally can manipulate them better than we can, but only those. That's true everywhere in the known world! A man *can't* . . . can't . . ."

"Correct, Highness," Dona Catalona answered moodily. "And yet, he does."

"He must be one of those unfortunate beings, what is the word, herma-frodies? Beings with both sexes in one body? That could explain why he's able to do women's spells, couldn't it?"

"Hermaphrodites, Highness," the priestess corrected politely. "And it might, except that he's been examined quite thoroughly by the diagnostic spells of a seventh-ranked priestess, and she reports that, physically, he is exclusively male. When he was an acrobat he performed in only hose and paint, not even a codpiece, as is the tradition in Silbar, and numerous observers testify that he, um, shows the correct features. The hose they wear is rather thin and clingy, you see. Besides, he was married for a year to a dancer of the DiUmbra clan and sired a son, though both mother and child were killed under mysterious circumstances during the Usurper's attempt on the Crown. Rumor places Sir DiUmbra deep in that particular chaotic event as well, but just what he did or didn't do is a matter of considerable dispute. His Highness, obviously, has his own opinion, and it is clearly positive."

The priestess shook her head in worry. "I wish we of the Temple could be so confident."

"I don't know whether to be horrified by this Left Hand, or to pity him," Callia muttered.

"Exactly the problem." Dona Catalona made the Sign Against Evil and sighed. "But I'd advise you to not let him know you do either of those, your Highness. He is reputed to get rather prickly when he is confronted on these issues. The King who you are to marry has chosen to send Sir DiUmbra to squire you across the ocean to Silbar. It would be best to be circumspect, when you deal with him."

"Yes, I see." Callia turned that one over in her mind. Her husband-to-be had sent a man with a demon inside him to escort her? But he trusted the man so much that he had raised him into the knighthood and given him one of the most important posts in the land. Why?

"Thank you, Dona Catalona. You've given me much to think about."

"I'm only doing my duty, your Highness."

~ ~ ~

That night Callia went to her mother's room before bedtime. It still seemed wrong for her father not to be there except as a black-bordered painting hung on one wall. Many of his possessions were still there too. His best dress sword hung on its usual peg with his favorite threadbare dressing gown beside it.

Queen Sephora wore her own dressing gown while she sat on a couch to read official correspondence. She glanced up and smiled, then handed the letter to her personal secretary and said "That will be all, Verena, file it with the others and go to bed. We'll resume tomorrow after breakfast." Then she turned to Callia and patted the couch next to her. "Come sit with me, darling girl. What troubles you?"

Callia curled up next to her mother on the couch and leaned her head on her shoulder. "Mother, I'm worried about this strange knight that Prince Terrell has sent to escort me."

"Sir Kirin DiUmbra? Yes, your betrothed sent me another message confirming the escort plans. He and I have corresponded by message construct on every detail. You'll be well protected on your trip to Silbar." Her mother patted her hand.

"Dona Catalona says the man has a demon inside him!"

"Prince Terrell warned me about his liegeman's reputation." Mother's tired eyes crinkled in a smile. "He explained to me his own beliefs about the situation. It's clear that this Knight has an unusual magical Talent, but he has an unbroken seven year record of using it for his liege's purposes and no others."

Callia caught the omission at once. "So the prince doesn't deny that his man carries a demon?"

Her mother pursed her lips for a moment. Her eyes gazed away as she often did while she consulted her memory. "Oh, he explicitly refutes that, but he does not pretend to understand the nature of the man's Talent himself. Nor has he hidden from me his own uncertainties, though he cited examples from what he says is a very long list of loyal actions his man has taken on their Kingdom's behalf. Which included what Prince Terrell calls 'crucial assistance' to claim his throne from that usurper seven years ago. He simply asks us to trust his own confidence in his servant. Which I would say to him if the situation was reversed."

"So he just says 'trust me' and leaves us at that?" Callia frowned.

"What else could he do, my girl?" Her mother cocked an ironic eye at her. "All of our communication has necessarily been by message construct and the one written letter that accompanied that cameo he sent to you. We've already given him our trust for far more momentous issues than the character and capacities of one of his servants. And he has extended similar trust to us. Our alliance will cost him a sixth of his Navy's strength, to our immediate benefit."

Her mother moved her hands in the air in front of her, up and down in opposition like the pans of a balance scale. "That is ultimately the foundation of all marriages, Callie. Trust."

Mother's eyes wandered to the black-bordered portrait of Father that smiled down from the wall. It had used to hang in another room but Mother had moved it in here after the war.

Impulsively, Callia kissed her mother and hugged her. "Thank you, Mother. I'll manage this strange knight, I know I will."

"Of course you will." Queen Sephora beamed at her youngest. "Remember that he's been sent here to answer your personal questions about your betrothed. Prince Terrell and Sir DiUmbra are close friends, by the Prince's own admission. Question the man, dear. Ask him whatever you've a fancy to know, weigh his answers, and form your own opinions. This is an opportunity. Take advantage of it."

"Oh I will," Callia answered fervently. "I promise you that, Mother. From the moment he gets here I shall badger him without mercy."

~ ~ ~

Chapter 12: Inner Ocean - Kirin

Forty-third day of Summer

I dangled my legs from *Waverunner's* mainmast lookout platform. The night air flowed almost cool this far above her deck while tropic seas stretched in all directions. The wind was light and the mast rocked in long lazy swings through the sky, an oddly pleasant motion. I raised my face to the Moon of Calm, presently a pale wraith behind clouds but not far from full, and tried to call some of its legendary soothing power down on me. It didn't help. The Dalbai words still danced in my head and sheered away with malicious little giggles whenever I tried to grab them. And this while the Moon of Madness yet lurked below the western horizon.

I'm gonna screw this up, I thought at Terrell. *I'll never keep all this crazy grammar and protocol straight. I'll insult somebody by mistake and they'll kick me out on my ass. You should have sent Pen. He knows when to bow and how deep and who to kiss and who to kick. Salim take it, hardly any of this is how Silbar does it!*

You're exaggerating, Kirin, Terrell answered inside my head. His mental voice came faint across the distance. Captain Velis' charts said we were almost seven hundred miles from Aretzo as the crow flies. *The Dalbai language has much more in common with ours than it has differences.*

But it's the differences I'll trip over.

So? You already speak Gwythlo and Bhinnish and a lot of Klinto and Duermu, too. It can't be that hard to add one more.

*Those are mostly gutter dialects that I picked up in the Sump and the Bazaar. Nobody cares if I mangle any of them. Now you want me to learn *Court* speech, and talk to *Royalty*! I'm gonna fall flat on my face.*

No you aren't. Don't worry, you've actually done quite well and you have whole tendays of time still to go. Remember that you'll have me in your head and Dona Seelie by your side to help you through the rough spots.

Haroun on a Crutch! She makes me more nervous than all of Dalbai put together.

I wish you'd be less blasphemous, he chided me for the hundredth time.

I ignored that. The One God hasn't proven to be my friend and the Seraphs are inseparable parts of that divinity. *How much do you suppose her grandmother's guessed about us?*

If you mean does she know who you really are, I doubt it. But we certainly can't ask her, can we? So there's no point in worry. Besides, you can be sure her deepest loyalty is to Silbar in the end.

Or to the Temple, anyway. You told me yourself about the century when the Priestesses kept the Kings prisoner and ruled in their names.

And they learned better. Don't worry about her.

So I'll worry about something else. Like that damn Mage. Was he one of Cathghar DiMerio's partners-in-crime?

It looks that way. DiMosil's hunch was correct, the same aura that burnt the Fehdaran ship was all over a piece of DiMerio's machine.

Any idea yet who he is?

The Colors have narrowed it down to someone from Xiphree. Unfortunately we know too little about any of their current high-ranked mages, a lapse which I'm going to have to correct. My ambassador to Xiphree has started discreet inquiries, I dare hope for a message from him any day now.

I felt him stifle a yawn. It must be past midnight in Aretzo.

Go to bed, I told him roughly, rather than hear about fruitless messages or get in another pointless argument about my swearing. *I've done all the learning I can stand tonight.*

I am in bed, he pointed out. *A nice still one that isn't swinging all over the sky like that crow's-nest you're perched on. You should go get some sleep too.*

I can sleep in late. I'm an ambassador with damn-all to do until we reach Dalbai. And anyway the suns rise and set later here than at home. It hasn't been dark for more than three hours yet.

More proof that the World is round, like I told you, he answered drowsily. *Very well, I'll talk to you again tomorrow night. Keep up your good work, you've almost got the language!*

He disappeared from my mind like a candle blown out. He must have been very tired. I suspected he'd strained himself to talk to me at this distance without using the Hill. Which he could hardly do every night, unless we wanted to attract the kind of notice that really would cause us trouble.

I leaned back against the mast and watched the stars wheel in the tropical sky. They were different here than I'd grown used to at home. The Hunter and the Bear were gone over the north horizon. The Ship, the Plow, the Kraken, those were the same, but shifted north now with strange new constellations rising in the south. I tried to swallow the notion that the World was a spinning ball. Why didn't we fall off? And could we really sail all the way around it?

Waverunner glided through the night in a long slow rocking-horse gait that moved the mast in endless ovals. I'd gotten used to it and even come to like the sensation. I especially enjoyed just being up here where I didn't have to take extra care to not destroy White's spells. He was asleep now and Captain Velis didn't hold with blind charges into the dark, so after sunset we sailed with the upper masts bare and just the mainsails up. That gave me a broad view from the lookout. And up here I also didn't have to worry about my Shadow eating the defensive wards laid at vast expense into the ship's hull. My Shadow perceived a cabin aboard *Waverunner* as a lot like a prison cage made of pies. Every night before I slept I made sure to tamp the monster down hard, and hoped it stayed cowed until morning.

The port stay ropes creaked against the movement of the ship. A few minutes later D'Auson's head appeared at the edge of the flat lookout platform. He casually swung over and seated himself at my elbow. He wore just trews and a singlet, his feet bare like he'd been about to go to bed.

"Couldn't sleep," he explained. "Not enough to do all day. Never thought I'd find a turn as a passenger so wearing. Every ship I've been on before this, I had a place in her command. Even if it was near the bottom."

I quirked a smile. "What, you're gonna pass up a chance to sleep without having to listen to me snore?"

"You don't snore, My Lord Ambassador, though I admit it is a little hair-raising to wake up at night and find you wrapped in Shadow. Good that I've got a strong heart."

"Ah." I winced, not glad to hear how poorly my discipline was working. "Yeah, it tends to ooze out when I don't watch it. Sorry about that. Don't worry, it's not dangerous to you and it has to stay near me, just not always inside." I turned my head to look at him speculatively, tried to keep the tension out of my voice. "I take it you don't swallow White's poison about me being a demon in disguise?"

He didn't flinch at all, unlike several of the ship's crew who still made the Sign Against Evil when I passed near them. Instead he shrugged.

"'Know them by their works', as the Writ says and our Donas repeat every night at dinner and twice at Holy Day service. I saw you teach the young middies how to fight hand-to-hand. You armed them with new skills without a hint of shame for their ignorance and you left all six more capable and eager to learn. That was well done."

"Eh." I ducked my head, felt my face grow warm. "I needed the exercise. I'm getting flabby here, not enough work for me either."

"I watched you climb ropes, do somersaults, cartwheels, situps, pushups, and more for three straight hours this morning. And another two in sword practice with the marines, where you beat most of them. And then you had the strength to teach six midshipmen to fight. Are you made of iron, man?"

"No, something more flexible. Catgut, maybe."

It was his turn to smile. It made his wind-weathered face look younger and I remembered he had barely forty years. "Like one of those magical golems they say Chisaad the Usurper used to make? Wood and leather and wire, if I remember, and cost as much silver to fuel as you'd pay three servants."

I shoved a bad memory aside and said lightly, "Which is why nobody uses them today except for swank. So why are you really up here, Captain D'Auson?"

"A little private talk. With the mainsail between us and the deck, if we keep our voices low the wind will carry them away and nobody can hear what we say." His own had dropped into a softer tone as he spoke. "And with you here, somehow I suspect no mage trick will overhear us either."

"I can promise that." I matched his voice. "What do you want to talk about?"

"When I take up command of the *Queen of the Seas*, DiMosil – Mage White – will be my Ship's Mage and you and the princess will be my prime passengers. This assignment will be tricky enough with a new ship and a crew that doesn't know her. Add to that half the nations of the Inner Ocean probably ready to sink us before the alliance comes about, and I can't afford the risk of any more uncertainties." His brown eyes bored into mine from a foot away, as black in the night as mine were in the day. "What's really going on between DiMosil and you?"

"You already know most of it. I'm the King's – I mean, the Prince's Left Hand. My duty is to keep the Mage Guild reminded of its place, in service to Crown and Country and not in mastery over the kingdom. Or any part of it; the Law governs the high as well as the low."

"And forbids both to sleep under bridges, yes, I know."

"Or to murder, or rob. If anyone in Silbar sleeps soundly in their own bed at night, secure that nobody will steal their life or their things, it's because our Kings have caught and hung those who try either." I tapped my chest. "I'm one of the reasons that only the very desperate or very stupid Mages try it today."

"And was DiMosil-the-White someone who was that stupid?"

"Partly. His main mistake was that he loved someone who saw Silbar as a tool and thought he could wield it."

"'He?' I wondered if he sacrificed to Sath." D'Auson referred to the minor seraph in the Temple pantheon who had the special charge to care for men who love men. "Well, he'll have company on my ship, a couple of my officers do too. So who was this lover? Another mage?"

"Yes to both." I closed my eyes for a moment. "Most of the details are a State Secret, but gossip gets around so you probably won't be surprised when I tell you his name was Cathghar D'Ivor DiMerio."

"Ah. The Hierarch's outcast nephew."

"Cousin, actually, twice removed. She probably wishes he'd been a hundred times removed now."

"Right, I remember I did hear something garbled about that scandal. Blood magic, wasn't it? She was livid, she'd have burned him at the stake for it, cousin or no, if he hadn't, hmm, died."

"That's part of the truth. It happened almost a year ago but there are, ah, side events still to unfold. Lives were at risk and I had to strip the man of his power in order to save them, and do it suddenly and with no warning. The shock dropped him like a puppet with cut strings, and unfortunately he stood in a bad place at the time. The fall killed him and DiMosil blames me. If DiMerio had survived capture and been executed, I suppose the exalted Mage White would still blame me."

"Hurrr. I suspected this had roots in a tragedy. 'Needs must, when Salim wields the whip.' So how much of a grudge does he hold against you?"

"You mean what'll he do for revenge?" I sighed. "I don't think he wants it so badly he'd be ready to die himself to get it, and he's proud of his art and his rank and probably wouldn't put either at risk."

"But if he could arrange an 'accident' with no direct connection to himself?"

"Maybe, though since I've got excellent magesight I don't know how he'd hide such a thing. Even if I was blind that'd be a mighty big trick to pull off on a crowded ship. Meanwhile he's certainly happy to bait me."

"Every chance he gets," D'Auson agreed. "You impressed me and Velis with your grace when you ignored White's demon jibes at dinner. It's pretty clear what he thinks of you. How do you feel about him?"

I thought for a moment, finally settled on the right word, one I'd learned from Terrell. "Irritated. He hopes I'll grow stupid if he throws enough sand in my craw."

"And will you?"

"Not a chance." I bared my teeth. "I can't prove he knew what his lover was up to. If I could, he wouldn't hold a seat on the Council of Colors. I'm not even sure myself; either he was truly shocked, or he's a great actor. But I'll still watch him."

"Wonderful. My Lord Ambassador, my crew will have to learn a new ship while we stand off whatever forces the enemies of this alliance decide to throw at us on the trip home. I don't need problems between my senior Mage and my charges while we're about it. Should I trade him to one of the other ships and get another mage for the *Queen*? How good is he anyway?"

I hesitated, tempted by the notion, but D'Auson plainly just wanted to do his duty. I owed him the truth. Little as I liked it, I sighed and resisted temptation.

"DiMosil is better at both attack and defense than any two of the other mages in this squadron. At one time or another I've seen all of them work. You should keep him and also Arlein and Rellir, the two best out of the rest, for the *Queen*. He got the 'White' post on the Council of Colors 'cause he earned it, they only take the best mages in Aretzo. Hell, the best in all of Silbar."

The words left a taste in my mouth like bad vinegar. Why isn't truth more comfortable?

D'Auson nodded thoughtfully. "Thank you, Ambassador. That will make my decision easier, if not the voyage."

"You're welcome." I glared out into the darkness. Now I'd have to put up with DiMosil's mouthy jabs on both legs of the trip. But if we met enemy ships we might need him very badly.

My jaw cracked in a sudden yawn. "Time for sleep, Captain." I reached for the starboard ratlines.

He nodded and did the same on the port side. "We'd all best stock up on it. I've got a suspicion there won't be much time for that on our way back."

~ ~ ~

Chapter 13: Aretzo - Hainin

Forty-third day of Summer

Hainin jerked like a puppet in the storm of his release. He felt Meltha's own pleasure course through her nerves and echo in his. He didn't know how she did that to him, and didn't care. The raging power of it was all he needed.

Afterwards they lay entwined in the rumpled bed of this discreet little rental. The proprietress was a crippled, deaf, and nearly blind widow grateful for the extra coins. Meltha softly brushed his unbound hair back and ran a finger around his left ear.

"Thank you," he whispered humbly, gladly bearing her weight across his hips and chest.

She chuckled quietly. "You are welcome. If your mage skill grows to match the rest of you, you'll be Archmage someday."

"You think so?" He preened. "Think I could match that Xiphree?"

She moved the finger to his lips. "Don't think of it. He's dangerous, Hainin, and at least as strong as any on the Council. Would you pit yourself against one of them?"

He licked the finger and considered. "Not yet, but if I'd learned enough from your cousin Cathghar, then maybe —"

Her whole hand covered his mouth and he obediently stopped talking.

"We do this my way," she admonished. "The Xiphree will deal with the Shadowmage, then the Council will deal with him. You just keep clear of both of them, keep studying secretly and getting better, and be ready when I need you. Understand?"

"I will, I will! I promised, didn't I?"

He pretended to be hurt, but she saw through that and smiled at him.

"You still want to jump in with both feet and start swinging, don't you?" she accused.

"Well, I get awfully tired of being a good little boy for my grandmother," he admitted. He stroked Meltha's back suggestively; it was too soon for a second round but he thought he might manage one before they had to vacate the room. After all, he was only eighteen, nearing the peak of his potency, and it would be a shame to waste any of this opportunity.

"Be patient and we'll have everything we want, Hainin." She grinned a happy grin and added, "Think of the shock on the old bag-of-bones' face when she finally finds out!"

Hainin grinned back and wrapped his arms around her. "All right, love, all right." He began to kiss her again, thinking, *Once we succeed, I can bed you every night! I can hardly wait!*

He failed to see the calculation in her eyes, or the grim determination that lurked behind her kisses.

~ ~ ~

Chapter 14: Inner Ocean - Kirin

Forty-fourth day of Summer

Next morning I awoke early after a dream-haunted sleep, still irritable over last night. D'Auson snored while I quietly pulled on some old hose and a shirt and went out on deck.

The first heralds of the suns barely lit the eastern sky. I stretched until my muscles were awake too and then climbed and descended each of the three masts by a different set of ratlines. Then I hand-over-handed my way between masts on the stays. I hung by my hands halfway between the mainmast and foremast and enjoyed the tremendous thrum from the tension that the sails put on the rigging that held them in place.

Rank on rank of swells ran out of sight in three directions while a huge fog bank stretched across the southeast perhaps five miles away from us. Waves frothed on a reef a few miles to our north. I saw a sloop near the western horizon, it must have passed us in the night. Small ships with large sails like that were the only ones that could outpace *Waverunner* and her sister warships. I watched it slowly vanish ahead. There were no other ships anywhere around us and not even a seabird to break the endless arc of sea and sky, wave and fog. The fog bank had crept a little nearer but it looked like we'd slowly angle ahead of it. The deck swayed back and forth far below my feet until I tired of the view and went back down.

White was at his station casting a complicated spell with silver and sulfur to shine up the ship's wards. He darted me a bleary hostile glance as he worked. I ignored him and greeted Captain Velis, who studied a chart with his helmsman and first mate. Velis answered civilly and pointed to the frothing reef.

"That's Whiteteeth, the last islet of the Lesser Continent and the start of the deeps for the Inner Ocean. We've made good time so far, My Lord Ambassador. Should be about thirty more days travel across the deeps to reach the outer islands of the Archipelago. We'll need another eight to ten to thread through them to Dalbai."

I remembered the map DiRovigo had shown me before I left. "Where will we make landfall, Captain?"

"I'm aiming for Volcano Island. Even if we end up a little off course we should be able to see the smoke plume from many miles away and we can refill our water casks there."

"Isn't that close to Khaitanial?"

"About three hundred miles north of their north coast, with Collirivar Island and several smaller ones in between. No guarantee they won't try to surprise us there, but we'll be coming in with the trade winds at our backs and the currents with us. Their window of opportunity will be very small." He flashed a sharp smile. "And it wouldn't be a bad opportunity to test our weapons against theirs. Or our mages."

"Thank you, Captain."

Forty more days of sailing. Plenty of time to get seriously bored, then the ship could play a game of run-and-seek among the islands while I stood by and waited some more. Eh. I wandered down to the fighting deck to look for something to do.

We had one and two-thirds companies of Silbari marines on board *Waverunner*, with the other third of the second company split between *Defiance* and *Stormrider*, which each had another company of their own marines as well. Only one of the four total companies would go with the new ship. The full company had filed up from the artillery deck below, a hundred and twenty men strong plus officers and staff. They unrolled practice mats on the middle section of the fighting deck under the muted commands of their officers. Their Lieutenant looked to be near my own age, he was the junior of the two commanders. D'Auson had told me he'd be taking this one to the new ship, the *Queen of the Seas*. My special version of magesight noticed a small glow under the officer's skin, one that shouldn't be visible to a normal Mage. I realized that he had Haroun's Gift, the inner resistance that shrugged off magic attacks as if they were gnats. It also let the possessor cut through any protection spell ever cast. The Gift was why Mages didn't rule our world. Pen had it and I'd met a few other warriors with it before. Terrell's Army and Navy recruited all they could get, which was not as much as he wanted because it was still a rare talent even in Silbar. I wondered how much that had to do with D'Auson's choice, and whether he understood that it wouldn't help the man against me.

The Lieutenant greeted me politely and introduced himself while a couple of grizzled sergeants hovered near and shamelessly listened.

"I'm Lieutenant Pallir D'Ibarra Viettar, commander of the First Sorianti," the officer explained, naming the city on Silbar's Vettore Coast where his company of marines had originally been recruited. "We saw you practice with the Second Rovigo the last few days, Sir DiUmbra, and we wondered whether you'd spend some time today with us?"

His words reminded me that in the Marines' eyes I would always be a warrior before I was an ambassador, and that he saw me as a man who his young battlers could learn from. I could hardly refuse, and besides, I didn't want to. I'd feel better after I chucked a few more soldiers about.

"Glad to, Lieutenant Viettar," I told him gravely and peeled off my shirt and sword belt. "Let's start with some unarmed combat."

Two hours and much sweat later I'd taught his soldiers a couple new tricks and learned one myself. They were good boys, Silbar's finest all wiry and tough and eager. They made me nostalgic for my early days in the DiUmbra Acrobatic Troupe. Their sergeants were tougher still, a real challenge for me. One with a grumbly North Vettore accent managed to almost pin me. He saluted me with a big grin and a thick "Thank yew sor!" when I let him up off the mat afterwards.

Lieutenant Viettar challenged me last. He had four fingers of height and reach on me and the muscles to match, he probably outweighed me by half a stone. But wrestling isn't about raw strength and weight, but how a man uses them. He still nearly pinned me before I broke his hold and set him on his back. Even then he bounced out of it before I could pin him. We fought back and forth a dozen times, his greater reach and weight against my greater strength and agility. Once he nearly kneed me and once I rattled his teeth with a chin strike. At last I slipped through his guard and tripped him, fell on him and mimed the death blow. He slapped the mat in submission, then laughed as I pulled him to his feet. He grabbed my right forearm in the Warrior's Grip, his face bruised and exhilarated while his troops cheered us both and pounded our backs.

It was a lot like the finish of a performance with my Troupe in the old days. I can't say I didn't enjoy it. Viettar had the same gusto for life that filled my DiUmbra brothers.

"Thank you, Sir DiUmbra. That was instructive!"

"You're welcome, Lieutenant Viettar." Something about his honest delight in the skin-to-skin struggle touched my heart and won my trust. I found myself adding, "When a man of your skill's nearly beaten me in the challenge ring, he can use my first name."

Viettar broke out in a pleased grin, not least because the honor I bestowed on him was so public. "And please you do the same with mine. Will you break your fast with my company this morning, Kirin?"

The galley's chimney had spewed smoke for an hour and the scent of cooked porridge had crept up from below to torment us. My own stomach rumbled as I said, most sincerely, "Pallir, I'd be delighted."

One of the marines handed me my shirt and belt. As I pulled it on I realized that White had watched me from his station, which gave him an elevated view over the crowd. He turned away immediately but I caught a resentful expression on his face. Maybe my strategy of refusing to rise to his baited comments was paying off. I silently wished him more frustration and went below.

The marines slept on the artillery deck, right below the fighting deck where the catapults stood and where we'd practiced. Second Rovigo, the eighty-man-strong fractional Marine company, had reset duty this morning and had stayed below to stow hammocks and unbolt *Waverunner's* knockdown dining tables and benches from the ceiling, set them up, and then get the first serving of breakfast. The last of them had just turned in their cleaned and dried bowls and spoons to the galley crew. They poured the used wash water out the opened artillery ports as First Sorianti filed down the portside ladder.

"Looks like they left the place neat and shipshape for you," I commented.

Pallir D'Ibarra Viettar grinned with a sharp edge. "They'd better. We switch off every few days. If they start to leave dirty dishes for us, they might find their mugs pissed in the next time. Though we officers usually crack down on that kind of behavior pretty quick. Both companies have to sleep in this room at night, so we keep rivalry in bounds."

He took a lead place in line – rank has its privileges – so I joined him. *Waverunner's* cook and crew dished us up warm bowls of pease porridge with bits of bacon and broken-up hardtack in it. A mound of oranges completed the meal and everybody snagged a couple as we filed by. The men all lined up at the tables, steaming bowls before them while they stood at attention with their purple and white uniforms buttoned up despite the tropic warmth.

"Men of Silbar," Dona Millente intoned from the front of the room where her portable icon of the One God had been set up. "Bow your heads and give thanks."

She ran through a mercifully quick prayer and then we all sat and ate before the warm spells on our bowls ran down. The porridge had softened the hardtack into a plain but filling meal and the oranges were at a peak of ripeness. Dona Millente and Dona Seelie moved among the tables to check on injuries. The yellow glow of their auras flowed over the men one at a time. The marines didn't hold back when they trained and there were plenty of scrapes and bruises and even a couple real injuries. Twice I noticed the brighter glow of power channeled into healing some young Marine whose stoic face relaxed under the Priestess' ministrations. It distracted me and I reminded myself yet again that nobody in this room but the two women and I could see the magic that they spread so generously. Except maybe the cook; he had enough fire talent to warm bowls so he might have magesight too.

I wondered if Pallir had magesight. Haroun's Gift isn't usually found with any other talent, but I didn't suppose it was impossible. So I asked him.

"No!" he laughed. "One magic talent's enough for me."

Before he could say more, Dona Seelie came to our table. She examined Pallir and touched a brief Heal spell to his jaw.

Then she turned to me.

"And what about you, My Lord Ambassador DiUmbra?" She rapped a finger on the board in front of me. "Do your old injuries trouble you today?"

"No, Dona," I answered truthfully. "Your grandmother does excellent work."

"So I've been told. Will you allow me to check on it just to satisfy my curiosity?"

I suppressed a sigh and answered, "As you wish." Then I forced my Shadow inward into a tiny space under my heart, and allowed her aura to enter through my skin. I held it away from only the deep-most private places of my mind and heart, and felt her spells churn about inside me before they withdrew. It tickled but I wasn't remotely tempted to laugh.

Her diagnosis was quick but thorough. "Bones quite healed, yes, and no internal scars, very impressive." Her face gave away just how much I'd really impressed her and I felt uncomfortably warm.

"Your grandmother is still the most talented healing artist I've ever met," I told her sincerely. "It was my great privilege to be her canvas." And I hoped I wouldn't have to be Dona Seelie's on this trip.

She looked at me in a way that told me she could guess that last thought, but merely said. "Indeed. The One God be with you, Sir Kirin." She went over to aid Dona Millente with her last patient at the far end of the room.

Pallir, who'd sat mute throughout this little show, rubbed his jaw and stared at me after she left. "I've never before heard a Priestess ask any man's permission before she examined him. Not even a Captain. Why'd she do that with you, if you don't mind me asking?"

"Because if I didn't *let* her under my skin, she couldn't 'examine' me at all," I admitted shortly.

"Right, you're a Mage of course, and the King's Left Hand too." He went two shades paler and lowered his eyes. "I didn't mean to presume, My Lord, and I apologize for forgetting my pla—"

I stopped him with a gesture. "Don't, please, Pallir. I get 'Sirred' and 'Lorded' enough to drive me mad. We're both soldiers for the Crown, while we're on the mats or at mess together or, The One help us, in a boarding action. Let's just leave it at that. Or I might have to flatten you twice tomorrow."

He grinned and looked at me eye to eye. "You can try, Kirin. So, please indulge my rude tradesman's curiosity, and tell me the story of just how you ended up with broken bones that had to be Healed by one of the highest-ranked priestesses in the land?"

"Ah. That was my own stupid fault. See, there'd been a Shade haunting this nowhere village on the Storm Pass Road, only there turned out to be two, and a demon besides –"

I gave them the edited version of the story, which means I left out little details like my dive into Hell and the way Terrell had rescued me. His physical eyes hadn't ever quite recovered from the damage he took then, but that secret we explained to nobody. Somehow the marines collected our bowls and washed them for Pallir and me even while they jockeyed for the best spots to hear. When I was done they uttered a kind of collective sigh. A couple of those who'd furtively made the Sign Against Evil when I started now looked as rapt as the rest.

"You tell a good tale, Kirin," Pallir acknowledged with frank envy. "I wish I had one half as –"

The voice of the lookout shouted overhead, faint through the open artillery ports. "Windwhales! Windwhales astern and three points to port! Out of the fog and closing fast!"

The bosun's whistle shrilled and his gravelly voice bellowed. "Clear the decks! All nonessential crew get below NOW!"

"Looks like you get your wish, Lieutenant," one of the older sergeants grinned at Pallir. "Sir, with your permission, I'll have the men grab the best places to see before the Second Rovigo gets here."

Pallir answered, "Make it so, Sargent." There followed a general movement toward the port artillery doors, all of which were open to let air in. *Waverunner* presently ran west-southwest across the trade winds and heeled several degrees to starboard. The twenty big arbalests that partly filled the long artillery deck, ten to a side, were folded up and covered in canvas. We crowded around them and Pallir ushered me to a front row spot. The bottom of the port was only two feet above the deck so I knelt down. That way Pallir could see over me easily and we could both stare across the waves.

A dozen huge shapes loomed out of the fog bank. They were flattened ovals, black above and pale below, three hundred feet wide and most of a thousand feet long. *Stormrider*, sailing a few hundred feet away and as much behind us, looked like a child's toy in front of their immensity. They floated perhaps seventy feet off the water and moved with the wind, which would take them across us at a sharp angle.

From their bottoms hung rows of fleshy strips like the tentacles of a jellyfish. They were ropy and the last few feet lined with suckers like an octopus. The ends trailed in the sea and one contracted to lift a big tuna out of the water. There wasn't any way to tell for sure the size of the flexing silvery shape but I thought it must be longer than me. The fish twitched feebly as it was raised up and up toward a bulge in the bottom of the huge body.

"Did the whale do something to that fish?" I wondered. "Shouldn't it struggle more?"

The old sargent nodded. "M' Lord, there be a stinger on the end of each tentacle, 'bout half as long as yer little finger. Anythin' it stings goes stiff and quiet-like, but not dead. They like live food so's they make it hold still while they eat it, m'Lord."

Smaller tentacles fringed the bulge, these helped push the fish into a hole that had to be a mouth; I could just glimpse white teeth. A moment later the tuna's tail fell back out and tumbled towards the water below. I suppressed the urge to shudder. It can be bad to be gifted with too much of what Terrell calls 'a rich imagination.'

"Do they just eat fish?" Pallir asked as he leaned over me to stare.

"No sir, also seals, and turtles, and whatever else they can catch, sir," the grizzled sergeant said. "Including nice pink babes like you young'uns. I once saw a sailor snatched right off the rigging."

Many of the younger marines surged away from the port, then sheepishly came back as he laughed. I pointed at *Stormrider*. Her smudge pots had been deployed and lit in hopes that the smoke would drive the whales away. Most of her crew had gone below. The handful left wrapped themselves in ropes.

"Sailors tie themselves to the ship?"

"Arup, sir." The old marine nodded. "Generally the whale 'all let go if it can't pull you in on the first try. But sometimes they keep pulling. Saw one little middie torn in half that way. Sure hope the blood loss kilt him before he got to the mouth."

All of the marines and most of *Waverunner's* sailors were packed into the artillery deck now, they crowded the ports. Somebody made a halfhearted suggestion to close them but was roundly shouted down. We all stared as Stormrider's skeleton crew hauled on ropes and her helmsman put the wheel over hard as he tried to dodge that fleshy curtain. Our own smudge pots added a tang to the air, but the way the wind blew the smoke would simply be carried away.

Then the suns' light dimmed as the forward edge of a windwhale passed over us. Hoarse shouts came from above. A leathery slapping sound reverberated through the ship as tentacles groped over the deck above our heads. A sailor screamed, then the sound was abruptly cut off.

A tentacle as thick as my arm came through the port.

I felt my curls parted as it passed above my head. Pallir uttered a startled yelp and stiffened as it stung him, then encircled him. There was no time to do aught else but grab my belt knife and stab upward. It was like stabbing a wet boot heel, the tentacle was so leathery and dense. I drove my knife in with all the strength of my body even as a foul stench washed over me. Several marines grabbed Pallir and tugged back before the monster could drag him through the port. For a moment the struggle wavered, then another knife came in from the side, and another. The tentacle abruptly released Pallir, splashed us with watery blood that tasted of seawater and acid, and jerked back outside. A moment later we sailed out from under the whale and full light returned.

"Sir!" One of the marines had caught Pallir before he could fall. "Lieutenant!"

He was as stiff as a board and had a red welt on his neck bigger than a coin. It dribbled blood.

Another marine helped the first and anxiously demanded "What's it done to him?!"

"Fetch the Dona," I ordered. "He looks paralyzed."

The men made a space and set Pallir on a bench. He breathed but couldn't talk or even move much, his limbs all stiff. Dona Seelie arrived and instantly started to work on him. To my surprise White elbowed his way through the crowd with a sliver of silver in one hand, began to drain it and feed the power to her. I stayed well back and squeezed my Shadow into a tiny space under my heart.

"Is 'e goin' to live?" asked the old sargent anxiously while he hovered at the magic user's elbow. White ignored him.

"Yes," Dona Seelie grunted, absorbed in her work. "This is a nasty poison, but it seems to attack only the voluntary nerves." She was silent for a while, her hands pressed against Pallir's neck. I could see her Healing spells wrestle with the paralysis inside his body. Pal's eyes rolled about mutely and looked from her to White to me and to his men. White finished wringing the last power out of his sliver of silver and stepped back just as Pal's limbs twitched and he let out a long groan. It was a few minutes more before Dona Seelie drew back her spells and let him sit up again. He dabbed futilely at the new stains on his uniform.

"You will have a scar where it stung you, Lieutenant,' the Priestess told him as she bandaged it. "And you'll probably be weak for the rest of today. If your men and Sir DiUmbra had not rescued you it would have eaten you. You're very lucky to be alive."

"Don't I know it, Dona," he answered, then nodded at White. "Thank you for your help."

The Mage made a curious little head bob and said nothing.

Then Pallir looked at me. "Thanks most of all to you, Kirin. You saved my life."

"Don't fret yourself over it," I told him lightly. "Someday you might get to return the favor."

~ ~ ~

Chapter 15: Xiphree – Zurtos

Forty-fifth day of Summer

Zurtos knew something was wrong the instant Captain Beliat's little sloop *Falcon* sailed into the harbor of Xiphree City. The city lay on the inside of a hook-shaped promontory that cradled a sheltered bay. It didn't need Aretzo's formidable harbor defenses to protect it against storms.

Though naval assault would be quite a different matter! He thought sourly, noting that work on the half-built guardian fortress at the harbor entry had been stopped again.

Then he saw the black banners hanging from every building. They glistened in the setting suns' light, and he understood. Black silk was reserved for the most pious expressions of grief. Such extensive signs of mourning could mean only one thing in Xiphree.

The King is dead!

Zurtos schooled his face to hide his sorrow. He had loved the old King, but he trusted the Crown Prince to carry on his father's wise rule. Right now he needed authorization to continue his assigned mission, and quickly, lest the cursed Shadow-mage get to Dalbai before him. He hastily cast a message construct and sent it to a trusted ally in the city, explaining the need and asking for his help to win an audience with the new King as soon as possible.

He was gratified when it was answered before they reached the docks, though the curtness of the response puzzled him. It wasn't until he reached his ally's home that he understood.

"They're *all* dead?" Zurtos couldn't keep the shock out of his voice.

"All but the youngest son," the other Mage confirmed. "Nobody seems to be entirely sure what happened. Rumors are rife, and hard knowledge scarce. Apparently the old king had ordered a fireworks display in honor of the Crown Prince's eldest son's birthday, and it went bizarrely, horribly wrong. An explosion leveled part of the palace and killed everyone in attendance, including most of the Royal Family. Leaving only one candidate to bestride the throne."

"Revallix," Zurtos muttered. He had little liking for the old King's youngest son, and suspected that the feeling was mutual. Zurtos was mildly amazed that some other mage family hadn't made an immediate play for the throne. This wouldn't have been the first time the Xiphree succession had been contested violently.

Unless, of course, they had, and this was the result.

His ally raised a warning hand, glanced significantly to either side. They were both master mages and met in a spell-secured room, but privacy was never guaranteed in Xiphree.

"Revallix has turned out to have surprising alliances," the Mage told Zurtos delicately. "Including three of the five Major Houses." He said no more, but his face assumed a suspicious expression. By which Zurtos guessed that the ill-fated birthday party had been under-attended by the members of those Houses, and rumors of collusion and assassination were flying.

Zurtos swallowed a queasy feeling, shook his head. "That just makes it even more imperative that I meet with His New Majesty. Xiphree has an opportunity to sabotage Silbar's play for power over the Inner Ocean, but it is a brief opportunity. You must get me into his presence as soon as possible."

"That I can do," his ally nodded. "Whether you come out again, well, that may be more difficult. Watch yourself, Dameon. Our new king is more – exuberant – than the old."

"I've no choice," Zurtos grated back. "Just get me face-to-face with him today."

~

Zurtos barely had time to bathe and dress in his stored finery before he was ushered into the new King's presence. He remembered Revallix as a callow youth fascinated by bizarre magical experiments upon animals and sea life. A dilettante to whom he and the other Master Mages had paid little attention.

That might have been a mistake, he thought as he beheld the young King bestriding the saddle of his father's elevated throne. Zurtos walked the echoing length of the teak and ivory throne room in dead silence. There were a dozen mages and fifty soldiers in the room and none of them so much as breathed audibly. *That's not a good sign.* When he reached the prescribed distance from the foot of the throne he prostrated himself to his young monarch. It couldn't hurt to start out humble.

Revallix let him lay on the floor for twice the usual time. *Just to show me who's in command here, may the Twelve–Horned God humble the brat!* Zurtos silently cursed to himself as he stared at the marble inlay in front of his nose. Then the King tapped the brass gong at his side, just enough to let Zurtos know he could rise to his knees.

The Mage did, sitting back on his heels and staring impassively up at the throne even though his mind screamed at the delay. Etiquette required him to wait for his king to speak first, and he had a feeling that this was a very bad time to violate tradition.

"Zurtos." Revallix spoke his name with a flat tone that was all the more threatening for its emptiness. "More than a year ago my late lamented father sent you to Silbar on a mission that did not go well. Now you return from another just after the bad word of this Dalbai alliance reaches Our ears. Have you further ill news for Us?"

Zurtos spared an instant to thank his god for such a gift of an opening. "No, your Majesty. Instead I bring the good news of opportunity. But it is fleeting. May I explain?"

The young king leaned forward slightly. "Do."

The hour that followed, sweating under the stress of Revallix' regard, was one of the worst of Zurtos' life. The young king was more than amenable to preventing Silbar's move for power over the Inner Ocean; too amenable. The fool wanted to challenge Silbar directly! Xurtos spent half of his allotted hour dissuading him, while the two mages closest to the throne quietly fed their Lord's reckless ambitions. Finally Revallix reluctantly agreed to the safer route of sabotage rather than open war.

"Which would be Xiphree's ruination," Zurtos found himself growling at the two court favorites. Both were younger than he, full of pride and still feeling the heady rush of early accomplishment. "Silbar is more than twice our size, has four times our ships, and the wealth to support them."

"Our Master Mages are more powerful than those of our northern enemy across the Sundering Sea," Revallix observed as the two glared back at Zurtos.

"On the average, Your Majesty, and slightly, but please recall that Silbari mages outnumber ours seven to one. Your Majesty, quantity has a quality that simply can't be argued with, if one wants to live."

Revallix shot him a questioning look. "But what of Osrick's known dislike of Terrell? Cannot something be done with that? Perhaps he would be glad to see Silbar's pride humbled."

Zurtos groped for words. Considering the Empire as a whole (and while Emperor Osrick didn't love his half-brother, he clearly would see Hell frozen before he'd give up Prince Terrell's annual tribute), the idea was beyond insane.

After far too much argument he finally convinced the twenty-year-old King. The two favorites retired from the argument a little too gracefully for Zurtos' peace of mind. Revallix had an ugly gleam in his eye when he agreed to authorize Zurtos to draw on Xiphree's connections around the Inner Ocean.

"I'll grant you the tools you seek, Zurtos, and a few more." The arrogant royal gaze bored into the Mage's eyes. "But I demand results. Stop this marriage alliance. Stop it dead."

"I will not fail, your Majesty," Zurtos recklessly promised. "Either I will capture the Dalbai Princess and kill her protector, or kill them both."

Revallix smiled at that. "Good. But if you manage to take her and also take the Silbari Shadowmaster alive, that would please me even more. I have a use in mind for that one."

Xurtos blinked. "He's an extremely dangerous man, your Majesty. And by all accounts, extremely loyal to his lord."

The King's smile broadened into a grin. "Do not underestimate the uses of pain, Zurtos. Any man can be broken, given enough will on the part of his captors. That one could be trained to make a splendid weapon, once the right persuasions have been applied."

The audacity of that vision boggled the mage for a moment. "Do you really think, your Majesty, that —"

Revallix' grin sobered and he nodded once, hard and decisive. "I do. I am not without experience in this area, Zurtos; in time you will see that. The gamble is worthwhile."

"I can promise nothing regarding that venture, your Majesty," Zurtos managed. "But if the Twelve-Horned God should send such an opportunity my way, I will remember your words, and strive to deliver. At the very least, I will take or kill the Dalbai Princess."

"Don't fail me," Revallix warned. "For if you do, I will have no choice but to send my fleet to intercept this Silbari squadron when it returns. This wedding must not happen."

"Understood, your Majesty." Zurtos bowed at the King's dismissal and left the throne room, relieved to have escaped with his mission, and his skin, intact.

~ ~ ~

Beliat was ready and eager to go. *Falcon* left Xiphree City behind before another hour had passed. The Klinto's relief at departing what was, to him, merely another enemy harbor, was tempered by apprehension over the largest of the King's parting gifts.

"Can it keep up?" Beliat quietly asked Zurtos as *Falcon* turned to the setting Suns. "I must make forty knots to catch up to the Silbaris."

The mage eyed the water behind the ship. The little sloop's wake was marred by a small swirl a few hundred feet back, a swirl that was keeping pace even as Falcon gained speed.

"Yes," he reassured the Klinto Captain. "It can sustain that speed for days, and even move faster if needed."

"Then will it *stay* where you put it? And go where you send it when the time comes?"

Zurtos sniffed. "It had better, or I will teach it regret."

Beliat looked like he was trying to find reassurance in those words, and failing.

Zurtos left him at his ship's wheel, casting wary glances back over his shoulder, and took himself below. Jos had a meal waiting for him, the first he'd eaten all day. As he dined, Zurtos hoped and prayed his young king wouldn't do anything stupid if the Dalbai mission did fail. The Silbari squadron had to sail more than five thousand miles on this trip, an effort that would strain the best ship and crew. By the time they were homeward bound on the final leg of their voyage they would be worn down, which he planned to aggravate at every step of the way. A simple attack near the end, pitting fresh ships against exhausted ones, would be more than enough. All Zurtos need to do now was make sure the enemy *was* exhausted by that time.

Though if he could seize the prize himself, so much the better. A dead princess who never left Dalbai was preferable. Add a dead Shadowmage and Zurtos would be satisfied.

Though there was a certain lure to imagining DiUmbra slowly broken.

Zurtos shook his head to banish the temptation. The man would be hard enough to kill. Capture offered insane risks. Though another of the King's parting gifts, resting as yet unseen in a chest brought aboard at the last minute, had interesting potentials.

Zurtos smiled coldly to himself. He had already decided that there was something to be said for inflicting a death by a thousand cuts. Soon he should be able to launch another attempt. And if it failed, there were the Beniyah sulking in their cabin, and other tools. He opened the coded packet containing passwords and contacts for Xiphree's spy network in the Archipelago. There were some surprising things in it.

~ ~ ~

"How close are we to the Silbaris?" Beliat asked three days later.

139

Zurtos shrugged. "Difficult to say. The location spells yield direction, not distance. They are still ahead of us, that much I am sure of, but they slowly shift to our south, which means we gain on them. If you can maintain this course and speed for two more days then we'll pull even with them. Hopefully we'll see their masts against the southern sky that night."

"So long as we see no more than that." Beliat patted the little ship's steering wheel protectively. "My *Falcon* is fast, but she cannot trade broadsides with a warship."

"They have no knowledge of us, and are not likely to gain any while under sail." Zurtos waved one hand in a negligent gesture. "It is chancy at best to send a message construct to a sailing ship. Their Circle of Colors would have to figure out who I am before they could even frame a warning. Chance is very much in our favor." He made a small prayer of aversion and blew a sacrificial pinch of kruff downwind in propitiation, for the Twelve-Horned God was notoriously touchy about his prerogatives where Fate was concerned.

"Let's hope so," the Klinto replied, scowling. "I am willing to take risks to kill this Silbari scheme, Zurtos, but I intend to return home to Klinto with both my ship and my skin. This is politics for Klinto, not vendetta."

Zurtos made a placating gesture. "I understand, Beliat. Have no fear, I'm as fond of my skin as you are of yours."

He turned away so that there'd be no chance the captain would read his next thought in his face.

But I will not only risk more than you dare, I will risk you and your ship as well. DiUmbra must be brought down.

~ ~ ~

Chapter 16: Inner Ocean - Kirin

Sixty-first day of Summer

A scent of cinnamon came to me just as I finished a round with one of Pallir's marines. The kid was good, fast reflexes and not afraid to get hurt in a fight. He even thanked me after I planted him face first into the mat. He'd serve the Crown well.

"I need a break," I told the rest. "Now you can all show your officers what you've learned."

The sergeants took over, some with fierce grins on their faces. My training sessions with the two companies of marines were very popular with the men. Nobody wanted to be stuck on punishment detail and forced to miss one. As a result discipline in the ranks was the best it had ever been on *Waverunner* despite two hundred marines crammed into a space meant for a hundred-twenty. Both Pallir and his opposite number in command of the Second Rovigo, Lieutenant Connir Ville Crebinet, were very happy.

I was having a wonderful time.

I swarmed up the ratlines to the foremast's lookout. The higher station on the mainmast was presently manned so this one was empty. I settled onto the crosstrees, careful that my Shadow didn't break the protection spells that kept wyverns and other pests from attacking men on the masts and rigging. The sky was empty of all save a single windwhale many miles to the south, and an albatross that loafed just off the starboard bow.

I opened my mind to my brother. *This is well before the usual time,* I told him. *What did you find?*

His voice was strong again. Every day that he practiced with the Hill let him reach me a little easier.

*Good news and bad news. First, my City Watch talked to the dock workers who cast off the docking ropes for that Fehdaran galleon, she was the *Hibiscus*. Two workers recognized her captain go aboard shortly before she departed, unusually late for him, and accompanied by a new helmsman. Only yesterday the Captain's body turned up in a canal in the Sump weighed down with stones. The fish had been at it but he still had his garb and gold ring. His throat had been cut so deeply that his spine was almost severed. Must have been very messy.*

I whistled. *Then that mage was good enough at disguise spells to pass for the Captain with his own crew!* I remembered the sailors on the doomed galleon and added, *Who he then murdered. This bastard is hard on his tools.*

And alarmingly good at covering his tracks. My Watchmen have no idea how he lured the Captain there. Somebody must have seen them meet, somewhere on or near Aretzo's docks, but we've no leads to him at all. Where he stayed, who he might have met, nothing.

But?

My Ambassador to Xiphree has good news! He's identified our enemy as Dameon Zurtos, one of the most powerful mages in their capital, who is currently 'away on Crown business.' Zurtos has a servant – slave, really – known only as Jos who is reputed to be a skilled assassin. And Zurtos is an Air-Fire-Earth-and-Water mage locally famed for his levitation skill.

*Sounds like the bastard on the *Hibiscus*. Servant-assassin, flying carpet, it fits. But what was he doing with DiMerio's bunch? Why was his aura on part of their machine?*

The Colors haven't figured that out yet. I could wish Cathghar D'Ivor DiMerio had been a little less closemouthed with his secrets. Did DiMosil tell you anything more?

Nothing. From the look on his face when I questioned him about it, I think his lover keeping that secret bothers him almost as much as the fact that I killed DiMerio.

You didn't kill him. With a little luck he would have survived that fall. You had no way to know he'd land on his head.

The White doesn't see it that way. He thinks I used my pet demon to break his lover's skull on purpose.

I brooded, remembering the horror of that moment. Sevan's scared face staring at me between the bars of his cage, the obscene spider of steel blades and crystals squatting over him and the other sacrifices, the water clock counting down time as a bizarre spell built up to a deadly discharge, and the rapt lust on thrice-damned DiMerio's face.

Terrell's mind brushed mine gently, a consoling touch.

He chose his path, and with it his death. If it hadn't been by your hand, it would have been by Pen's, or he would have been burnt at the stake for the sin of blood magic. And either way, the final responsibility was mine.

I sighed wordless agreement and changed the subject.

One thing still bothers me. I know I broke a couple bones in that assassin's hand, but he could use it almost normally the next day.

Then he received highly skilled healing from someone in Aretzo. No little hedge-witch healed two broken bones overnight. None of the Temples reported a patient with that kind of damage, and we've asked every ranked Priestess in town. It might have been a visitor, but nobody known to be that powerful paid an official visit within that time.

*Great, there's an unknown woman involved too. *

Odds are this Zurtos brought a Xiphree Priestess with him and his servant. And kept her hidden too. He has to be a master at disguise spells.

Might have known. I shook my head.

We also have one solid link, if I may call it that. The Council of Colors have tried for days to tease something out of those fragments they scraped off the wreck, and they've finally succeeded.

They traced it to this Zurtos?

No, but they were able to trace his carpet. So well that Mage Green, after nine failed attempts, finally persuaded a location spell to seize the fragments and point to its current whereabouts.

I reflected that Green was stubborn enough to try such an exhausting and expensive spell nine times, too. The man was like a badger that way. *You gonna make me ask?*

It's less than a day's travel north of your squadron and moving in the same direction. Since it's very unlikely that any mage could have made it fly for that long, it must be aboard a fast ship.

Salim's hairy arsehole! I'll bet it's not in a cargo hold with a bunch of rejects headed for some island chieftain.

I'll decline that wager, thank you very much. Whoever he is, Zurtos or someone else, it's likely he knows where you're bound and he plans to beat you there.

Can we – Damn! I can't tell Velis to go faster, can I?

Not unless you can come up with a reason that doesn't include me whispering in your ear from twelve hundred miles away. I'm going to send a message construct to Velis and D'Auson alerting them to all this, it should get there in a day or two and you can ask him to crowd on more sail then. But remember, we've no idea what Zurtos's ship looks like or how big it is, where it's actually bound or whether it's alone. I doubt the practicality of stopping and searching every ship on the way to the Archipelago.

Damn Ifni's Luck. Damn, damn, damn!

Must you slide into blasphemy? It may come back to haunt you one day.

I'll worry about that when it does. So the bastard is sure to get there before us, and I can't even tell anybody what to watch out for; we already know he's good at disguise. Are there any hints at all? About the ship he's on, I mean.

Very few, and all ambiguous. A fast packet left Aretzo the day after you did, with an official destination of Alibar. They should have arrived by now. Snowdon came up with a sufficiently ambiguous tax question that we could plausibly send an inquiry about them to the Alibar Port Mages in the monthly message construct. With luck we'll get an answer this tenday. A Klinto sloop left the night after you did on the last of the evening ebb bound for Haresalaam, picked up passengers there and left with a claimed destination for Holbinnh and Klinto, neither of which will answer a snoopy message construct from Silbar. A fishing boat vanished three days after you left, but there was a squall in the area and they may have simply gone down or been wrecked somewhere in the eastern islands. And I doubt any fishing boat ever built could pass Waverunner and her sisters on a trip across the ocean. There could easily be another ship involved – if it didn't dock in Aretzo's harbor it'll be a lot harder to find, though it would also have attracted local attention wherever it did land.

Salim take that Zurtos. What if he tries to assassinate Princess Callia next?

I already thought of that. I had Aytin send a message construct to Queen Sephora with a carefully-worded precis of our discoveries and concerns. I had to minimize your role in it all, I'm sorry about that, but I hope it'll inspire her to be very careful with her daughters.

Good. I brooded for a moment but the next step was obvious. *Velis says we should sight Volcano Island in a few days. He thinks we're only ten to fifteen days from Dalbai. I guess I get to stew until we get there, then I go ashore expecting the Xiphree bastard to try to do me dirty at any moment.*

Not necessarily. He's failed at three assassination attempts and you're now surrounded by hefty magical and manpower defenses. He may plan to even up the odds. He may be headed for Khaitanial, or about to talk or trick somebody else into attacking you on the way back. That's more or less what I expect. After all, his real goal must be to destroy the alliance. Killing you is just an incidental added handicap.

There's another happy thought. You're just full of good news for me today.

Sorry, Kirin; it goes with the mission.

I know. I'm just cranky. I hope this Zurtos tries to go hands-on with me. Right now I'd really like to lay my hands – and my Shadow – on him. Hard.

Careful. Vengeance is a bitter fruit.

I know, I know. But I can dream.

One last thing before I go.

What?

Mage Green says you owe him a favor now.

Damn.

~ ~ ~

Chapter 17: Inner Ocean – Zurtos; Barlen; Kirin

Sixty-first day of Summer

The Klinto sloop *Falcon* sped westward under the Wheel of Stars with all sails set. Her deck constantly heaved up and down as bursts of spray broke over her bow. Now and then bigger waves surged onto the deck and swept it clean. Zurtos slammed the companionway door shut behind him just in time to keep one of those out of the cabin.

Captain Beliat grinned at him from his place at the wheel. "Trouble sleeping, Mage?"

Zurtos scowled. "Say rather trouble breathing. The stench down there, by the Twelve-Horned God! Four Beniyah stink bad enough when they aren't puking. Together, I don't know how they stand themselves."

"You thought it important to fetch them," the Klinto pointed out.

"And still do. When I go up against *these* enemies, I want the most skilled assassins I can hire on my side."

"I hope they'll still be able to stick a knife in their target when we get to Dalbai." Beliat adjusted the sloop's wheel slightly. "An assassin who can't even stand isn't much use."

"Give them three days on dry land again and they'll be as fast and deadly as I could wish. Less, if we can find gentler seas or cross them with less haste. I myself feel like a seed in a maraca!"

"It cost us a four day delay to sail to Haresalaam to get these Beniyah for you, and another day to pause in Xiphree on the way back. If you want me to catch up to the Silbari squadron, I have to make up that lost time somehow."

"I understand the necessity, Captain, and I am not arguing with it." Zurtos smiled. "Indeed, I would urge you to still greater haste right now."

"How close are they?" Beliat asked.

Zurtos' smile sharpened. "Very close. By sunset we'll see their masts against the southern sky."

"I'd prefer that we see no more than that." Beliat patted the little ship's steering wheel protectively.

"Now is not the time for fear, Captain. When we are in sight of them I can launch what follows behind us."

Beliat's jaw tightened at the implied insult, for a moment he hesitated. Then his face turned stony and he nodded. He turned the wheel toward Zurtos' indicated closing course with the yet-unseen Silbari squadron.

Zurtos nodded. "Very good. I'll prepare our nighttime surprise for our enemies."

~ ~ ~

Burlen Crasset DiMosil, Mage White, quietly slipped out of the cabin he shared with the other two mages. Rellir was on duty tonight and Arlein was snoring in his bunk. Burlen carefully shut the door behind him and stepped several paces down the dark companionway until he could see into the artillery deck. The marines were sacked out in rows between the folded arbalests. Lieutenants Pallir Viettar and Connir Crebinet had their heads together over some paperwork lit by a lonely night lantern.

Burlen silently cast a small spell, sent it drifting into the artillery deck just under the ceiling. The tiny spark crept along, virtually invisible in the dark, until it reached Pal Viettar. Then it dived and stung him behind his left ear.

Pal scratched at the annoyance, then told Connir, "The rest of these are fine with me. How about you take care of the men tonight and I'll return the favor tomorrow and the next day, aye?"

The other lieutenant squinted at him suspiciously. "You gave in pretty easily, Pal."

Pal stretched his arms over his head and affected a yawn. Burlen admired the artistry of it.

"I'm just tired and want some sleep. I'm going to sack out in the hold tonight. Deal?"

"All right. Pleasant dreams, Pal."

"See you in the morning, Connir."

Pal strolled down the narrow aisle left between the ranks of sleeping men. Burlen stepped back into the hallway and when Pal entered the narrow space, flicked a small light spell to illuminate his own face.

Pal smiled and quietly said, "I hoped that was you."

Burl looked up at him – the marine was half a head taller than the mage – and whispered back, "One worshipper of Sath can recognize another."

"Nobody's sleeping in the tiller room tonight," the marine suggested.

The mage nodded happily. The two of them made their way down the companionway steps to the hold and the little room where the tiller controlling the ship's rudder was housed.

~ ~ ~

I had bad dreams.

That's usually my Shadow's fault. It was this time, too. The monster wanted my attention. D'Auson snored in his bunk while *Waverunner* rocked across the seas in the way that gave the ship her name. I finally gave up trying to sleep, pulled on my hose and a shirt again, and went up to the command deck. I passed Rellir on duty in the Mage Station as he yawned while adjusting the nighttime ward spells. He nodded cautiously to me.

The officer on duty, First Mate Cassaret, greeted me quietly while the night helmsman bowed to me in tongue-tied awe. I answered the Mate in monosyllables and he wisely recognized that I wanted to be alone. I went to the starboard corner of the stern, where the shadow of the huge gaff sail covered me like a blanket, and leaned on the railing.

Calm's waning crescent was poised to slip below the western horizon. Madness had already risen and crossed paths with the larger moon to shine like a baleful eye ahead of *Waverunner. Defiance* sailed a little ahead and to starboard of us, *Stormrider* behind and to port. Moonlight barred the long rolling swells and put their troughs in darkness.

I gazed aimlessly over the striped seas, not seeing them as I wrestled with the thing inside me.

What do you want? I growled silently at it. Occasionally it answered my questions, though rarely in any way that left me more comfortable. More often it didn't, but pressed me with an unfocused longing that could drive me to distraction. That was tonight. I leaned my elbows on the ship's railing and rested my forehead in my hands. This looked to be one of those nights when I got no sleep at all.

~ ~ ~

Zurtos struggled to direct the enslaved creature. It was one of the Xiphree mage guild's newer efforts and had been well trained to fear the lash of magical pain. Unfortunately, that did not make it any smarter than the average seagoing beast.

The situation was made even more awkward since he could not magically scry for his target. The damned

Shadowmaster's presence aboard made his ship effectively invisible to most scrying. Only the locator device, with its link to the hair of others on the ship, escaped the effect, and it was too imprecise for this purpose. But *Stormrider* and *Defiance* were not so masked, and by tracking them he had figured out that *Waverunner's* captain tended to sail between the other two ships. If he could keep the beast focused on the central ship, there might be a chance to disable or even sink it.

He urged his monster forward.

~ ~ ~

Cold images flowed up from my Shadow's lair under my heart. Pressure, chill pressure on every bit of my skin as if I was squeezed by an enveloping fist. Darkness filled with vague swirling shapes that I couldn't make out no matter how hard I stared. That was the most unnerving feature of all, for I've been able to see in the dark ever since my Shadow first blossomed in me.

I gripped the ship's rail hard enough to make my fingernails hurt. *What does it mean!* I shouted back silently. My Shadow roiled within me, struggling. M*ean, mean, mean,* it echoed back at me.

Then the darkness and movement flowed past me — no, I was moving, through something that felt like water. I was filled with a great hunger, and prodded by a great terror, something that would hurt me unless I did its will. I was rising, and moving forward under ripples of light toward something that could sate my hunger; three somethings. I started to turn toward the nearest and the terror behind lashed me again. Ruthlessly it whipped me toward the thing in the middle, a long narrow shape moving away from me, pointed at the front and flattened at the back. It cast a complex shadow on the ripples above me —

~ ~ ~

The creature had found the target. Zurtos couldn't see the ship through its eyes but sensed from its reactions that *Waverunner* must be right in front of it. The creature was baffled by the spell-sheathed hull, instinctively realizing that the ship wasn't food. It was ravenously hungry, wanted only to turn away and find flesh to gorge upon.

Zurtos sent pain to prod it forward. There was warm tasty flesh aboard the ship, and the beast could climb, even right out of the water if necessary.

~ ~ ~

Burlen DiMosil, Mage White, sighed happily and snuggled against the marine's side atop a flattened-out pile of spare sailcloth. It made a tolerable bed despite being wrapped in waxed canvas to keep damp at bay. A few feet above them the tiller, the big lever that controlled the ship's rudder, swung a couple degrees as the helmsman three decks above adjusted the ship's course. The thick ropes descending from the steering wheel ran through huge pulleys on either wall of the tiller room to tug the lever back and forth.

"That was wonderful," the mage whispered to the marine.

Pal grinned back at him in the feeble illumination of the mage's light spell. "You're pretty wonderful too. Such an unexpected talent for lust! I haven't had any man make love to me so skillfully before. Did you discover that on your own or were you gifted with a past lover who taught you so well?"

Before the mage could answer, the tiller suddenly jerked above them. The rudder groaned and shuddered on its mountings. Seawater splashed through the gap where the lever pierced the hull and brought with it a foul stench.

"What in the nine hells?" Pal tried to leap to his feet and narrowly avoided bashing his head on the tiller.

"Something's attacking the rudder!" Burlen scrambled to his knees, grabbed the big lever with both hands and sent a surge of lightning along its bronze reinforcements. Whatever had seized the rudder let go with a thrashing that sent more foul smelling water through the hole.

"I've got to get to my men!" Pal grabbed his sword belt, scrambled through the door into the orlop deck and ran for the stairs.

"Wait!" Burlen called fruitlessly. "You forgot your clothes!"

~ ~ ~

I realized almost too late what my Shadow was trying to tell me. Waverunner suddenly heeled and began to sheer off course to starboard. Something was dragging at our hull.

"Sound the bell!" I bellowed at the First Mate. "Wake the mages! *Waverunner's* being attacked from under the sea!"

Blessedly, the man didn't question or argue. He seized the bell rope and began ringing it with all his strength.

~ ~ ~

The rudder proved to be better protected than Zurtos had guessed. The shock from the guardian spell almost frightened the Kraken free of his control. He let it dart to the side and grab onto the hull while it recovered. It tasted the water and its tiny mind recognized a familiar flavor, for it had been fed on convicted criminals while being raised, and had developed a taste for the salty flesh of Man.

Zurtos was relieved. Now that the monster had discovered the ship's crew, his job would be easier. He prodded its hunger to flare up. The creature's arms were fifty feet long, easily enough to let it pluck men from even the highest deck. It pulled itself to the surface and reached.

~ ~ ~

A glistening pale tentacle rose from the Inner Ocean towards me.

"Goddamnit! Has everything in this ocean got tentacles?" I groped for my blades, and only then remembered that I'd left my sword belt in my cabin.

The tentacle lunged. I dodged.

The horrible rubbery length of the thing came over the railing and slapped down where I'd been. It stank of salt water and death and splattered me with cold wetness.

I ran towards the First Mate and the helmsman.

"Weapons!" I shouted. "We need swords!"

The officer whipped out his key ring and clattered down the port ladder to the fighting deck to unlock the cutlass cabinet. The tentacle groped around the command deck. It was getting nearer to the night-helmsman, who bravely stayed at his post even as he trembled and prayed. I had to keep the creature away from him.

I grabbed a belaying pin from the mizzenmast and hit the nightmarish thing as hard as I could.

That shifted its attention. The questing tip whipped towards me. I smashed it against the deck with my belaying pin, putting every bit of strength I had into the blow. The tentacle recoiled, I must have hurt it, and I knew a burst of hope.

Then four more came over the rail.

Just then Rellir cast a light spell onto the mizzen yardarm and the sail too. In the blue light the marines poured onto the fighting deck. They'd armed themselves in answer to the alarm bell, some not even taking the time to dress. Blades raised and an animal roar rose from them as they attacked. Steel bit two of the new tentacles in ten different places and they threshed in agony. The coils knocked twenty men down and flying blades cut two more. Rellir hurled a fistful of fire darts at a third tentacle and it recoiled. Then the fourth one seized a fallen marine and dragged him over the rail. He screamed all the way to the water.

I couldn't spare him any attention. The tentacle I'd hit before had come back for me.

~ ~ ~

Xurtos urged the kraken on. It tore at the first man and the taste of blood roused its appetite to raging hunger. It scarcely needed his prodding after that. The creature pressed itself against the side of the ship and let out a mighty squirt from its muscular water-pump to propel it half out of the ocean.

~ ~ ~

A monstrous shape rose above the rail of the fighting deck, a giant spearhead of glistening flesh sporting eyes bigger than my head. The monster sent more tentacles onto *Waverunner*'s fighting deck.

Pallir was there, clad in nothing but his sword belt. He rallied his men and a wall of steel met the probing arms. The other marine lieutenant led his men in a charge from the forward part of the ship. The kraken caught a second marine and twenty swords hacked the man free.

"Sir Kirin!" The First Mate shouted. "Catch!"

He tossed a ship's cutlass at me hilt first. I snatched it out of the air and slashed with the same motion. The tentacle was barely deflected as blood splashed. It caught the helmsman's leg as he fought to keep the ship on course.

He'd had the good sense to tie himself to the ship's wheel mountings with the ropes used to guard against windwhales. The kraken tugged; the ropes tugged back, but this creature was vastly stronger than a windwhale. The helmsman began to scream as the tentacle strained.

I chopped right through the damn thing.

Watery blood sprayed me as the severed stump thrashed. The helmsman kicked desperately at the bit still stuck on his leg. The suckers left round marks in his skin as they peeled off.

Rellir had launched more flights of fire missiles at the exposed eyes. The monster reacted with a jet of black ink that splashed several marines, including Pal.

Mage Arlein staggered on deck and DiMosil followed close behind, both half dressed. That slowed neither of them. They began hurling fire darts from their fingers towards the looming body beyond the ship's rail.

That maddened the beast. It seized the mainmast with two tentacles and bodily pulled itself onto the rail. The ship groaned at the sudden addition of tons of weight and the deck tilted. Two men lost their footing and slid straight towards the invader. A tentacle lashed at one of them and Pal's twin swords pinned the end to the deck, then slashed it badly before it tore itself free. The rest of the men rescued their comrades and pressed the attack while the mages kept up a rain of fire against the hulking monster. Tentacles writhed, revealed a mouth wide as my arm span with a hard beak that clacked angrily.

"We're hurting it!" DiMosil bellowed. "Why is it still attacking us?"

Oh. Of course. I could have kicked myself for a fool.

I gathered my Shadow and sent it at the creature.

Black as the creature's own ink, my Shadow spilled across it, lapping over tentacles, beak, eyes, and the great triangular body. There were spells on the beast, some implanted so deeply I could barely find their roots. But I didn't need to find a whole spell, any piece of it was enough.

My Shadow bit. Spells shattered.

The monster shivered and released the mainmast. Tentacles curled over its trunk as though trying to hide it. The railing crackled and groaned as the creature toppled backwards off the ship. The last few fire darts quenched themselves in my Shadow, then the sea surged and the monster was gone.

I drew my Shadow back inside my chest as everybody gaped at me.

"Thanks for your help," I told the marines. "If you men hadn't kept those arms busy, that fight would have gone badly for me and the helmsman."

The helmsman gulped out a loud prayer of thanksgiving. Several of the marines preened at my words. I didn't mind; they deserved it.

"What was that damn thing?" Pallir demanded, still dripping black ink. He let the tips of his swords drop toward the deck, speared a severed bit of tentacle and held it up. "Looks like octopus, only a hell of a lot bigger!"

"Kraken, Sor," his grizzled sargent answered. "Big un, usually they're not mor'n a dozen feet long, but I've heard tell of some as big as ships."

Mage Rellir shook his hands to quench his firedart spell. "Twelve years at sea and I've never seen the like!"

"Do they often attack ships?" Mage White asked the old sargent.

"Only ever heard of that happenin' oncet, Ship's Mage," he answered with a dip of his head. "An thet was a fishin' boat wit a full load. Musta smelt the fish or sumthin."

"This one wasn't after fish," I said. "And it wasn't any blind chance that it came after us instead of *Defiance* or *Stormrider*. There's an enemy mage nearby. I tasted his magic on the kraken."

"Same mage who attacked us outside Aretzo?" asked Captain Velis.

I jerked my chin in a sharp nod. "Yeah. Stubborn bastard. He's got to be on a fast ship somewhere out there." I waved at the night-dark ocean.

Velis looked at the mages and me. "I will be relying on you gentlemen to shield us from him."

Rellir and Arlein looked at DiMosil. He looked at me, glowered, but said, "A task we'll gladly undertake, Captain." His glower turned into a vengeful smile as he added, "Next time I want us to be the ones who surprise *him*."

First time I agreed with him on that trip.

~ ~ ~

Zurtos pounded a fist on the sloop's rail. Control over the creature was completely lost, the spells so badly shredded that he could barely tell where the monster had gone. It sulked in the depths to gorge on squid and fish, and ignored his every attempt to control it. Soon Falcon would leave it behind. But if he ordered Beliat to turn back and stay near it, the Silbaris might make it to Dalbai before him.

With an aggravated sigh, he released the link and let the creature go. Another Xiphree mage might be able to reclaim it someday. For now, there were other plans to lay.

~ ~ ~

Chapter 18: Aretzo - Penghar

Eighty-first day of Summer

Penghar didn't like the Old City of Aretzo. It was too crowded, too decayed, too chaotic. Men and women jostled together in the winding streets and alleys with little respect for rank. Donkeys brayed and the pavement – when there was pavement – was a horror. His boots would require serious cleaning when he got back to the Palace. He hoped that whatever servant got stuck with the task would at least deserve it.

The alley he currently followed bent sharply right where the instructions said it would. He ducked through the low arch at the left. The brick-vaulted tunnel made him squirm. It would be hard to draw Irreneetha in this narrow dark space and the smelly little stream running down its center made footing chancy. Fortunately the tunnel soon opened into a squalid courtyard and he could stand upright again.

Tenements on either hand loomed four stories high, sagging balconies festooned with washing and loud with the sounds of children and women. Most men in this neighborhood were laborers elsewhere, the few ground floor shops were shuttered. The fountain in the middle of the long narrow space burbled anemically. Pen guessed the input pipe must be partly blocked, since this place was close enough to the Great Quanaat that water pressure should be adequate. The water overflowed the basin in a green sheet to fill a laundry trough, then dumped into a gutter choked with the contents of too many morning chamber pots, and finally ran out the tunnel toward the nearest sewer.

On the far end of the courtyard the buildings were lower, only three stories, and behind them a wall reared another dozen feet. The top of a tree could be seen beyond it. Another arched tunnel lead, not into a tenement, but through it. The keystone of that arch was made of red porphyry that gave a lonely splash of color to this drab slum.

Pen swallowed to ease a sudden tightness in his throat. He knew what lay beyond that wall, through that tunnel.

I am proof against their worst, he thought. *Against* her *worst. Terrell would not send me here if I were not.*

Irreneetha hummed slightly below the audible level, at least to any ears other than his own. Reassuring him.

He pulled the concealing hood further over his face and clutched the nondescript cape around him. Then he stalked across the courtyard and into the second tunnel before he could think better of it.

A spell rippled over him, probably something designed to exclude the uninvited. The tunnel's floor was dry and clean and did not stink, quite at odds with the courtyard. After a few paces the floor began to slope upward. It was dark for thirty paces and then turned sharply to the right. A mage lamp ignited to shine on a stair a dozen paces ahead of him. He took the steps two at a time to find another bend, left this time. Six more paces under the light of another mage lamp led him to another left turn and a second stair new-lit by a third mage lamp. He was fairly sure he'd just passed through the high wall that had once marked the uphill boundary of the Old City. This stair also featured two more spells, the second a visible barrier of silver strands that made Irreneetha grumble. Pen paused a step below it, pulled the sword far enough from her sheath to let her pommel touch the sheen of the spell. It parted like a curtain and the sword's grumble faded back to her watchful hum. She was no more pleased by this place than he.

A final turn and a short stair brought him into a garden. He barely noticed the last two spells as beauty caught his eyes.

Beds of flowers spread to either side, orange and crimson poppies and purple delphinium and pink elephants' head, dashed with yellow sunstar and blue and white daisies. A path of circular stones lead through a turf of thyme. The tree he'd seen from outside arched overhead, its spring blossoms faded so that small green seed pods peeped from their withered petals. A delicate gazebo of white marble interrupted the path directly ahead.

A woman sat under its cool shade. Or . . . not quite a woman.

She wore a flowing dress of ocher-tinged brown that covered her from throat to wrist to toes. One small slipper peeked out from under the near edge. A bland color, a modest and antique style, but the fabric was Sulucid spidersilk and woven through the entire dress, skirt and bodice alike, were strands of crimson. She petted a black cat with one pale hand, white as the northern snows he'd known too well through the Gwythlo winters of his youth. The cat surveyed him with incurious eyes, yawned to expose fierce little teeth, and commenced licking a front paw. The woman gestured gracefully with her other hand at the opposite bench, and spoke.

"Welcome to my garden, Baron Sir Penghar Verhys DiLione, Right Hand of His Majesty – pardon me, His Highness. Please be seated."

Pen abruptly realized that the last spell he'd walked through had been some sort of cleaner. His boots were immaculate. He couldn't stop his eyes from darting around the garden in search of listeners.

She chuckled. "We're quite alone. None can enter this garden but you and I, nor can anyone outside it see within, nor hear any sound we make. I would not compromise your . . . reputation."

Pen forced himself to take a step, then another. Thyme leaves crushed under his cleaned boots and the pungent scent battled the sweetness of the flowers. He entered the gazebo – the roof was high enough that he didn't have to duck – and warily swept his cloak aside as he took the bench opposite her. He did not put his hand on Irreneetha's hilt, not yet, but he kept it close. She had made it a point to pretend to adhere to Emperor Osrick's petty restriction while also acknowledging Terrell's claim to the ancient Silbari title, but that meant little.

"Madam Ymera," he ground out, intentionally stressing the first word. "You sent my Lord a message."

"And he honors me by sending you in response." She smiled, revealing perfect white teeth. None of them were pointed, as legend said they should be, but he wasn't fooled. She could probably change her own shape to suit her whim. "I am flattered."

"Only one other would dare," Pen growled back. "And he's not here." For a moment he wished otherwise, this was an assignment he'd gladly have handed to DiUmbra. Who'd probably have hated it for completely different reasons.

She raised one exquisite eyebrow, midnight hair stark against her white, white skin. "True, I'm sure by now he's rather closer to Dalbai than to Aretzo. And he would have come to me by my front door, being less concerned with reputation than yourself."

"Or having less of it to lose." Pen immediately regretted the words.

Her smile became just a little sardonic, then smoothed back to the bland mask it had been. "You are both remarkable men, Sir Penghar. In seemingly different ways, but in the end equally remarkable."

That sounded like a subtle payback for the 'Madam' reference. "Is he the reason you asked for this meeting?"

"Part of it." Her smile became enigmatic. "Indulge me for a moment, Sir Penghar. Who are the great powers of Aretzo, and Silbar itself?"

"My Lord Prince Terrell," he immediately answered. "The Hierarch and her Circle of Septissimas. The Archmage and the Council of Colors." He paused and honesty made him add, "Kirin DiUmbra. And you."

When he didn't continue she raised one eyebrow in almost mockery of his own habit. "And yourself. Let there be no false modesty here, my lord. The aristocracy and the merchants guilds might also be counted, but let us stay with those who wield raw power, the stuff of magic, and leave aside those who wield power over men through authority or wealth. Although neither is to be despised, those are not my concern today."

Mystified, he objected. "I am no mage. For that matter, neither is my Lord."

This time she raised the other eyebrow; he was sure now that she mocked him subtly. Irreneetha sang softly to him alone so he put his anger aside and listened.

"There is no other soulsword in all of Silbar, unless the fables about Cahir's Tomb are true. Concerning which I remain skeptical. Say better that there is no living bearer of such save you. And is She not a device of power? That it flows to you from divine means rather than arcane is of little import. Further, his Highness has gradually learned to control that enormous artifact under the Hill bequeathed to him by his ancestors, and learned to persuade the wight within it. He may not be a Mage in the sense that Aytin Cervisi is, but he certainly wields Power. So. What is the relationship between the powers we have named?"

163

"My Lord Prince Terrell rules Silbar from the throne of his ancestors, wearing their Crown. I serve him, body and mind. The Mage guild and its Council of Colors serves him too through their Archmage. You are oath-sworn to him as you were to his ancestors, though the particulars of that oath seem rather more to your advantage than to his. And the Temple serves him in so far as it serves anyone outside the Hierarchy, which is not very much. Kirin DiUmbra is sworn to my Lord much like myself. Does it amuse you to make me recite like a schoolboy, so that you may correct me?" Pen asked irritably.

"I find little to amuse me in a threat to my home and life."

Her words were so cold it shocked him. Her smile had vanished and the face it left behind held no trace of good humor.

"Name this threat," he said, keeping his voice steady.

"I cannot. I can state with certainty that it comes from a woman, a high-ranked woman of the Temple Hierarchy. She is willing to ally herself with enemies of Silbar to further her aims, and she has a youthful spy inside your Prince's Court. Beyond that I know little, but I will venture to guess that, at least, she is displeased with the marriage arrangements of His Highness."

Pen shook his head. That last part could fit at least half the Hierarchy, more like three-quarters. He knew that the Inner Circle had voted down or deadlocked on a dozen other marriage proposals, most sponsored by one Septissima or another, before finally approving the Dalbai alliance. And even then he suspected that many of the Septissimas had voted for it simply because it didn't reward any of their rivals. "Can you describe her?"

"An adult woman of medium height, completely covered by a hooded robe and a veil."

That fit most of the Circle and the Hierarch too, plus several thousand other Priestesses.

"A simple 'no' would have sufficed," Pen groused.

Ymera shrugged elegantly, a slight ripple of her shoulders and hands. "My cats do not see colors well, and have little memory for voices." Which was the closest she had ever come to acknowledging how she knew so much of the goings-on in Aretzo. "But such a woman met with a foreign mage in an abandoned garden here in the city, twice. The second time a Klinto ship captain was also present, though not one known to me. Her name was not spoken, but that of the mage was – Zurtos."

Pen felt his face betray him. "You knew this and waited until now to tell my Lord?"

She tilted her head and moved her free hand in an exquisite expression of irony. "'Knew' is too strong a word. The name meant nothing to me, their plots were not obvious from the small snatches of conversation I received – less than a tenth of what they spoke, unfortunately. It was only when I learned, just this morning, that Prince Terrell was seeking a foreign mage of that name, that I understood this was more than the old stale rivalry between the Temple and the Colors. Perhaps if I had been consulted earlier?"

For the first time in years Pen was tempted to curse. "You dare to punish my Lord for not confiding in you, you creature of Darkness! Isn't it enough that he grants you his protection and a free reign over this festering sore on Aretzo's body?"

The look she gave him then was drier than the desert winds. "So narrow, your perspective is, and so arrogant your judgements. Compare my Red Street to that of any other port city in the Empire, or outside it. Are not my women healthier, safer, more kindly treated by the men who seek them out? None is ever beaten here, not more than once, and any man who harms one of my women regrets it very deeply indeed. It is because of my rule that all who enter are on their best behavior; soldier, sailor, tradesman, merchant, mage, noble, all men. I protect more citizens of Aretzo every year than you will in your paltry human lifetime. Do you think that mitigation a mere coincidence?"

Pen scowled and fought the temptation to squirm under her gaze. "I know nothing of whores, in this or any other city. But I know you buy your long life with those of the unborn."

"Say rather, that Silbari women gift me with those tiny lives when they buy my protection spells. I do not compel them to pay me for this service, yet they flock to me by the tens of thousands, the hundreds of thousands. They send me lives forced into being by men seeking satisfaction of their lusts. Yet you blame the women alone for their state, don't you?"

Irreneetha hummed, a long lamenting descant for the lives that would never be, and Pen shuddered as the note grated down his spine.

"Enough," he managed. "You've added a little to the small scraps we've found so far. Thank you for that. But why do *you* feel threatened by this plot?"

Her alabaster face assumed the expression of a grandmother talking to an exceptionally dense grandchild. "This dynasty is young and fragile, yet I gave your lord my fealty. If those who wish him to fall should succeed, where does that leave me? I have very limited ambitions – to hold what I have. Prince Terrell, young as he is, understands that. Those who would supplant him or his betrothed may not. A threat to him is a threat to me."

Pen blinked, nodded. "I . . . had not thought you would see that so clearly."

The grandmotherly expression faded, replaced by a cold regard. "Then think more. It will do you good. I have passed such warning as I have. Now it is up to your lord to profit from it. Fare you well, Sir DiLione."

Pen didn't quite know how he found himself once more descending the stair, spells closing behind him like iron doors and mage lamps blinking out in his wake. He pulled the cloak once more close about him and made his way back to the palace with his mind in a whirl.

"Someone in the Hierarchy wants to sabotage my Lord's marriage," he whispered to himself on an empty stretch of street. "Wants it so badly that she allies with Silbar's enemies. But who? And how do I stop her?"

For one of the few times in the past seven years, he wished that DiUmbra was here.

~ ~ ~

"I don't know that we here can stop her, Pen," Terrell answered him an hour later. "But I find solace in the thought that at least some of her sisters will be irate when they know. We must trust Kirin to manage the trip itself; all we can do here is try to find more answers, and prepare for Princess Callia's arrival. Did Ymera give you any hint who this spy might be?"

Pen scowled. "No. I don't think she had any idea."

Terrell looked thoughtful. "Keeping Ymera so isolated eases conflicts with the Hierarchy, but limits her usefulness to me. We would know more if she could recognize more of my court and the Hierarchy by sight. I'll have to give thought to that."

"Terrell," Pen said urgently. "Remember, she's a vampire and an abortionist! And cunning as an old crocodile in the Poison Marshes."

"I know, old friend, I know." Terrell gazed into the empty air. "There must be a way."

"Well, it will be half season before the princess gets here, so I suppose we're not in a hurry."

"Yet." Terrell shook his head. "But I'm starting to suspect that we will be. Somebody is playing a game for stakes that we don't know about, and that worries me."

Pen studied him for a moment. "What are you thinking, my Lord?"

Terrell slowly said "There may be a way to tease some more answers out into the open. A way to stimulate others into launching their own inquiries. The bigger the fleet that scours the sea, the better the chance to find an enemy ship. A great many ships can be launched with a single word, if it is uttered in the right place."

"And where would be this 'right place'?" Pen asked, mystified.

"The most watched 'unimportant' place in Aretzo. This is a risk, but one I think is worth taking."

"You know I don't mind risks."

"Not to you. I imagine the only danger you'll face is some disrespect, which I expect you to endure. Time for you to make another visit to the Old City, my friend, with no disguise. To Kirin DiUmbra's home."

~ ~ ~

Chapter 19: Aretzo – Penghar; Meltha

Eighty-first day of Summer

The Sulfur Serpent Inn had repelled Penghar on first sight, seven years ago, and every time since. It didn't look any better today. The tall brick tower on the corner was built to look like a snake. Shaped bricks mimicked scales and a terracotta viper-face loomed five stories above the junction of Sulfur Street and the Serpentine. A ceramic tongue protruded between the eroded jaws and cracked fangs, its forked tip long ago broken off. White birdlime streaked the tower's upper works. The roof bulked high and sprouted three rows of dormer windows. The slates were ragged as broken teeth, many time repaired without concern for appearances. It looked as seedy and down-at-the-heels as an old whore on the docks.

DiUmbra chooses *to live here? That shouldn't surprise me.*

The broad street was jammed with wagons and men intent on their business, many oblivious to anyone else. Pen managed to cross without getting run over and was almost glad to climb the steps to the corner entrance and enter the vestibule. The thick brick walls cut the fierce outside heat almost as well as a spell. His eyes needed a moment to adjust to the darkness within the round entry.

This is the first time I've ever come here when I knew he wouldn't be present, Pen thought to himself. *It feels strange.*

An arch to his left opened to the foot of a staircase and another on the right revealed a broad taproom. High narrow windows admitted dim beams into the tavern through actual glass, wavy and dusky green. The big room was mostly empty at this hour. A man polished mugs behind the bar and a small group diced in a corner. Those carefully studied him and he saw their tension rise as they recognized him. It could be an advantage to have one of the most famous faces in Aretzo. He deliberately looked away. Nobody down here was likely to answer his questions with anything but lies anyway. Upstairs, perhaps, he might find a little truth.

He climbed the three flights, conscious of the tall well of open air above that ran right to the floor of the Serpent's attic. Today he took the time to examine the place more closely than he ever had before. The second and third floors were rows of anonymous rooms lining long straight hallways that ran north and west from the stairwell, both hosting the faint odor of chamber pots and vomit. The fourth floor was different. The north wing was closed off from the stairwell by a door sporting a carved and painted wooden sign that said 'DiUmbra Acrobatic Troupe.'

A child sat on the top step playing with a cat. Her large brown eyes watched him as he approached and her face went carefully blank when she recognized him as a noble.

"Girl, I need to speak to the leader of the DiUmbra troupe. Please take me to him."

"Sir, who shall I say wishes to see my grandfather?" Her voice was as wary as her face but her manners were decent. She made a little head-bow just deep enough to acknowledge that he had rank without asking what it was. Someone had trained her to deal with important strangers. Pen didn't remember ever seeing her before. Had she been posted here as a lookout because Kirin was away?

"Baron Sir Penghar Verhys DiLione." Pen heard his words echo faintly in the stairwell.

"This way, sir." The girl's face betrayed nothing as she stood up and led him through the door with the sign. The cat mewled in complaint and followed her, weaving in and out of Pen's feet as he walked. He managed not to step on it.

Inside was a long hallway of doors, but she turned immediately into another stair not part of the big well. It went up at a steep angle and opened into a vast high-ceilinged space lit by those dormer windows. There men swung through the air on trapeze bars and children walked on tightropes rigged knee-high off the floor. Pen paused to stare up at the huge spiderwork of wooden trusses arching overhead to enclose the vast space, over thirty feet high, half again as wide, and six times as long. Wooden ladders ran up support pillars to ropes that crossed parts of the room. A huge net was suspended waist-high off the floor with two trapezes swinging above it. As he watched, a lithe youth launched himself from one trapeze and somersaulted in midair. His hands slapped into the hands of a bigger man swinging upside-down on the other and together they swung back and forth twice, then the catcher tossed the young flyer into the air again. The youth touched finger to toes and arched back in time to grab the same trapeze he'd leapt from.

Another man slid down a rope and landed with a thump a few yards away. He was as muscled as any knight but wore only patched hose and a scowl, no weapon in sight. The acrobat demanded, "What do *you* want here?"

There's the disrespect Terrell warned me about, Pen thought. Aloud he said only, "To speak to your Magister. I am Baron Sir —"

"I know who you are." The man's glare was furnace hot. His fists were balled so tightly the blood had fled them.

For an instant Pen wondered if the churl was actually about to strike him. But Irreneetha was quiet, she saw no danger here. Carefully Pen said, "Then you have the advantage of me. Are you —"

"Sevan Sule DiUmbra. Sevan the Younger, Kirin's older brother. I know who you serve. What does *he* want of us now? Isn't it enough he took Kirin away and sent him into danger? What else will he take —"

"Sevan." The new voice was older, calmer, and heavy with authority.

The angry man stiffened, then after a moment turned and made a little head bow to a squat man with gray sideburns who had just approached with the girl. "Papa," he said through gritted teeth. "It's not right!"

"Baron Sir DiLione." The authoritative voice greeted Pen in much warmer tones. The older man's bow was correct as he added, "I am Sevan Sule DiUmbra, Magister of the DiUmbra Troupe, also called Sevan the Elder. Please pardon my eldest son's lack of proper manners. He is very worried about his brother. Come with me to a private place that we may talk, My Lord."

"Gladly, Magister," Pen answered, dropping the younger DiUmbra from his attention.

Sevan the Younger turned on his heel and stormed away while his father led Pen to a round room in the Attic's corner.

"Please be seated, Baron." The Magister ushered him to a shabby chair with a seat padded by a tattered rag cushion. "We've little of civilized comforts to offer you, but I do have tea, and I could have biscuits sent up from the tavern if you like. Anything else would take a while, I'm sorry to say, My Lord."

"Thank you but no, I'm not hungry. Tea would be pleasant."

While his host busied himself pouring two mugs from a gently steaming kettle on a small hob, Pen looked around. He realized this must be the top floor of the tower that gave the building its name. The brickwork bulged and curved to echo the serpentine face displayed without. Brick piers jutted into the room from the walls to support the domed roof overhead. That had a round skylight in the middle that would be invisible from below. It was propped open and blue sky shone through the gap. The oval windows of the snake's eyes were a full yard across, half again as high and filled with stained glass; their centers pivoted on bronze rods. Two more windows were set on either side of the little entrance hallway behind the viper's face. All were braced open to let a welcome breeze into the room and out the skylight.

A cat lazed on one windowsill and gazed at him insolently while outside the other a raven perched. Pigeons could be heard cooing beyond the eyes and a hawk flapped to a landing on the rim of the skylight.

Pen stared back at the cat sourly. "Do you know –" he began when the Magister handed him a steaming mug. The aroma was plain and a little harsh, not softened with the spices one would typically find in aristocratic teas.

"Of course, Baron DiLione." The elder acrobat gave him a sardonic look. "Did you think Kirin wouldn't have warned his father about the spies? They must get dreadfully bored, listening to an old man haggle over contracts and grumble about bills. I occasionally try to do something to entertain them, probably without success. These days I'm a better manager than performer."

Pen held the mug in his left hand to touch Irreneetha's hilt with his right. The magesight she conferred revealed spells on the cat, the raven, the hawk, and three different pigeons. Plus half a dozen spells in the walls, though some of those looked like parts of the building's own wards.

"How do you keep your wards going with Kirin living here?" He couldn't help asking. "His Shadow eats such, it's been a problem at the Palace and the Chapter House several times."

"It's eaten these a couple times too!" The Magister gave a fond chuckle. "Gave me quite a shock the first time, Baron DiLione. We didn't know *what* had caused the wards to vanish. Expensive to fix! Fortunately the Serpent was built before such spells were common, so it doesn't really need them. We figured out that his room has to go unwarded, which it is now. Kirin just leaves a Shadow to guard it and that's more than sufficient against anything any Mage in the City can do. The last several years he's gotten much better at controlling his Shadow while he sleeps, my Lord. We haven't had to replace a single ward for over five years now."

Pen blinked at this casual reference to living in close proximity to a Shadow. "This dark Talent of his doesn't concern you?"

"Of course my son concerns me, my Lord, as do his brothers and cousins, every hour of every day. How could it be otherwise? They are all my children, by blood or adoption or marriage."

"I meant, if it gets out of his control. Shouldn't you be afraid of the consequences to everyone else here?"

"You don't understand, do you, Baron Sir DiLione?" The old acrobat gave Pen a look that made him feel like a new-minted squire again. "My Kirin is the Master of Darkness, not its slave. He would never allow it to hurt those who love him. The Shadow knows that, and must submit to his will. Thanks to him we are safer than we have ever been in this chance-wracked world. Ifni may roll Her dice as She will, but there is one combination we DiUmbras no longer need fear. Is that not a fine gift for a son to give his family?"

The notion of Kirin as part of a real family made Pen feel oddly jealous. He shook his head to banish the unwelcome sensation. "I'm not seeking an argument, good Magister, I'm just surprised. But I am glad to hear that he has been so open with you, as it may make my task easier. Let me first share some news with you, then ask a question."

Penghar quickly outlined Prince Terrell's suspicions about the attempted assassination and the way the assassin had found healing so quickly. "That is why I've come here to ask you if you know of any powerful woman, Priestess or not, that Kirin considers his enemy."

DiUmbra Senior was obviously taken aback by the question, but he thought it over before replying. "Enemy? No, he's never mentioned any woman that way. He's a little bit afraid of Madame Ymera; well, who wouldn't be? But not of her powers. I suspect it's her overwhelming personality that he finds upsetting. He is somewhat irritated by Dona Seraphina, His Highness' Confessor and Healer, even though my Kirin is quite grateful to her for the way she healed him after that Dalmatzo incident. Which also should not be a surprise to you, I suppose. Rumor is not kind to the woman, perhaps not entirely without justice. While it's true that Dona Tiniea caused him considerable pain when she tried to Banish his Shadow, she did it with his permission, and meant no ill to him personally. Nor did he take any ill from it, or any damage beyond a blow to his hopes."

"What?" Pen felt his jaw drop. "When did this happen?"

"Mmmmmm, perhaps nine years ago now? When he first became interested in marrying my daughter, though I don't think he knew that was driving him at the time." The old man smiled with a mix of pleasure and pain. "He wanted to be worthy of her, and didn't understand that he already was."

Pen closed his mouth on further words for a moment. DiUmbra, trying to get rid of his own Shadow? The thought made Pen dizzy.

"He never mentioned that to you, My Lord?"

"No. I suppose this Dona Tiniea must not have been strong enough."

Old DiUmbra gave him a pitying look. "Strength was not the problem, My Lord Baron. Tell me, can the link between you and your sword be broken by a Priestess?"

"Of course not. Irreneetha is an angel, she cannot be compelled by anyone mortal."

The acrobat stared at him with a small smile playing about his lips, waiting.

Pen sucked in a breath from sheer astonishment. "You think his Shadow is an angel?! That cannot be. The Living Darkness is nothing but evil. The Writ says so! Surely that can only mean he is bound to a demon."

"Does it? But the Writ also says every demon can be banished. I am no scholar, but I can read words on a page as well as a more lettered man. You might benefit by reading again, with your mind a little more open, my Lord."

Pen resisted a flash of anger at the old man's presumption. "We have wandered from my question. Does your son-in-law have any enemies who might have strong Healers in their families?"

"Oh, that gets impossible to tell very quickly, Baron DiLione. You aristocrats are so heavily intermarried with both the Priestesses and Mages, you know, that one can't pick out loyalties just by tracing bloodlines." The magister shrugged. "I believe two of the Colors are married to high-ranking Priestesses, for example. Mage Yellow's mother-in-law is the chief of the Inquisition, and the new Mage White is cousin to the Hierarch, while she also had another cousin who was a brilliant mage, though they had quite the falling-out when he joined the Young Rebels. Tragic situation, that, but Kirin only did his duty."

"I know." Pen scowled. "If he had enlisted my aid it needn't have ended so badly."

"He's not entirely fond of you, my Lord," the old man admitted, "Though he respects you a great deal and even finds you admirable, most of the time."

"'Most of the time?' That's generous of him," Pen growled.

The old man smiled like a cherub. "You might be surprised. To answer your question, there aren't many Healers or Mages that he trusts, especially after the way Chisaad betrayed him. But I don't know of any that he's ever hinted he considers an actual enemy."

Pen made a noncommittal sound. He suspected that Terrell hadn't really expected anything more, but the point was to ask the question where it would be heard. He drank the last swallow of tea and set the mug down on a cluttered table. "Disappointing, but not surprising, I suppose. Thank you for your time, Magister."

"Don't despair of an answer quite yet, Baron DiLione," the elder DiUmbra said with a smile. "I don't know everything he's said inside these walls. I suggest that you go ask my other children. When I'm not there they may remember something that I never heard. By now my eldest son has probably calmed down enough to be civil, though I'll caution you not to expect grace or even good manners from him today."

"I can handle a little rudeness, Magister," Pen answered, standing up. "Or, if necessary, a lot of it, in pursuit of my liege's orders. Thank you again."

He left the office and found the big practice room just as busy as it had been when he came in. Sevan the Younger leaned on a wooden brace for the big net, watching two others swing on the trapeze. He turned at the tread of Pen's boots on the plank floor.

"Papa sent you to badger me." He crossed his brawny arms and stared at Pen, radiating hostility like an oven radiates heat.

"I'm pleased to find that you possess ample wit," Pen answered evenly. "Your father suggests that you may know a possible answer to my question." He outlined it again for the surly acrobat.

Sevan the Younger narrowed his eyes and frowned. "If I do, why should I tell you?"

"Because I seek to help your brother, as His Highness commanded me to do," Pen answered reasonably, ignoring the churl's repeated lack of an honorific when addressing his betters.

Sevan snorted disbelief, put his hands on his hips and leaned toward Pen pugnaciously. "Kirin doesn't trust you as far as he could throw you. Less, since he could throw you two or three yards. I trust you not at all, *noble* man. Your kind treat us like cattle or dogs, expect us to cater to your whims and thank you for it, and cheat us of our pay even when our performances move you to laughter or tears. Anything we tell you just becomes something you use against us."

Pen choked down his own temper before he answered. "You don't know me as a man at all, yet you judge me falsely and with more arrogance than any noble."

For a moment Sevan flushed red as mahogany. Then he growled, "I don't know you as a man? Then let me find out." He jerked a thumb towards a big mat on the far side of the huge room. "Beat me at wrestling, *noble man*, and I'll answer your question. Lose, and you'll leave that fancy garb here when you slink home with your tail between your legs!" He grinned nastily. "Don't worry, I'll let you keep your sword and a loincloth. All else stays."

He wants to humiliate me before his folk, Pen thought, studying Sevan. The acrobat was two fingerwidths taller and a good stone heavier, his waist thick as a tree and his chest and limbs brawny with muscle. *He's strong and he must be skillful, but he's not a trained warrior. This won't be easy — but it's possible.*

"Agreed." Pen strode to the mat, drew his blade and stuck her point into the floor. "Don't anyone touch Irreneetha, she's very particular and tends to sting the unwelcome." He kicked off his boots and began to strip, piling his clothes on a long rough bench set against the wall. When he was down to his loincloth he carefully laid the jeweled sword sheath atop his pile of clothes, then stepped barefoot onto the straw-stuffed mat. "I'm ready, Sevan Sule DiUmbra. May The One grant that the better man win."

Sevan stepped onto the other side of the mat, a hard grin on his face. Others had drifted over with their faces eager to see what was going on. "Uncle Ger. You judge."

An older acrobat nodded, stepped to the middle of the mat, looked at both of them in turn. "I want a decent fight. No biting, no eye gouging, no face punching, and no crotch hits. First man gets pinned and can't break out of it by my count of ten, loses. Step up."

Pen stepped forward an instant after Sevan and imitated his opponent's crouched stance. They were face to face with their noses barely a foot apart. Sevan's face was lit by an angry glee.

"On the word three." Ger stepped back to the edge on the mat. "One, two, three!"

The acrobat exploded at Pen, tried to take him down with sheer weight in one motion. His grip on Pen's shoulders was strong but not enough. The knight ducked sideways and dumped him. Before Pen could pin him, Sevan bounced aside and up. He regained his feet just as Pen closed on him. They grabbed each other's shoulders this time, arms straining and feet pushing against the lumpy straw mat like two bulls in one pasture. Pen ignored the excited yells of the onlookers and strained for advantage. Abruptly Sevan shifted a fraction of a second before Pen was ready and the knight found himself falling. He hit the mat and tried to roll but the acrobat was already on him. They struggled back and forth, Sevan not quite able to pin him but Pen unable to get out of the grip. Then he remembered the movement Terrell had used on him, the one he'd gotten from Kirin. It went like —

Sevan's face showed his shock as Pen flipped him completely over and slammed his back to the mat. Pen almost got him in a scrambling lunge before the acrobat backed away, newly wary, and they both got to their feet again. They crouched, having completely switched places, and panted as they eyed each other.

"Where'd you learn that move?" Sevan demanded, feinting slightly to the right.

Pen matched him and answered "From His Highness, who learned it from your brother."

Sevan glowered. "Another thing your kind took from us!"

He lunged on the last word, caught Pen around the waist. Pen barely managed to break the grip just as the stronger man lifted him and slammed him to the mat. Sevan scrambled for the pin, but Pen eeled out of it and they grappled. Muscles strained and each gasped for breath as they surged back and forth while the watchers cheered. Sevan had more raw strength and was superbly coordinated, but Pen nearly matched him on both counts and wasn't half-blinded by anger. They swayed back and forth, neither quite able to bend the other to his will.

He relies too much on strength and suppleness, Pen thought. *Let's see how he handles true leverage.*

He twisted abruptly, caught Sevan's arm in a lock and forced him down. The acrobat twisted back and heaved desperately. Pen barely managed to hold against him. He kept up the pressure and slowly bent his opponent flat as they both strained and pushed. Pen's own legs spread wide for leverage and his toes dug in as he gradually forced Sevan against the straw, both their faces contorted and gasping. For a while Pen thought Kirin's brother would let his own arm be broken rather than concede. Uncle Ger evidently thought so too for he began to count, but just before he reached ten Sevan slapped the mat with his free hand and went limp. Pen held him an instant longer, felt Sevan's gasp of shame as he accepted defeat, then released him. Pen rolled over on the mat beside his opponent, gasping for breath himself.

"You're – good," he panted. "Better – than most – I've ever – fought."

"Damn – you," Sevan panted back. "Kirin's – only one – who beats – me."

Hands pulled them both to their feet. Ger stepped between them, stared intently at their faces and nodded approval. "Match to Sir Penghar," he declared. "Go rest, both of you." He pushed them both off the mat toward the bench. "Somebody bring them water."

Sevan flopped onto the hard wood and gave a halfhearted glare as Pen fumbled to a seat beside him. A younger version of Sevan brought a bucket and dipper, offered them both a drink. Pen pushed the dipper at Sevan with one trembling finger, splashing them both a little.

"Drink first," he mumbled, and Sevan did. Pen accepted the second dipper and they traded after that. The youth set the bucket on the bench between them and strolled away, looking back once with a big grin.

"You won," Sevan said at last. "I promised you an answer. You probably won't like it."

"It isn't my place," Pen answered carefully, "To like the answers I find, or to dislike them. It is my duty to my Lord to gather them and bring them to him."

Sevan stared at him for a long moment. "He must be something, your prince, 'cause both Kirin and you give him so much loyalty."

Pen raised one eyebrow at that and chose to say nothing.

"There's a woman," Sevan said, so quiet Pen could barely hear. "A priestess. I think maybe she's something to Mage DiMosil, who's now the White. Maybe relative, maybe enemy, maybe even lover for all I know, though she sure didn't look happy to see him! Or maybe she was something to Cathghar, since she barged into his sanctum unannounced. But when Kirin took down Cathghar – you know about that?"

Pen nodded, his mouth gone suddenly dry. "Cathghar D'Ivor DiMerio. The leader of the Young Rebels. The most promising young Mage in Aretzo since Tagir the Traitor, and inclined much like him, only worse. He committed blood magic, or tried to. Your brother killed him before he could succeed."

"And am I ever glad of it," Sevan growled. "Since I was one of the men Cathghar was going to sacrifice to make himself blood-strong. Kirin saved my life that day, and the other seven men in that cage. But I think I was the only one looking in the right place at the right time to see her. She'd come in through a side door just a moment before. She looked confused, I don't think she knew what was happening, and just then Kirin broke through the main door dragging DiMosil at his heels. She saw them even before Cathghar did. Then things got confusing. Cathghar threw a spell and Kirin threw a Shadow back at him, there was lots of screaming. The look on her face when Cathghar fell and DiMosil started screeching, and then the look she gave Kirin – yeowtch! I'd never seen true hate before. Everybody else was busy screaming or crying or, in Cathghar's case, dying, and Kirin was busy breaking us out of that damn cage before the water clock ran out and the blades came in, so I think I'm the only one that saw her. She turned and left right away. Kirin never saw her, and DiMosil was busy blubberin' over Cathghar's body so I don't think he saw anything else."

When Sevan paused for breath Pen asked softly "Can you identify her?"

Sevan snorted. "A priestess wearing robe, veil and hood? You must be joking. She was a good thirty feet away and all I saw was her hands and her eyes and forehead. I couldn't even tell you how tall she was, or how old, though I'm sure she wasn't either very young or very old. Maybe I'd know her again, if I saw her angry like that, or maybe not."

Pen bowed his head in frustration. So close . . .

"See," Sevan continued in a normal voice. "I told you that you wouldn't like it."

"You have my gratitude," Pen answered with formal politeness. "For your words, and for that bout of wrestling. And I'm sure His Highness will be grateful too, and will find a suitable way to express it."

"The only thing I want from him is to have my brother back," Sevan said sadly. "Is that too much to ask? I miss him more every time your lord takes him away from us. Our act is less without him in it. I'm afraid that someday he won't come back at all."

"That . . . is not under my control," Pen told him heavily as he began to dress.

Sevan watched him. Only when Pen finished pulling on his boots and stood up to tug Irreneetha out of the floor and sheath her did the acrobat speak.

"Then whose control is it under, noble man? Your King? That angel who lives in your sword?"

"The One God," Pen told him, sliding Irreneetha into her sheath. She glowed a misty gray that communicated nothing. "The weaver of Fate. You know the answers."

Sevan looked sad. "I do. They're the same answers you *noble men* usually give to people like me. Goodbye, Baron Sir Penghar Verhys DiLione."

"Fare you well, Sevan Sule DiUmbra."

The acrobat sat there silent as Pen walked to the stairs and descended, leaving the Serpent's Attic to its denizens. And as he left, his mind worried one thought over and over.

How does a man with a demon inside him command that much love?

~ ~ ~

The bird patiently waited on Meltha's windowsill until she could make certain she was undisturbed. Then she opened the glass and let it fly in and perch on the special stand she kept for this purpose. She smoothed its feathered head and touched an ensorcelled bit of worked silver to the matching stud set in its tiny skull. The bird held perfectly still while she reviewed its memories. Then she released it back into the outside air with trembling hands, shut the window, and sat very still on her favorite upholstered chair.

He suspects. The Prince suspects, but he does not know. I must plan this very carefully.

She thought it through several times before she even took the first step, for that would be irrevocable. If she failed, her fall would be swift and far, one from which she would never recover, if indeed she survived it at all. But played right, then, oh then, much that was unobtainable now might move within her grasp. The temptation . . .

Meltha D'Ivor DiMun took a quill in hand and set ink to paper.

~ ~ ~

Chapter 20: Daleray - Kirin

Ninety-first day of Summer

I stood on the lookout platform and wrapped my fists in the rigging. *Waverunner* forged steadily ahead under reduced sail, parallel to and only a few hundred feet from the shore of green Dalbai. Clouds of red-and-blue parrots and yellow finches drifted through the trees. Pink blossoms as big as a man's head starred the leaves of great moss-shaggy giants that ruled the ridges. Orange nasturtiums braided the lower trunks of swaying palms on the white sandy shore. The suns lit the huge island like a lantern.

For the first time in seven years, I dared to open my mind completely to my twin.

There was a single flash of dizziness — mine or his I didn't know — and he was there inside my head. My eyes opened wider and colors leaped at me.

Gorgeous! Terrell whispered. *I have always heard that the Dreaming Isles were beautiful. I am glad to see the truth lives up to the tale.*

Can you smell that? I asked as I inhaled deeply of the wind from the shore. Flowers, green growing things, an earthy richness from tilled fields, the odd whiff of animal manure or wood smoke. A storm of gulls passed near and added a dash of their rank fishiness before they departed. Then the heady perfume of a million blossoms drowned all else.

Yes! Wonderful!

My senses expanded again after tendays of shipboard privation. I was very glad to flush my nose free of the smell of tar and saltwater, stale sweat and the stink of *Waverunner's* bilges.

I can smell those too! I feel the wind! Kirin, I'm there!

Good. I relaxed into the sway of the ship even as my own mind soaked into his. I could feel cool unyielding marble under his ass, the sharp dry scents of Silbar's summer in his nose. We were so far apart now that only the Stone Throne atop the Hill of Sight let him reach me. He had his eyes closed and had pulled a cowled robe close over his face to minimize distractions, with Pen on the steps to keep interruptions away. The One alone knew what the palace servants thought of all that, but it worked.

They think I use the Hill to check on the squadron and make sure nothing bad has happened to it, he told me. *Which is completely true, though not the complete truth.*

True enough, I answered. My anxiety began to rise again as I looked west toward Waverunner's bow. *Captain Velis says Daleray City is on the far side of that peninsula dead ahead. We should reach their anchorage in a couple hours. Then this dance really begins.*

I'll be with you through every step of it. But right now you should go get ready.

I don't need two hours to wash and dress.

In full Ambassadorial garb? You will be surprised.

He chuckled, his humor like a tickle inside my heart. For a moment I tensed, almost overcome by the sheer intimacy of the sensation. Then I fought my way back to balance. I panted and clung to the ropes so hard that my knuckles went pale.

Kirin? Are you well?

Sorry, I mumbled. *This is just so — I've never — I can feel you there, sitting on that rock, feel all the Power that runs through you, even feel the Node all the way down there under the Hill. I can taste what you ate for lunch, feel it there in your stomach, the bruise on your knee and the fit of your clothes, and every thought that flies through your mind — and — it's a lot to take in. You're, you're so real right now. Maybe too real for me to stand.*

It's only a little easier for me, he whispered back. *I think we can both cope with it. Thank you for this gift of sharing.*

His gratitude was like one of Sevan's bear-sized hugs, only enfolding me inside rather than out. It almost overwhelmed me.

You're welcome, I managed to think back. Then I had to take ten deep breaths before I dared climb down the ratlines. I could sense him in every movement I made, my legs felt sluggish and slow while his feet twitched against the Hill's marble pavement. But the long descent gave me time to grow accustomed to it, enough that I could walk normally once I regained the deck. It helped that he sat completely still. If we'd both been moving I don't know how I'd have coped.

I went back to my cabin to find young Crevi, one of the midshipmen D'Auson had brought for the new ship. He was some sort of cousin of the captain and stood barely four feet tall. He looked up at me, his twelve-year-old face the picture of earnestness as he saluted.

"My Lord Ambassador, I bring you Captain D'Auson's compliments and I am ordered to provide you all you need to get ready. I've already prepared hot water and a tub."

I looked at the broad tub he indicated, rather like a wooden bucket four feet wide but only two feet tall, and the steaming urns of water. It smelled odd.

"Wait, that's not seawater, is it?" The waste almost shocked me. The ship had carefully rationed fresh water all the way here so we wouldn't have to stop for more. The times we'd been able to wash it had been with salt water scooped up in big buckets on spare yardarms rigged like cranes, which were sometimes dumped over five or six men at a time. The only thing familiar about that was the coarse soap and rough sponges. Though one day it had rained hard and everybody and their clothes got soaked. That had lasted long enough to do our laundry.

"No, My Lord, Captain Velis has authorized me to use some of the ship's fresh water. We'll drain the tanks and refill them in Daleray later today anyway."

"Ah. All right."

"Do you want assistance?" He pointed to a long-handled scrub brush and a bar of soap set next to the tub.

"No, Midshipman Crevi," I told him definitely. "I can bathe myself."

"Then I'll wait outside your door, My Lord. Call me when you're done and I'll have the tub removed and assist you with your laces. I'm trained to assemble noble garb."

"Oh. Thank you." I shut the door firmly after him. *What is all this about?*

Terrell chuckled inside my head. *You didn't unpack the formal clothes I had made for you, did you?*

Not till now. I wasn't gonna take the chance they'd get damaged on the trip. I remember how I had to stand there like a fool while your tailors fitted me. I guess there were a lot of laces. I stripped as we talked and stepped into the tub, it had just enough room to sit. I grabbed one urn, broke the warm spell with a flick of my Shadow, and slowly upended it to pour the steaming water over me. Bliss!

Terrell enjoyed the sensation of the hot water as much as I did. *You'll find you can't get into or out of those clothes without help. Since you don't have servants of your own –*

And that's all right with me. I don't want a bunch of snoops around to pry into my things. I picked up the soap, smelled it; a sweet scent that I couldn't name.

Gardenia. I ordered Captain D'Auson to loan you one of his midshipmen if you needed help. Crevi is the younger son of D'Auson's sister's husband's sister. He's a well-mannered boy who is developing into a fine officer. I think he'll suit you.

Gah. I took up the scrub brush and worked over every inch of my skin, then my hair as well. The sensations echoed weirdly back from his mind. *I don't have to keep him when this is over, do I?*

No, he'll stay with the new ship. But you could learn a great deal from him if you allow yourself to do so.

Scolding me again? I meant it when I told you I don't want to be a high nobleman. Being a knight is as much as I can stand. I don't know how you stand servants fussing over you all the time.

I dunked my head in the tub, which required some contortions, and scrubbed the soap back out of my hair.

To be a proper lord you have to let your servants take pride in their work, the same as with any other craft. And you have to be willing to be the canvas upon which they practice their art, too. It's not so different from the way you used to let the women of your acrobatic troupe paint you before your performances. And with the same purpose; to present a good show.

Urk. I spat out soapy water. *Never thought of it like that.*

You'll find that a little help from a servant at strategic moments makes a big difference. Such as now. How can you pour that second urn of water over yourself and still scrub the soap off? You'll need both hands to lift it.

Damn, I sighed. *All right. You've talked me into it.* "Midshipman Crevi? I require assistance."

"Certainly, My Lord."

He came back inside, shut the door and immediately picked up the urn, though it was clearly a struggle for his strength. He poured it over me in a long slow stream while I scraped off suds and felt horribly self-conscious. I'd grown up washing with the men of the DiUmbra Troupe in the public baths and after every show, but they were family and he was a stranger. I carefully knelt so that he couldn't see the slave tattoo on my thigh. I really didn't want to explain that unhappy bit of my history to him. But he kept his face averted and handed me a strip of cloth to dry myself while he politely turned his back.

See? I told you he has good manners.

Yeah, yeah, you were right. I dried off and pulled on clean white hose, made from a fine cloth that felt like a second skin. *What is this?*

Silk.

Can't be, I've felt silk before.

Sulucid spidersilk, to be specific, imported from southern Xir.

Wow. I've never worn any hose this smooth and alive-feeling.

I can tell. Your physical reactions are astonishing.

The echo of my own sensations returning from him became a shout.

Hey! Don't embarrass me, dammit! This is hard enough!

Sorry. Please believe that I am very grateful to you, my brother, for allowing me use your senses like this.

He was too. I could feel the truth in every thought that flicked through his busy mind. As he felt mine. That should have made it all much harder, but instead somehow it was easier to know just how overwhelmed he was too. *Yeah. Well, you should be.*

I surveyed the array of clothes that had been laid out for me by Crevi. "All right, midshipman, let's get started on this damned harness."

"A moment, My Lord, while I have the tub removed."

He called in two sailors who had clearly done this before. They poured the water back into the urns without spilling a drop and took it all away. Then he picked out different garments and helped me drape myself like a tailor's clothes tree.

"The breeches lace up the back and the front, My Lord. The purple leg goes on your right and the white on your left, please turn them the other way round. Hold a moment, let me get the back laces while you do the front. Be sure the codpiece is comfortable before you tighten the cords, My Lord. There. Leave the knee laces, they tie onto the slippers. Now the shirt, you want the blackwork to show well."

"I'm gonna roast in all this cloth," I complained to both Crevi and Terrell as I held up the white shirt heavily embroidered with black thread.

"That's why it has the slits in the underarms, My Lord," Crevi explained. "It's made of mixed thread of silk and cotton, very finely spun; must have cost a mountain of coin! But it will breathe better than you might expect even through the fabric. Before you put it on you should shave and apply the perfumed lotion."

"Shave my beard?" I put a hand over it protectively. "I don't want to look like a boy again, it took me long enough to grow it."

Terrell chuckled inside my head while Crevi said, perfectly seriously, "No My Lord, it only wants a trim, but you should shave your armpits. I can see that you used to, but you haven't done it in a while. With hair as dark as yours you really should do it right before you put on the garment."

"Right." I glared at the innocent shirt while I thought at Terrell, *Just like a show.*

As I said. I suspect that if you treat this like a stage performance you will find it all much less uncomfortable.

Another sailor brought more warm water and soap and a brush and a straight razor. Letting Crevi shave my face, neck, and armpits with that wickedly sharp blade took both Terrell's persuasion and a self-discipline that I hadn't exercised since I had starred with the DiUmbra Troupe. But the kid had genuine skill, he didn't once nick me. And as promised, he merely trimmed around the edges of my beard.

"I usually shave Captain D'Auson," Crevi explained. "His beard is much heavier than yours, so I get a lot of practice." He studied my head critically. "Your scalp wants to form curls, and it looks like they'll just about cover your, umm, ears, My Lord, so with your permission I'll just fluff your hair out a little."

"Right," I said hollowly. "The show must go on."

"Beg pardon, My Lord?"

"Never mind. Continue."

Once I'd been laced into the shirt I discovered that it had clever arrangements for air movement against the back and up the sleeves. Those required even more lacings. All of the cords were silk braided with gold thread. The vest was half white silk and half purple silk, with a pattern of birds worked into it in silver and black thread. With the black-embroidered white shirt and the purple and white trousers quartered opposite the vest, and a rolled-brim purple chaperon hat with a long tail and a white and gold tassel, I was half afraid to move for fear I'd tear right out of all that expensive cloth.

It's stronger than you think. Don't worry, you'll get comfortable after a while.

"Now the slippers, my lord." Crevi urged me to sit on my bunk while he bound my feet into them. They were a fine purple and white leather laced together with black and gold cords that braided up my legs to tie onto the bottom of my breeches.

These soles are too slick, I complained to Terrell. *I'll fall flat on my face.*

You're supposed to walk deliberately and slowly in them.

Rot that. "Give me that razor for a moment, Midshipman."

I took it and made a crosshatched pattern of shallow scrapes in the soles. "There, now I won't slip so easily."

Overhead I heard the bosun bellow and the rattle as *Waverunner's* mainsails came down. D'Auson rapped on my door and stuck his head inside just as I stood up and buckled on a new sword belt inset with gold. My belt knife and knight's sword hung from it in new scabbards encrusted with amethysts and more gold. He whistled.

"You actually look the part now, My Lord Ambassador."

"Hooray."

D'Auson grinned; he already wore his own purple and black dress uniform and had bathed and shaved while I watched dawn over Dalbai. "Captain Velis invites you to join him on the command deck, My Lord, that you may observe Daleray from the sea. We're only a few miles outside their harbor and the tide is near the cusp."

"Wouldn't miss it," I told him with a hollow feeling in my gut.

Neither would I, my brother told me cheerfully. *Please relax, Kirin, and allow yourself to enjoy this. It's a wonderful new place neither of us has ever seen, filled with interesting new people. How often do either of us get to do anything half as exciting?*

Eh, not every tenday, I admitted. *Or every season.*

So why are you so gloomy?

You mean aside from the good chance that there's a damn assassin mage waiting like a snake somewhere ahead?

Which no amount of worry can prevent. You've got platoons of marines and a Mage to guard you.

A Mage who also wants me dead.

No, a Mage who wants you disgraced, so that he can hold it over you for years to come. That's how I read Burlen Crasset DiMosil, Mage White. The absolutely last thing he wants is to be publicly seen to fail, and your arrival is plenty public. He's the type who'd far rather grind your face into the mud than kill you.

What a wonderful thought. I feel just great about having him around me now.

He's been at your elbow for the last forty-eight days, almost half a season. And for all that time he's served the ship well. What's really upset you?

I . . . don't know. I stopped and leaned against the ship's rail to really think about the question. *I really don't know. I just have this nervous, hell, apprehensive – see, there's one of those big words you like – feeling about me meeting your bride.*

I haven't had any visions about her, or about you meeting her.

We both knew that was actually no bad thing. When the One God choses to haunt my brother's dreams it just about always means somebody's in deep manure somewhere, and usually not so far away. On the other hand, no news is not the same as good news.

I'm confident the Dalbai Palace won't collapse on your head. So let's not worry?

All right, I answered reluctantly. *Maybe I just expect trouble because I deal with trouble so often.*

So today, let your retinue do their jobs, which are to not allow trouble anywhere near you, he cheerfully replied. *Now look at that view!*

Waverunner and her attendants had rounded the mountainous peninsula I'd seen earlier. This side cradled a long white sandy beach spotted with fishing boats and a string of villages separated by plantations and groves. It ended at the mouth of a broad river. Beyond that a huge rock thrust up out of the sea. The flat top bristled with walls and towers that ran for a good mile. Beyond the rock more beaches stretched into the distance. Inland two rows of mountains marched away. Dalbai is an island but it's a *big* island, the largest in the Dreaming Isles.

Our ship coasted along under topsails alone. We flew the red banner of the Gwythlo Empire atop our mainmast and Silbar's purple and silver banner immediately below. Mage White contrived some air magic trick that made the purple stream forward while the red hung limp. I could almost like him for that.

A picket galley rowed toward us with Dalbai's blue flag proud atop her bare mast. The galley executed a smart about-face and fell in parallel to us on the land side. Her commander bellowed a welcome amplified by their own air mage. The White managed Captain Velis' reply the same way and I kept my Shadow under tight control while he did his work. The galley's captain told us that the tide would change in less than an hour and urged us to ride it into the docks rather than fight the river current. Two merchant ships waited at anchor for the same opportunity. Our squadron joined them and the galley politely bid goodbye and went back to its endless picket duty. As it left I saw a blue spark leap from it and fly directly to the city's guardian castle.

Message construct, I thought at Terrell. *In moments the Dalbai royals will know we're here.*

Good! I'm pleased to see our new allies are alert, he answered. *And prepared, too. Look at that fortification that guards their harbor.*

The fortress on the rocky cliffs bulked high. Those big catapults had enough reach to easily cover the mouth of the river and probably much of the city too. I could see that the rock ran back from it some distance to the north –

I believe their royal palace is those white buildings back there, on the lower part of the cliffs.

– before it dropped suddenly into more city behind the other sandy beach.

The city looks big, I thought at Terrell. *But it's narrow, isn't it? Yeah, I can see right down that canal there into the marsh behind.*

The western part is little more than a long strip of levee along the riverbank, he agreed. *But the part behind the rock is much larger. I am told the whole contains ninety thousand souls, perhaps a few more, with a third of them packed in very densely on the river's levee. Look along the waterfront, you can see that many buildings are four or even five stories tall.*

And this is their capital? I thought of Aretzo's quarter-million. Daleray seemed small next to our home.

The reports I've received say that there are three more cities as big or bigger on the other sides of the island, but here is the center of their shipbuilding industry, thanks to the river. Those mountains in the distance yield straight trees over a hundred feet tall, similar to the best we get from our Vettore Coast. They float the logs downriver to their shipyards here.

I could see miles of docks that gave way to at least another mile of shipyards. There were so many that they followed the bend of the river out of sight. On the west side of the river-mouth behind the sand beach I could barely make out marshes that stretched north and west. The river reappeared in them as silver crescents now and then. I scowled.

Aren't marshes supposed to be unhealthy? I've heard talk about bad air.

They go to considerable lengths to keep these safe. I think it has to do with bats, which are sacred to their Gods and protected by powerful injunctions against harm to them. And fishes too, they have long channels that run deep into the marsh and they raise big schools of fish in them. Whatever it is, it seems to work; they rarely have much disease here.

That's good to know.

I studied the shore and city until the ship shifted as the tide changed. *Waverunner* raised anchor and coasted slowly into the mile-wide estuary, only her topsails set. White and the other mages carefully manipulated the winds to keep us on course as we passed the Rock of Daleray and its turbulent airs. They stopped the wind entirely as we approached an empty pier with the Silbari flag on a pole. Two long boats rowed out to meet us, caught ropes and took our ship under tow as the last sails came down. The twenty oarsmen aboard each one chanted a work song in Dalbai, I only caught about half of it but it seemed cheerful enough. Like Silbar, Dalbai didn't allow slavery, which had made me like them better since I heard about it.

Look! Said Terrell, and I felt an internal nudge that made me turn my head to the left. *That has to be the *Queen of the Seas*!*

The many docks along the broad river hosted dozens of ships, but I had no doubt which one he meant. My eyes widened as I stared. I'd seen big ships in Aretzo's busy harbor before, but none like this. She stretched out longer than the pier beside her, bowsprit thrust almost into the shoreside road and her stern jutted out into the river. Tall too, the smallest of her three masts must reach better than a hundred feet above the deck. But not very wide, narrower than most merchant ships I'd seen, and lined with covered arbalest ports. She had a look of deadly grace even at rest.

That's a warship if I've ever seen one, I thought. *Even her wards look sharp as a razor.*

Definitely, Terrell agreed. *She's got too little hull volume to be profitable as a merchantman unless she loads only high-value cargo. Look at her decks. She carries at least sixteen catapults on the fighting deck and twice that in arbalests on the artillery deck. I see two sternchasers too, even though her hull is narrow compared to her length. And look at that sail plan, she's got six yardarms on the main mast, five on her fore and three plus a huge gaff sail on her mizzen! And the lower three on the main each have outriggers for extension sails. How does her hull take the strain?*

You're asking me?

I apologize, I'm just excited. Kirin, our shipwrights will learn dozens of techniques just by looking over that ship. This is an unparalleled opportunity.

I get that, I do, I just wish I didn't feel like a pig trussed up for the slaughter.

You'll get used to the clothes.

Sure, it's the rest of it that worries me.

Dona Seelie joined D'Auson and me at the rail. She wore her elaborate form of clerical dress. It included a big jeweled pectoral to depict the many-armed swirl that is the closest that Silbari faith comes to an image of our unknowable god. The angel wing sleeves were scalloped with fine lace and several pounds of embroidery, with more on the skirt that fell to her ankles. It looked warmer than my own suit.

She cast a critical eye over my garb and nodded approval, then said in Dalbai, "Beautiful day for ceremony. A comfortable breeze off the sea and just enough high clouds to cut the suns."

I resisted the temptation to point out that I was already nearly melted and the day was bound to get hotter.

Good restraint! Terrell whispered his approval. *You're learning diplomacy!*

You're learning wiseassery, I grumbled under my breath.

"Did you say something, My Lord Ambassador?" D'Auson asked with a perfectly straight face. But he didn't hide the twinkle in his eye.

I also resisted the urge to slug his shoulder for baiting me and instead said, "No."

The towboats brought *Waverunner* to the end of an empty pier, then they cast off. Our ship rode the rising tide into the slip. Ropes were tossed and made fast as we came to rest with a bump. A big rickshaw trailed several others as it clattered up to the dock. Purple and white pennants flew from all of them and the lead one bore the royal arms of Silbar.

"That's Silbar's regular ambassador to Dalbai," D'Auson pointed. "I met him once."

Pallir and three platoons of his marines were the first down the gangplank. They took up stations around the cleared space in the middle of the pier. White and Rellir followed, conferred briefly with Pal, then carefully set several prepared wards around the perimeter. Only when they had signaled their readiness did Pal beckon us to land. Following D'Auson I stepped out on the gangplank and walked down to the pier.

And for the first time in five tendays, set foot on dry land again. Unmoving land. My knees betrayed me by trying to shift in response to wave motions that weren't there anymore and I stumbled. D'Auson caught at my arm and missed. I found my balance again just after I stepped in a pile of fresh horse dung.

"There's a great omen," I grumbled as I tried to scrape my slipper off against the planks.

"An unfortunate event is not necessarily an omen from the One," Dona Seelie snapped at me. "Some are just carelessness. Hold still, my Lord Ambassador, let the guardsman clean it off."

I did and he did, then I managed to make it to the rickshaw without any more calamities. Silbar's ambassador had dismounted to meet me, he stood slightly taller than me and thin as a rail with a wash of gray at his temples and in his beard. He had piercing eyes and a long face that looked like his mother had just died. I suddenly realized that I'd completely forgotten his name –

Serman Marati DiTorian.

– but my brother rescued me.

"Ambassador Serman Marati DiTorian, I presume," I greeted him formally.

"Lord Ambassador Sir Kirin DiUmbra," DiTorian bowed with an impressive flourish. "I am honored to meet my prince's Left Hand. Please permit me to offer my credentials." He presented a white stick capped on either end by gold and heavily inset with silver runes; it glowed with spells.

What in the Nine Hells is that?

His baton of office. The spells testify to its authenticity. He's inviting you to check that he's bona-fide, but you don't need to worry. I recognize him from when I appointed him. He's been there almost seven years.

I took the stick gingerly while I suppressed my Shadow, which sulked down in my gut. Then I pretended to learn more from the stick than how tasty my Shadow thought it would be, and handed it back. I said cautiously "I'm very pleased to meet you too, Ambassador. I'd better warn you that fancy language is not my best skill."

He smiled and suddenly looked a lot less dour. "Have no worries about that, My Lord. I was warned thirty days ago. His Highness sent me a message construct, it contained much good advice."

You did what?!

I helped you. Let's see how it works.

"Oh. Ah. So, where do we go first?"

"Since I see that you are already suitably prepared, my Lord, I suggest we immediately go to the Palace to meet her Highness, Princess Callia. Your ship's approach was noted and the Dalbai's Ministry of State has spent the last couple hours activating preparations made tendays ago. The princess requested that you pay her a visit as soon as you are ready. Shall we go?"

Yes! Terrell cheered.

I gulped. "All right."

DiTorian gracefully bowed me into his rickshaw. It was plush with silk cushions and sheltered by a broad sunshade. A gymbal spell gentled the ride and a protection spell wrapped it, woven into a string of silver baubles among the roof fringes. The spell was strong and resilient, probably proof against rain, insects, bird dung, arrows, or most other unwelcome nuisances. But not proof against me. My Shadow nearly ate the magic before I stopped it and locked the blasted creature inside me. The ambassador joined me after speaking a few words of Dalbai to the puller, a squat peasant bulging with well-fed muscles. I caught what sounded like a personal name.

"Jins is a very skilled puller," DiTorian explained. "He's served me since I arrived at this post, I'm fortunate to have him." He glanced behind us, where D'Auson and Dona Seelie, White and Pallir, and two platoons of marines settled into other rickshaws. Rellir and the other platoon stayed on the dock to check its wards and keep the curious at a distance. White cast a protection spell that extended over the entire row and anchored itself on my lead rickshaw – my Shadow almost ate it before I forbade. "Everyone's loaded. Let's go, Jins."

We moved off smoothly and the others followed in more rickshaws behind us. DiTorian had two of his embassy guards ride horses ahead of us. The beasts must be seriously expensive to maintain in this packed city, I didn't see many others.

Traffic swirled around us a bare arm's length away. It was thick with pushcarts no bigger than our rickshaw and hundreds of men and women on foot. The local Priestesses dressed a little different from Silbaris. I saw a pair of them who wore headbands instead of wimples and their robes were saffron instead of the yellow Priestess robes I knew at home. A Temish merchant stalked along in the proud plumage of an iridescent feathered headdress and half-cloak over gold-webbed black body hose. His sword and belt knife were more practical and looked like they'd seen plenty of service. A group of Breen sailors in cotton pantaloons and thick leather belts topped by crossed sashes sang a drinking song at an open air tavern. Teamsters steered a flatbed cart bearing a huge iron anchor toward the shipyards behind us. The four pygmy elephants that towed it trumpeted shrill complaints over the massive weight until a groom offered them snacks of water hyacinth. A solemn Derbite monk peered out from under his broad straw hat woven with the Seven Maxims. He waved his hands in blessing over a one-eyed one-legged beggar. The beggar didn't look too skinny but I noticed that his left hand had only half of a thumb and no fingers. I winced in sympathy and tossed him a coin that he dexterously caught with his right hand, which boasted three fingers. Two boys bounced a rubber ball between them, absorbed in some game.

Silbar's purple and silver pennant snapped in the air above our rickshaw and now and then someone in the crowd would cheer it. Not as many as I'd have liked. About half as many frowns came our way as the cheers.

I don't like that, Terrell remarked. *Kirin, please ask him how the Dalbai people feel.*

"Is there much resentment in Dalbai over this alliance?" I asked DiTorian as we trundled along the shore road. We rattled over a canal on a two-part wooden drawbridge, each half of it able to be lifted by counterweighted arms on towers. The towers and their arms were carved and painted to resemble redheaded cranes, right down to the tail feathers. The sound of our passage echoed back from the stone-walled channel below where fishermen poled little boats on the rising tide and cried their wares to the passersby on shore. DiTorian waited until the cacophony fell behind before he answered.

"I wouldn't say so, my lord." He pursed his lips judiciously. "After Dalbai's costly victory over Khaitanial at the Bay of Sharks last year, everyone with any sense knew the Queen would have to make a strong alliance. She not only lost her husband the king and their only son the crown prince, she lost ten ships and most of their crews and officers – nearly a quarter of her Naval strength. If Khaitanial hadn't lost more – sixteen ships, I'm told – it would have been a devastating defeat for Dalbai."

"So instead it was a devastating victory?"

"Rather an apt description, my Lord. The Dalbais couldn't even take advantage of Khaitanial's weakness to extract compensation for the losses, though the queen certainly tried. Since then she and her ministers have thrown several fortunes into the shipyards, but it will take longer to train new crews. Years, probably, through which they will be painfully vulnerable to another attack. But Silbar has thirty-two ships in our Vettore Coast Fleet alone. His Highness indicated to me that he plans to dedicate a third of it to bolster the Dalbai defense once we have a basing agreement, which is part of the marriage contract. That will still leave us a strong defense for our own western shore, and deter any more adventurism from Khaitanial. We were truly Dalbai's best choice, which was a great aid to negotiations, let me tell you. His Highness' modest goals made my job delightfully easy."

That was essentially what Terrell had told me, so DiTorian knew better than to start off with a line of bull.

Prudent of him, Terrell chuckled. *But that's why I appointed him. He's very sensible. I had to have a man like that at such an important and distant post.*

I thought for a moment as our rickshaw rattled past a meat market. Flies bounced off protection spells that held them yards away from the abundant display of bloody flesh. Sarong-clad housewives bargained with the butchers.

"You said anyone with sense could see this. What about those without sense?"

"Mmmm. Yes, there are a few of those. The Gwythlo Empire is not, dare I say, any more well-loved west of Cape Woe than east of it. Some here think Prince Terrell is just a stalking horse for his alarming brother. Ever since their father stopped his western conquests with Silbar, there's been wide fear in the Isles that the Klinto, Fehdar, and Silbari fleets would combine and sweep the entire archipelago into the Empire."

I felt Terrell's frustration over that as he grumbled, *Osrick will never combine the fleets. He doesn't trust any of them enough, he'll always want them separate. Besides, I'd never agree to give up Silbar's fleet to his control, and our oath reserves that decision to *me*.*

Aloud I asked DiTorian, "Don't they understand that Emperor Osrick can give orders to the Klintos and Fehdars, but not to Silbar? Prince Terrell makes his own choices."

"Oh, most do understand," DiTorian soothed. "They're no strangers here to dynastic politics. I've done what I could to counter the more foolish local notions, with reasonable success. Certainly most of the aristocracy and the merchant class seem to have understood the truth. And however much the empire might worry them, they purely hate Khaitanial." He grinned happily, a remarkably shark-like expression.

"You said most."

He shrugged slightly and made an expressive gesture with his hands. "Unfortunately a couple of the minor houses still loudly spout nonsense about Prince Terrell's intentions. Even a few men close to the throne express occasional concern; the queen's brother-in-law Count Harren is probably the most prominent. Though I strongly suspect that he may actually play demon's advocate to help his sister-in-law extract better concessions. Certainly he hasn't raised any objections since the announcement. I suspect he only *acts* the fool, and that only when it suits himself or his – now her – Majesty."

He glanced at me for a moment. "The Dalbai court is quite sophisticated, my lord DiUmbra, and has plenty of very shrewd men and women in it. I find it's necessary to keep that in mind at all times when dealing with them."

"I'll remember it," I told him, while Terrell gave me a wordless touch of encouragement.

That too is to our advantage, he whispered inside my head. *I dare to hope that Callia is no neophyte to court maneuvering, and thus she won't be overwhelmed by Silbar's own intrigue.*

I wish you'd dismiss that whole nest of vipers you've got toadying around you, I grumbled.

Not possible; too many of them are really quite competent at their tasks and would be much harder to replace than you think. Talented administrators are hard to find, Kirin. It is worthwhile to accept a few character flaws in order to keep a good one. But only a few. Haven't you noticed that I don't let the truly venal, brutal, or incompetent stay for long?

Ah, no, I, um, haven't kept track.

He let silence stretch for a while as I thought back over the past seven years. There really had been a lot of turnover in the court, but it had mostly been quiet and I'd paid it little mind. Maybe that was a mistake.

Maybe, he agreed cordially. *But we can talk about that another time. Meanwhile you're in one of the most beautiful cities I've ever seen. Let's enjoy it!*

Daleray looks nice, I agreed, glad of the change of subject. *Flowers everywhere and practically every bit of wood is carved and painted. These folks sure love to make stuff pretty.*

And they keep it all impressively clean too.

I glanced at the sky – there were puffy white clouds. *Must rain a lot here.*

Our rickshaw jolted onto another wooden drawbridge twin to the first, save that these carvings resembled blue and gray herons instead of cranes. DiTorian looked like he had been about to speak but the thunder of our wheels on the planks again stopped speech.

Then I heard a horn blatt. A gate descended behind us and cut off our retinue. A shudder went through the rickshaw as the bridge began to rise under us. A gap appeared in the two halves right in front of Jins' feet.

~ ~ ~

Chapter 21: Daleray - Kirin

Ninety-first day of Summer

Jins the puller put on a burst of speed and hurdled the opening gap. Our rickshaw bounced across with a jolt that lifted DiTorian and I off our seats. DiTorian's mounted guards stopped on the far side, then saw us coming and spurred their horses out of our path. Jins dashed down the other half of the bridge and bounced again off the bottom end of the plank span. The forward ends of the puller handles hit the flimsy wooden gate and snapped it right off, luckily throwing it to the roadside instead of under Jins' feet. We rolled several paces down the road while he tried to kill our momentum, the mounted guards cursed, and the bridge rose into the air behind us.

"Ooof! What are those idiots –" DiTorian began.

Someone in the crowd screamed and I saw one of DiTorian's guards fall to a crossbow bolt that trailed blue fire. A twin to it appeared in Jins' ribs. The puller collapsed, the rickshaw's towing-arms dropped with him and dug into the road. The vehicle rammed to a stop just before it ran over him.

I was thrown right out.

My acrobat's reflexes saved me. I tucked into a roll, then flipped onto my feet. Another scream from the crowd and I saw DiTorian sprawled atop Jins. I guess diplomats don't get taught how to tuck and roll. Two more crossbow bolts stuck out of the seat cushions about where my chest had been seconds before. They both glowed with blue fire - ensorcelled to penetrate the protection spells.

Four men with crossbows stood at the edge of the road. Two rapidly cranked the cocking mechanisms while two others tossed their bows aside and charged me with drawn knives.

I managed to draw both my sword and my gauche before they got to me. Then I drowned rickshaw and street in Shadow.

The world turned to glass in my vision. The beasts and wagons around us became ghosts in fog as my Shadow blotted out the suns' light. The lead assassin had a double-edged dirk in his left hand and a stiletto in his right. My Shadow didn't faze him, he plunged in blind. The bastard even had his eyes closed, so someone must have warned him about what I could do.

He still ran right onto my sword.

The second attacker came at me from my left side. He leaped at me as I jerked my sword free of his dying partner. He had two knives too, one nearly as long as my sword, and to face him I'd have to turn my back on the two crossbowmen.

So I flung my gauche at him.

Even a highly disciplined man will lose his focus when a sharp point rips into his left eye and jams in the bone behind it. His hands jerked up in reflex and he paused just long enough for me to dodge his longer blade. I caught the wrist that held his dirk and jerked his throat onto the point of my sword, then spun his fountaining blood away from me as I yanked my gauche free of him.

Two down, two to go.

Terrell had been swept from my head by the sudden release of my Shadow. My ghosts clamored. I stared around wildly. Just outside my Shadow one of the embassy guards gasped out his life on the pavement. DiTorian's other guard sported a crossbow bolt in the meat of his left arm. He had managed to stay atop his panicked horse while the beast kicked and shied but had no attention to spare for the fight. If the third man wasn't there, then —

I dodged barely in time. He had thrown his crossbow at me, it cartwheeled through the space my head had occupied an instant before. A blade sliced my sleeve as he leaped at me from behind. His stiletto came for my ribs just as I kicked out sideways and caught him full in the crotch. The stiletto point missed my thigh by a whisker as he doubled over. I brought my own sword around in a slash that almost removed his head. He fell and bled on the stones.

Then it was over. Four men had fired four crossbows, but hard as I stared I could find no fourth attacker. He'd already fled.

Several people stumbled around inside my Shadow and wailed in terror. To them it must have been like being struck blind. Luckily no other horses had been within range to panic and run wild, but one pushcart man had spilled his load of firewood and fallen to his knees to shout prayers. I hastily drew the Shadow back inside me and shut up my ghosts.

Terrell immediately came back into my mind. *Kirin! What happened?*

Assassination attempt. Failed in my case, and I think DiTorian's unhurt too, but at least one of his men is dead.

Terrell's shock rippled through me. *How? You're protected!*

Notice how much good it did? They had bolts ensorcelled to penetrate the rickshaw protection spell, even penetrate White's spells.

A wave of thoughts spilled through me from Terrell — anger at the assassins, guilt at having sent me into this mess, fear for me and shame that he had to ask me to face this risk while he remained safe, fury at his faceless opponents who thought murder an acceptable tool of statecraft. And behind them all a painfully cold calculation of relative advantage in the balance of power between Silbar and the world. The last triggered a deeper wave of shame again.

Stop it, I told him roughly. *You are the King! You must do what the King must do for Silbar's sake. I swore to help you do it, and I'll not betray that oath now. Don't you betray yourself inside that busy head of yours.*

I knelt and rolled over the nearest assassin's body, the one with his head folded sideways. His weapons were plain and serviceable, they could have been made by any blacksmith anywhere. He wore an undyed homespun shirt and breeches much like most Dalbai sailors, nothing that would catch anybody's eye, and had a battered leather carrysack in which the crossbow must have been hidden.

But when I pulled his shirt open I discovered white crescents tattooed on either side of his sternum and a carved jet amulet on a string about what remained of his neck. *Aha! The clothes are a disguise. This one's really a Beniyah from Annubhinh, see the marks? I'll take a gamble and bet the others are the same.* I snapped the string and examined the amulet closely, found a name carved in Bhinnish. *This one's from a famous family of assassins, the Oyam. They don't hire themselves out cheaply. Zurtos must have brought them here and equipped them too.*

That explains why Beniyah are in Dalbai, more than three thousand miles from their home.

Only how'd he get them here?

I think we know why that Klinto sloop that the harbor mage mentioned went to Haresalaam. Zurtos picked up these assassins before he raced across the ocean to Dalbai. Then he loaded their weapons up with spells designed to counter White's protections and sent them against you, and probably hoped to kill DiTorian too.

It almost worked. I'm alive only because the rickshaw's handles dug into the road and I got thrown out. If I had kept my seat there'd be a bolt stuck in my chest.

The heady rush of a fight for my life had worn off and left me a-tremble. So close. Even if the bolt had merely nicked me I might not have been able to beat all three knifemen. Five tries now. Zurtos wanted me, or at least my mission, very dead.

This makes no sense, Terrell muttered. *Callia is the essential person in this alliance, even if they kill you the marriage will still go forward. Yet they're spending disproportionate effort attacking you. Something deeper is going on.*

Deeper? A wave of dizziness swept over me.

I felt Terrell's wordless support buoying me up. It was enough to get me back to my feet. I stuffed the Beniyah amulet in my belt pouch and looked around. *I can't spend time thinking about 'deeper.' I've got to find the fourth man.*

Agreed. If we're lucky he'll be the leader and will lead us to the mysterious Zurtos. Uh-oh, Kirin, look over there.

A priestess stood in the crowd just outside the area that had been engulfed by my Shadow, her hands raised in the act of casting a spell. Her eyes had followed the retreating Shadow to me and now she stared at my face in horror.

Quickly, Terrell urged. *Show her you aren't a demon or she'll cast a Banishment on you!*

"Dona!" I called then remembered to use the Dalbai words. "Soer! Men are hurt. In the Names of your Gods —"

Seleph, Algol, and Merduk.

"— Seleph, Algol, and Merduk, please help them!"

She blinked, clearly surprised that a man she thought demon-possessed would call on her gods. I turned away from her and helped DiTorian while my back itched in anticipation.

212

A Banishment wouldn't harm me physically, but neither would it free me from my Shadow. And as I knew from previous attempts, there would be pain. A lot of it.

DiTorian managed to get to his own feet with only a little aid. Some dirt on his left knee and a general air of shattered equilibrium seemed his only damage. He stared at a smear of Jins' blood on his left hand.

"I – I didn't expect that," he said in a dazed voice as I knelt next to the puller.

"Me neither." I checked the big vein in the fallen man's neck for a pulse but found none. "I'm sorry my lord, but he's gone."

He saved me when he dumped me out of the rickshaw, I thought bitterly, *and I can't even thank him.*

He may have family, Terrell whispered back. *Find out, and use your authority to see that they are taken care of.*

Damn right I will.

"I felt him die," the regular Silbari Ambassador babbled. "Why – how – I don't –"

I stood up again and grabbed his elbow, gave it a little shake. "What about you, Ambassador? Did you hit your head? Your limbs whole? Joints work?"

With a visible effort DiTorian pulled himself together, moved his arms and legs to see if they all worked. "I'm undamaged, My Lord Ambassador. Are *you* hurt?"

"Not even scratched." I checked my ventilated shirt sleeve to be sure it was true, but the fabric was all that got cut.

"The – my guards – how are they?"

The priestess was working on the wounded one, who had his horse under control now and had dismounted. She had already extracted the bolt from his arm and stopped the blood flow. From the look of the guard's drawn back lips and

213

clenched teeth that must have seriously hurt even with her numbing spell. Maybe she hadn't quite got it right, since she also kept one eye on me even as she worked.

The other guard was clearly dead. Nobody can bleed that much and live.

"One dead, one alive." I checked the other two bodies. Both had prominent Beniyah tattoos and black amulets, which I collected. The priestess saw the tattoos and made an expression of distaste as she worked. Silbar's Holy Writ forbids such bodily disfigurement and the Dalbais are against it too. "I think there was a fourth attacker but I couldn't spot him."

The crowd had drawn back from us but several folks still gawked. A wooden whistle made a throaty shriek and a Dalbai man in a blue tabard and peaked hat arrived, apparently a city constable. He sorted out the situation at a glance and demanded an explanation from us. While DiTorian provided it, with occasional comment from me, the drawbridge clattered down again amidst a glow of spells. Feet thundered across it as the majority of our party finally rejoined us. There were loud expressions of dismay, except for White who just looked angry.

"Lord Ambassador!" Pallir shouted.

"Assassins." I held up a hand to forestall him. "We're both unhurt. There was a fourth crossbowman."

Pallir wasn't slow. "He can't have gotten far!" He snapped orders to his men and pointed out the dress of the three bodies. White began to cast a scry spell. While the marines fanned out Pallir turned partway back to me while his eyes roved the crowd. "Not much chance with all these people and an unfamiliar city, but The One might favor us, My Lord."

"Thanks. The bridge operator may also be in on it. That span went up awfully fast and I didn't see a boat in the channel."

"I'll tackle him myself!" Pallir strode away to call more orders.

Dona Seelie had taken over care of the injured Silbari guard while the constable interrogated the Dalbai priestess with exquisite politeness. The bridge operator turned out to be very dead, knifed in his little shack.

"Then who lowered the bridge?" Pallir wondered aloud. "Burlen was still groping for the controls when it came down."

"Probably the killer, then used it to escape. Did you notice anyone go the other way while you rushed across?"

"I wasn't watching." Pallir answered, ashamed and frustrated. He redirected a couple of his men to check the far side but I wasn't surprised when they found nothing.

White had extended his scry spell for hundreds of yards overhead in every direction. When Pallir looked at him with a question on his face the Mage shrugged in frustration and collapsed the spell. "Too many people," he growled. "Dressed too much alike. I need a linkage."

I handed him the three amulets. "There will be a fourth one of these. If you can derive a link between them, a location spell might work on it."

White's face lit up in a smile like a lion scenting prey. "Excellent!" was all he said, but he started to cast immediately.

"Does the assassin know that?" Pallir asked. "Won't he simply ditch his amulet?"

"Probably," I answered. "But it may take him a while to think of it. If we move fast enough –"

More constables arrived before I could say another word. I had to repeat my story twice more and wasted time when I tried to convince the city watch to help track the missing man. I finally sicced DiTorian on them in the faint hope that he could drive them into motion.

But it had taken too much time. White began to swear in four languages when his cobbled-together location spell suddenly collapsed.

"Somebody grew wise," he snarled to Pallir. "The fourth amulet has just been destroyed."

We all looked at each other and gritted our teeth. Which helped not at all to get the City functionaries to move, though now there was little point.

Eventually the guardsmen collected the bodies, bowed their regrets that such a heinous crime should have been committed in their city, and we could finally stop blocking traffic and leave. Dona Seelie looked at the mess on my back – I'd rolled through plenty of dung and mud when the rickshaw pitched me out – and bullied me to stand still while she and White used magic to clean me off. It wasn't quite as good as I'd started but it would do.

I glanced at the suns. The whole mess had eaten more than an hour. "Let's go. I still have an appointment with the princess to keep."

Yes! My brother cheered me.

"You want to continue to the Palace?" DiTorian's voice squeaked in astonishment.

"You bet I do. Somebody wanted me not to, wanted it so badly they were ready to kill me and your guards, and maybe you too, to stop me." I snarled silently inside and Terrell sent back wordless agreement. "I am damn well not gonna to give them what they want. Take me to see Princess Callia. Now."

~ ~ ~

Chapter 22: Daleray - Zurtos

Ninety-first day of Summer

Zurtos paced the confines of a wickerwork cabin on a tiny sampan docked in a canal behind the riverbank strip of the city. His servant Jos, disguised as an old fisherman, crouched on the front deck to jiggle a baitless hook on a line and pretend to be intent on fish that weren't there.

A glance at the scry spell he'd installed in a glass globe told the mage it hadn't gone well. Three of the four life-lights he'd linked to the Beniyah assassins had winked out and the last was dimmed. There might be a hue and cry raised even now for the fourth, a mob might already have closed in on him. He told himself he wasn't worried even as he checked his weapons, a very sharp knife in his sleeve and another in each boot, and of course the subtle spells that wreathed the little craft.

Footsteps slapped the dirt path. Zurtos peered out through a screened window of crisscrossed split bamboo. The fourth Beniyah ran towards him, his disguise spell reduced to ragged shreds more likely to draw attention than divert it. The Shadow mage must have almost got him. The man caromed aboard the rear deck of the sampan and made it rock. Zurtos cursed silently and raised the rough curtain that passed for a door, dropped it behind the man.

"What happened?" he demanded.

The Beniyah panted, leaned his hands on his knees for a moment to catch his breath, then stood back up and spoke.

"Demon of Night! He was fast as a serpent and twice as deadly. The Shadow of which you spoke was so quick, we were overwhelmed in a heartbeat and then could only move as men blinded. I put down my assigned guard and dropped my crossbow, prepared to leap on the carriage, only to find he had already killed my brothers!"

Zurtos stopped him, made the man breathe deeply, then questioned him for every detail. The man finally ran out and shrugged as he said, "That Shadow, waugh! It was to freeze the soul! There was naught I could do but flee, oh mighty Mage."

The assassin moved as if to bow in apology. Zurtos's blade caught him in the throat to slice through cartilage and arteries up into his brain. The mage swayed aside as the fool's life fountained out, then shoved the twitching corpse to the floor before it could splash his clothes.

"You were not worth your pay," he growled at the corpse, a vile insult to Beniyah ears.

Jos had pulled in his line and stowed it, now he stepped through the front curtain, deftly avoided the body and blood, and stepped out the back. In moments the sampan was untied from the shore and Jos stolidly poled it down the canal. Zurtos made a few more knife strokes, the last to remove the dead fool's amulet which he immediately broke to free the spirit link inside. That would halt any trace spell that relied on linkage to the other three. He tossed the halves over the side to vanish in the tea-colored water. Then he cast a small spell on the corpse, stepped over the pooled blood and out through the stern curtain.

"Find us a channel in which to hide this craft," he told Jos in a language spoken by no one else on Dalbai. "One with water deep enough to swallow its hull. The fishes will feast while we go about our business."

Jos cocked his head slightly, nodded, then added, "The local ally?"

"Yes." Zurtos brooded. The Shadow-mage was unreasonably lucky, or very subtly protected. Zurtos distrusted claims of luck. In his experience thorough preparation counted for far more, and was more reliable. But how to counter the preparations of a man who couldn't be studied by magic, or even seen by the simplest spell? It was a conundrum. A puzzle.

A challenge.

Zurtos's lips drew back from even white teeth. He liked challenges.

~ ~ ~

Chapter 23: Daleray Palace – Callia; Kirin

Ninety-first day of Summer

Callia decided that he did not look plain after all.

She had studied the Special Ambassador as he crossed the marble throne room, watched him through a screen of sandalwood pierced with holes shaped like alternate stars and hexagons as he bowed deeply to her mother. He was really rather handsome. The tone of the whispers in the throne room seemed to agree. More women than men had spoken and she heard several delighted giggles among them.

To start, Ambassador DiUmbra was clearly young and energetic. As a knight, she had expected him to walk with the sort of controlled power that Dalbai's own military men displayed. But most of them had heavy musculature in the legs and shoulders, rather like the water buffalos that plowed Dalbai rice paddies. The ambassador was powerfully built but much more lithe, his walk like a cross between a prowl and a dance across the floor. Her brother's sword instructors had been much like that, but not quite as – sensual, she thought. He reminded her of some jungle beast, exotic and mysterious with a hint of danger.

He's a leopard. The idea went well with his pale skin, golden instead of the usual medium-brown common to Dalbai and Silbar both. *He has very black hair, very curly too. Dona Catalona said he has pointed ears like the Klintos, or an Imp, but I can barely see them among his curls. I wonder why he has those two thin white stripes in his sideburns? Is that a fashion in Aretzo?*

~ ~ ~

I looked at the mob spread in front of me as I entered
the throne room and tried to perform a 'stately walk.' Dona
Seelie and Captain D'Auson strode two paces behind me and
Ambassador DiTorian at my right. I struggled to listen to his
whispers about who was who even as Terrell's words dropped
into my mind.

*They certainly have some clever architects here. This
room is designed to draw attention to the thrones.*

*Eh. It's big and showy all right. I hope I remember
my lines.*

Don't worry, I'm here to help.

I see Queen Sephora. She looked to be around fifty
years old, a handsome woman with a stern yet kindly face. She
wore a spiky gold crown above a gown of some sheer blue
cloth that draped from her proud shoulders all the way down
her throne and the dais beneath it and spread across a few yards
of floor. The throne she sat on was one of a pair, the other –

That's Princess Alliet on her father's throne.

The girl wore a smaller crown and a dress nearly as
impressive as her mother's, but she looked faintly uncertain.
Alliet probably hadn't expected to ever find herself there, since
her brother had been the heir until two seasons ago. I noticed
that the two thrones were identical.

*Exactly. Queen Sephora and King Baint ruled as co-
monarchs, and very effectively too.*

DiTorian whispered, "The Queen's older brother,
Duke Admiral Abemar Abn Sandello, is the fellow at her left."
A tall acetic noble in an obvious military uniform, hawk-nosed
and proud but his left sleeve ended below the elbow. "He lost
the arm in the same battle that killed the King and Crown
Prince. His wife and younger children are at his left, with his
daughter-in-law Elina. Her husband, Sandello's eldest son
Vimmal, is in command of a ship out on patrol right now but

is due back very soon. That side of the family has been prominent in the Dalbai Navy for as long as there's been one."

"On Alliet's right, is that her husband?"

"Yes, Prince Jarreth, younger brother to Breen's Crown Prince."

"And who's next to him?" That burly muscular build had to belong to a swordsman.

"Count Yare Abn Harren, King Baint's younger sister's husband, therefore Princess Callia's uncle. He has two daughters and three sons. That's them on his right, with their mother Princess Gadet, who holds their newest, a boy just born eight days ago."

The older girl looked perhaps thirteen. She tried to be solemn while obviously so excited she could burst. The younger held her sister's hand and stared with wide four-year-old eyes. The boys seemed likely lads perhaps seven and ten years old. Their mother the princess met my eyes with a smirk that sent my gaze running elsewhere in a hurry.

"Is this the whole royal family?"

"There are quite a few cousins. Several are over there to the right in that clump."

I counted twenty heads and cringed inwardly at the thought of learning all their names.

He continued, "And there's a dowager aunt who took religious orders, I don't see anyone that looks like her here, but otherwise, yes."

"Where's Princess Callia?"

"Probably behind that screen to the left," DiTorian made a slight motion. "They'll most likely call her out after the formal presentation of your credentials."

My fingers tightened on the scroll that Dona Seelie had put into my left hand just outside the throne room. Fortunately my Shadow wasn't too hungry and hadn't tried to eat the magic in it yet.

Kirin, Terrell whispered. *You're ready for this, you'll do fine.*

Here we go. I stopped in front of the two thrones, bowed, and began.

~ ~ ~

Her mother had almost finished the formal greetings. They were marred by the need to express everyone's shock at the attempted assassination.

An assassination right here in Daleray! Callia thought, still shocked herself. *Who would dare? It's probably Khaitanial, but why? We're bound to suspect, and then strike back. They gained nothing! Or could it be some trouble the Ambassador brought with him? Does some enemy of Silbar reach across the ocean? I think I'd rather it was the old enemy we know, than some new and faceless threat.*

She pushed the thoughts away with an effort. The unidentified enemy had failed, and that was what really mattered. She reminded herself: *today is the start of something happy. I will not let our enemies cloud it.*

Her mother beckoned. Callia followed her handmaidens to sweep from behind the screen in her own stately walk, aware that hundreds of eyes were on her. Her women had spent extra hours to get her washed, perfumed, combed and curled, draped in yards of fine fabric, and then decorated. Thank heavens it was high summer and the heavier makeups couldn't be used. She'd never liked the feel of caked-on powders and pastes on her skin. And she adored the light saris that were traditional court wear in summer. This one showed her off especially well since it was made of the sheerest Sulucid spidersilk dyed gold and pale green and trimmed with embroidered flowers. Her handmaidens held giant feathered fans around her until she was an arm's length away from the Ambassador, then gracefully pulled them aside.

From the way his mouth fell open, he liked the dress.

~ ~ ~

By the One, she's gorgeous! The thought shot through my brain and I didn't know if it was mine or Terrell's. Then her perfume reached my nose and for a moment all was confusion as my blood and Terrell's both roared.

Her face —

-hands —

-breasts —

-body —

-eyes!

Ah!

Somewhere I found the strength, maybe from him, to bow courteously over her extended hand. When I kissed it, touched her living warmth and inhaled her scent again, the cascade threatened to start over and I had to fight the desire to sweep her off her feet. I was profoundly relieved that there was extra space in my codpiece.

Terrell found his way back to sensibility before I did. *Say something to her, Kirin.*

What?

Say something!

I heard you! What should I say?

Her name!

"Princess Callia Abn Serziza," I managed in my clumsy Dalbai as I straightened up, then I looked in her eyes and was promptly tongue-tied again. My face grew warm and I'm sure some damn mage made my collar shrink to choke me.

Her smile grew wider and she answered me in very good Silbari. "Sir Kirin DiUmbra, Lord Ambassador of Silbar.

I am very pleased to meet the Left Hand of my betrothed. Welcome to Dalbai, my Lord."

Her voice played me like a lute. For a moment even Terrell was stunned into silence.

~ ~ ~

Well this is very flattering, Callia thought to herself as she resisted the temptation to laugh. *I think I've overwhelmed the poor man. Indeed, I'm sure of it. I'd better give him some help before he falls over. Mother said this was my chance to ask questions. I suspect he would tell me anything right now!*

~ ~ ~

"Would you like to take a walk in the Garden Courtyard, My Lord DiUmbra?" Princess Callia asked in Silbari. I still held her hand and she didn't show any sign of wanting it back.

This is the opportunity we planned for. Say yes! Terrell hissed.

I'm gonna! "Yes, please," I mumbled in my own language, not trusting myself to be able to get hers right. Then I wondered if I'd be able to walk in a garden without tearing my new clothes or tripping in those damned slippers.

She slid her hand around my arm and just in time I extended my elbow to her at Terrell's urging. As she led me away I glanced back at her mother. The Queen's face had a slight frown and she made a gesture to her guards. Two of Callia's handmaids trailed us discreetly and a couple guardsmen joined them.

Terrell, she's noticed me drooling over her daughter! Is she gonna have me strung up?

No! You're my Ambassador, you're perfectly safe. She'd just being cautious. Don't worry, pay attention to Callia. Sweet heaven, she's amazing!

She led me through a side room and out an arched doorway into a long arcade. Walking turned out to be easier than I'd feared but if I kept staring at Callia then stairs would be trouble. I was grateful for the shade of the arcade and the plantings outside it. My own Shadow had drawn into a hard ball inside me.

Can you believe this? Terrell babbled inside my head. *I've never felt so powerfully attracted to any woman!*

Tell me about it, I answered fervently.

I thought I was past this sort of intense reaction. Delighted to know I'm not!

I'm glad you're enjoying it, but it's too damn much, I told Terrell. *I'm getting your body's feelings piled onto mine and I can barely cope. You've got to pull back a little, give me some breathing room.*

But this closeness is what I was hoping for!

Terrell, you're about to wreck me. Give me a little less of what you're feeling so I can control what I'm feeling. Please, damnit!

Very well; I'll try.

My answer was a strangled mental grunt. I was surprised my sleeve didn't smoke where Callia's hand touched it. But that intense echo from his senses faded until it was merely very strong instead of overwhelming. I hoped that would be good enough.

"There's a lovely view from just ahead," she told us.

Terrell and I both nodded speechlessly.

She guided me into an opening in the arcade. There was the flight of stairs I dreaded. I wrenched my attention away from her and managed not to trip as I went up the marble treads. The steps led to a little stone gazebo perched above the gardens, carved marble benches around two sides and a vine-draped railing to which Callia drew me. I leaned on it at her elbow, my eyes fixed on her and only dimly aware that the handmaids had arranged themselves on either side of the steps with the guards below.

Callia smiled at me again and I forgot about her escorts. "My great-grandfather had this built for great-grandmother. She was a Silbari princess, you know, and sometimes missed her home. After he died she spent a lot of time here, and when I was small I'd sit with her while she brushed my hair and told me stories. I've always loved the place." She turned her gaze away from me and waved a graceful hand at what lay beyond.

Let me see what she's pointing at, Terrell demanded.

My eyes followed her gesture as if they'd been made slaves to her will, or maybe his. I had to fight down a stab of resentment before I could finally pay attention.

I managed not to gape at the place. It wasn't nearly as astonishing as her, after all. Terrell's attention was divided and some part of his mind waxed lyrical about it even as the other part tried to catch its breath. I was relieved when some of that aching pressure in my groin subsided. I'd lusted after Maia this way, but I'd married her — that sure wasn't going to happen here!

The courtyard was sunken a few steps below the arcade and must have covered more than an acre. Four broad paths lined with date palm trees converged on a central fountain that threw four watery arcs skyward. The four huge beds between the paths were each cut in turn into four more by cross paths.

That makes sixteen beds, Terrell burbled. *See how each of them has a quartet of fruit trees — orange, lemon, fig, pomegranate, the Four Trees of the Holy Writ? A Silbari gardener was definitely involved here. What a magnificent creation!*

Beneath the trees' raised branches flowers rioted. The arcade circled three sides, each draped with different vines;

bergamot, bougainvillea, nasturtiums, morning glories, and plants neither Terrell nor I could name. Tall slender cypress trees made green pillars along the fourth side. That was the fortress, a cyclopean wall much taller than the Palace.

All right, the place is gorgeous too, I thought as my eyes wandered back to her. She was just as stunning as before.

Tell her that.

"It's gorgeous." I gulped and added "Really pretty. So many flowers, um. Very pretty."

No, tell her she's very pretty too. Come on Kirin, I'm trying to work with you, now focus!

I am focusing, damnit! If I stare any harder my eyes are gonna fall out!

Not on her body! Her mind!

You're not helping!

~ ~ ~

Callia decided that this Sir DiUmbra must not have much practice at courtly talk. He looked like a man who had been given formal training and now struggled to remember it. She wondered if this was his real personality, shorn of pretense. Shy, a little clumsy with words, very aroused and horribly embarrassed to be so obvious about it. It was flattering but on the edge of being coarse. What was it Soer Catalona said about his past? Raised out of a gutter, right. But he *was* embarrassed about it and wasn't trying to paw her, so that was good – he had that much restraint. It was interesting that he could be so vulnerable to her charms. She wondered if his prince would be too. Could she get Sir Kirin to talk about himself, or better yet his master? Perhaps one could lead to the other.

~ ~ ~

"I heard," she purred to me, "That you were once some sort of entertainment performer before Prince Terrell raised you into the knighthood?"

"Um, yes." I relaxed a fraction – a question I could answer, hooray! "I was what Silbaris call an acrobat."

"Is that like a jongleur?"

"Partly." I plucked three palm-sized blossoms off a bush and tossed them in easy loops for a moment while her eyes followed, bright and curious.

Why are you doing that? Terrell asked, mystified.

To please her, of course. I hope it works.

I caught all three and hid them between my hands, then presented them to her with a bow and a flourish.

I'd thought her smile was brilliant before. Now it just about melted me. Her fingers touched mine as she took the flowers from me and my blood pounded so hard I thought I'd burst.

I think it worked, Terrell whispered in frank admiration.

I answered with a mental smirk that wasn't quite lost in my giddiness.

"So an 'acrobat' juggles?" She asked as she tucked the flowers into her hair.

"And does other things."

"What kind of other things?"

"Oh, dance, walk or swing on ropes above a stage, do somersaults and cartwheels, sing lines from the stories we performed, the usual."

"You did *yaleys* too?"

I hesitated over the unfamiliar Dalbai word and Terrell rescued me. *It means plays, like the scripted parts of your performances but usually with less movement.*

"Ah. Sort of. In Silbar acrobats also tell stories. We use both the movement of our bodies and spoken lines to carry the tale."

Inspiration rose up and slapped me in the face. "Here, Princess, let me show you a bit from one story that I used to do a lot. It was the most popular show our troupe ever had. Have you ever heard of 'Malik and Mercia'?"

She looked thoughtful for a moment, then she caught it.

"That's a story from the Silbari Holy Writ, isn't it? The Dona read it to me while she taught me to speak this language."

"Yes, exactly. Salim the Tormentor sends his Imp Malik to seduce the Angel Mercia away from the service of Umana the Mother Seraph, but the Imp falls truly in love with the angel and refuses to carry out his assignment at the last, even though he knows Salim will destroy him for it. This is the scene in which the imp confesses his shame and his love to Mercia and refuses to betray her."

"I remember!" She brightened visibly. "Yes, I remember every line in the whole passage."

"Good! You'll recognize some of it, though the poet who wrote this play gave Malik a lot more lines. Just sit on that bench. Your maidens can watch from the stairs, they won't be in the way."

I took off my hat and vest and set both aside, tied back my hair so that my ears showed plain. "I don't have the right costume but I have a few tricks that will help. Give me a moment and think of yourself as the Angel and me as the poor Imp."

I called my Shadow into my fancy clothes, turned the white silk to night, remembered the lines I'd said so many, many times, and once more became Malik.

"O agony of heart's desire,

"O bitter irony,

"That I now here before thee come,

"To confess perfidy.

"My Master sent me to betray thee,

"Through cunning treachery,

"But I instead am now betrayed,

"By my true love for thee . . ."

I ran through Malik's fear and grief for the love he had thought to fake, that now had become real. And his shame for the betrayal he'd planned, that he now revealed. At the last I collapsed at her feet and begged her to flee before Salim appeared.

"Oh," Callia breathed as her maids burst into spontaneous applause. "My. That was amazing."

I got up off the floor of the little pergola, thankful that it was clean marble, and drew my Shadow back inside me as I bowed. "A small entertainment, Princess."

Very small. Terrell's mental voice was flatter than I'd ever heard it.

What's wrong? I was still excited and flushed from my performance but his words stopped me in my mental tracks.

You're there to help me make a marriage, and you just advised her to flee your 'Master'. Do you think there might be some chance of misinterpretation there?

Oh. Oh dung!

~ ~ ~

I wonder, Callia thought, *If he did that spontaneously, or as part of a plan? There are so many possible levels of meaning in that particular choice. Hmmm. Looking at his face, I think that problem only just occurred to him. Sweet gods forgive me, but if I've ever seen somebody who's put his foot in his mouth, this is him! The poor man — oh, I mustn't laugh, I mustn't —*

~ ~ ~

"Princess," I began, as my tongue tied itself into knots. "I didn't mean — it's just a — you see, I mean, umm, ah —" I could feel the blood mount into my face as my heart fell into my fancy slippers. *Oh dung oh dung oh dung!*

Wait, don't panic, Terrell told me. *I think —*

Then her smile stretched into a grin and she burst into laughter.

"It's nice to receive a gift offered from the heart," she told me, eyes twinkling. "Without guile, scheme, or hidden intent. Thank you, Ambassador."

"Umm. You're welcome, Princess. I'm not usually this big a fool."

Not usually, Terrell agreed. *Today must be an exception.*

"So I trust." Her smile grew again and with it the heat in my body. I blushed like a beet.

She took my arm again, and this time it didn't burn so strongly. Terrell had drawn back just enough that I wasn't overwhelmed by his sensations running through my nerves. I managed a deep breath and didn't shake.

"Let's continue our walk," she said. "You tell me about my husband to be."

I swallowed relief strong enough to melt me. "Gladly."

We strolled through gardens and halls and talked. The Daleray Palace was even more of a labyrinth than Terrell's own in Aretzo. I told her about it and about Terrell, his courage and curiosity, his discipline and dedication. Talking about him helped me control my own reactions to her, which was a relief.

"He wants to do the right things for Silbar," I said. "Things that our people really need. And he knows so much more than I do, about a King's work anyway."

"'King's work?' What do you mean by that?" Callia asked.

"I mean making laws, and knowing how money moves and what it does—"

Economics.

"—economics, that's the word, and how to make the taxes fair so everybody pays what they can afford—"

Tax policy.

"— tax policy. And being a lord over people, giving orders and seeing that work gets done by the people who are supposed to do it, or make others do it—"

Management and supervision.

"—supervise people, so they do good for Silbar. Especially the parasites in the Palace—"

My administrators! Somebody has to be accountable to see that money goes where it is actually needed and the roads and canals and harbors and ships and bridges get built and maintained!

"Well, he doesn't call them parasites. Not out loud – I guess he thinks of them differently than I do."

That's certainly true.

"But if they do a bad job he sends them home in disgrace."

Callia laughed with a little catch in her voice. "He sounds like my father – I remember that Papa was unhappy with two of his ministers once so they got sent home to their provinces. It was years before they were allowed back."

There was sorrow under her smile. I nodded and almost touched her hand with my free one, but didn't quite dare. Her two guards were several steps back but they never took their eyes off me. It made the back of my neck itch, which was actually a welcome distraction.

"Terrell does pretty much the same with his if they don't behave. The ones that steal too much or laze about ignoring their work –"

The venal, the under-performers.

"–the ones who can't even pretend that they've done what they're supposed to do, they don't last long. And they don't get second chances, not in Aretzo. Which is good. The streets are cleaner now and all the fountains run regularly, fewer babies die; the priestesses say those go together. Our Navy's as big now as it was before the Conquest."

And the commercial fleet has doubled while the number of Silbar's tradesmen and artificers has increased by half. Tax revenue is vastly improved even though my rates are lower.

"The merchants love him, there are more of them than we used to have and they don't squawk nearly as hard about taxes now. He won back control of the sulfur mines from the Empire and ended slavery there, and made the new Gwythlo nobles stick to the old limits on how much they can tax the peasants and townsmen, so more people can afford shoes. And he made all the nobles keep up the roads again, too. In a lot of ways life is better now. People are proud to be Silbaris again."

"Interesting," Callia spoke the word softly, and for a moment she sounded so much like Terrell that I was startled. "He's a very competent and capable ruler then. Father said a noble who could tend his own province well was better than a chest full of gold, because in a year the gold would be spent but the noble would still be there paying taxes and raising men for our Navy."

Ahhh! I could feel Terrell's joy in my own heart. *She understands!*

"You understand," I told her seriously. "You are very like him that way."

Callia colored slightly. "Thank you, my Lord Ambassador. Tell me about his other interests."

I thought for a moment, aware that Terrell wondered what I'd say. "He likes to learn new things, even when they don't look useful right away. He likes it so much that I even like to do it now, because it pleases him and it's fun too." Terrell glowed at me without words, a burst of affection that cheered me down to my toes. "He's still got his tutors, and he keeps adding books to his library, and he buys all kinds of curiosities. He's got a whole hall of strange things brought from everywhere, dragon bones and dried animals and stranger stuff—"

"Oh!" Callia clapped her hands delightedly. "Father had one of those! We still have it right over there, let me show you!"

She grabbed my hand and dragged me down a side path to the arcade, and along it to another corridor that lead to a large room in another wing of the building. The place had a high ceiling and tall windows on two long walls and was crammed with cabinets large and small, big tables loaded with bones and odd minerals, and shelf after shelf of books. It smelled of dust and odd scents, some pleasant and others vile but most just strange. An elderly scribe sat at a table in a beam of light from tall windows, scribbling on the margin of a dusty scroll. Callia introduced him as Domas.

I looked up at the ceiling and Terrell gasped inside my head.

What is that?!

I simply pointed up and the old man smiled and answered the question before I asked it.

"That is the skeleton of a northern sea-unicorn, My Lord. The body is a full twelve feet long and the horn adds another six feet. Note how it grows from one side of the upper jaw, much like a tooth? His Majesty bought it a dozen years ago from a Vinelandia trader who traveled the northwest coast of Greatland, who in turn got it from some tribe of savages who hunt such creatures in the Ice Islands north of there."

That might as well have been on the moons as far as I knew, but Terrell was excited.

Ask him what holds it together. Most of those bones don't even touch each other! Is that thread?

When I repeated the question Domas beamed like a child. "The bones are held together with copper wire. 'Tis said that those people have a great boulder of pure copper upon the shore of a lake in their country, which they worship. The boulder, not the lake. Their shamans have Earth talents that let them draw threads of copper wire from the boulder and the rocks beneath it, and this they fashion into fine decorations for themselves and even trade south for such little as they need. They made this as a present for a northern chieftain in Vinelandia, whose widow sold it to the merchant who sold it to His Majesty."

"Amazing!" Terrell and I said as one.

Callia looked pleased. "There are many treasures here. Domas, open everything, I want to show Ambassador DiUmbra all the best ones!"

He smiled at the princess and dragged out a huge ring of keys, began to open locked cabinets for us. Several times he had to blow dust off an item so that we could see what it was. Callia's maids opened windows on both sides and let the breezes in to sweep the air clear again, her guards helped with the higher ones. There were fantastic minerals in colors to rival any flower; skeletons of bizarre creatures preserved under glass domes; pickled fishes and other creatures with fantastic shapes preserved in bottles of distilled wine spirits; branched antlers and curved horns of creatures both known and unknown, and much more. Terrell and Callia were delighted and at each new revelation I shared their pleasure as my own.

Hours later the tap of rain on the real glass windows drew my attention and I realized that we had lingered straight through whatever noonday meal must be customary here. Callia's maids had closed the windows when the worst of the dust was gone and the breeze became too hot. Now a warm tropic rain tapped the panes.

My stomach rumbled.

Callia caught it and stopped in mid word as she admired a tiny clockwork bird made of gems and metal. She smiled at me happily and then turned to Domas and said, "I think this is enough for today. I'll speak to Mother about getting this room cleaned more often. A scholar like you shouldn't have to work amidst squalor."

Domas stammered appreciation. Given the state of his clothes, I doubt he'd noticed the condition of the room until she mentioned it.

We took our leave and returned to the arcade where the air was much damper. Somebody had set out a light lunch in the little gazebo where I'd recited for her earlier. Curtained by the steady rainfall, we had an oddly private meal together despite the vast gardens beyond. I made sure Callia had a selection that pleased her before I devoured my own plate as slowly as I could force myself. And realized as I ate, that I had thoroughly enjoyed every moment I had spent with my brother's betrothed, in a way that hadn't happened since Maia.

Me too, my brother whispered. *I can hardly wait for whatever this afternoon will hold!*

~ ~ ~

Hours later I settled into a luxurious bed in a guest room of the Dalbai Palace, my belly stuffed with a magnificent dinner feast. It had followed introductions to all of the royal family that had strained my knowledge of etiquette. If Terrell hadn't juggled names and ranks and titles for me I'd have offended most of them. I'd been so overwhelmed that I had eaten more than I meant to. As I settled onto the soft sheets it dawned on me that I still felt a vague hunger. It came from Terrell. He'd muted his own sensations so thoroughly, the better to share mine, that I'd forgotten he really wasn't here eating with me.

Terrell, I'm an idiot! I just realized you haven't eaten in hours.

Actually, I didn't realize it either until just now. How strange. I can still taste that fabulous sugar and almond confection we – I mean you – ate, but my own stomach's growling.

While I stuffed myself like a pig. I'm sorry.

I've fasted before, it won't hurt me. I'd go without food for a week to gain what I learned today.

His presence inside my head was as comfortable as an old shoe. I wondered why I'd feared this so much.

You thought you'd disgrace yourself in my eyes. You never needed to worry.

Didn't I? I said to my brother, remembering my stupid choice of a recitation. *I told you I'd screw it up.*

Yes. But you rescued it too. And as I said you would, overall you did fine. In fact, better than fine. Without that bit of a misstep earlier she might not have believed as much of your later words, true as they were. And would she have shown us quite so much about herself, her delights, her pleasures, without the sympathy that your honest error brought forth in her? I think not. Considered together, you did very well indeed. Thank you, Kirin.

You're welcome. I snuggled into the bed. The silk sheets were deliciously cool thanks to clever air scoops in the ceiling that funneled night breezes into the room. *After that, the rest of this trip doesn't look nearly so hard.*

~ ~ ~

Chapter 24: Aretzo - Terrell

Ninety-second day of Summer

Disengaging from the massive magical construct inside the Hill of Sight left Terrell's mind raw as a bloody scab. He pushed back the cowl on his cloak and sagged in the stone chair, suddenly aware solely of his own body and how much it hurt. Night was well advanced and a sharp dry breeze blew out of the heart of Silbar towards the sea. Scents of acrid desert weeds and millennia of dust and ash warred with night-blooming flowers on the Hill. The dry air scorched his throat.

"Pen," he croaked.

Penghar was already there and raising a mug to his dry lips. Terrell clutched it, drank greedily.

"More," he begged.

"Slowly!" Pen cautioned as he poured watered wine from a leather sack. "I was worried about you. Midnight has passed and the bells already rang for the first hour. You haven't eaten or drunk in more than fourteen hours!"

"It was worth it," Terrell whispered back, his throat still sore. "Kirin did it, Pen, he gave me *everything*. I saw her, heard her voice, smelled her perfume, touched her hand, talked to her. She's the woman for me, I know it, I've made the right choice. Thank The One and all the Seraphs!" Joyous tears leaked from his eyes.

"I think that's more than I want to know," Pen said carefully. "You probably better not talk. Can you stand?"

Terrell tried to rise, nearly fell as his legs gave way. Pen caught him, helped him stand, held him up until he could walk a few paces.

"You can't manage five hundred steps that way." Pen called down the hill. Soon a team of litter bearers appeared and Pen ruthlessly bundled Terrell into the canvas device.

"Everything's perfect," Terrell whispered as the six bearers began to lug him down the long stair.

At the bottom of the five hundred steps Pen saw Dona Seraphina arrive, fear and fury in her every movement. "Let's pray it stays that way," he muttered.

~ ~ ~

Chapter 25: Daleray – Callia

Ninety-second day of Summer

"Mother said I could take the collection with me," Callia remarked to Dona Catalona. "We'll have to start packing it right away, and find room for it aboard a ship. And I must bring Domas too. He'll be so excited to show it off to Prince Terrell!"

"It sounds like the perfect wedding gift for you to give to your husband," the little priestess nodded.

"Yes, I'm so glad I thought of it!"

As her women peeled her out of the sari and undid the ornaments in her hair, Callia idly remarked, "I never did ask Sir Kirin how he changed the color of his clothes like that."

"Changed the color of his clothes?" asked the little priestess curiously.

"Yes, he changed his shirt from colored to black, and then changed it back again, perfectly. It was an impressive trick. I suppose that would be some kind of Earth magic, to turn colored dyes to black?"

"Ahhh." Dona Catalona raised an eyebrow at her. "I take it that you've never seen a living Shadow before today, your Highness?"

Callia paused as the world seemed to tilt slightly around her. "What?"

"That was almost certainly his Shadow being exposed, just a little, your Highness." The priestess sniffed. "Evil, used as a costume effect."

"I didn't know," Callia said slowly. "I didn't know."

~ ~ ~

Chapter 26: Daleray Palace - Kirin

Ninety-second day of Summer

Dawn barged into my bedroom uninvited. The first rays of new-risen Fathersun peeped through my room's eastern window to paint the opposite wall with a stripe of crimson and gold.

The servant was more polite. He knocked first and called out, "My Lord Ambassador?"

I grunted and he took that as permission to walk in. I saw a skinny man a dozen years older than me if I could judge by his close-cropped beard. He wore the same blue pantaloons and vest embroidered with the royal sigil that seemed to be the uniform of the Dalbai palace staff. A white turban topped his head.

I was not used to any of that, uniform, turban, or servant. But the terrified look that came over his face a moment later was all too familiar.

"M-m-my L-lord Amb-b-bassador?" His eyes bugged out.

My Shadow had leaked out again overnight.

"What's your name?" I asked him calmly as I sat up in the luxurious bed and dug the night-sand out of my eyes – and drew my Shadow back inside me. I felt strangely empty after I'd spent so long yesterday with my brother's mind inside mine.

"L-Limis, m-my Lord." He cast me an apprehensive glance and then his eyes skittered away, terrified by what he wasn't sure he'd seen. He actually shivered, though the morning air was hardly what I'd call cold and promised a day much warmer to come. The door had sighed shut behind him and he had backed right against it. At least that would make it hard for him to run away screaming.

The risk that he might just stand there screaming instead made me flog my sleepy wits awake.

"Limis," I told him quietly, my face twisted up in what I hoped was a wry smile. "I've never hurt a servant in my life and I hope to the One God that I never will. So please don't tremble like a leaf in the breeze. It makes my stomach queasy just to watch you."

He blinked, seemed to notice his own shivers for the first time and visibly forced himself to stop. He made a mighty effort and ground out the words, "I've b-b-been s-sent h-here to serve you, my Lord Amb-bassa-sa-sa-dor."

I stopped him before the panic could get set in any deeper. "Please, Limis. You saw my Shadow. Yes, it's a living Shadow, and sometimes it wraps me when I'm asleep. Think of it as a sort of Mage protection spell." It wasn't remotely the same but he might understand the idea. "It's no danger to anyone as long as they don't attack me." That was even less accurate but the truth was no help at all right now.

My explanation seemed to comfort him. He managed to twitch less and actually looked at me for an instant, though he avoided my eyes. His hands stopped wringing each other and settled into a pose closer to supplication and farther from panic.

"I'm sorry My Lord, I didn't know I was intruding on – on –"

I held up a hand again to stop the flow of words. "I'll guess that's not all that's scared you. Somebody told you I'm a demon in disguise and if I discover that you know it, I'll rip your soul out and eat it, didn't they? No, save the denials, I can see it on your face. Well here's what I have to say to that idea: Yuck!" I didn't have to make a show of gagging, I just remembered the taste of my ghosts. "I have it on the highest authority that souls taste terrible. I'd prefer a nice juicy orange any day."

That was unexpected enough to get through to him and he suddenly laughed explosively. I joined him with a few forced chuckles and he relaxed enough to look at me for two whole breaths before his gaze ran away again.

"You've been played, Limis," I assured him with a sad smile. "Whatever you may have heard as gossip below stairs, I don't go around ripping people's souls out for amusement. You are safer around me than you are in your own bed. So please, give over the fear. It's all right for you to look at me."

He swallowed hard and his gaze came back to my face. I held my Shadow inside and well away from my eyes and let him stare. His own eyes soon dropped again but most of the tension went out of him after a couple deep breaths.

"That's better. Someone unpacked my clothes for me last night, maybe you?"

"Yes, My Lord." A quick nod.

"Good, but I don't know my way around this huge room. Where is everything?"

At that question Limis relaxed still further and finally moved from his rigid pose just inside the door. He explained where he'd put my things yesterday and offered me one of the fancy new garments. I chose comfortable old tights instead and put them on myself while I sent him back to the wardrobe for a pair of sandals.

"Not the fancy slippers, just the sandals. The green vest will do – wait. What are the usual arrangements around here for breaking one's fast? Do my hosts expect me at table with them?" I might have to dress up again. "Or can I just get a bite from the kitchen?"

Limis told me that I was not required to break my fast with the family, whose members evidently rose at different hours. And if I wished he could arrange for the cook to make me my very own meal.

"Better yet, help me find some fruit somewhere, and then show me to the fencing yard. I need exercise after that huge meal last night. May I use whatever place the palace guards use to train?"

Limis blandly said, "Count Harren practices his sword work most mornings in the Court of the Cats; he and Princess Gadet have apartments in that wing. He directed me to invite you to join him, if you wish, my lord."

"Count Harren," I repeated thoughtfully. I'd barely had time to exchange ten words with the man at the dinner last night, it would be useful to catch him without other people to distract both of us. "Yes, that would be excellent. Forget breakfast, fighting's better on an empty stomach. Please show me there." I belted on my sword and followed him out.

A half-mile of corridor later Limis ushered me into the Court of the Cats, which didn't have even one visible cat in it. It did have four high walls, two of them parts of the blank fortress and the others made of carved arcades that held up rows of balconies. The floor was mostly a level paved space with flower-filled planters around the edges. Racked weights under one arcade, an unrolled wrestling mat and a row of pells revealed the normal use of this space.

The burly man that I'd seen at dinner worked at the pells, stripped to a loincloth and swinging a two-handed longsword. His cuts were strong and clean and the bunched muscles in his arms and back testified to his strength. He hadn't been at it long, he'd barely begun to work up a sweat. He saw us approach and paused, handed his blade to a servant.

"My Lord Ambassador Sir DiUmbra," he greeted me. "Welcome! Care for a little exercise to start your day?" He had a wide brown face with dark eyes and a ready smile only slightly marred by a scar that started next to his nose and ran down to his jaw. A few more seamed his ribs, clearly he did more with his sword than just practice. He wore his black hair long and clubbed back in a fighting braid, and looked to be perhaps ten or twelve years older than me. If there was an ounce of fat on his body it was hidden well.

"Gladly, Count Sir Harren," I answered as I clasped his wrists in the Warrior's Grip – the custom was practiced across most of the Continent and had plainly spread to the Dreaming Isles too. He was almost exactly the same height as me but broader and more heavily built. "But please just call me Kirin – the Ambassador post is a temporary one, without it I'm just an ordinary knight."

"Or perhaps a not-so-ordinary knight," he grinned. "And call me Yare, at least while we're at practice, Kirin." His eyes had flicked over me to take in my own build, and his hand slid down to mine and tested my grip; not like a bully, just checking before he released. "Would you enjoy a little sparring?"

"I'd love it, but do you mind if I stretch first? That fabulous feast last night has left me slow as a steer fattened for slaughter."

"I know that sensation," he laughed. "Call me when you're ready."

I ran through my own limber-up exercises, a combination of the acrobatic preparation the DiUmbra Troupe had taught me and the lessons that had been drilled into me when Terrell knighted me into the Old Order. I kept one eye on Count Yare who had continued to work the two-handed broadsword. He chopped several times each through twelve pells made of water-soaked bamboo mats tightly rolled and bound with thongs. By the time he was done the ground was littered with bits of bamboo and leather. His strength and control were impressive, but any forester can chop down a tree. I wondered how he was against moving targets.

When I was ready he put the broadsword aside and his servants brought out a pair of padded arming doublets with neck and groin protectors and padded legs. Though both were clean they had the familiar smell of old sweat and rancid oil that no amount of washing removes. It made me nostalgic for the Old Order Chapter House in Aretzo. Limis appeared from wherever he'd been and helped me into mine with the expertise of someone who'd done it many times. I wondered who he had been servant to before me, then remembered that Callia's brother had died in the war.

Yare's servant opened a case and displayed two wooden longswords and two wood parry knives, what Silbaris call main-gauche, all battered by frequent use but well cared for.

"Your choice, Kirin." Yare magnanimously swept a hand over the pairs. "I use both and switch off every couple days to keep them equally worn."

I picked one pair and hefted them. They were good hardwood with lead cores to give them similar weight to the real version. Both had leather-wrapped grips and were beautifully balanced. He took the other and we entered a practice circle marked by a ring of black stone set into the buff limestone of the courtyard. I noted the way he moved. There was plenty of controlled power in that walk.

"To seven touches?" I suggested.

"Agreed. On your guard," he said, and we began.

He moved immediately, a smooth draw and crosscut that would have slit my belly if I hadn't deflected it and moved aside, and if the swords had been steel. I turned the deflection into a return slash that he blocked and we exchanged twenty blows in thirty seconds. I barely managed to deflect them all. The strength in his arms made me wary and I was glad I hadn't tried a direct block. It might have broken the sword, and surely could have broken the lighter gauche.

Yare chased me around the circle for ten more blows while I learned his style. Then I began to get my own in, and soon forced him into a more even exchange. He was clever and quick as well as strong. Soon we both panted like oxen dragging stones uphill. By the end I got five touches in for the seven he got on me.

"Very good, Kirin!" he saluted me as he stepped back and out of the circle after his seventh touch. "Not many do so well against me on a first try!"

I saluted him back as we got our breath down to normal. The servants brought us water and I raised my helmet to gulp down a dipper. Yare took his helm off, poured his first dipper over his head, shook his hair till droplets flew, and laughed before downing the second one. I poured my second down my neck. My own doublet was half soaked with sweat already and the day would only get hotter.

"Want to try for another seven?" I offered, unable to suppress a grin. He was a real challenge but a fun one too.

His own grin matched mine. "You're on!"

This time took longer. I had a sense of his reach now and stayed just at the edge of it as I darted in for quick taps and stabs. That cost me four solid whaps from him, the last delivered just as I landed my seventh touch and made his helmet ring.

"Woooo!" he puffed and returned my salute. "Magnificent! Though I'd have bled you some before you took my head."

I laughed happily. "A break, and then one more set to settle the tie?"

"Perfect!" he answered.

The servants collected our weapons again and helped us out of the padding to cool down. This time they brought us a bucket each, and I gladly dumped most of mine over my head. I could faintly hear music; someone strummed a lute inside the palace. A few servants had moved about the edges of the Court of the Cats while we fought, but none had disturbed us.

"Where did you learn to fight like that, Kirin?" Yare asked as he ripped an orange in two and handed me the larger half. "Were those all Silbari techniques? Some felt more northern."

I squeezed sweet juice into my mouth, then told him. "Mostly Silbari. I learned the basic traditions from Sir Menandir Libran DiCati, my chief teacher in the Old Order, and a fair amount of advanced moves too. But I learned those Gwythlo moves from Pen. Sir Penghar Verhys DiLione."

"You trained with DiLione?" His eyebrows went up. "What's it like to fight against that magic sword of his?"

"Never done it," I answered frankly. "Never plan to, you can make book on that. She could probably cut me in half without trying."

If I was ever stupid enough to let Pen actually swing Irreneetha against me in a fight, I'd probably die. My Shadow might not mind that at all, or it might fight for me, I didn't know. And I definitely didn't want to find out.

"You think so?" He looked dubious. "Never met a soulsword myself, understand, but I don't have a lot of trust in the words of any bard." He tossed his empty orange husk into a flowerbed and broke open another, passed me half of that. "Does it really have an angel in it?"

"Yes. I've seen her."

"Hunh. What's 'she' look like?"

I struggled to frame my memories with speech. "Like an essence of womanhood. Like a statue of steel. Like nothing else I've ever seen. I can't even remember what color she was. All colors, maybe. I, I don't have the right words."

He snorted softly, as if I'd confirmed a guess for him. "And does he actually chop through walls with the blade? Seems like a crazy way to treat a fine piece of steel."

"I've seen him do that too; it was a rock wall." I savored the memory. "The blade's insanely strong and unbelievably sharp. He's cut other swords in two with it. And the edge doesn't get dulled, ever." I shook my head. "For once the Bards don't exaggerate."

"Hmmm." Yare thoughtfully finished his orange while I worked on another. After a while he asked me, "How does any swordsman fight such a weapon? Does the wielder even have to be any good, or does the sword do all the work for him?"

I thought I knew what could fight Irreneetha, but I'd rather not talk about it. I sidestepped the question by telling him, "I've fought Pen in the practice ring, with wooden swords like these of course. He's very good. He usually beats me two out of three times or better. The few times I've won I suspect he hadn't tried as hard as he should have. With Irreneetha in his hands – Salim's Tail! He's deadly. Never lost a real fight. And I've been with him in a couple where our lives were in the balance, too."

Yare's eyebrows twitched and he grunted. "Sounds like a powerful recommendation."

"It is." I found it a lot easier to admit that here than at home.

I hadn't practiced with Pen very much over the years. Three bouts was usually enough to make me want to strangle him with my bare hands. Though I had to admit that I'd learned some good tricks from him. If only he'd ever been willing to learn anything from me.

I finished my orange.

"Ready for the tiebreaker, Count Yare?"

He grinned fiercely and waved to the servants. In moments we were suited again and faced each other across the circle.

"On your guard, Kirin!" he called to me gaily. "Get ready for a thrashing!"

"Yours!" I shot back.

We moved toward each other, wooden blades poised and ready, and began. The power in his strikes, the speed of mine, both of us pushed to our limits. We thrust and cut and blocked and parried until my blood hammered in my veins. This was as exhilarating as the finest trapeze work, the same steel-sharp focus on the dance of muscle and motion.

Six touches we traded and the next would end it. He'd slowly worked me back against the edge of the garden. He knew this place better than I did. But I'd noticed how rarely his feet left the pavement. He was a 'grounded' fighter, powerful and quick, but not nimble.

Not like me.

I lured him into a leg strike. When he went for it, I leaped straight up and came in over his defense with a long stab. The point of my blade rammed his chest hard enough to rock him off balance.

"Seven!"

And even as I shouted the word his counter slipped past my gauche and rapped me in the belly.

"Dung!" I landed on my feet and had to take two fast steps to keep my balance.

Yare laughed as he staggered upright again and gasped for breath. "Mutual kill. But I'd have died first, your point was dead on my heart. By Danner's Dick, that was a good fight! I declare you the winner, Kirin!"

The servants took our weapons and stripped us out of the padded outfits. I was flushed and dripped sweat, as did he. The day was still young but neither of us had held back during our bouts.

He grabbed my wrist in the Warriors Grip again and looked me in the eye with a grin of pure happiness.

"My thanks for that fight. I haven't had so much fun in seasons!"

"Same here." I squeezed his wrist back and liked him greatly at that moment.

"Come talk with me while we wash up, my *hamman* is right at hand and Limis can fetch you clean clothes."

"Sure!" Maybe I could get him to share his real thoughts on the politics of the marriage alliance. His opinions must have some weight here.

He led the way through a door in the fourth wall of the Court of the Cats into a small but well-appointed set of wash rooms.

"I've got the full suite," Yare explained as he stripped off his loincloth and tossed it to a servant. "Steam room, cold plunge, tepid pool, and solarium."

I hesitated only an instant before I peeled off my hose and followed his lead. The servant collected my sword and belt as well, bowed and left. Yare's eyes flicked at once to the Klinto slave tattoo on my thigh.

"Yes, it's exactly what it looks like," I said quietly, chin up. "The red line means I was freed."

"I'd heard a rumor that you were once a slave," he confirmed as we stepped into wooden clogs to protect our feet and walked through a heavy door into the dim steam room. "I'm not so big a fool to think the less of you for it, though some would. You may not know, but my great grandfather Yare, who I'm named for, was enslaved by Khaitanial in the Channel Wars."

The steam room's tiled floor, walls, and vaulted ceiling radiated a fierce heat that reminded me of Silbar's deserts. There had to be a fire behind each or else he had a fireworker on hand to keep it hot. Since I had smelled charcoal smoke in the courtyard I guessed the former. A mage lamp at each end was the only illumination and tiled benches on either side of the central pit the only seats, a lot like a Silbari *hamman* would boast. Yare poured dippers full of water over hot stones and splashed more on the walls. The room was instantly thick with vapor. I took the bench opposite the one he chose. The wet tile was warmer than my skin but not hot enough to be uncomfortable. Some herb in the water perfumed the steam. It was delicious and I inhaled it with pleasure. My already-open pores streamed sweat as my body purged itself, but I remembered to keep a firm rein on my Shadow.

"I didn't know that about your ancestor," I admitted as I reclined on the bench.

He nodded, frowned introspectively as he propped himself on one elbow while he lounged. "He was chained to an oar in one of their galleys, whipped and forced to work against his own people. His son Eril, my grandfather, stormed that same ship later in that war and cut some of the slaves free. One had been chained with great grand and told Eril about an uprising that Yare had staged earlier in that same battle, when the Tanny captain called for ramming speed. Half the left-side rowers revolted then and instead the ship slewed sideways to miss our ship completely. The Tanny bastard massacred the rebels then and there, and great-granddad was gutted and hung on a hook from the stern. He was still there when our ship came around later in the battle and grappled on. Grandpa Eril reclaimed his sire's body and brought him home to bury with the Tanny captain's head to rest beneath his feet." He glanced at my leg again. "You fought back too, didn't you?"

"Damn right I did, and left the bastard who bought me dead behind me." Gerlach's ghost writhed inside me. The memory was both bitter and triumphant, for that was the first time I used my Shadow to kill and knew what I did. "It was a long time ago. I was a child." He could probably tell as much, as I'd grown the mark had stretched and the number become distorted. "I was young, to learn to kill."

"No age too young for that if you can hold any kind of blade at all," he nodded. "And I'll bet you hate slavery above most anything else now."

"Truth."

He poured more water on the rocks and through the hiss of the steam added, "You've come to the right place then."

"I've been told Dalbai doesn't allow slavery any more than Silbar."

"Yes, we hire our servants here instead of buy them," he agreed. "Though most of mine have been with my family for generations. It's our pride to always reward our own very well. They've grown to know what we need and deliver it perfectly. Sometimes I feel like a stone nested in a mossy bed, so pampered I don't want to leave it! But sooner or later Lord Duty pries me back out again."

He delivered that cheerfully, as if not the least bit bothered. "Luckily, some of my duties are more pleasure than burden. Fighting, for instance, or making heirs, that part's pretty good. And from the way you reacted to our little Callia yesterday, I'd bet half my lands that you enjoy it too!"

I laughed, amused and embarrassed. "Was I that obvious?" Then I was more embarrassed as my loins stirred in memory of her nearness. I was amazed that I'd managed to sleep through last night and didn't wake up sweaty and bothered.

"Hah!" His laugh was friendly and inviting and I couldn't help joining in. "Obvious to me, certainly. My niece set out to charm you, and I knew right away that she succeeded. By The Mother, that girl's grown up to be a beauty, and is she ever *ready*! Your prince is a lucky man. Though you better warn him, if she turns out like my Gadet she won't want him in her bed from fifty days before each birth to fifty days after."

"That bad?" I jibed back. "Your balls don't look blue."

"There's more advantages to a title than good swords and fancy bath suites!" He preened like a rooster.

"And speaking of that, this is great, but I'm cooked," I told him.

"Same here, let's take a dive in the cold plunge."

Yare led the way to the next room, which had no floor, just a glass-smooth sheet of water. He dived in and I followed. The shock of the cold water after the hot steam cured my little arousal problem. I swam the length of the pool – it must have been forty feet long and half that wide – and back on one breath, then came up whooping. Yare had paralleled me on the surface, he shook the water out of his eyes and pointed to the far end where a wide arched door opened to the next room.

"This is bracing, but a little's plenty for me. Tepid pool next."

There was a narrow flight of steps up to the broad stone sill but Yare just surged out of the water and hand-vaulted himself over into the next pool. I followed and found it was comfortably warm. The ceiling here was open to the sky and the room bright compared to the dark cold plunge, but I could see the pale blue of a shield spell arched above. There'd be no bird droppings to befoul this pool. In fact the water was wonderfully clear and so clean that I could see fine details in the fancy tile patterns set into the floor and walls.

We swam a dozen laps, then lolled in the shallow end while we talked of Island politics, most of which Terrell had outlined for me. Yare had a shrewd grasp of the diplomatic situation and how narrow Dalbai's choices really were.

"We can either ally with someone more powerful than our traditional allies, Tem and Breen," he explained, naming the two smaller isles to Dalbai's northwest and south. "Or strike a bargain with Khaitanial. That probably means we betray Breen, which is pretty weak without us. The Tannys have wanted to dominate them for centuries, old grudges there. Only nobody here's wildly excited about that alternative, let me tell you! It's not just our honor, though we don't take that lightly, but if Khaitanial could base ships in Breenport they'd be within a day's sail of our south coast. That's a risk we've no appetite for, unless we're really desperate. Fortunately, we have a couple princesses to offer in marriage. Callia of course, or if she doesn't please your lord there's my own Bettina."

"Your eldest daughter? She doesn't look more than thirteen."

"She'll be ready soon enough." He waved a hand dismissively. "Your prince can use his concubines until then, if he prefers riper women. Or if he's satisfied with Callia, then all's well. My Bettina's an obedient girl, she'll please whichever husband she ends up marrying."

I didn't much care for that suggestion and thought Terrell would like it even less, so I changed the subject. "Do you think Prince Terrell's offer is a trick to get Emperor Osrick a foothold in the Archipelago?"

Yare snorted. "My sister-in-law isn't much pleased with your prince's brother. Nor am I! But we look at it this way; the man hasn't got the sense that the Gods gave a duck! Sooner or later it's a sure bet that he offends somebody strong enough and stupid enough to think they can challenge him head-on. Then the Empire shatters like a dropped melon. Silbar'll probably suffer some, but odds are you'll survive as long as you can beat the Klinto and Fehdaran fleets at sea. And with our ship designs, you can. That'll leave Dalbai and Silbar as the two biggest navies in the known world. We've got a very good chance to whip Khaitanial's ass in a few more years. If it wasn't for sheer bad luck we'd have beat them last time. Then we take Khaitanial and end the real threat to the archipelago."

I nodded, more pleased than I'd been by his previous suggestion. He was smart and funny and open and I couldn't help liking him, mostly. Though his willingness to offer his young daughter as an alternative bride bothered me. Maybe it was a sign of how desperate Dalbai was for the alliance? I knew royalty sometimes had to make such bargains, but she was just a girl.

Yare interrupted my thoughts. "I've got another treat for you, Kirin. This way!"

He waded out the far end of the pool where a broad set of steps lead to a marble terrace with a table on it. I followed and he tossed me a luxurious towel and began to mop himself dry with another as he walked toward a door.

"Don't worry about getting completely dry," he said. "The solarium will take care of that."

We stepped through another heavy door into a warm room with an actual glass ceiling. The suns struck through it like twin hearths. The place wasn't very large, just big enough to hold four heavy wooden tables a little less than waist high. Each had a padded leather cushion draped in a cotton sheet on top and with a shelf underneath for oil flasks, strigils, and the like. I recognized the arrangements. Terrell's palace had masseurs on the staff too, a family of seven that ranged from a youth not yet in his third decade to two gnarled grandfathers. All had hands like iron and a talent for finding every knot and strain and soothing the hurt places. Of course his hamman was four times the size of this place, and handled the entire Palace Guard in shifts as well as himself and privileged guests like me and Pen; I'd never seen it empty. Yare and I had this solely to ourselves.

He hopped up on one table and tossed his towel to the same servant who'd collected our clothes at the start. I imitated him and took the next one. I laid face down on the contoured cushion to get relaxed for the masseur. Then I wondered if he had one or two. I didn't mind waiting for a turn and I said so to Yare.

He turned his head sideways to look at me. "No worry, I've got a matched pair, raised on my estates and trained by the best." He glanced behind me and smirked. "And here they are."

Two women entered the room.

Now, I'd met masseuses before. Duke Cerrai's castle hamman was ruled by a stern pair of fiftyish matrons with arms and legs like trees and no patience for young men's nonsense, By The One! But these were young, no older than me and probably younger. And beautiful. And nearly identical; possibly sisters or even twins, I couldn't quite tell while lying flat on my belly. And nearly naked themselves, which I know was sensible in the warm room. But –

Yare chuckled at me. "Never had a masseuse before? Please be my guest and let mine show you what they can do. Reela, Thami, this is Lord Ambassador Sir Kirin DiUmbra from Silbar. Treat him as you would treat me."

The two chimed some words in counterpoint that I had to puzzle out, their Dalbai had a thick accent as bad as any deep rural Silbari. About the time I got it – 'Happy welcome to the Blessed Isle' – Reela dribbled warm olive oil on my back and began to work it into my shoulders with strong sure strokes. I dropped my face back down on the pad as bliss claimed me. Maybe they were just masseuses.

That illusion lasted for half an hour while Reela worked her way from my neck and shoulders down my back and buttocks to my toes, then back up. The return trip involved more detours of her hands, more whispers and giggles between her and Thami, and an end to my pretense. In moments I went from fully relaxed to as aroused as I'd ever been. I lifted my head enough to catch a look at Yare, who grinned and rolled over then. Thami had shed her halter somewhere along the way and now she dropped her skirt and climbed naked upon him.

Reela urged me to turn over too.

Terrell hadn't mentioned this when he'd filled my head with Dalbai customs, which meant it wasn't a common one. But I was Yare's guest, and he was one of the most important and influential men on the island. From the look of this he'd done it often before; both women were obviously practiced. And seemed to enjoy their work too, with a happy abandon that said they didn't fear whatever might happen here. I doubted there was any chance his wife didn't know how he dealt with his lust while she was birthing their children.

And it wasn't like I'd never used a servant woman to satisfy my own lust, when guest manners called for it in a lord's castle. But —

That had been private, between her and me, and sometimes I'd begged off with tiredness as an excuse, which wouldn't work here. This wasn't anything I was prepared for. Only I was pretty sure walking out now would be a slap in the face to Yare. Did I dare offend him that way?

If my wits had been quicker I might have thought of a third choice. Instead I cooperated with the situation, and rolled over.

~ ~ ~

Afterwards Yare and I went back to the pool to wash.

"That was a great performance, Kirin." He winked lasciviously. "I should arrange an orgy for you before you leave. I bet you'd put every one of my friends to shame and leave all the women sated."

"Umm, I don't think I'm ready for that, Yare." I felt myself getting red and toweled my head to avoid looking at him.

"Another time perhaps." Yare sighed happily as he dried his own hair. "I'm a lucky man. A beautiful wife who likes to bed me except for a hundred days out of every two years, and some very talented servants who'll take me any time. Thanks for sharing my good fortune with me, Kirin."

"Umm, thank you, Yare. It was, ah, an eye-opener of an experience."

"I don't doubt that!" he smirked. "T'was the same for me!"

He opened another door out of the solarium into a changing room with the biggest mirror I'd ever seen and servants standing ready by garb tables. I found that Limis had laid out one of my fancy Ambassadorial sets. He silently helped me into it while Yare's own servant did the same for him. Limis had brought me an airy shirt with ribbon sleeves in alternate strips of green and yellow. The vivid yellow spidersilk hose were also as light as clothes could be in this humid heat. I stuck to the same sandals I'd worn here this morning since I didn't want to suffocate my feet inside another pair of fancy silk and leather slippers. I was glad to buckle on my sword belt again, it was a familiar and welcome weight in all this strangeness.

Yare dressed in loose silk pantaloons, an elaborate vest, a big leather sword belt, and an odd three-cornered hat. He smiled at me as his servant settled it on his head, then he held out his hand.

"You were great company this morning, Lord Ambassador. Care to join me again tomorrow, same time?"

I took the hand and shook it, remembered enough diplomacy to say, "While I could use the exercise and much as I'd like to, Princess Callia and her mother have plans for me. I'll have to see what they allow."

"Fair enough." He nodded his head genially. "Enjoy your day with my niece and my sister-in-law." Then he breezed out.

"Limis, I think I'd like that breakfast now."

"This way, My Lord." He led me off through long corridors and arcades. He remained silent behind a shield of formality.

I broke that silence as soon as we crossed an empty courtyard. I stopped him with a hand on his sleeve and he gave me a look simultaneously distant and attentive.

"Limis." I tried to control my resentment. "I think you knew what Count Harren would lead me into this morning. Damn it, why didn't you warn me?"

He stared somewhere over my left shoulder. "His lordship expressly forbid me to do so, my lord."

That took me aback. Yare didn't feel dangerous to me, even while we fought. Then I thought what he'd look like to a servant. You don't have to be a slave to fear a man with power. "Oh. Was he your master before you were sent to wait on me?"

"No, my lord, that was Crown Prince Mikkal, may the Gods keep his soul."

"Then why did you heed Count Harren?"

"He's quite a forceful man, my lord. He doesn't anger often . . . but when he does, the results tend to be, um, unfortunate for those that draw his ire. And you are a man grown."

Meaning I didn't need protection like a child. I winced at that. "Grown a fool, more like. The clues were there, and I didn't see them. Maybe I didn't want to see them."

I was very glad that Terrell hadn't yet spoken to me today, and wondered how I would explain myself when he did. Debts and obligations; he'd always kept ours very clear and simple, and never complicated them by offering to share his concubines with me or anything similar. I thought I must have resented that sometimes, but now I was glad of it.

Unexpectedly, Limis volunteered, "Some of the last words Prince Mikkal said to me the day he left for the war were these: he found his own soul harder to explore than the bottom of the sea, and other people's souls more filled with strangeness than a forest at night."

That made me blink, and think. "Limis, did you ever bring the prince to the Court of the Cats the way you brought me?"

"No my lord; he knew the way. Count Yare has lived here since the prince was a boy, and he installed his private bathing suite soon after he arrived." Limis finally unbent enough to add, "King Baint required his son to practice sword work with his own sword master in the barracks each morning, until he turned twenty-one years of age. Then he gave him leave to 'be wise or foolish as he chose'. So the prince accepted his uncle's invitation three times in a row, and then never again. His Majesty seemed to take pleasure in his heir's fourth choice, and his cares seemed to be less after that."

I frowned. "It was a test then, for Prince Mikkal; and maybe for me?"

Limis was silent for a moment, then said, "Princess Gadet has always been quite pleased with her husband and supportive of him. He worships her and loves their children, you see, even though he's not traditionally faithful. Her brother the King made it plain to any who questioned the, ah, situation that her wishes controlled and he would not go against them. While he also made it clear to his children that neither he nor the Queen were happy with some of their brother-in-law's choices. Since the King's tragic death Her Majesty has maintained those understandings."

"She's not about to rock the boat while the Kingdom is at risk," I translated. "But later that might change." And I thought Yare was plenty smart enough to see it, yet he'd lured me in anyway. Was he trying to win an ally of some kind? Or was this an indirect bribe? "I think today I crossed a border that I didn't know was there."

Limis looked me in the eyes. "My lord, there is a Dalbai saying that the road to Hell is paved with single stones, and step by step, they each lead downward. Unless you turn around."

"Thank you, Limis," I told him. "You've given me a lot to think about."

Including the most worrisome thought of all, which came to me as he led me towards breakfast. Why had Yare gone to such efforts to snare me? I was just a visitor who'd be gone in a few days, probably never to return. Yet he'd spent the time and flattery – a lot of flattery, I'd begun to realize – and women too, all to seduce me into trusting him like a close friend.

What was he hoping to get in return? When he made that offer of his own daughter as Terrell's bride, did he intend to advance his own line at his niece's expense? Did he think he could get me to support such a betrayal by offering me his women?

I didn't know whether to be outraged or disgusted. Or ashamed.

That led to another thought. What would his sister-in-law the Queen think of me? I was already worried about the way she'd sent those two soldiers to follow me and Callia around the garden. If this had been a test, and I'd failed it, would I even get a third chance?

And most important of all; what would Callia think?

~ ~ ~

Chapter 27: Aretzo Palace - Seraphina

Ninety-second day of Summer

"Your Highness, don't be a fool!"

Dona Seraphina wished back the words as soon as they left her withered lips. Her joints ached abominably today, a sure sign that she didn't have many more years before the Gray Judge would claim her. It probably clouded her judgment. But Prince Terrell had frightened her half to death last night with his antics atop the Hill of Sight and she was still exhausted from the aftermath. And still frightened. A third of the Royal bloodline had been slaughtered in the Conquest and half a dozen more by the Usurper. The present opportunity to reinforce it with an advantageous marriage was too precious to lose, and then this idiot prince had to risk his very life because of some romantic vapors.

Prince Terrell frowned reproachfully at her. "I believe I have gone about my plans perfectly sensibly, Dona," he countered in the reasonable voice that could be so infuriating.

Seraphina glared at her charge, fought back her exasperation and returned to manipulation by reason. In a slightly calmer voice she added, "Please don't waste your breath to deceive me. I have healed your body a dozen times in the past twenty-five years, and last night was one of the worst. You can't hide from me what a mess you've made of yourself. The channels of your mind are dangerously strained from excessive contact with the deep Node. Your spine is traumatized, your nerves badly over-stressed, your sinuses near to bleeding internally, your inner ears inflamed and your eyes – your poor wounded eyes! They're dangerously inflamed too.

Only the Seraphs know what long-term damage you've done to your heart, lungs, and liver."

She paused for breath and he let her continue. "The Hill wight is not your guardian and it won't protect you from yourself. That monstrous construct it lives in is meant to be used sparingly, and only in extreme need. Too much use will *kill* you, as it killed two of your ancestors before you. It certainly shortened your mother's life, too. I insist that you rest and heal before you try it again!" She barely managed to keep her voice below a scream.

"But you do agree than it is possible for me to use it again without excessive danger to myself?" The prince pressed the point.

Aggravating boy. She took a deep breath before she answered as quietly and yet forcefully as she could manage.

"Not today. Not for at least twenty more hours, and you should spend at least half of those asleep. And you must let me and your other Healers undo some of the damage you've done to yourself. After that, perhaps." She glared again. "You *may* be able to safely withstand an hour of time per day with that infernal device. Possibly less."

"Very well, Dona." Terrell sighed mournfully. "I'll take your advice."

"Good! And spare me the theatrics! Just get back in your bed while we do our work."

An hour later, with Prince Terrell asleep and two healers meshing their spells to carefully soothe his damage and coax his body to mend, she felt able to leave his side for a few minutes. She gave Sir Penghar a harsh stare, pointed to the next room and managed to get him to follow her out. A servant closed the bedchamber door behind them, then at her gesture bowed himself out by another route to give them privacy.

"Why in the name of all holiness did you aid him in this folly?" she demanded.

Pen did his trick of raising one eyebrow. "Because he required it of me."

"If he required you to throw him off a tower, would you do that?" she tartly shot back.

"Of course. I would trust that he knew what he did and had some plan under way."

"Ah! Knights!" She spit out the word like an expletive and massaged her aching forehead with one hand. "Pen, obedience must be informed and wise, lest it become blind and destructive. There is no honor in 'helping' him to his own death."

"I beg to differ with you on that last point, Dona." He made an apologetic little half bow. Then, cautiously, he asked, "Is he really in danger of death?"

"This time? Probably not," she admitted grudgingly. "He is still healthy enough to heal from what he inflicted upon himself yesterday. The damage would have been less if you'd stopped him sooner. Fourteen hours, Pen! Didn't you worry? When I returned from my Conclave and found out he was still up there after midnight I was ready to crawl up all five hundred steps on my hands and knees!"

"Thank you for meeting us at the bottom."

She noted that he hadn't answered her question, so the answer was probably yes. "Another ten minutes and I'd have found enough bearers to have myself *carried* up there," she growled. "I had better have them ready tomorrow. If he will try this foolishness again, then by all the Seraphs I shall have to be there too."

"I'm not sure he will accept that," Pen said with a worried look. "I think it was a very private experience, one he's not willing to share."

"Don't get cryptic on me, boy," Seraphina frowned at Pen. "You were there. What did he try to do anyway?"

"Look across the ocean to Dalbai."

"Waugh! Madness!" She sputtered, aghast. "No King has ever managed to make the Hill project his vision that far. His mother barely managed the five hundred miles to Black Pass, and that for mere minutes!"

"Two and a half thousand miles," Pen said proudly. "For all fourteen hours. He did it."

"Two. . .for. . ." Words failed her and for a moment she just stared, stunned. "How? In the names of all the Seraphs great and small, *why?*"

"I don't actually know." Pen's eyes shifted away and he stared at the windows.

"But you've got a good guess, don't you? What is it?"

Pen just shook his head. "I'm not sure I believe it, Dona Seraphina, and anyway it's his choice to give or withhold, not mine."

"Knights!" Seraphina spat the word twice as hard this time. "Blessed Saint Palena save me from foolish young Knights."

A corner of Pen's mouth tugged up. "I'm not sorry that we're all stuck with each other's company, Dona." More seriously he added, "I am glad you persuaded him to rest today. I was worried too."

"But not enough to stop him." She eyed his sword with disfavor. "Did Irreneetha express any opinion?"

Penghar just shook his head. "Not about this. She understands my duty."

"Might have known," Seraphina grumbled, choosing to ignore the implied dig.

Then she stopped herself from saying words she'd regret later, forced herself to recite the Litany for Calm and followed it with five deep breaths, then five more. Pen stood by impassively and waited. She had to admit that he did that exceptionally well.

"What's done is done." She let it go with only one twinge of regret. "I should have anticipated that he'd try some venture of this nature. Though I thought he had learned better than to fool with that thrice-damned underground monstrosity after the last debacle. If he remains determined try it again tomorrow, I want myself and the Archmage close at hand." She raised a hand to forestall words from Pen. "We'll wait on the first landing below the top, fifty steps away. I insist that you call us to him at the first sign of danger, and I'll instruct you and him both quite clearly in how to recognize such signs. Agreed?"

"I agree." Pen nodded once. "You'll have to ask him whether he agrees after he wakes."

"Oh I will, you may be certain of that."

She left Penghar with a final glare and returned to the prince's bedchamber. The two Healers who worked on him were among the best in the entire kingdom, she had trained them herself. But nobody else had as many years practice as she did at repairing the wretched boy's carelessness with his own body.

Seraphina settled herself on a padded chair, close enough to reach him with her diagnostic spells but out of the Healers' way, and studied him inside and out. Inside, she sensed the strains and stresses that had been so dangerously close to a cascade of failure last night. They were much reduced now, but not nearly back to what a priestess would call normal. Why couldn't the fool boy stick to lesser dangers like swordplay and horses, instead of playing with power? He was as bad about that as any Mage.

On his outside . . .

He slept deeply, his face smooth save for the fine blond hairs that coalesced at his eyebrows and mustache, the natural smile lines that got too little use, and the tiny scars that he wouldn't let her remove. The shock of yellow curls above added to his exotic look. There was a strength and beauty there that made even her aged heart sing. In his awake hours he'd shown a wisdom that had eased fears and raised hopes across twenty million people. Seven years of hard work and brilliant governance; Silbar hadn't been so prosperous, just, and secure in centuries.

She thought *He will either be the greatest King that we've known in the last thousand years, or our worst disaster. And the list of our disasters is long indeed.*

Seraphina simultaneously thanked and excoriated her God for putting this boy in her charge. No, in the privacy of her thoughts she had to admit that he was a man in every way that counted, or would be as soon as he could produce heirs. She grimly settled down to wait for his next appalling action. Sure as the suns rose in glory every morning, there would be one.

~ ~ ~

Chapter 28: Daleray Palace - Callia

Ninety-second day of Summer

Callia woke restless from half-formed dreams. Dreams of a yellow-haired dark-skinned face and a paler black-haired one. Dreams of touching and being touched. Dreams of urgent importance; dreams that fled as she tried to grasp them.

She threw off the sheet and stalked to the window, pushed back the spell screen, and took in a deep breath of dawn air. Salt sea and flowers, the famous scents of the Dreaming Isles, but they didn't help her find more meaning. Instead the dreams faded further, and she felt obscurely sad at their loss.

Her maid came in yawning.

"I need to ride," Callia declared. "And then swim. Arrange both please, Junia."

Half an hour later she strode into the royal stables. A groom brought her favorite horse, dappled gray Sassy, and minutes later she clattered down the dim tunnel to the Coast Gate. Bars of sunlight filtered down through the murder-holes lining the roof and the clash of horseshoes on stone echoed thunderous. Today forty guardsmen and their lieutenant rode with her, alert and more heavily armed than usual, and a Healer and two court mages besides.

It was because of the assassination attempt, she knew, and a tiny part of her shivered. But most of her rebelliously shoved the thought aside. *I will not live in fear.*

The tide had turned and the wet sand stretched broad and sun-washed before her. Dunes hid the city beyond, no one would build this close to the chancy sea unless they made their living from it. The first mile of the beach was reserved for use of the castle folk and walled off from the city. Sassy tossed her head eagerly and whinnied.

"Go, girl! Go!"

Sassy launched herself like a bolt from an arbalest. In moments the salt wind was roaring in Callia's ears. The lieutenant shouted but Callia ignored him and crouched low in the saddle. Sassy was lighter than the soldiers' heavy warhorses and gained rapidly. Only when they approached the first village just over a mile down the strand did Callia slow the horse to a canter and let the guards catch up. One of the mages, lighter in the saddle than the armored soldiers, had managed to stay close behind her, but everyone else straggled.

"Your Highness!" the lieutenant spluttered, not quite angry enough to swear at her but clearly thinking about it.

"I needed a run, and so did my horse," she not-quite-answered him while slowing to a decorous trot. He took several deep breaths as if considering a real outburst, then the mage wordlessly shook his head at him and the officer subsided. Good, she'd judged them correctly. While she wanted to do more, this was as much as she could get away with this morning. She stopped watching her escort and cast an appreciative eye over her surroundings.

A few blue and white painted fishing boats were drawn above the high tide line and more bobbed offshore. Nets flew black against the suns' light, raised froth as they hit and came back up squirming with silver. Fishwives bowed their heads to her, hands busy with their endless mending and gutting, children playing at their feet. Callia nodded acknowledgement to the women, for how could she have dignity if she didn't give them theirs as well?

The guards stared about edgily, nervous beyond the normal alertness.

Afraid of Khaitanial assassins, she knew, and couldn't help casting a more wary eye over the dunes. But her mages were at work, protection spells floating overhead so thickly that a bird couldn't have gotten through. The sense of restless irritation still afflicted her so she stubbornly rode on. Finally at the fourth village, just before Uncle Yare's fishing retreat, she did consent to turn back, riding at the edge of the surf this time. But no crossbow bolts flew from the waving dune grass, no mad swordsmen leaped from concealed hollows in the sand or rose out of the sea itself. Only the cool splash of water kicked up by Sassy as she danced with the rhythmic waves.

This is silly, she decided. *Nobody knew I'd ride here today, I didn't even decide to do it until a couple hours ago. An assassin would be crazy to wait here day after day and risk discovery by the fishermen just on the chance that I'd go for a ride!*

But both she and the guards relaxed slightly once she was behind the wall again.

Too soon Callia was back at the foot of the ramp that led to the Coast Gate. The gaily striped changing pavilion had been pitched and her maids awaited. Most of the guards dismounted and took up positions between gate and pavilion in a wide arc. They faced east with their rigid backs turned to her and her maids to grant a sort of privacy. Two soldiers climbed into a boat with one of the mages and four oarsmen took them out to patrol parallel to the shore. Two other soldiers stripped to loincloths and waded into the water, ready to guard her against any hostile sea life that evaded the patrol. Both of them had knives and short wicked tridents thrust into their waist straps.

Junia and Sharme helped her change into a swimming costume. It was the bare minimum that court manners would allow, and twice as much fabric as Callia would have preferred, but she was resigned to it. Then she ran out on the beach to glory in the rough wet sand under her bare feet before she splashed into the warm sea. The two swimming guards formed a live screen against sharks and any other creature that might lurk in the waves.

When the water reached her waist she dived into a wave and under the next, then came up with a happy laugh. The river beyond the Rock fed a long sandbar four hundred feet off the shore. Her two guardsmen waded knee-deep onto it and carefully did-not-quite-look at her in between their scans of the open water. The longboat patrolled but the nearest fishing boat was miles away and no threatening fins split the little waves. For a while she swam back and forth in the warm sheltered water behind the bar, but it was too tepid to suit her restlessness.

She waded up onto the bar. The waves were not more than a couple hands high and on the far side the sand shelved rapidly down into deeper water. Both guards moved closer while they still faced away from her. They were only a little older than her, chosen for their swimming prowess and as muscled as any wrestler. And nervous as cats over the risk she took with herself, out here in the chancy waves. They wouldn't speak unless in dire fear for her, but she could feel their watchful tension even so.

She dived off the bar into the deeper water and the two promptly bracketed her thirty feet to either side, powering through the water with strong strokes.

She thought that they looked like trolls compared to the leonine grace of Sir Kirin. He had said his prince was only a little taller than himself but had broader shoulders and was more handsome. She thought that last was probably flattery. He had said it just the way Mikkal used to speak when he knew his sisters could hear and he wanted to tease them. She suspected such speech must be a habit for Sir Kirin, since Prince Terrell certainly wasn't here to be teased.

But did that mean Sir Kirin told her the truth, or did he tell her only what his lord wanted her to hear? Yet he had not said one word that sounded practiced or forced. Instead he had almost been bantering.

I think they must be very close, she reflected. *Like brothers, even.*

She surfaced and blew out stale air, inhaled several times to get clean air well into her lungs, then exhaled most of it and dived. There were rocks in the dim depths, crusted with barnacles and thick with sea life. Her guards drew in closer. A brilliant and poisonous sea slug rippled through the depth from one rock to another. Branched corals reared like the horns of monstrous beasts and delicate sea fans waved in the currents. Tiny damselfish and rippled green eels darted among them. A dog shark as long as her forearm scattered a school of yellow parrotfish. The dog shark suddenly discovered that much larger creatures were near and fled with a too-slow parrotfish in its jaws. Sea stars crawled slowly over coral and clams alike, and spiky urchins clustered in groups of many small ones around one large one.

Like sycophants at a court, she thought, and suddenly the depth was less wondrous.

She returned to the surface and gasped fresh air, her attendants did likewise. With all but her head and hands hidden below the water they dared look at her more directly as they transparently wondered how much longer she would practice such dangerous stunts today.

Even here there's no escape, she thought sadly, and began to swim back toward the beach. In the warm shallows behind the bar she rolled over on her back and sculled slowly, thinking.

I will have forty to fifty days on the trip to Silbar. I will ask Sir Kirin many questions. I think he is not as practiced at guarding his tongue as he believes himself to be. I will know more about his prince by the time I get there. Yet does it really matter? Dalbai must have this alliance. I have no choice. Even if Prince Terrell should prove to be a monster I must marry him. But I don't think he is a monster, I don't think Sir Kirin could hide that — or would. He sounds like a good man. I dare to think there is a chance for happiness with my betrothed.

I wonder if Sir Kirin has a wife? Perhaps she could become my ally. I would not feel so alone in a strange court if I had some allies.

The waves told her she was near shore. She stood up in water barely waist deep and splashed through the wavelets to where Junia waited with a dressing gown. The guardsmen splashed out of the waves behind her and immediately headed for their comrades' line. Callia noticed the last one give a lingering glance at Junia, who returned it with interest. The man strutted the rest of the way to his clothes while Junia paused outside the pavilion to watch.

Inside, Sharme helped Callia out of her wet swim costume and washed salt off her skin with a basin of fresh water, then gave her a fluffy towel. Clothes were laid out on a dressing table. Junia came in with a happy smile to help Callia dry her hair.

"Mother says I may choose four guards to accompany us to Silbar," she told Junia while Sharme giggled. "Would you like me to ask for him?"

"Yes!" Junia sighed happily. "His name is Aber Peng. His father is an officer in the Navy! He's so —"

"Handsome?" Callia suggested with a sly smile.

"Virile?" Sharme leered. "That one wants to put a baby in you, girl!"

Junia blushed and tossed her head. "In time, maybe I'll want him to!"

All three of them dissolved into giggles and it was several more minutes before Callia's raven hair was dried, braided, and readied for her day.

Love is all around me, Callia thought as she smiled privately. *Surely I can find some for myself.*

278

~ ~ ~

Junia, Sharme and two guards accompanied her into the Palace again. She went to the small salon where the members of the royal family typically broke their morning fast. It was unoccupied at the moment but the sideboard was lavishly filled. An elderly woman servant stood by to tend it. Baskets of whole oranges, figs, and pomegranates, a platter of cooked bacon with heat spells to keep it hot, a tureen of coconut milk pudding under a cold spell, plates of biscuits, a crock of dates in honey and another of shelled and salted nuts, bowls of cut fruits, shredded coconut, peeled mangoes and two kinds of exotic berries. She was instantly hungry.

Even as she looked over the morning's offering, Limis brought in Sir Kirin. He had the relaxed and self-satisfied glow of a man who had recently exerted himself to his limits and was happy to find them considerable. He had looked pensive before he noticed her, then his face blossomed in an appreciative smile. He had dressed well and moved with his usual leonine grace to bow over her hand. Along with the scent of a healthy clean male, she detected a faint perfume emanating from him. Probably some exotic scent applied to his clothes, she suspected. Perhaps they had been packed in it for travel.

He's quite attractive. Impulsively she said "Will you break your fast with me please, Sir Kirin?"

"Gladly, your Highness. Despite that amazing feast last night, I've worked up an appetite this morning. What would you like to eat?"

"Junia will assemble something." She gestured to the sideboard, where Junia and the old woman had their heads together over a pair of plates. "Let her surprise us. Come, let's sit here."

He gallantly held the chair for her and then took one himself. She studied his face across the little table. Despite his obvious robust health and energy there was still a faintly sad air about him this morning. The twin white lines in his sideburns stood out sharply against his black hair and beard.

"Sir Kirin, may I ask you a personal question?"

His face became guarded, which probably meant he'd rather have his teeth pulled. How like a man! "Of course, your Highness."

"Do you have a wife?"

Now he looked startled and one hand made an abortive reach for his chest as if it sought an object hung about his neck. but she saw none there. "I did once, your Highness. Seven years ago. She was killed by the Usurper's men." Both hands brushed the white lines in his sideburns as if that explained much more. At her confused look he added, "When a Silbari man loses his wife, it's our tradition for him to cut himself on both sides of his head at the funeral. The scars often grow out with white hair afterwards."

Callia blinked. Dona Catalona hadn't mentioned this little tidbit. "I apologize if I have offended you, Sir Kirin."

"No offense given, Highness." He smiled again that slightly sad smile.

Callia realized she tread on the thin edge of propriety, but couldn't resist the question. "Why have you never remarried?" He was handsome, energetic, held a high office, and seemed an attractive prize. Were Silbar's women all blind?

He shrugged. "At first I missed my Maia too much. I was two years mourning her. Then the life of a travelling Hand of my ki– prince, left me little opportunity."

Callia doubted that. She'd seen the way court women often threw themselves at high-ranked men.

It must have shown on her face, for he continued, "I don't mean *that* kind of opportunity. That hasn't been lacking! But I had had a *marriage*, a true love in my life as well as our bed. I wanted that again. But I have no lineage I can offer a ranked woman, and Klinto was Silbar's great enemy for a thousand years before the Gwythlo Empire came and swallowed us both up. Many Silbari families of any rank have trouble seeing beyond my Gwythlo skin and Klinto ears."

He stopped as Junia set two plates before them. "Thank you," he said to Junia, then to Callia, "My, this is a beautiful meal."

It was quite true. Each plate had a piece of broiled fish surrounded by sliced figs mixed with wedges of papaya, pomegranate and orange, a fan of crispy bacon and little fried rice balls, and a small dish of rice pudding mixed with chopped nuts and honeyed dates. But Callia knew blatant prevarication when she heard it. Her stomach signaled its own hunger and she signed her meal with a Dalbai breaking-fast prayer and began to eat, letting him do the same. He watched her for a moment, then made his grace in the Silbari way. His table manners were perfect; if he'd really been raised in a gutter, he'd learned better since then. Junia had loaded his plate with half again as much as hers since vigorous men tended to require a lot of feeding.

As usual, Junia gathered a plate for herself and took a table nearby where she could keep an eye on her mistress while she broke her own fast. Limis made sure his charge didn't need anything, then joined her. Sir Kirin noticed. Callia wondered what the traditions were in Silbar regarding servants. Presently she paused, her meal mostly demolished, and asked him, carefully waiting until he had swallowed.

"Sir Kirin. How do Silbari lords and ladies behave toward their servants? What are the customs?"

He blinked in obvious surprise. "I'm not sure what to say, Princess. I can tell you how Terrell treats his own servants, and I've seen the households of a few of the great nobles. Will that do?"

"Tell me about your own too."

"Oh, I don't have any servants."

Callia stared at him in disbelief. "Then who cares for your house? Washes your clothes, cleans the linens, sweeps the floor, that sort of thing?"

He grimaced as if he was embarrassed. "I guess I'm not quite being honest with myself. When I stay in my assigned room as a knight, at the Old Order Chapter House, it's cared for by the Order's own servants, who also clean what little garb and equipment I store there. When I'm at home with the troupe, the wives and daughters do the washing and feeding, and all of us do the cleaning twice a tenday."

"Troupe?" Callia grasped for sense in his words. "Wives and daughters? I thought you said you weren't married."

"They're not my wives and daughters!" He chuckled. "My adopted family, the DiUmbra acrobatic troupe. My brothers, Sevan and Attir, are both married and have children, as well as my father-in-law Sevan the Elder and mother-in-law Carmina. And aunts and uncles and cousins, there are more than forty all together. The family fills the whole top floor of an Inn in Aretzo." He glanced away and added "My wife Maia was sister to Sevan and Attir. Their uncle Pater DiUmbra adopted me and brought me to live there as a child. It's the only home I've ever known."

Callia remembered Dona Catalona mentioning that he had been raised by acrobats. "It sounds like a big family, and a busy one," she ventured. "Is living in an Inn very much like living in a palace?"

"Yes, if you mean 'living like a servant in a palace.'" He smiled, visibly remembering. "On every Thirdday and Eighthday our Grandma DiUmbra lines us all up right after breakfast and sets us to cleaning. The men have to carry buckets of scrub water up all four flights of stairs from the courtyard fountain. The only running water in the Inn is in the ground floor kitchen and the latrines. The women scrub the floors and everything else, it seems like, and then the men have to mop up the water after them and dump it out the gutters. Then the women wash all the bedlinens and clothes in the courtyard's fountain trough. The men clean out the chamber pots with the overflow water before it runs down the sewer. Then everybody has to carry the wet cloth up in baskets and hang it out to dry in the Attic and from the balconies. If we take too long then lunch has to wait, so everybody works as fast as we can. Generally we're done by noon."

"You do that twice every tenday?" She thought uneasily about the many times she had seen the palace servants cleaning in the mornings, and couldn't fit him into the same image.

"Yes, and on the other days the men still have to carry water if it hasn't rained enough to fill our rain barrels, which happens about two seasons of the year." He flexed one arm. "I remember when I started, the stairs that seemed to go on forever, the weight of the yoke, the buckets swinging from the ends and spilling a little on every step. It took me days to learn how to balance them so they didn't spill. Now I carry them up without losing a drop."

Callia knew pages and squires were required to do menial service as part of their training for knighthood, since one couldn't know how to give orders unless one had first had to receive them. But – "You mean you *still* carry water?"

"Of course." He shrugged. "I'm still a DiUmbra. The family still needs water. The others have to make more trips when I'm not there."

"But you're a knight!"

"Well, it does strengthen my legs, which is good for sword work, too. A flat-footed swordsman is a dead swordsman." He grinned impishly at her.

For a moment Callia was tempted to suspect he was telling her an elaborate joke, but he didn't have that kind of smile. "So you have no experience with servants at all?"

"Not as their master. But Terrell has herds of 'em, he was born to a Lord's life." His thoughts seemed to turn inward once more. "You know, even though there must be two hundred or more in his Palace, I think he knows all of their names? He's always polite, too, even when the new pages make mistakes or somebody spills the tea. And he never allows them to be beaten. He says there's better ways to keep their minds on their tasks."

Callia decided that was good. A husband who was kind to his servants would probably be kind to his wife as well. But the notion of Sir Kirin with a yoke over his shoulders and water buckets hanging from it still boggled her. "Thank you, Sir Kirin. I apologize for being so inquisitive."

"Not at all. You are quite welcome to ask me questions, Highness. Answering them is part of my duty."

He returned to his meal and after a moment Callia did likewise. She thought, *He still works like the lowliest servant for these people he calls family even though he has a high rank? That's so very strange. I think it says something important about him. And that's not the only thing; even though he's had flings with noblewomen he's looking for a wife he can love. And be faithful to? I think so. He's not at all what I expected of a bastard. I think he might be a lot like Father was.*

For a moment the memory was pain, even after half a year. Then she set it aside.

I lost my father, Sir Kirin lost his wife. We both must go on. He knows what he wants. Do I?

The uncertainty wasn't welcome.

Junia cleared their emptied plates away and Limis brought rosewater-scented towels to clean their hands. Callia decided that the breakfast salon was too public for more talk.

At any moment Aunt Gadet or Mother or someone else might appear.

"Will you walk with me in the garden for a while, Sir Kirin?"

"Gladly." He stood and moved her chair as gallantly as before. He offered an arm and she took it, slipped her fingers through a gap in the woven ribbon-sleeve of his shirt to touch the smooth movement of muscle beneath. His appreciative glances throughout the meal had already told her that he was well aware of her as a woman under her sari.

Well, he is a man, Callia thought with amusement, then pushed aside the distracting thoughts that followed and firmly focused her mind. *If I can hold Prince Terrell's attentions as thoroughly, then hopefully I can make him forget his concubines.*

Sir Kirin didn't have to be told the way to the garden, which showed that he learned a new place quickly. Callia hoped she would do as well in Silbar. She didn't speak until they reached the arcade entrance, then directed him to the long axis of the garden. The fan leaves of the date palms kept the walk shaded at this hour and the day promised to be a hot one. Gardeners worked on beds along the outer edge, and sentries could be seen along the fortress wall, but there was nobody near the central promenade. Sharme and Junia walked with Limis two dozen paces behind, close enough to be easily summoned yet out of earshot, with the two soldiers pacing behind them. Sir Kirin matched his own pace to hers as they strolled down the shady promenade.

For a while they said naught of consequence, just admired the flower beds and enjoyed the varied scents lofted on the midmorning air. An orb-weaver spider had built a huge web in one of the palms. The spider sat in the center eating a moth while the strands around it glinted in the sun. A saucy little lark trilled a late aria from a fig tree while a hawk circled overhead. A bower-bird scolded them when they walked beneath her pendant nest of soft down. The central fountain splashed a cool mist from sprays that leaped a dozen feet in the air before they fell back to shatter the surface of the pool. Bone white ghost carp swam languidly through the shivered waters.

Sir Kirin paused to blink at one of the exotic flowerbeds. "I'd swear that's a pear tree, but it's growing figs on it."

Callia nodded. "Father had the gardeners explain that one to me. It is a pear tree, and a fig too, growing on the pear and in it. We have insects in the isles that feast on pear trees, we can't grow them here without magical protections – an endless expense – or else grafting on this special type of fig tree. The fig gives protection to the pear, something in its scent keeps the insects away, and so the pear lives and flourishes at the cost of also supporting the fig. Both give us fruit in their seasons, and both are stronger for the marriage."

Sir Kirin nodded his head thoughtfully. "That's an interesting arrangement, Princess. There's probably a lesson in there."

Callia smiled at his wry tone. "Yes, my tutors love to find parallels in this garden for anything they think I should learn. Our priestesses too. I suppose one could get tired of such moralizing, but they usually manage to be reasonably inventive about it."

He chuckled. "Terrell feels the same about his own tutors. And priestesses." He resumed walking without saying anything more.

I must know what he really is, Callia thought. *And if no one else is close enough to hear, then he may tell me the truth.* She signaled to Junia to fetch a drink. Sharme and Limis took the hint and fell several more paces behind, signaling the guards back. Neither man looked happy but they obeyed, while still keeping her well within their sight.

"Yesterday," she began, "You told me so much about your prince. I almost felt as if I had met him myself."

"I suppose indirectly you were meeting him, your Highness," Sir Kirin answered with an enigmatic little smile. "I have spent a lot of time in his company and know him better than most other men do."

"And you not only hold an important post for him, but he trusted you with this very intimate mission."

"More true than you know, Highness."

"This causes me to wonder," Callia continued doggedly. "Why does my husband to be place so much trust in a man reputed to carry a demon inside him?"

She felt his arm tense beneath her hand. They strolled on three more steps in silence.

Strange, she thought. *I have just challenged a leopard, yet I am not even slightly frightened of his response. Am I mad, to be so brave? But something about him tells me I am perfectly safe. I roll Ifni's dice like a Silbari!*

Suddenly he laughed, a full-throated laugh that ended in a rueful chuckle. "I should have known my reputation would have reached your ears. Do you think *I'm* a demon, Princess Callia?"

She considered him carefully. His eyes were very opaque and she could still feel the tension in his arm.

"No. But you are certainly different from any other man I've ever met, and Dalbai has sought allies for years. The list of diplomats and nobles who've passed through our palace is very long."

"Different in what way?"

"At least two ways. To start, even if you had not told me so and despite the fact that you are well trained and have made no errors of etiquette, I can tell you were not raised a noble. Your actions are too studied, as if you followed someone's directions rather than aristocratic habits trained into you as a child. Secondly, when you recited that glorious scene yesterday, you changed the color of your clothes to black. I thought that you must have some sort of Earth Talent to change the dyes in the cloth, but that wasn't what you did, was it?"

"No," he admitted while he looked down at his feet. "It's my own unique Talent. I simply wrapped shadows through the weave. It's as if I poured water on a cloth and let it soak in. Let me show you again." He gently disengaged her hand from his arm, then stroked his left hand up the right ribbon sleeve of his shirt. Again the colorful fabric turned to black. He paused at the shoulder, reversed the motion and stripped the black away again.

Callia struggled to *see* what he did, strained her own magesight to the fullest, but the darkness was simply there, and then not there. As if he somehow poured it out of his empty hand, and then took it back again.

"Where does the black color come from? Where did it go?"

"The answer to the first is, many places." He reached out to a laden date palm that leaned over the promenade, passed his hand through the shadow in the lee of the trunk – and came away with a handful of inky night.

She blinked. He had literally pulled a piece of the tree's shadow free, though more filled the hole instantly. Now he divided it between his two hands, rolled it into two balls, and began to juggle. Then he switched to juggling both with one hand, snatched a blossom from a hibiscus bush and added it to the shadow balls. The heavy blossom shed a few petals as it circled through the air, then he deftly caught it in one hand and the shadow-balls in the other. He presented the blossom to her with a flourish, but she kept her eyes on his other hand and saw the spheres of shadow melt into his palm.

"You." she hesitated. "How did you do that?"

He held the blossom cupped in one palm and gazed at her over the soft petals. "I command Shadows, your Highness," he said, and this time she heard the capital letter. "I've been able to do it since I was small. Most of the time it's little more than an amusing stage trick such as I just did for you. Indeed, when my Maia and I danced the tale of Malik and Mercia, I would wrap myself partly in Shadows and trail them through the air like black silk kerchiefs, while she danced with very real white silks. The audiences loved us." He smiled in memory.

"Most of the time?" she asked.

"Ah," he said, then looked over her shoulder toward the skuff of sandals on the pavement that heralded Junia's return. "I'll show you that in a few minutes."

By unspoken consent they moved to a bench set between two date palms, where the far-spread crown of an old fig tree added to the shade; the morning grew hot. Junia set a sandalwood tray inlaid with a geometry of mother-of-pearl and ebony between them. It held a pitcher of cooled tea and two glasses with cold spells. Callia admired the blue-glowing frost that covered the thin silver rims which powered the spells.

Sir Kirin accepted a filled glass from Junia. As his hand touched it, the spell died.

Callia stared. She hadn't been mistaken; the cold spell was clearly gone. And by the look on his face he knew that she had seen.

Junia handed her the other glass and Callia took it mechanically as the maid bowed herself away and retreated to where Sharme waited back along the path.

"Do you have magesight, your Highness?" Sir Kirin quietly asked. His eyes were very black, so much so that she had a hard time distinguishing the iris and the pupil.

"Yes, and more." She called Healing into her right hand and touched yellow-glowing fingers to her left shoulder, soothed a slight strain from the morning swim, then let the spell fade. She wore very little silver to use for Power and the Node under the Rock of Daleray was small and heavily committed by the defenses for Palace and Fortress. She knew better than to draw on it for trivial purposes. "I have all of the Life suite; Healing, Diagnosis, Empathy, and the rest, though none at a very high level." She didn't mention the obverse; the Talents that could put a man back together could also take him apart. "I thought once to train as a true Healer, but my Talents aren't great enough for more than ordinary things. What Talents are yours?"

He nodded, still meeting her gaze. "Magesight also . . . command over Shadows . . . and one that is truly unusual."

He glanced at his drink, drained it in a long quaff, then reached out with his other hand to touch her own still-untasted glass. Again the spell went out like a blown candle, but this time she saw what happened. The spell had stretched, flowed like water right off the glass and onto his finger, and then vanished within his flesh.

"Like water soaked into cloth," she repeated. "You absorb magic."

He nodded, twirled his emptied glass and wrapped it in Shadow like wrapping it in a napkin. She could dimly see the outline of the glass within, like a charcoal sketch of a glass turned end over end in a slow circle. Then he absorbed the Shadow once more and set the glass back on the tray with a wry remark. "I shouldn't take risks with such a beautiful goblet. I'd be ashamed to drop it."

"Could you mend it?"

"No. I have no Earth talent at all. Nor Water, Fire, or even Air." He shrugged. "But magic cannot harm me, or even find me, unless I wish it to."

She hesitated, took a drink of her own tea while she tried to frame the question politely, but he anticipated her. He held out his left hand to her.

"Feel free to try, your Highness. Don't worry. You can't hurt me."

Callia knew she was a limited Healer but her magesight had always been quite good. Her Diagnostic talent was even better. She could look under anybody's skin with ease, see the interplay of bone, muscle and organs, and had learned to recognize healthy flesh from diseased or injured. She took his hand in hers. It was warm, dense with the solidity of trained muscles and calloused all across his palm and fingers, the hand of an active young man. But when she looked beneath the surface –

He was completely opaque. She could see the bare surface of his skin readily enough, but could not see so much as the thickness of a fingernail beneath it. Even the mages that served the Dalbai court were more transparent, and most of them had at least some ability to blunt magesight or diagnosis. But not to block it.

"How can you do that?" she blurted. "Block my Talent so completely? No man, not even a Great Mage, should be able to do that!"

He looked briefly sad. "I haven't yet done anything, Highness. This is the way I'm made. It takes me a serious effort to be otherwise." He stared at his hand for a moment. She felt her talent slowly begin to penetrate his skin and that special awareness within her followed the corded muscles and bones and sparkling nerves inside. Then his opacity snapped back in place and she once more felt naught but a healthy young man's calloused skin against her own.

"The cold spells," she said slowly, releasing his hand. "You absorbed them somehow? Are they still within you?"

"No; they're gone, or at least broken. I guess you could say that I ate them, your Highness. Ate the power in them, at least." He made an open-hands gesture. "I can do that with any magic that comes into contact with me, I don't even have to think about it. It just happens unless I'm careful to *let* the spell affect me. It makes me just about invulnerable to mages, which is why Prince Terrell made me his Left Hand."

He looked directly into her eyes as he spoke the words. She wondered if this was some sort of challenge, then realized that other emotions roiled there. Fear? Hope? Not for the first time she wished her Empathy talent was stronger.

"I noticed that you did not quite answer my question," she said as she watched his eyes. "Do you carry a demon inside you, as the Silbari Priestesses think?"

For a moment he didn't answer, only stared back at her as complex emotions flitted across his face. "I call it that sometimes myself. But demons can be banished, and my Shadow can't. It's been tried."

He frowned, visibly remembering. "Even two priestesses working together couldn't remove it. It hurt a lot even to try."

His attention returned to her face. "So my answer is, I don't know what I carry. There are days when I hate the monster. It's always hungry for power, you see, so I have to keep it under control whenever I'm near a strong source, or it will try to reach out and eat until the source is destroyed. Small ones too, like those cold spells, though I deliberately let it do that so that you could see. But it also protects me. A mage once threw a lightning bolt at my back. I was caught flat-footed and should have been fried, but my shirt wasn't even singed. My Shadow ate the bolt before it touched me. I think a demon would have let me be killed. My Shadow didn't."

Callia couldn't help the question. "What did that mage do then?"

"He was very surprised, very briefly, then very dead." He smiled grimly. "Since then all the Mage Guilds of Silbar have been very well behaved around me, which makes Terrell's work easier."

"Yes, I'd think so." No wonder his prince valued him so highly. Callia had heard that Silbar had tens of thousands of mages, Aretzo alone was said to be home to twenty thousand. She doubted there were as many as ten thousand in the entire Archipelago and less than a third of those dwelt in Dalbai. Dalbai's dozen court mages were far outnumbered by her mother's swordsmen and archers. While they were no strangers to intrigue, there had never been any hint that one or even all were foolish enough to think they could overthrow the Crown.

"Ah," she perceived suddenly. "There's another reason why your prince sent you here. As a reminder to our mages of the power he could wield over them, if he wanted to."

Sir Kirin nodded. "He supports your alliance with more than just his fleet, your Highness. On the other hand, there's only one of me, and I have to be near a mage to affect him. So I'm another weapon in Terrell's hands, but one that has to be used sparingly."

"I see." Callia sorted through the implications for a moment while she drank. *He just disclosed something very important to me. Unless this is something everybody in Aretzo already knows? Even if it is, I'm not sure anyone here knew it, even Mother. He's making a point about trust. No, I suspect it's his prince making the point by ordering Sir Kirin to reveal this. I will be included in at least some of Prince Terrell's most important confidences. That's good.*

She finished her tea, set the glass down gently. "Shall we walk some more, Sir Kirin? Our weather mage says this noon will be unusually hot so everyone will rest during the worst hours; we call that *revesh*. Normally at this season it rains in the later afternoon, so Mother has ordered an indoor entertainment for after *revesh*."

"Delighted, Highness," he answered and offered his arm again.

Callia took it and once more slipped her fingers through the ribbon sleeve to touch his skin. As they resumed their stroll she thought, *I touch a man who likely carries a demon inside him. Yet he feels like an ordinary human, and a very attractive one too. I was right about their closeness; he even uses his prince's personal name casually, though he has been entirely polite and correct to me. How very odd. I go to a truly strange place with some very strange people.*

"You mentioned two things about me that were different from most men you've ever met, Highness," he reminded her as they walked. "Was there another?"

Before Callia could answer, a palace functionary ran up and bowed.

"Your Highness, please pardon my interruption, but there is an urgent message for the Ambassador," he gasped. "He is wanted at the shipyards immediately. Something has happened to the *Queen of the Seas*!"

~ ~ ~

Chapter 29: Daleray - Kirin

Ninety-second day of Summer

Callia came with me. She insisted.

"The *Queen of the Seas* is my ship, Sir Kirin; my dowry. No one has a greater interest in her than I do," she told me in a way that let me know argument would be useless. "And some of my personal guardsmen have skills that might be helpful."

I bowed to her wishes. "Very well, Princess. But let's hurry."

She called to Junia, "Fetch Aber Peng and Dal Morengal to accompany us. Sharme, tell my mother where Sir Kirin and I have gone, and why."

Callia's decision actually saved me time, since she could order up a large carriage and a couple platoons of soldiers immediately. In minutes we rattled through cobblestoned streets down to the royal shipyard with a herald in front to shout, 'Make way! In the Queen's name, make way!" and a thicket of steel around us. Two master mages rode along. From the density of the protection spells they wrapped around the carriage I suspected neither was as powerful as the White, but they seemed more than capable.

The guards at the shipyard gate waved us through. The *Queen of the Seas* loomed huge at her berth, tended by painting barges and a mob of riggers to install her last miles of cordage. Covered sheds overflowed with all the necessities that would soon be loaded aboard her.

I jumped out of the carriage first and helped Callia down, then the two of us and her maid and personal guardsmen trooped up the gangplank. The ship looked no different than she had yesterday save for the additional rigging and paint, but four men on her main deck showed that something wasn't right. They were all mages and their spell auras boiled about them angrily. The White and Arlein were among them.

D'Auson stood nearby. He saw me approach and hurried toward me as shouts broke out behind him.

"Foreign fool!" A Dalbai man in the local version of mage robes snarled at Arlein in the Dalbai tongue. "You know nothing of our ship construction arts!"

The other Dalbai man wore an elaborate surcoat and feathered hat. He did outrage in great style with gestures and bitter sarcasm. "You expect me to drop all of my numerous duties and hold your limp hands because our ship is greater than you ignorant barbarians can understand? Impossible!"

Arlein answered hotly in his halfassed version of the Dalbai tongue. "I know when found I have a thing not rightness!"

"Arlein's skill at detection is second to none in Silbar's whole fleet," White declared, his own grasp of the language much better. He crossed his arms as he glared eye to eye at Feathered Hat, then added in Silbari, "So stuff your arrogant twaddle up your own ass and listen to us!"

D'Auson told me in Silbari, frustration in his face and voice, "The ship's architect and the shipyard's chief mage both think we're fault-finding out of envy, because we don't understand their work. Arlein says he detects a wrong spell in her keel, but the architect won't listen."

Feathered Hat was about to reply to White, probably with some choice profanity, when he noticed Callia stepping on board. He visibly bit back whatever he'd been about to shout even though it made veins bulge in his skinny neck. Instead he turned to her and bowed with an exasperated,

"Princess! Please excuse these bad-mannered barbarians. How may I help you today?"

"Baron Abn Cleng," she said in their own language while she gave him her hand to kiss. "I've come to visit my ship. I thank you for all your hard work on her design. I'm told it was your most excellent insights that led to her many advancements. I understand that our allies have expressed a concern about her?"

Cleng's veins throbbed again and his face went an interesting shade of mahogany. He looked torn between gratification at her compliment and fury at the need to defend his work. "There is no flaw in her wards! None! Highness, I oversaw every cast myself, they knit together perfectly!"

"Whoa!" I raised a hand and caught their attention before shouts could start again. In Silbari first, I asked, "Mage Arlein, are you sure you've found a flaw, or have you found something else?"

"I – I don't know, my Lord Ambassador," the mage stuttered. He was a good two decades older than me but skinny and short, and plainly overmatched in any argument with the much larger Cleng. "Whatever it is, it's below the bottom deck planks and the bilges in the keel, just starboard of dead center."

"Are you sure it's *in* the keel, or might it be some loose thing in the bilges?"

Arlein hesitated. "I – I – I'd better check again."

I smiled at them all with just a hint of my Shadow in my eyes. Cleng blinked in surprise and White squinted back angrily.

"Gentlemen, I propose we all go see for ourselves." I turned to Callia. "If your Highness wishes it so?"

"I do. Please show us the way, Baron Cleng." There was a ring in her voice and willpower in her gaze. That was a Royal Command if I ever heard one.

Cleng knew when to shut up. He bowed and obeyed. We all trooped down into the ship's hold through decks fragrant with new wood and paint, where carpenters still hammered at last-minute tasks. The loading ramps had been set up on one of the deck hatches that led down through deck after deck, like a long winding stair with cleats instead of steps. I gave my arm to Callia as we walked down side by side and she stared around with great interest. First we passed through the artillery deck with its thirty-two arbalests lined up in a double row. Then the orlop deck below where partitions obscured most of the space and the medical station was being installed with much noise. The whole ship smelled new and clean, cleaner than she ever would again once sailors began to live in her.

We descended to the very bottom deck just above the bilges, which didn't stink and might not even have any water in them yet. The long cargo hold would be crammed full of supplies for the actual voyage. Right now it held only the two huge built-in wooden tanks for the ship's fresh water supply. The long space was lit only by beams of light that speared down from the fighting deck through the open hatches above.

White flicked his fingers and cast two mage lights into silver pins he'd taken from his collar, held them up so we could all see better. The ship's ward spells wrapped under and around us through the wood, a net both dense and fragile. I controlled my Shadow tightly.

Arlein stopped at a specific point only a few feet from where the mainmast was stepped into a socket above the keel. He knelt on the rough planks, touched his hands to the floor, and said, "It's here." A glowing maze of magical lines appeared between his hands, a view under the floor. "It's very small, I only noticed it by chance."

White stuck his lamp-pins into a beam overhead and extended his own spells in concert with Arlein's. He provided support rather than took over, which surprised me. Now he said, "Which thread do we seek, Arlein?"

"This." The skinny mage brightened a single line in the matrix. "Look, it's not anchored to the rest. That can't be right!"

I called my Shadow into my eyes and stared down at the complex mass of ward spells under our feet. They flared blue-green and red and purple. The offending thread was gray, and part of it was *below* the matrix embedded in the ship's keel. "Are you sure that's not under the hull instead?" I asked.

The four mages blinked at each other, bent closer to study the line.

"Possibly," Arlein answered. "At least, part of it could be, though this end is definitely sunk into the timber right next to the keel. But that could mean—"

"Sabotage." Baron Cleng and D'Auson spoke the word simultaneously.

"Gentlemen, can you determine what it is from here?" D'Auson asked sharply.

White scowled, shook his head. "Probably not, it's much too close to the wards. They'll interfere with any analytical spell." He darted a look of challenge at the Dalbai construction mage, who reluctantly nodded in agreement.

Cleng looked even angrier than he had been as he stared at Arlein's scry. Through clenched teeth he managed to say, "I'll have to fetch a crew for underwater work. It'll take a day to assemble them, another two or three to repel enough water for us to get under the ship and examine her."

I could see him and D'Auson mentally review schedules and wince at the cost. Water magery tended to eat silver like nothing else.

"No need for all that," I told him pleasantly. "I can swim under the ship and look. If there's any bit of silver on her keel that doesn't belong there, I'll find it."

Cleng looked pained. "My Lord Ambassador, that is far easier said than done. While the *Queen's* hull is new and clean, it is also very large. You won't have any point of reference to find an object that is probably little more than a finger length in size, and may well be disguised."

"I'll have plenty of references, if two of you will simply stand here to bracket it." I smiled and looked at the mages individually with my Shadow in my eyes. "I am confident that mages of Master rank can manage such a small task."

White shot me a venomous look, then his face turned blank and he blandly said, "Of course, my Lord Ambassador. Arlein can represent Silbari interests."

Cleng looked at me like a bug he wanted to step on, then jabbed a finger at his construction mage, who rolled his eyes and nodded.

Princess Callia nodded regally. "We shall try this. Thank you for your cooperation, gentlemen."

D'Auson followed me, Callia, and her maid and guards back to the deck. Cleng and White trooped after. Before the Captain could speak Callia said, "What do you need for this, Sir Kirin?"

I looked over the ship's outer side and pointed at the nearest painters' barge. "That. It's close enough to the main mast that I won't have to swim far. Tell the workmen to do something else for an hour."

"Do you want a magelight?" D'Auson asked. "It'll be very dark under the hull."

"Oh, I'll be able to see all I need," I assured him and grinned as I started to untie my fancy shirtsleeves. "A magelight would just distract me."

White made a tiny sound in his throat and ostentatiously turned his attention to an examination of the ship's wards. They were fully engaged to form a net of blue fire over the wooden surfaces, and again I had to forbid my Shadow to eat them. Cleng extended his own spells and the two mages fell back into an uneasy parallel examination that pretended to ignore me.

"Aber, Dal, you'll go with him," Callia ordered and began to help me with the laces. "They're both excellent swimmers and divers, Sir Kirin."

"Princess, that will just endanger them for no reason," I started to protest while the two guards set aside their weapons and stripped off their mailed tunics.

She cut me off. "I don't want you to try this alone. Now hold still while I get these ties, you don't want to ruin this beautiful shirt in the river." She began to unlace my collar while her maid captured my left foot and removed the sandal. Quietly Callia added, "Please take them. I still have many questions to ask you about my betrothed, so I need you to come back alive."

I shivered slightly as her fingers brushed my throat. Her nearness, her scent, her touch reawakened that intense longing from yesterday. "Yes, your Highness," was all I could say.

When I was stripped to my hose I went over the ship's side and climbed down a rope ladder to the barge. The *Queen* floated high out of the water since she carried only her own weight, which would reduce how far we had to swim. Aber and Dal had already stripped to loincloths and armed themselves with knives. I went over some hand signals with them for use under water.

Then I said, "One more thing."

They stood side by side, strong brown men barely a fingerwidth taller than me, and watched me with obedient expressions.

"You will see me do a thing that may frighten you. It will not harm you. I won't let it. I'll show you now so that you know." I raised my left hand and called my Shadow into it, then filled my eyes with night.

Aber's eyes got wider and he stiffened up for a moment, then with a quick glance up at the deck where Callia, her maid, and D'Auson watched us, he forced his body to relax. Dal had a harder time with it; he flinched back half a step and stared at me in undisguised horror. Then he glanced at Aber and seemed to draw some strength from his comrade. Dal stepped back to Aber's side and schooled his face. Callia leaned over the railing, watching us silently.

"Good men," I told them as I pulled the Shadow back away from my eyes. "Let's go."

We stepped off the barge and swam along the side of the ship to the point where the shadows of her mainmast fell across the water. I breathed deeply several times, then half-emptied my lungs and dived into the brackish flow. Aber and Dal flanked me.

Daylight was different under water, softer and fading, but with both suns nearly overhead it was enough. The river was forty feet deep here and the *Queen* drew less than a third of that when empty. We swam down and under the turn of her bilges, below the ship and into dimness. Her hull was still clean, no barnacles or shipworms gnawed at her pristine timbers, no weeds attached to drag at her forward motion. Cleng claimed that her wards should prevent that for years to come. I could see the spells laced through her wood like juice in an orange. I let my Shadow take my eyes fully, and the ship above me turned to smoked glass lit by lines of fire.

Her deep keel was a wall of light ahead of me. It knifed down from the bottom of the hull for nearly five feet and glowed bright blue with the power of her wards. That glow spread sideways along the ribs like hundreds of fingers to clasp the ship in a benevolent grip. Only a few feet away and almost above me, the mages standing on either side of that mysterious gray smudge were visible as two brighter glows. I swam towards them. Between them there was a small shiny bit of metal.

A silver spike. Half its length had been shoved up into the wooden hull. The spell on it was subtle, almost lost in the greater glow around it. I didn't know what it was, but it shouldn't be here. I wrapped my hands around it, planted my bare feet against the Queen's hull, and started to pull.

And then, as I hung upside-down under the ship, I saw a long lean shape swim towards us from barely twenty feet away. I'd seen sharks before, but never one that glowed red to my Shadow eyes. It swam straight for Aber with jaws agape. He had stayed near me but some movement in the water warned him. Even as I looked up he turned and saw it. Instead of trying to dodge, he pulled the puny knife at his waist and faced those rows of teeth to block its access to me.

I remembered the sea-unicorn in the hall of curiosities. Instantly I grew myself a six-foot horn of Shadow and launched myself past Aber as he jerked in surprise. My Shadow-horn met the shark barely a yard from Aber's chest and the red spell died. The shark arched as if I had harpooned it, reduced to merely a natural creature now and confused to find itself so near two humans. The wash of its tail buffeted me, then the flank and tail itself struck Aber as the shark swerved away. The rough sharkskin, more coarse than a stone, stripped his own skin from his shoulder.

Aber nearly lost his control and breathed water from the shock of the blow. Dal had drawn his own knife and kicked towards us but arrived too late to matter. The shark swam away as fast as it had come. I signaled Dal to help me help Aber.

We three burst through the surface together and sucked air. Aber could swim but skin hung from his shoulder in shreds and his blood stained the river.

I coughed water, gasped deeply and told Dal, "Get him onto the barge!"

He pointed down, made the signal for danger and shouted the Dalbai word for shark.

"I can handle one shark, just get him out of this water before his blood draws another! That's an order!"

D'Auson and Callia shouted something above but I ignored them and dived again.

I found the spike easily enough, and this time covered myself with Shadow while I pulled. My Shadow desperately wanted to eat the wards so close to my feet and I fought to hold it even as my back and legs strained against the spike. For a long moment I thought it wouldn't give and I'd have to let my Shadow eat the gray spells and leave the metal behind. Then the spike jerked free.

Its magic stabbed at me.

I nearly lost control over my Shadow as it ate whatever the spike threw at me. I tumbled head over heels under the hull of the Queen for a moment and fought disorientation, my Shadow, and my lungs' urgent demand for air. But I lost neither my control nor the still-glowing spike, found my way out again and back to the surface. Dal waited on the edge of the barge. He reached out and heaved me up onto the deck, checked me for shark bites and muttered Dalbai prayers of gratitude to find me whole.

"Thanks," I said in Dalbai between gasps. "That was . . . well done."

We helped Aber up the rope ladder to the deck, where the maid uttered a little cry at the blood running down his ribs. Callia promptly went to work on Healing his wound while her maid tried to stanch the flow. From the way the maid stared at the guardsman's stoic face I thought he meant more to her than just a guard.

"What did this, Aber?" Callia asked. Her hands glowed yellow as she knit bits of his skin back together. "It doesn't look like a bite."

"Shark," he laconically replied in a deep voice, added "Tail hit me, shark's got skin like little teeth."

"It was also sorcelled," I explained grimly. "Almost certainly set as a guard by whoever planted this in the *Queen of the Seas'* keel, to keep us from taking it out again."

I held up the spike, spell intact, and laid it atop a barrel at the end of a row set to be loaded down below. Cleng and White both tried to reach for it but I told them "Don't touch it. I think we need our other two mages up here now. This little silver bastard is nasty."

It took time for the four mages to examine the spike and the spell, squabble over three interpretations of it, and reach a consensus. Aber's blood had clotted, his wound was bandaged, and my silk hose had dried enough for me to dress again. I'd spent the time to study the many windows in the row of four-and-five-story buildings that faced the shipyard. There must be two hundred rooms up there and at least half of them had some magic trinket or Talented resident to set a blue glow behind their walls. If Zurtos was up there looking back at me – I couldn't be sure. D'Auson helped me with the laces on my shirtsleeves while I questioned the mages.

"So spill, all of you. What is it?"

White and Cleng tried to talk at the same time and for a moment nothing could be understood. Then White visibly bit his lip, stopped his tongue and let the architect-nobleman speak. Baron Cleng started over with a sniff.

"It is a sabotage spell, as we suspected, my Lord Ambassador." His tone managed to be both haughty and apologetic at the same time. "It is designed to awaken at a planned time or in response to a specific signal, or possibly both or either. Then it would have chewed at our wards from beneath, where it would have been devilishly hard to stop while the ship was under sail."

"Impossible to stop," White interjected. "At least before it damaged the _Queen's_ wards beyond what we could repair at sea. Somebody planned that placement very carefully. Somebody with a thorough understanding of ward spells." His eyes rolled toward Cleng and then away.

Cleng darted him an aggrieved look and continued. "It appears to have had a locator spell attached. Your countryman has stopped that, so the caster doubtless knows now that we have discovered his little toy. It also had two defensive spells." His gaze at me sharpened. "One is unclear, but the other was triggered when you pulled it free. You should be most thoroughly dead now, with all the blood in your body solidified like a boiled egg." He stared at me like he wanted to prod me to see if I was still squishy. "I am curious as to why you are still alive."

I ignored that and demanded, "What else can we learn from it? Can you trace it back to its maker?"

"Not now that the locator spell has been stopped," Cleng managed to insinuate.

White growled. "Not even if it was still operating. I could smell a double backbite on it. That location spell was itself a clever trap. If any of us had sent a snoop spell out to trace that locator to its origin, what would have come back at us – well, the caster is extremely skillful and a very nasty piece of work. We still wouldn't know where he is, but one of us would need a priestess. Or a coffin. That's why I killed the spell rather than trying to trace it."

"There's nothing more to be learned from it?"

"The most important thing we already know." White glared at the shining metal. "This is another piece by the same bastard who attacked this mission before, who was likely behind the assassination attempt too. I recognize his touch, work like that leaves subtle marks in your aura that any master mage can find. He's strong, he's damnably clever, he's dangerous, and given how fresh this work is, he's somewhere here in this city."

Cleng glowered at the spike. "He tried to destroy my beautiful ship. For that he must be caught and hung!"

"You'll get no arguments from us, Baron," I told him, then addressed the mages collectively. "What should we do with his trap now?"

"Now it's just a dangerous chunk of metal." White's gaze shifted to D'Auson and he added, "Captain, I advise you dispose of it as soon as possible. There's no safe place for that spell inside the ship. I don't think it can be externally triggered any more, but I wouldn't care to bet our lives on that."

D'Auson looked at me. "Sir Hand?" he asked, pointedly invoking my other official function for Prince Terrell.

"Right." I picked up the spike and curled my fist around it. Cleng and his mage tensed and drew in their breaths sharply, but White and Arlein merely watched. I let my Shadow pass through my palm and it immediately ate the final spells. The power in it buzzed along my veins like a swarm of bees. Then I held the spike up for the mages' inspection. "It's harmless now." White and Arlein nodded, Cleng followed more slowly, and the little shipwright mage stared at me in awe. "Captain, we're at least a little richer in silver for our trouble."

"The shininess tells us one more thing," Callia commented. "It hadn't had time to use up the power in the silver, so it had to have been placed recently."

"You're right, Highness," I agreed. "Certainly since the *Queen* was launched and perhaps this very day." I tossed the spike to the Captain.

D'Auson caught it easily. "I'll put it in the keeping of the Purser."

"Princess?" I turned to her. "Since we're here, would you like to take a tour of your ship? I think Captain D'Auson might like to show her off to you while these four gentlemen go over the rest of her as closely as magic can."

D'Auson smiled. "If it please you, your Highness, I'd be honored."

Baron Cleng looked like he wanted to explode in outrage at this usurpation of his usual privilege. But his chief mage tugged at his sleeve and he suffered himself to be led below in silence. White looked savagely pleased as he and Arlein followed.

Callia looked me over. "I quite like that idea, but you should finish dressing first, Sir Kirin. Do hold still."

Her maid waited with my sandals. I bowed and let the two of them lace me up again. The two guards had dressed as well, though Aber looked uncomfortable under his stoic surface. His skin loss must hurt like fire.

D'Auson plainly enjoyed squiring us about the *Queen of the Seas*, showing off her armaments and her luxuries. The ship was an eyeful even though the busy carpenters and painters made some areas inaccessible. We finished shortly after the mages did. Baron Cleng and his shipyard mage had already left to set the Daleray Mage Guild to hunting Zurtos before we came back to the deck.

"No further sabotage detected, Captain," White reported to D'Auson. "With your permission, I shall set up preparations for screening all of her cargo to make sure something else isn't smuggled on board during loading."

"Make it so, Ship's Mage," the captain replied, and then looked at me and the princess. "We are scheduled to leave in five more days. It is likely that this won't be the last trouble we encounter before your wedding day, your Highness."

Callia was quiet for a moment, looking over the ship past the rooftops of Daleray to the white palace and black fortress towering on the Rock. Her hand tightened slightly on my arm and without thinking I put my other hand over it.

"That is a measure of how important my marriage is to our countries, Captain," she answered. "All the more reason that we must overcome any opposition to get to Silbar. I trust you and all others concerned with my safety to make it happen."

She looked at me as she spoke the last words. I raised her hand to my lips and kissed it in a silent promise.

~ ~ ~

Chapter 30: Daleray - Zurtos

Ninety-second day of Summer

Zurtos cursed with weary annoyance as the royal carriage drove away with his two targets inside. He could penetrate its guardian spells readily enough. Even though both mages were skilled and watchful, they were no match for him. But any magical attack would be worse than useless with the Shadow-mage inside. Useless because his infuriating and too-competent opponent would simply devour whatever Zurtos threw at the carriage. Worse because it would alert the dog to Zurtos's location here on the top floor of a sailor's flophouse that overlooked the dockside road. Jos had the carpet ready for escape but that would be chancy, his enemy's tame Shadow might catch them first. In Silbar Bay Zurtos had been shocked to see how far the demon-ridden son of a baboon could hurl his Shadow. Only luck had saved Zurtos then. He didn't intend to rely on it again.

A gaudy butterfly landed on his windowsill. He smashed it with a fist, then felt a little better as he shook its iridescent powder from his skin.

No, best to swallow this loss like the others. His attempts to penetrate the Palace had failed. None of Dalbai's mages were his equal but they outnumbered him enough that it didn't matter. There wasn't enough time left for a subtle assassination scheme and his best trap had just failed. He would have to try some new course of action.

His local ally had raised a most intriguing possibility that looked well worth exploration. It also reeked of desperation, but the negative consequences wouldn't fall on

Xiphree in general or Zurtos in particular, so that was of little matter.

What happened to Dalbai didn't matter at all.

"Jos," he rasped. "I go to meet our contact. Prepare your knife. It may be time to try close work again."

Jos smiled and bowed.

~ ~ ~

An hour later Zurtos, disguised as a well-dressed merchant's factor, entered the back door of a prosperous sword seller's shop in a much wealthier district of Daleray. The owner, long in the pay of Xiphree and cowed by blackmail over a past indiscretion, nervously showed him to a special seat in a tiny back room. The wall that separated it from the much larger and more sumptuous customer area had a few embedded spells that Zurtos customized for today's use.

When Count Yare came in for a private showing, Zurtos was ready for him. He had to wait while Yare tested three new blades, practiced cuts and thrusts upon lifelike dummies, then selected one and ordered special adjustments to the grip. While the count waited for the shop to complete his work, he lounged on a chair against the same wall and picked at a light lunch.

"Your Excellency," Zurtos purred into the spell that would carry his words to Yare's ears alone. "Madness ascends."

"And Calm fades," Yare answered instantly, his own words likewise captured by the spell and audible to Zurtos's ears alone.

"Yet opportunity is to be found," the Mage continued.

"In twilight," finished Yare. He snorted. "Pretentious drivel you spies like to use. Whoever you are, make it quick, I've little time."

"Sabotage has failed," Zurtos reported baldly. "May I hope that your negotiation with the Ambassador was more successful?"

"It was not." Yare bit the words out and took a long gulp from a waiting drink. "He was willing enough to fuck my servant, quite enjoyable to watch in fact. But then he went all distant on me. I pretended not to notice, but I'm not stupid. His damn loyalty to his prince is too strong."

"Such a pity," Zurtos sympathized, unsurprised.

Yare snarled silently. "Sephora 'asked' me to make a surprise inspection of our South Coast bases; I'm to leave on the morning tide. I'm going to try to lure him to my service once more tonight, but I doubt it will get me anywhere."

"A depressingly narrow window of opportunity," Zurtos commiserated. "You are wise to exhaust all of the easy avenues before attempting the more difficult and dangerous routes."

"'More difficult and dangerous routes?'" Yare snorted moodily. "What's left to try? I'll be out of the game entirely after dawn." He gulped down the rest of his drink. "The opportunity of my lifetime, gone like that." He snapped his fingers.

"Perhaps not completely," Zurtos suggested. "My lord, is it true that you have a fishing lodge along the north coast just outside the city?"

"Eh? Yes, just past Fourth Village. On a pier of its own."

"Perhaps if you were to entrust its key to your niece? Ask her to look after the servants there, as you suspect pilfering?"

"Ah." Yare looked thoughtful. "Say no more. I imagine you can't make any promises."

"Unfortunately true, my Lord, but many things are possible."

"My cabin steward is old and his hearing and eyes are fading."

"Useful to know, my Lord. Where will your inspection trip take you first?"

"Crescent Fort, then through the Mangrove Islands. I'll likely anchor for two nights in Ring Cove."

"I'll bring you word, my Lord. Perhaps it will be word of success; if not, you can make a more informed decision then."

Yare chuckled. "A 'more informed decision'? I like that. I will be interested to know your face, spy. I'll look for you there."

"At your service, my Lord."

Zurtos gracefully withdrew from the conversation, carefully terminating his listening spells behind him. He had prepared warning spells in case anyone used this meeting to ambush him, but nobody did. He made it several blocks away, turned aside into an alley that led to a laundry. There he switched into clothes that lowered his station a couple ranks, and then made his way several miles across Daleray.

"All clear, Master?" Jos asked quietly at their designated meeting place.

"He's not trying to magically trace me nor have me followed," Zurtos concluded. "Interesting. I'd guessed him for a less calculating sort."

He tapped his lower lip with one finger. "Let's see what's possible. Prepare to move, Jos; we're going fishing."

~ ~ ~

Chapter 31: Daleray Palace - Kirin; Callia

Ninety-second day of Summer

"What's this play called, your Highness?" I asked as we entered the vast throne room after the afternoon nap the Dalbais called *revesh*. I'd had time to change my clothes and bathe so I didn't smell like river water any more.

"I don't know," Callia answered. "Mother asked the best *yaley* company in Daleray to give us something from Silbar. I suppose it's a comedy or love story, or perhaps a history. Let me ask."

The rays of the afternoon suns sloped under drizzly clouds through high windows to light a low stage built against the east wall. A sketchy framework held banners and similar set pieces. There were no ladders or tightropes or other acrobatic tools, which meant this entertainment would be presented in the Dalbai style.

I escorted Callia to a seat in the front row at her mother's left hand. Queen Sephora bestowed a welcoming smile on me, which unaccountably made me blush. I hid it by bowing deeply. Callia's maid folded the tail of her sari aside for her and she sat. Another maid whispered in her ear and she brightened.

"Aha, I've just learned the title. 'Azerin and Zablok' by a Silbari writer named Valleon. Do you know it? Is it a romance?"

I almost choked. It was the most infamous play about the worst disaster in my country's last thousand years. I sat down harder than I'd meant to and the chair creaked.

"You do know it," she said. "What is it about? From the look on your face I suspect it is not a comedy or a romance."

"It's a history of the Twins War." I tried to figure out how to condense a two-hour production into a few pithy sentences and quickly gave up. "It happened three hundred years ago. It was a very bad time in Silbar's history."

"Why?"

Her simple directness left me no graceful way out.

"Because the king at the time was weak and indecisive." There was another one of Terrell's big words. I briefly wished he was in my head to help me explain, then considered the subject of the play and was intensely glad that he wasn't. "And then twin sons were born to the Royal House."

"I think I've heard about that part. Twins are usually regarded as bad luck in Silbar, are they not?"

"Yes, and this birth is a big part of the reason why. You see, they were so alike that the nurses confused the babies and lost track of which was firstborn. Their father had named them Azerin and Zablok, but nobody was sure which was really which. There were arguments about it all the time as they grew up."

"And factions at court backed one against the other?"

"You got it."

"It sounds tragic. But why did it shock you to hear the title? Does it have special meaning to you?"

Like a blind shot in the dark that finds the heart, her keen words stabbed me. I couldn't tell her the truth. The musicians saved me when they started the opening and I could say, "Watch and you'll see."

The DiUmbra Troupe had several of Valleon's plays that we did year after year. Though it was many years since we had done 'Azerin and Zablok', I still remembered every word. Sweet flutes at the first scene carried us through the long-awaited birth and the nursemaids' confusion and almost comical effort to cover up their error. Meanwhile I remembered the hard truths that Terrell had shown me while I watched that last performance, more than six long years ago. His story fit together too well for me to doubt a word of it.

He had told me that our Mother, Queen Shyrill, had done all she could to hide the truth of her double pregnancy from her husband the Emperor, and especially from his firstborn son Osrick, who fiercely resented his Silbari stepmother. The midwives could detect Terrell as he grew within her womb, but not me, and so she was able to conceal me even from my Father. When I was born she risked all in a gamble to win life for one of her newborn sons. Halfbreeds we might be, fusion of Gwythlo and Silbar, but Terrell and I were her hope. Her chaplain priestess and her loyal ladies-in-waiting helped Mother lay plans to smuggle away the mystery son that could not be detected by magic.

On stage in Dalbai, the King of Silbar had to make a decision as to which baby bore which name. He opened the door to tragedy wider still by dithering for three days. Lutes and tambourines played up his hesitation and the acid doubt that spread from it to eat away at his courtiers' trust.

My mother found that no secret can be kept when seven people know it. My half-brother Osrick learned that he had two rivals for his father's affections instead of one. The Crown Prince of Gwythlo hadn't dithered. Though he was only fourteen years old that day I was born, before sunset he'd suborned Mage Tagir to help him murder at least one of his newborn brothers – me.

Drums boomed on the Dalbai stage and the long struggle began while the birth of Azerin and Zablok's sister

Gayla and the death of their mother went almost unnoticed by either boy. The actors were excellent, the script and staging superb. Gitars added to the tension as spat turned to feud and feud to burning hatred.

I hid my wince. I knew little about my own blood sisters beyond their names, and my mother died while I still thought her the weakling Queen who had surrendered Silbar into the hands of an enemy. Terrell had shamed me down to my toes when he showed me his memories of her grief and struggle to save what could be saved from the Conquest. Which didn't include herself, sacrificed through marriage to ransom her captive nation. "Sacrifice," he had told me, and the memory still burned, "Is what we royals are made for."

Then more drums and bugles, banners flew above the makeshift stage as the twins entered adulthood and their struggle sharpened. Young Gayla belittled and neglected, finally married off to a northern nobleman. The schemes, the anger, the acid hatreds as bad faith joined bad choice to birth worse outcome.

And twenty-five years ago, Penghar's mother laid her own newborn son in my cradle and with my mother's aid, smuggled me out of my Father's northern castle-city to board a secret ship. She dared a risky night voyage down the Gwythlo River to the sea and the long ocean route to Silbar, that I might live. And Tagir's vengeful spells followed, seeking and seeking until, well out to sea, they caught her ship, and brewed a storm about it.

An oboe sobbed on the shrouded stage in Daleray as a Silbari King died and the throne fell vacant. The gleaming crown waited there on the high seat, waited to choose the new king. Pipes skirled and kettledrums thundered as the Twins went to war, each to stop the other from being chosen. Portents screamed through dreams and pleas were cried from temple pulpits, and ignored. Battles boiled through Silbar, canals were broken and cities sacked by both sides. Famine stalked the land, the Amm flowed red to the sea and bodies washed up in Aretzo's harbor.

Pen's mother bound me to her breast as waves grew mountainous and the warped skies split open under the assault of Osrick and Tagir's magic-fueled hate. Then came the moment they had not foreseen. Their hidden treachery escaped them and their storm grew monstrous. It rang the sky like a bell as big as the Moons, pealing across sea and continents alike. Ten thousand mages across my Father's Empire looked up from their work at the torment of the heavens and began to scry. Out in the Sundering Sea our ship broke into shards. Nameless sailor hands tied the woman and child to flotsam before they themselves sank beneath assassin waves. And whatever lives inside me made a tiny oasis of safety around that flotsam, safe within the storm's concealment, while on land fingers pointed and accused.

A wooden Dalbai stage became Silbari fields and ancient battle was joined across them. Azerin and Zablok screamed hate against each other as their swords flashed and spilled the blood of each other's followers. And Silbar's God at last took a direct hand. An earthquake split the battlefield and indeed the whole valley from edge to edge as the land itself tried to separate the combatants. Azerin, lifted high on a clever piece of tilting stage, screamed defiance and hurled himself upon his brother-foe, and the dynasty fell with them in mutual destruction.

Twenty-five years ago my Father the Emperor sat in judgment over Osrick and Tagir as my weeping Mother cradled survivor Terrell. His wife a deceiver, his heir a fratricide, his most powerful mage doubly a traitor; and himself a fool oblivious to warnings. Voices cried for executions, of the fratricide, of the Queen, of the mage.

The suns were shrouded by sad rains outside Dalbai Palace. The stage was a dark silent ruin, the empty throne stood above all with the gleaming silver and purple crown still atop.

Then Gayla and her husband enter, pick their way through the dim wreckage. She, pregnant with a son, submits herself to the test of the Crown, and it chooses her! Light returns to the stage (nicely handled by a nervous junior mage). Her husband's men bury the bodies and she sheds a tear over her dead brothers before she turns her face to the work of the kingdom. Curtains fall.

My Father issued his decree, and it included no more deaths. His heir pardoned at the price of a binding oath sworn before all the nobility of the empire assembled; that Terrell should have Silbar with no other duty to Osrick than payment of an annual tribute. Our mother pardoned for her deception, driven by fear proven justified. Tagir subordinated and enslaved to the very spells he'd woven to support the empire, bound there by a hundred mages. And I, consigned to melancholy memory, I am the blood price of the peace he thus bought for his dynasty and the shaky young Gwythlo Empire.

But I'm not dead. With three words I could end that peace and give the world to new bloodletting. I still live.

"Did you say something, my Lord?" Callia whispered to me. "Please applaud, it's expected in Dalbai. And the actors deserve it."

I came back to myself with a start and hastily stood and added my applause to the rest of the audience —the queen was on her feet, so we all had to be as well. The actors bowed and Callia's mother tossed a fat purse onto the stage, which the young man who'd played Zablok dexterously caught and promptly handed over to the young woman who played Gayla. Both male leads bowed to her amid renewed applause, then the troupe left the stage with many bows to the queen and the rest of us.

"Found the production fascinating, did you, Ambassador?" inquired Crown Princess Alliet with a smile. "You were positively rapt all through it!"

"Ah yes, it certainly stirred old memories," I answered as I bowed over her extended hand and then escaped as soon as I decently could.

Callia guided me to a corner partly sheltered behind the sandalwood screen that had concealed her the day I arrived here. Was that only yesterday? At a signal her women moved to buy us a few moments of privacy by impeding anyone who approached.

"What is wrong, Sir Kirin?" She stared at me intently.

"What makes you think anything's wrong?" I babbled, then silently cursed myself for a fool. "No, I should tell you. That play, it calls up unhappy memories of my wife's death. From before I was knighted. If I'm not careful I start to dwell on them. It's stupid of me, Highness, and I know better, I apologize. Please forgive me."

Her stare unnerved me. I don't know why I had to struggle to meet it. Every word I'd spoken was the truth. Just not all of it.

"Forgiven," she said. "You should circulate among the guests. There are people here you should meet."

I bowed myself away with relief, exchanged pleasantries with three courtiers and two military officers, and tried for ten agonizing minutes to tactfully escape a gushing noblewoman and her husband who were eager to dissect the play with a native Silbari. Then I found myself facing Count Yare.

He was beaming and jovial as he gripped my hand. "Kirin! I'm glad I caught up to you tonight. Sephora has ordered me to check over Dalbai's south coast defenses in case Khaitanial tries a sneak attack. Which from the gossip I heard, they did earlier today! Attempted sabotage on our new warship, eh?"

"Yes, My Lord Yare, though we can't prove the spike's origin." I scowled in frustration. "There's too many possible villains behind it." Though I was sure I could guess the name of one.

"But one name's more likely than any other," he nodded. "Tanney bastards! We'll nail them someday. Say, I don't have to leave until the dawn tide. A couple Navy friends and I, and four very attractive women who are eager to meet you, will be having a private party in my hamman in an hour or two, one that will last well into the night. Can we hope that you'll grace us with your presence?"

I hoped my face didn't give away my thoughts while I scrambled for a polite way to say 'hell no'. "Unfortunately, my Lord, tempting as that offer sounds, I have other commitments this evening. The sabotage attempt only adds to the urgent need to get my charge safely to her betrothed husband. I must speak tonight with Captain D'Auson and your Admiral about speeding the princess' departure —"

"About which I also wish to be consulted tonight," Callia interrupted, sweeping in to join the conversation with an attendant at each elbow and two guards at her back. "My maids already have much to arrange before I can be ready to leave. Plus there's the promise you made this afternoon, Sir Kirin, to help train my guardsmen in Silbari fighting techniques tomorrow morning."

Yare's answer was smooth as spidersilk. "Dear girl, I wouldn't dream of taking the Ambassador away from you. I just wanted to convey my regrets that I won't be here to say goodbye when you set sail. I'll have to hop around South Coast for the next tenday."

"I'll be sorry to miss you, Yare," I assured him and hoped I sounded sincere. "We'll meet again someday."

"I'll count on it!" He grinned that infectious grin, squeezed my wrist in the warrior's grip once more, gave his niece a 'best wishes on her marriage' and a peck on one cheek, and left.

Callia looked at me with her head tilted a little to one side. "Will you walk with me for a moment, my Lord Ambassador?"

"Gladly, Highness." I wondered how much she had heard and what she thought of it.

She set a hand on my arm and we strolled around the edge of the party. "My uncle Yare is not typical of us, Sir Kirin."

"I guessed as much, Princess. Thank you for, ah, rescuing me from his attentions."

"Perhaps I should have arranged for that this morning as well?"

"Ah." I swallowed a sudden lump in my throat. "Some warning would have been helpful, yes. I felt trapped when I realized – so. Tell me, was that a test?"

"Not an intentional one on Mother's part. Uncle's intentions are harder for me to understand." Callia glanced at my face, her own expression chilly. "Did you find it so?"

"Yes." I let that hang in the air for a moment, then felt forced to explain. "It's hard to know what to do when guesting with a strange Lord. I didn't want to give offense to a powerful man without strong need."

"That is sensible." Her voice was neutral and I wondered what that meant. Then I wondered what her mother thought, and my collar felt tight again.

At that moment Lieutenant Pallir and Captain D'Auson caught up to us to report that the squadron's mages had set up wards around and under the *Queen of the Seas* to warn if any person, thing or creature came near the ship again before we left. They would finish doing the same for *Stormrider,* *Waverunner,* and *Defiance* tonight.

"They also want to spend my squadron's purse dry to buy magic toys and stockpile silver for spare power on the return trip," D'Auson confided with a sigh and a beseeching look at Callia. "Your Baron Cleng is urging them on right now, Highness. I swear he and White have gone from enemies to conspirators in a heartbeat. The man probably wants to bankrupt us as a petty revenge."

She merely smiled. "I wouldn't dream of intervening in the day to day management of any ship, even my own, Captain. I'm sure you will handle this problem adroitly."

Pallir grinned. "So he's assigned me to 'guard' the mages and the Purser on their shopping trip tomorrow, to keep us solvent. The Purser gets to say 'No!' and I get to back him up." He slid his sword out of his scabbard for a fingerwidth and clicked it home again.

D'Auson added to me "Would you by chance care to go along and back my Marine commander up too, Sir Hand DiUmbra? These are mages after all. I am not sure I trust them to resist the temptation to try a little sorcerous persuasion on my men in pursuit of some glittery toy. Admiral DiRovigo will be very annoyed if I return the squadron bankrupt and trailing creditors."

"Tempting," I chuckled. "But not very; it sounds deadly dull, and no sorcery will work on the Lieutenant."

Pal preened for a moment and D'Auson made a conceding gesture.

"Though if you've time in the early morning, Pallir," I continued. "I'd like to have you here for sword practice with Princess Callia's personal guardsmen. She asked me to prepare her men against attackers who use Continental or Silbari techniques, and I could use some help."

D'Auson rolled his eyes as Pallir looked to him hopefully. "Yes, Lieutenant, you may. I need my Purser with me in the morning for other work, the mages will have to wait until after noon anyway."

We settled on a time and they drifted away. Callia looked thoughtful and slightly mischievous as she drew me over to Princess Gadet, who was seated at one side chatting with a retinue of court ladies.

"Oh Aunt," she asked sweetly. "I've asked Sir Kirin and his Captain's officers to help train my guardsmen tomorrow morning. Since Uncle Yare's to be away on a mission for Mother, do you think they might use the Court of the Cats for practice, and his hamman to clean up afterwards?"

Princess Gadet gave me an outright leer. "Certainly, dear, I'll order the staff to prepare. Of course, my dear Yare will be taking his 'masseuses' with him, so your men will just have to do without."

I managed to thank her amidst the titters of the other noblewomen, and persuaded Callia away as fast as I could.

"You did that on purpose," I accused as soon as we were out of earshot.

"I did," she agreed smugly, her eyes alight with laughter. "It'll do you no harm and my men will enjoy a sample of Uncle's more innocent luxuries." Her smile faded as she added "I only chose unmarried men and Mother plans to promote all four of them before we leave. But I'll still take them far away from their families and they may not be back for years. Rank and good pay and even the new weapons and armor that are being prepared, are not enough. I'd be grateful if you'd help me show them that I want to equip them with the best skills, too."

"That's very wise of you, your Highness," I answered slowly. "And very good, too. I'm glad to help you however I can."

Ambassador DiTorian diverted me then with a plea for the story of the sabotage. Callia and I told the tale and he speculated over a long list of potential suspects.

I shook my head at most of them. "It has to involve a very talented and knowledgeable mage with access to information about the ship. He may not be here anymore, but he was here within the last tenday. Add the Beniyah assassins and you can bet that Khaitanial's found an ally east of the Inner Ocean. One that I've met before."

DiTorian's gaze sharpened. "Who?"

"A Xiphree mage, his name is Dameon Zurtos. He tried to sink *Waverunner* right in Silbar Bay, when we were still in sight of Aretzo." I told them both about it.

"That is disturbing," DiTorian muttered, his face creased in worry. "I wish I had known those details about it earlier. Do you have any idea what other tricks he may be getting up to?"

Callia and I looked at each other. I shrugged helplessly.

"I don't know, Highness," I told her directly. "We'll just have to deal with whatever comes."

She nodded slowly. "Yes. The good and the bad together."

DiTorian excused himself and the rest of the party passed in a blur. It was late before I was able to retire to my guest bedroom.

Limis helped me out of the Court garb and left me alone with my basin and water jug to wash. Afterwards I crawled into the big bed again and curled under a light sheet.

Have I offended her badly? I wondered, thinking how distant she'd been after discovering my visit to Yare's hamman. I wished that I knew. *Terrell would have a better idea than me. He understands noble women better than I do.*

Terrell hadn't touched minds with me all day. I tried to reach for him in the dark.

Brother, are you there? Can you hear me?

I called a dozen times with no answer. Whatever our gift of mind-speech was, it could not cross two thousand miles unaided. I had no Hill of Sight to help me, only my too-weak voice.

It was a relief when sleep claimed me at last.

~ ~ ~

Callia lay in the darkness, listening to the night doves coo.

He as much as said he's had flings with noblewomen. So why do I resent him for having one with Uncle Yare's women? It's Uncle I should be angry at, for tempting him. But that's what Uncle does, try to tempt the young men into his orgies. Father said it was useful to have someone around like that to test the young men's character, so as long as we have to put up with Yare for Gadet's sake we should make use of him.

She tried unsuccessfully to discipline her spiraling thoughts. *Why should I be angry with Sir Kirin anyway? He's a man, doing something men do. Even Mikkal did it, three times, Sharme said the women told her! Then he never went back again; Father was pleased. But I think he'd have been more pleased if Mikkal had stayed away entirely. I wonder why Mother didn't have someone warn Sir Kirin about Uncle's ways? Maybe she's just been too busy. Maybe I should have warned him. He felt trapped, I could tell. He didn't want to go back there even once. He was embarrassed about it too. Maybe that means he learned better, or faster than Mikkal anyway. He's older; if he was born after the Gwythlo conquest of Silbar then he must be twenty-five now. I'm still surprised how handsome he is, Dona Catalona really didn't do him justice in her description. That light golden color to his skin, and the graceful way he moves.*

Yare's women were lucky they got to have him. I wonder —

"Stop," she said aloud. "Get your thoughts under control, Princess of Dalbai. You are marrying his lord, Prince Terrell, and everything Sir Kirin and everybody else has told you says the prince is a good man who'll make you a good marriage. Think only of that."

Only of that.

~ ~ ~

Chapter 32: Aretzo – Penghar

Ninety-third day of Summer

Penghar carefully checked over the troops assigned for Terrell's escort this morning. It wasn't necessary, every man in the Palace Guard was fanatically loyal to the Crown and would give his life for its wearer. But habits were good things, they sustained you when Fate threw unpleasant surprises in your face. Like the one that had been eating at him all night.

Terrell came out of the Palace into the stable yard. Pen noticed that he had dressed in casual riding clothes of leather and plain durable cloth with almost no ornamentation, just the royal crest on each shoulder and a little piping along the seams. He wasn't wearing the Crown this morning but instead had a broad brimmed hat held on with an adjustable cord. He mounted his horse and rode past the two Mages and two Healers already settled on their steeds to join Pen.

"Let's go up the center valley today, at a nice brisk trot," Terrell directed. "To the Marble Spring. That will be a good place to water the horses."

"As you wish, your Highness." Another habit, Pen mused, not using the title his brother-in-all-but-blood deserved. But this was one of the concessions Terrell made to keep Emperor Osrick calm, so Pen obeyed.

They passed through the Sunset Gate, over a causeway above the sunken road circling the city, and through an overgrown wall on the other side. The vast park maintained for royal riding opened before them and Terrell urged his horse up to speed. Pen maintained position next to him easily enough, a mage and a healer on either side of them. The troops fanned out into a huge circle surrounding them at a distance. It was nothing like privacy, but the air was clear and sweet with flowers and birdsong. They rode west beneath huge spreading oaks a fifth as old as the kingdom, across a little stone bridge and up a long meadow that climbed steadily. In an hour they were higher than the Palace roofs. In two they could look east and down on the Hill of Sight with the rooftops of Aretzo spread like a patchwork cloak below it.

Terrell reined in and his horse blew and stamped as he dismounted onto the lowest step of the little marble pergola that surrounded the spring. A groom took his and Pen's horses to water them at a stone trough filled by the spring's outflow. Terrell mounted the steep stair to the double ring of pillars and the dome that topped them, went to the small shrine at the pool's edge and made a quick prayer. Then he strolled between the two rows of pillars to a jutting balcony that offered a sweeping view.

"Vallit," he said to a servant hurrying toward his side, "Fetch a horn of spring water for Baron DiLione and I, then pass the word to leave us in peace for a while."

When the man had brought the water and left, and the rest of the party had carefully positioned themselves well out of hearing, Terrell leaned on the balcony rail and took a long drink from the horn, then looked at Pen.

"Out with it, Pen. You've been broody as an old hen all morning and I swear you're lacking a few hours of sleep. What's bothering you?"

Pen heaved a sigh, planted his feet in a parade-rest position, and looked his best friend and lord full in the face. "Do you remember what you said to me just before we carried you down from the Hill of Sight that night?" He didn't have to specify which night.

Terrell looked thoughtful, slowly shook his head. "No, I'm sorry to say that I don't. Everything was rather a blur there at the end. What was it?"

Pen stepped closer and lowered his voice even though nobody was close enough to hear and Irreneetha would warn him if anyone tried to use magic to spy on their speech. "You said 'Kirin did it, Pen, he gave me *everything*. I saw her, heard her voice, smelled her perfume, touched her hand, talked to her.' I've been trying to forget it ever since."

Terrell closed his eyes, held out the horn. Pen took it, drank deeply.

"It would be better if you did forget," his liege said softly, opening his eyes and staring at Pen's own. Terrell's eyes were plain brown, like Pen's and those of twenty million other Silbaris, but there was a chill distance there that wrung Pen's heart.

"I can't forget it. I love you, my Lord, my life is yours and while there is breath in my body I will serve and protect you. But I can't forget this. You touched minds with him, didn't you? Across all that distance, risking your very life to open your mind to that – that –"

"Pen, the Hill can do marvelous things, I was straining both it and myself –"

"Don't try to mislead me, please, Terrell. Don't hurt me that way. I've known you better than anyone else alive, even Dona Seraphina. I've been at your side, seen how you talk to him, and seen when you don't talk, and yet he knows what to do without instruction. I didn't want to see it, but since that night I can't look away. You've been talking mind-to-mind with him for years."

Terrell hesitated, a hesitation that nearly broke Pen's heart, then said, "Yes. Kirin has unique talents and this is one of them."

"And that's the problem, for if he really is unique then there's only one man he can possibly be, and that's not Duke Cerrai's bastard. He told me once that he came to Aretzo from an island in the Sundering Sea. That's the same sea where a ship sank twenty-five years ago –"

"Don't speak it aloud, Pen." Terrell made a small negating gesture with his right hand, glanced from side to side to be sure no one was near.

"I'll be cut apart a fingerwidth at a time before I do," Pen vowed. "I swear that to you on my eternal soul, but I can't *not know*. His invisibility to magic, his apparent age, the way the bones of his face so nearly match your own in the right light, it's so obvious once I let myself see it. Someone else will too."

"Yes, and no." Terrell took off his hat, ran his fingers nervously through his curling yellow hair. "There have been a number of unusual Talents found in halfblood children born in Aretzo over the past generation, and more in the last few years. I've played them up to the Guild, offered training funds to such youngsters and generally made it plain that I believe there are more like Kirin out there, if not exactly like him. People are coming to expect something unusual of mixed-blood children. He's less remarkable every year."

"But still unique, because none of those children can do the things he does. And when I think of our history, all the tragedies that came from sons like him, I can't help wondering what evil he is destined to visit on Silbar."

"No!" Terrell paused and visibly mastered himself, then signaled for the watching attendants to draw back still farther. After a moment he said, much more quietly, "The One God does not enslave us to a destined path. We are free to choose our steps, every moment of every day. Kirin has chosen to serve me, and I, him, and together, We serve Silbar. I need him, Pen, and he needs me even more. He is the Darkness that cools my searing Light and lets me see, unblinded by myself. I am the Light that leads him out of his dark Hell, the anchor that brings him to harbor again every time he sails into Night. Which he does again and again for me. I give him Purpose, he gives me Perspective. We are lost without each other. But together – do you think I would have, could have, accomplished so much in seven years, if I'd been alone?"

"You haven't been alone," Pen said dully. "You have me."

"Yes," Terrell answered him steadily, his gaze never wavering from Pen's eyes. "Your service, your *self*, is the greatest gift and treasure of my life." Terrell took the drinking horn out of Pen's hand, drained the last drop and set it aside, then stared into his face again. "One that drives me every day to try anew to be worthy of you."

Pen's knees went weak and he sagged to the pavement, crouched and shivered even as he bowed his forehead to the cold marble. "My Lord!" he choked through a throat gone tight, while thinking, *I'd hoped that was true, but you never said it before now.*

Terrell gently touched him on the back of his head. "Rise, my brother, and face one last truth before we end this conversation."

Pen had to try twice to get his legs under himself before he could stand. He swayed and Terrell grasped his shoulders to lend him strength.

"Kirin is neither gift nor treasure, sometimes he's so aggravating I could scream to The One for relief. But his soul and mine are linked in a way that I can neither explain nor escape. A link that I cannot share with you or anyone else, though I have wished that I could. He and I can only follow the twisted skeins of our lives until we come to the end of each other. Despite what I said about destiny, neither of us has any choice in that, and you cannot help me in this search any more than you could help me find my bride. I'm sorry for that. It seems grossly unfair for The One to have laid two such burdens on your shoulders. But there it is."

Pen nodded mutely while his thoughts whirled and Irreneetha sang softly in his ears.

Terrell released him and picked up the drinking horn again. "Dona Seraphina says I'm well enough to use the Hill today. This afternoon I'd like to hear Callia's voice again."

"As you will, your Highness," Pen answered and signaled the grooms to prepare.

As he mounted his own horse and Terrell directed the party onto a path that led through Shady Glen and back to the Palace, Pen's tangled thoughts settled around one certainty. He briefly gripped the pommel of his sheathed sword.

If my Lord ever needs me to cut the knot that binds him to Darkness, I know how to do it.

Irreneetha hummed softly in what he told himself was agreement.

~ ~ ~

Chapter 33: Daleray Palace - Callia

Ninety-fourth day of Summer

"Callia? Are you in here?" called a female voice.

Callia looked up from the back of the Collection room, saw her cousin's wife Elina peering in though the bustle of the busily-packing servants. "Over here!" she called gaily and waved, in the process smearing dust on her sari.

Elina dodged through the crates and barrels being filled by servants and meticulously recorded by two scribes, found her way around the mob of men slowly lowering the sea-unicorn skeleton into a padded cradle, and made it to Callia's side. They exchanged glad hugs, then Elina coughed.

"There's so much dust in here! Might we step out of it to talk?"

"Certainly!" Callia drew her over to an open side door that led to the Court of the Banyan. The two of them sat on benches in the shade of the giant tree that dominated the courtyard and enjoyed the gentle breeze. "So good to see you! How was your trip to Falls Valley yesterday?"

"Oh no trouble at all, thankfully, and grandmother was her old self again, back on her feet and pottering about the gardens. She swears the estate will fall to ruin if she doesn't supervise everything personally. I don't know how her poor Seneschal gets anything done. I didn't get back until after dark and was too distracted to attend the party. I hope the *yaley* went well. No, it was what Silbaris call a 'play', wasn't it?"

"Yes, a historical one, quite a tragic tale really, but wonderfully staged and very absorbing. The actors did a magnificent job and everybody applauded. Mother even awarded them a fat purse at the end."

"I wish I'd arrived home in time to see it, but I probably still wouldn't have had enough time to change. Travel is so filthy in the hills this time of year. It's been three whole days since they had enough rain up there to lay the road dust."

"Sir Kirin told me that's the usual state in Silbar. Two seasons out of four there's almost no rain. He said anyone who can afford air magery pays to have their windows and carriages shielded from dust." Callia shook out the tail of her sari and dust drifted on the breeze. Junia produced a brush and began delicately cleaning the garment while her mistress talked.

"I envy the time you've gotten to spend with him," Elina said. "He looks so handsome and fascinating! Of course, my Vimmal's ship returned yesterday and he reached the house shortly before I did, so we found other things to do." Elina wore a complacent expression.

"Aha, I thought you had a glow about you this morning!" Callia teased. "So that's why you were so 'distracted' last night, hmm? Still pleased with marriage to my cousin?"

"Oh yes, 'pleased' doesn't begin to describe it." Elina smirked. "He had been away at sea for nearly three weeks, we had to make up for that lost time! But you've known Vimmal your whole life. I'm sure you're bored with hearing me talk about him by now. Tell me about this Prince Terrell that you're going to marry. What did the Ambassador tell you about him?"

"A great many things, nearly all of them good." Callia's face acquired a thoughtful expression. "If I assume that Sir Kirin's words can be trusted, and I feel I can safely do so, then Prince Terrell should be considerate, kind, loyal, and interesting. He's only twenty-five years old, and quite handsome and energetic."

"As husbands go, those all sound like points in his favor," Elina ventured. "What did you hear that you didn't think good?"

"The concubines, for one." Callia twisted her lips in a wry smile and shrugged her shoulders in a fatalistic gesture.

"Oh dear, will you have to put up with those after you're married?"

"No, they will all be pensioned off before the ceremony, according to both Dona Catalona and Sir Kirin. Mother wrote it into the marriage contract too. I'm not worried about them competing for his affections, at least not directly."

"Then what are you worried about?" Elina asked the question in a way that let Callia know that she had already guessed the answer.

"I'm concerned," Callia answered slowly, hands clasped in her lap, "That he may have expectations that I won't know how to meet, at least not initially."

"But Soer Tiresa taught you the same marriage preparation as she taught me. We talked about it before I married Vimmal. I've told you before that it all went quite well that first night and I've enjoyed his love ever since. I still do!" Elina gave an exaggerated little shiver and laughed.

"You also told me you were glad to find that he wasn't too experienced and how much you enjoyed learning together. But Prince Terrell is very experienced. What if he thinks me naïve and ignorant?" Callia uttered the last all in a rush, relieved to finally reveal her fears to her friend.

Elina proved her own worth by getting to the heart of the problem. "You're worried that you can't trust him to understand your inexperience? That he may not be considerate enough to help you through your first few nights of learning? That he may be disappointed or annoyed with you?"

"Exactly." Callia clutched her hands together and stared at her fears. They didn't seem any smaller once spoken out loud.

"It seems to me that you only have two people available to you for counsel about the prince," Elina thought out loud. "Your language teacher Dona Catalona, and Sir Kirin. And from what little I've heard about either one, the Dona has no personal knowledge of the man, but Sir Kirin does. That's a difficult situation. Wait, wait, what about the other people in the Silbari squadron? Vimmal was reading a dispatch about them this morning. He had orders already waiting for him when he got home. His Father-the-Admiral is sending him to Silbar with you as our Navy liaison, which means I'm to go as well!"

"Oh! That's wonderful!" Callia cried, immeasurably relieved. "I've been so afraid that I'd have nobody I know over there but my maids and my guards."

"Well, eventually your uncle will call Vimmal home and I'll have to leave too. But by then you'll have had time to get to know your husband and establish some new friends in Silbar." Elina paused, visibly remembering something. "Don't the Silbaris have priestesses serving as Healers on their ships like we do, including one who they sent especially for your ship?"

"That's right, that Dona Seelie. I met her briefly the first night after they arrived, but I haven't had a chance to talk to her since."

"I think," Elina suggested archly, "That you should talk to her sooner rather than later. She must have highly-placed family in Silbar to get such an important posting. She might know your prince personally too."

"A very good point. I'll send her an invitation to wait on me tomorrow. Heavens, did you know that we're supposed to leave in only three more days?"

"What? But Vimmal's orders said five!"

"After the assassination attempt on Sir Kirin and the sabotage attempt on my ship, Mother told Uncle Abemar at breakfast this morning to push up the departure as soon as possible. He said three days is the best we can do. That's why I've set everybody who can be spared to packing the collection and getting it on board. It's going to be my personal bride-gift to Prince Terrell."

"That sounds like an excellent idea, but it reminds me that your mother gave me a message for you. She told me to remind you about your Aunt Gadet wanting the ivories."

"I've set them aside for her already. I suppose I should deliver them to her myself to make sure she gets what she wants. I did ask her for a favor last night so I owe her a consideration today."

"Oh?" Elina gave Callia a curious look. "What could you want from her?"

Callia smiled at the memory. "I'd already asked Sir Kirin to give my guards extra training in Continental fighting techniques today, since we'll be in Silbar. So I asked her if he could use the Court of the Cats for it this morning, and Uncle's hamman afterwards." At Elina's puzzled look she added "Uncle's not here. He left on the dawn tide for South Coast and took his women with him."

"I see. But why did you ask her for that place?"

Callia's smile faded. "Uncle Yare privately invited Sir Kirin to join him for sword practice early the first morning after the Silbaris arrived, and nobody thought to warn the Ambassador about what might happen. He said he felt trapped because he didn't know what was expected, so when uncle brought out his 'masseuses', he stayed." In a dry voice Callia added, "Afterwards the two women boasted about him to Sharme in the servant's quarters."

Elina chuckled. "And you were cross with him and wanted to embarrass him?"

"Well, yes." Callia tossed her head. "I imagine he's gathered my guardsmen together with whoever else he's using as instructors. The Silbari Marine Lieutenant is one, I believe. They are all probably quite cheerfully trying to cut out each other's livers about now, preferably with blunt weapons. I should imagine my cousin would love it."

"Oh! Vimmal was grinning when he read his orders this morning. All he would say is that he had to get to the Palace right away and did I want to ride with him to visit you. I just bet he's there, and probably up to some mischief involving swords."

Callia gave her a slow grin. "In that case, we should definitely take those ivories to Auntie ourselves, and see what's going on in the Court of Cats."

~ ~ ~

Chapter 34: Daleray – Kirin; Callia

Ninety-fourth day of Summer

"Good move, Kirin!" grunted Lieutenant Pallir after he landed on the straw mat. He sucked in air again and I gave him a hand to help him back to his feet.

"How'd you do that?" demanded Lord Vimmal, Callia's first cousin. He had shown up just before our practice started with a letter of introduction from his father the Admiral identifying him as their Navy's liaison to Silbar's Navy. I hadn't hesitated to include him in the practice.

"I used his own movement against him," I explained. "Here, you try to put that spear through me."

A moment later Vimmal hit the mat the same way Pal had. The blunt imitation spear with the stuffed 'blade' cartwheeled into a planter where the chalk-impregnated cloth left a white mark on the stone. Aber Peng, his shoulder still bandaged, reclaimed it.

"Ufff!" Vim bounced up again. He was only a couple years younger than me though not quite as vigorous. "You dodged, I saw that much, and then you grabbed me somehow, and then I went flying!"

"My Lord Ambassador, please pardon me for asking, but may I try it next?" asked Corporal Dal Morengal tentatively.

"Yes, the rest of you watch." I waved him forward and gave him the same treatment, though Dal managed to hang onto the spear and roll with it. While I helped Dal up I said to him, "Did you feel what I did to you?"

He nodded, smiling. "I think so, my lord. Almost took it right out of my hands!"

"Good man." I turned to the watching men "Did any of you see what I just did?"

Pal nodded vigorously. "You changed your balance from one side to the other as he came in, then moved so that he had to shift the spearpoint to track where you were. But you moved faster than it did. You grabbed the shaft somehow, only with Lord Sandello it was his arm I think."

I nodded, pointed to Vim's left arm. "You had your hand too far advanced on the shaft, so I was able to grab your wrist and pull you off balance. Lieutenant Pallir's hand and Corporal Dal's were both back in a safer position where I couldn't get a good grip, so I went for the spearshaft instead. You were already falling forward as you ran, I just moved you faster than your feet were ready to go, and down you went."

"But how did you dodge so fast!" Vim asked.

"Practice. Lots of it."

"Then let's get some more!"

The seven of us went through several more rounds. Callia's four guardsmen worked as hard as any, though Aber Peng was badly slowed by his wound and I refused to let him work after it broke open again on the fourth throw. Aber argued that it was all right if he bled a little since Princess Callia had stationed one of the Palace Priestesses with us to repair damage, but I didn't swallow that nonsense. Pallir, already very good, soon mastered the trick well enough to throw me a couple times. Vimmal had a steeper hill to climb. He kept at it with dogged determination and finally managed a couple throws of his own. Dal and the other two guardsmen caught on about then as well, and soon all of them could manage to counter the trick at least a third of the time.

Then I shifted us to sword practice and we traded off two and two. We used Yare's two padded practice suits and the guardsmen had brought extras, so we had two pairs. Those who weren't in any particular fight stood by and called out the touches. Vimmal and Pallir were in their element there, both excellent swordsmen who could beat me as often as I beat them. None of the guardsmen were less than very good either, so we all thoroughly wore each other out.

~ ~ ~

"Good morning, dear!" Aunt Gadet cheerily welcomed Callia to her second-floor parlor. "And Elina, so good to see you too this lovely morning. To what do I owe this visit?"

"Mother said you wanted some of the carved ivories from Father's collection hall." Callia waved forward a servant who set down a wooden box in front of her aunt. "I brought them all to make sure you get the ones you want. I'll be giving the rest to Prince Terrell as part of my personal bride gift."

"How thoughtful of you, dear." Gadet beamed. "Just let me look."

A few minutes later her aunt had chosen several of the carvings and Callia sent the servant back with the much-reduced box.

"Thank you so very much for fetching those here personally, my dears. Now you simply must have tea with me in my solar. Come!" Gadet led them into the many-windowed room. "Do both of you sit here with me by the windows and enjoy this view."

Callia and Elina looked through the expansive glass windows, made of dozens of small panes cleverly joined, and turned grins to each other.

"As I predicted. Trying to cut out each other's livers and having a wonderful time," Callia remarked as she took a seat next to her aunt's chair.

"They make quite a handsome set, don't you think?" Gadet observed. "Vimmal's grown up to be an impressive man even in a loincloth, or perhaps especially so. And the Ambassador is quite as much a man even in that worn-out hose. That Marine lieutenant is also a pleasant eyeful."

Elina took her own seat and leaned forward to watch. "I wonder what Vimmal thinks will happen afterwards, the rascal? I shall have to twit him about this."

Gadet chuckled as a servant passed out cups and saucers and poured the tea. "If you'd like to hear it in his own words, I can open one of the windows. They are well oiled and don't squeak. But do keep quiet while you listen, for voices travel both ways. He can't see you through this spelled glass, but he'll be able to hear you if you speak."

"I promise to be quite mute, Princess Gadet, at least until I meet him again. Then I shall give him an earful!"

~ ~ ~

By the time the suns crept towards noon the seven of us had worn out two practice swords and were tired enough to stop. The Priestess checked each of us over for injuries and I held my Shadow tight while her aura probed me. She set an extra Healing into Aber's shoulder before she removed his bandage to let the now-closed wound air. It looked likely to develop an impressive scar, over which she tut-tutted before she left us.

"And now for Uncle Yare's notorious baths," Vimmal remarked cheerfully. Two of the guardsmen looked intrigued and more than a little eager, the other two uncertain. Yare's servants smiled as they took the armor and weapons away.

Pallir made an inquiring sound. "Notorious baths?"

"Uncle Yare keeps a pair of very talented women, officially they are masseuses," Vim explained with a grin. "They're trained in all sorts of techniques, especially those that get and keep your soldier at attention!" His grin turned sly. "Gossip says Ambassador Kirin had a chance to thoroughly explore their talents yesterday morning."

"Salim's Teeth and Toenails!" I swore. "Does everybody know about that?"

"I'm sure there's a deaf gardener somewhere who hasn't yet heard the news," Vim laughed. "I learned of it on the way here this morning."

"Well, there'll be nothing notorious about the baths today," I quashed that idea. "We'll be the only ones there other than the menservants. His 'masseuses' have gone with him to South Coast."

Pal looked oddly relieved at that.

"I know, else I'd never dare enter that door," Vim grinned as he waved at it. "Elina would have my left nut in a jar for going in there any other time."

The four guardsmen looked hesitantly at the door. They were plainly excited and a little overawed at being invited into their lords' privileges. Vimmal was the only one who didn't seem entirely at ease with their presence even though he tried to hide it behind his boisterous behavior.

"Look here, all of you." I stepped in front of the door and used my imitation of Terrell's command voice. Their heads turned to me before their ears had quite heard. "It's time for me to make several things clear. You're all going on the *Queen of the Seas* with Princess Callia. Captain D'Auson will command her, Lieutenant Pallir is his commander of marines, and Lord Vimmal will serve the Captain as Special Adjutant for Navigation on loan from Dalbai's Navy. Lieutenant Dal and Sargents Girr, Aber and Benor – yes, you four are getting promoted tomorrow – will report solely to the princess. But thanks to Prince Terrell's appointment I will rank every last one of you, including the Captain. Since I'm not stupid I won't be throwing that around."

Vimmal unsuccessfully tried to hide his relief.

I smiled grimly. "That doesn't mean there will never come a time when I have to exercise it. We don't know what we're going to face on this trip. Magic attacks, physical attacks, ship-to-ship fighting, even fighting off boarders may be part of it. Anything might happen. We may not all live to reach Silbar, but the princess must. That is our sole charge; to get her there come what may."

The five Dalbais showed fire in their eyes at my words. Good, they'd each already thought about this and made their own peace with their souls. Pallir looked at me with new respect and simply nodded.

"To that end, among us rank and blood and nation will all be distant seconds to our mission. I worked you all hard today in part to get you used to working together. I'll be continuing that training on the ship, as will others, of whom Pallir is not the least. And you'll be working with the hundred-twenty marines and two hundred sailors that make up the crew of the Queen, and her officers and mages and priestess. But every moment of every day, waking or sleeping, remember this; you will guard each other's backs like brothers. And you will live and die for Princess Callia, not for your bloodlines or clans or families. Understood?"

Six pairs of eyes stared back at me as six heads nodded solemnly.

"Good. Now a lesser thing; me. I'm a knight, I'm my King's Left Hand, and I'm his Lord Ambassador for this trip. I'm also the strangest sort of Mage you'll ever meet, and some people will tell you I carry a demon inside me. And maybe I do."

The Dalbais' eyes got bigger at that and two of the Guards' hands twitched as they suppressed the urge to make the Sign Against Evil. Only Aber and Dal, who had seen my Shadow yesterday, showed no reaction.

"You'll see and judge for yourselves. Living Shadows obey me and I can make them kill a man without me even touching him, and do worse things. I was born and raised in a gutter and sold into slavery as a child, you'll see the slave mark in a few minutes. Good people rescued me, raised me as one of them, and taught me most of what I know. I don't fit anywhere in the ranks and bloodlines that shaped your lives. I stand outside them all. But I know where my loyalty lies, and that is to Prince Terrell of Silbar."

Vimmal blinked rapidly, nodded his head once. "I think I see, My Lord. This is a lot to drop on me so suddenly. That means you're testing me, the way King Baint used to test us by whether we spent time with Count Yare's women, or didn't."

"Yes." I nodded to him.

"I won't fail my cousin Callia," Vim answered steadily. "On my oath."

"Good man." Then I looked each of them in the face one at a time. "And the testing won't stop here. It'll last every day of your service to the prince and princess."

The four guardsmen glanced at each other. To my surprise it was stoic Aber who spoke for them.

"We're ready, My Lord."

"And you already know I am," Pallir finished.

"Thank you," I told him, and to the guardsmen, "Thank you all. Now let's enjoy this place. After the noon meal it's back to duty for all of us." I opened the door and led them inside.

~ ~ ~

"That was a pleasant distraction," Gadet remarked as the men filed through the door into Yare's *hamman*. "Though I'm afraid your husband is more virtuous than you had feared, Elina."

"Which I'm quite happy to learn, Princess Gadet, believe me. But what did the Ambassador mean by that last part?" Elina wondered. "I could hardly hear it, but did he really say he has a demon inside him?"

"No," Callia said. "He said 'maybe I do', like boys say when they're daring each other. I think he wanted to cow them a little."

"Or a lot, with that claim he can kill a man without touching him," Gadet sniffed. "Men are always on about 'whose is biggest' and who hits hardest and such."

"And he said he was a slave!" Elina's voice was hushed. "Was he captured by the Khaitanials?"

"Probably the Klintos," Callia guessed. "They keep slaves and they were Silbar's enemy long before the Gwythlo's Empire."

"I wonder where that slave mark is, the one he said they'd see in a few minutes," Elina speculated.

"Under his hose, obviously." Gadet snorted. "He wasn't wearing anything else, was he now?"

They all giggled a little over that.

"He claims to stand outside all of our ranks," Elina noted. "I can't decide whether that's the most arrogant thing I've ever heard, or the simple truth."

"And at the same time he says he's loyal to Prince Terrell," Callia said. "From the time I spent with him yesterday I am quite sure they are very close friends. I'd never realized a man could be raised out of the gutters and become an aristocrat."

"His manners at dinner were impeccable too," Gadet noted. "Dear, didn't you mention that he's an acknowledged bastard of one of their dukes?"

"Yes, that's what my language teacher told me."

"Then that probably explains the friendship and the good manners, dear. I suspect he was exaggerating to shock the men. Most likely he was really raised from the beginning to join the court when he came of age, and all that Bards' twaddle about 'humble beginnings' can be ignored. Likely his father paid for training and had him introduced as a safe companion for the prince. A bastard can't inherit in Silbar any more than here, so there'd be much less danger of dynastic ambitions." Gadet nodded her head in satisfaction over devising this neat explanation.

"That could be so," Callia answered slowly, not sure why it immediately felt wrong to her.

"I think you can rely on it, dear," Gadet said firmly. "Now, we saw that he's quite athletic. If he's had the right teaching he might make a skilled lover too. Are you thinking of bedding him?"

"What? No!" Callia answered, flustered.

"Your body's certainly thinking about it," Gadet laughed. "And why not? As long as you take care to avoid your fertile times and use a good protection spell you won't get pregnant. A baby with his skin and ears would be an undeniable disaster for you, but simple precautions will keep you safe."

"But I'm betrothed," Callia protested weakly. She remembered that dream last night . . .

"And your husband-to-be has had concubines to satisfy him ever since he took up his throne," Gadet pointed out. "It's only fair that you get some practice too."

Elina frowned. "I didn't, Princess, and I don't think my Vimmal did either, or at least not often. I would be very cross with him if he were to seek out other women while he was away from me. And I won't do the opposite either!"

"Faithfulness is all very nice," Gadet answered deprecatingly. "But men aren't made that way."

"Perhaps not," Callia answered. "But some of them choose to be, I've seen that. Sir Kirin is a trusted servant of my betrothed, and will still be so after my marriage. I'll not strain his loyalty by trying to seduce him. Besides, I'm not at all sure I would succeed. He's looking for a wife, not a lover, and he cannot become my husband. Dalbai needs this alliance and I will do nothing to jeopardize it."

"How very responsible of you, dear," said Gadet in a disappointed tone.

Later Elina and Callia walked back to her quarters through the hallways, the maids trailing a discrete distance behind. Elina said quietly "I wonder why your mother still keeps Gadet here in the palace, and hasn't exiled her to some provincial city."

"She and Uncle would be harder to watch if they were somewhere else," Callia answered. "And they need watching." Her steps slowed for a moment as realization struck. "And Mother may want her here as a test for us, like Father used her husband to test the young men."

Elina frowned. "I can't decide if I'm angry about being treated that way, or if I admire your mother's cleverness."

Callia's face turned pensive. "Both, I think."

They walked on in silence for a few yards, then Callia added "I'm very glad it's you that will accompany me to Silbar, and twice as glad that it's not Gadet."

"This way I get to be with Vimmal and with you. I'm going to miss you dreadfully when we come back and you have to stay, Callie."

"I'll miss you terribly too. I hope I can find a friend even half as close as you, 'Lina."

Then to herself, Callia thought, *what if I don't? What if I'm alone there?*

~ ~ ~

Chapter 35: Daleray - Kirin

Ninety-fourth day of Summer

Terrell finally touched my mind in the afternoon as I returned from a visit to the *Queen*. I'd borrowed a carriage and had barely settled onto the cushions for the trip back when I heard his voice. It was faint and weak.

You're back! I was getting worried, I scolded him. *Why were you silent all yesterday?*

I did too much, he confessed. *The Hill took more out of me than I thought it would. Dona Seraphina was furious, and beneath that I suspect she was frightened. I agreed to rest for a day, and to limit my use of the Hill for a while. I can't talk long. How is Callia?*

Doing well. This morning she watched while I put her bodyguards through some training, though I don't think she knew I could see her. Queen Sephora is sending her cousin and his wife along for a few months so that even in Silbar she'll still have friends from her old life.

Good. I want to make this marriage as happy for her as I can. I remember how I felt when I arrived in Silbar. If I hadn't had Pen with me it would have been a lot harder. Any new word about our enemies?

Yeah, that bastard Zurtos tried to sabotage the ship. I explained quickly. *We've got her thoroughly guarded now by magic and men, and the rest of the squadron too, so I hope he won't be able to try it again.*

I suspect he's more likely to try something else, Terrell agreed. *He strikes me as an imaginative man fond of springing surprises on his opponents. Thank you for stopping that one.*

His voice sounded fainter and he hadn't opened his mind fully. Worried, I asked him, *Just how much hurt did you take from doing this?*

Nothing I can't recover from. But I've got to go, I don't want Dona Seraphina to get suspicious – more suspicious. I'll contact you again in two days, and then again the day you set sail.

That's only three days from now. The Queen ordered it moved up and everyone's packing furiously. Wait if you need to, Terrell, and be sure you take good care of yourself meantime.

I will.

And he was gone.

I turned his words over in my mind, uneasily recalling the exhaustion that colored his thoughts. But I was glad I hadn't had to explain the rest of yesterday's adventures.

Back at the palace I found Callia dressed in riding clothes and wearing a broad-brimmed hat with a low crown. She beamed at me with a frank happiness that warmed me down to my toes. So alive, so desirable, no wonder my brother was already in love with her.

"Sir Kirin, will you ride with me along the beach?"

"Certainly, Highness."

I had worn one of my practical old tunics and tights for the ship inspections, so I didn't even have to change. She found a well-trained horse for me at the Royal Stables and we were soon clattering down a long stone tunnel to the beach. With forty troops, a Healer and two court mages for escort, of course. I wondered if she ever got to do anything without a mob of guards around her. Though I didn't mind being one of them today; her smile lifted my heart.

The tunnel was lit by tall slits in the outer wall, none more than a foot wide and most of them several feet deep — the route followed the outer side of the Rock as it descended. I craned my neck to look at the rectangular murder holes in the ceiling.

"Cheery place!" I called to her over the echo of a hundred-eighty-four horseshoes on stone.

She gave me a wry grin. "Not very. But worth enduring to get to ride on the beach."

"I'm looking forward to that part." I grinned back.

Soon enough we rode out the bottom end past more guards and onto grassy dunes next to a broad sandy beach. South it narrowed quickly where the outthrust Rock shut it off, but north the white expanse ran for miles. Inland a tall blank wall extended from the end of the Rock, separating beach from city. In places the dunes reached halfway up its height.

The lieutenant commanding the troops issued brisk orders and in moments Callia and I were surrounded by a moving wall of horses and armor. Two court mages and a Dalbai priestess in a divided riding skirt much like Callia's rode behind us. The mages wove protection spells that arched over the whole mob like a translucent blue dome. The tide was retreating so we rode on the hardpacked wet sand just above the water. Foot-high wavelets foamed on our right, grass-covered dunes on our left, and an endless golden expanse unrolled ahead.

"This is beautiful!" I enthused, delighting in the sun and air.

"Have you beaches in Aretzo?" she asked curiously. "Or near it?"

"Outside Southgate there's a large one, though not so pretty nor as long as this," I explained. "Otherwise no, nothing north of the city but marshes right to the mouth of the River Amm. South you have to go past several miles of cliffs to the next beach, and it's not very long either. Most of the coast south of Aretzo is cliffs and rocky islands. But Terrell has a big riding park west of the city, the Palace stables lead right to it. You can ride for miles up into the hills there."

"That would be nice," she sighed, still looking a little sad despite the beautiful day.

I decided to try to draw her out of it. "Where are we riding to, Highness?"

"Uncle Yare's fishing cabin." She waved vaguely ahead. "It's just beyond Fourth Village, on a pier he built for it. Aunt Gadet asked me to make sure his steward isn't drinking up the wine cellar. Apparently the man's become a bit of a problem this year. A shame. Father quite liked taking us all to fish there, at least when Uncle was there with his boys. Aunt hates the place and won't visit it for anything, says it makes her seasick."

"Seasick?" I shot her a questioning look.

Callia merely smiled. "You'll see."

The beach unrolled before us. We passed a tiny village of conical-roofed huts tucked behind the dunes amid a litter of beached boats and excited children, then another and another. Somewhere along the way the wall had disappeared and I caught glimpses of the city set well back behind the dunes. Then that too disappeared and we were miles into the countryside when we reached the fourth fishing village.

"Aha," I said to Callia as enlightenment dawned. "*That's* your uncle's 'fishing cabin.'"

A wild balloon of wood perched on hundreds of spindly pilings driven into the seabed. Balconies and rooms bulged from every side, including the tiny third story. A long narrow bridge of planks held up by more pilings connected it to the land. Gulls soared and danced on the breeze around it and dove for their meals in the shadow of the 'cabin'.

Callia shaded her eyes and gazed at the place as our horses plodded closer. "It looks the same as ever. Uncle Yare's steward has the House pennant raised on the topmost pole, but not his personal pennant, good. If the man's been drinking, at least he's carried out his duties first."

"Let's take that as a good sign." I waved at the structure. "I'm impressed. That thing must have taken as much wood to build as a ship."

She nodded. "Uncle's estates include some of the best lumber on Dalbai, which we're buying from him for the new ships. He didn't spend even one part in fifty of the annual harvest on this. Father thought he was pretty frugal, considering. And Mikkal and I both loved spending days here fishing with Father and Uncle's boys. I think it helped Father to tolerate Uncle's other behaviors."

I winced. "If I lay down on the sand and let you ride your horse over me, would that be enough to prove that I'm sorry?"

She gave me a sideways smile. "Nothing so drastic is required, my Lord Ambassador. I believe you."

I resisted the temptation to say 'that's a relief', which would probably have gotten me right back in trouble. Instead I pointed to a mound of glittering glass on the shore, mingled with the seaweed wrack at the high tide line. "Looks like wine bottles."

The pile was only a few yards away from the start of the long bridge connecting the house to the land. I guessed that they'd simply been dumped off a balcony during the night, without a thought to their probable landing place. Callia directed her horse close enough to see them for herself. A soldier hurriedly climbed down from his own horse, picked up one and poured seawater out, then presented it for her inspection.

"Uncle's best," she reported dismally. "I'm going to have to punish his steward."

"Highness, if you wish, I could carry out that task for you," the guard commander offered.

"No, Lieutenant," she signed. "I let Aunty fob the duty off on me, which was reasonable enough considering she just had a baby a tenday ago. This requires family, and I'm the only one here."

The soldier led her horse to the land end of the wooden bridge, tied it to the railing, and helped her down while the rest of the troop spread out and took up guard positions. I tied my own horse beside hers and one of the mages joined me, carefully scrying around.

"Count Yare left all the defensive spells alert and on guard, Highness," he reported. "None but those keyed into the house can enter."

"Which is another reason that Aunty asked me to do this," Callia sighed. "I'm the only one here who can get in to lower the barrier spell."

The Court Mage gave her a little head bow of deference. "Highness," he said. "It's not my place to question Count Harren, but something in his protection spells doesn't seem to be installed quite right." The other mage, still on his horse, began scrying.

I frowned at the silent house. It was layered with spells, including three different protection spells, two wards, and half a dozen other more specialized things that I could barely make out through the overlays. There was enough that it must require a noticeable bit of silver to power them every day. That seemed like expensive overkill for such a seasonal-use place.

Doubly so when Yare had known he was going away for an extended time, and his wife wasn't likely to visit in his absence.

"You are not the only one who can enter here," I reminded her quietly. "I hope you'll pardon me if I invite myself along? A drunk steward caught red-handed might make himself an uncomfortable nuisance."

She stared at me in surprise, obviously minded to refuse, but something of my unease must have made itself felt. Her guard commander managed to urge her to accept without opening his mouth; I'd seldom seen more eloquent eyebrows. After a moment she nodded to me.

I followed her down the long plank bridge. It had wooden railings on either side and felt secure enough under our feet, but the planks squeaked as we walked. Callia slapped her feet down almost fiercely. I thought she must be nerving herself for the coming confrontation. If the steward had done more than drink, she might have to dismiss him on her uncle's behalf. I moved as lightly as I could.

The waves monotonously washed the shore, intermittently drowning everything else. Gulls screamed and the sea breeze drew a dozen different whistles from the elaborate woodwork. Even so the looming structure seemed disturbingly quiet.

The front door was secured by a simple rotating latch-lock, backed by a triple pile of spells. Callia hesitated. Before she could put out her hand I reached past her to grasp the latch and twist. The spells didn't notice me. The bolt drew back and the door clicked free. I gave it a small push and the carved wood panel creaked open. Then it thumped against something that sent a metallic sound through the house.

"Entry gong," Callia said. She hesitated on the doorstep, squinting into the comparatively dark interior.

I called my Shadow into my eyes, and made the interior as bright as daylight — to me.

The hallway ran back perhaps half the depth of the house, gorgeously carved and painted but otherwise barren. Half a dozen doors and two stairways opened off it.

"Seems empty," I whispered, though I was not sure why when we'd just announced ourselves. "Where's the spell controls?"

"Closet under the second stairway," she answered as quietly.

I nodded and drew my blades. We stepped inside together.

~ ~ ~

Chapter 36: Daleray - Kirin

Ninety-fourth day of Summer

We were in a hallway plenty wide enough for us to walk abreast, but I followed her instead with my blades held ready.

The building creaked constantly in the wind, a soft groaning chorus of wood and nails. The air inside the closed house was stale. It had a faint iron tang like dried blood.

First door on the right was labeled 'storeroom' in Dalbai lettering, the door shut and bolted. First door on the left was open to a large kitchen, where something had spoiled. The next two rooms were dining rooms and their wide doorways had no actual doors in them, just beaded curtains. I glanced into each; the right was elaborately decorated, the left plainer with a 'servants dining room' look. Their window curtains had been drawn to protect the fancy carpets from fading. The beaded curtains stirred slightly as we passed.

The first stairway appeared on the right, a grand affair folding upward through dimly-lit space. Dust motes swirled there in a vagrant breeze, from the sea scent I suspected an open window somewhere above. Beyond it another open door led to what looked like a man's study, with comfortable chairs, trophies on the walls, and a suit of armor on a stand in one corner. A door in the far wall must lead to one of the balconies.

The sixth opening proved to be just a dogleg for the hallway, dodging around the second stairwell. That was a more utilitarian flight that practically shouted 'servant's stair'. A narrow nook held the short door that served the dead space under the steps.

The perfect place to get trapped.

I gestured silently to Callia. She moved slowly towards the little door, the oppressive air of the place weighing on her spirits too. The sooner she could lower the spells and admit the rest of her guards to this house, the better. I took up station facing the hallway, trying to watch both branches and the stairwell at the same time.

She opened the closet door. I caught a glimpse from the corner of my eye of a nested set of glowing blue spell crystals.

Then something hurtled down the stairs with a banshee shriek.

I met it with my sword and my Shadow. It expired in a burst of spilled Power; some sort of construct, noisy but impotent against me, more of a distraction than a threat.

Distraction –

I swung too late and missed the assassin's dart.

~ ~ ~

Callia opened the closet door. The silver-wrapped crystals that held the house wards glowed normally. She had just started to furl the guardian spell when something came shrieking down the stairs above. She ducked into the too-small closet as Sir Kirin moved against the thing. A moment later a dart scratched her thigh before thumping into the open closet door. Its needle-nose stuck in the wood, dripping.

Drugged! She felt the creeping numbness in her leg. She squeezed herself into the tight space to give the assassin as little target as possible while she sent her Diagnosis into the wound. *Poisoned!* Her Healing aura followed, grappled with the spreading toxin. The numb patch on her thigh grew.

~ ~ ~

I knocked his second dart aside. A man had come down the grand stairway behind us, I could see the familiar outline of Zurtos's assassin-slave crouched behind the balustrade.

"Beware – he's using poison!" Callia told me.

I hurled my Shadow at the man even as another construct screamed down the stairs above. I killed it and realized that I couldn't charge at the assassin without exposing Callia to the mage upstairs – and I couldn't move on him without letting the assassin get a clear shot at her.

~ ~ ~

Callia grabbed the guardian spell control and twisted to shut it down. She wanted as many of her Mother's men around her as fast as possible. Then she furled the other spells in rapid succession. The glowing crystals obediently winked out, but her magesight showed the house spells still in force.

"The spells didn't shut down! These controls aren't working!" she told Sir Kirin while the numb place on her leg grew bigger.

~ ~ ~

"Salim take the bastards," I swore as I knocked a third dart out of the air unpleasantly close to my face. The assassin was firing blind into my Shadow now but still dangerous. "They've taken control of the house. I can turn that back on them." My Shadow started to grope for the ward spells even as I sent it at the assassin.

~ ~ ~

The darts stopped flying and Callia heard pounding feet on the other stairwell. She hoped that meant the assassin had fled. Prudently she stayed crammed into the closet until she could be sure it was true. The already dim light faded further as Sir Kirin's Shadow plugged the stairs above.

Then red light sheeted into the hallway from the windows of the study and dining rooms, and she realized what else the enemy mage had under his control.

~ ~ ~

I wanted to call myself ten kinds of stupid when the outside of the house lit up like a torch. There wasn't time for that so I sent my Shadow through the walls and floors to bite the protection spell that was being twisted into a fire spell. Maybe I could kill it before the wood had time to catch.

I almost succeeded. Parts of the fire died, but not enough of it. The study's balcony was burning and the front door burst into flames on the inside. I could hear roaring crackles from elsewhere too. I sheathed my sword and grabbed Callia's hand.

"We've got to get out before the whole place goes!"

"Fire burns up, so we need to go down!" she yelled back. "There's a hatch in the kitchen floor!"

We hurried through rising heat and only then did her stumbling reveal that she'd been hit.

"Highness?" I fought panic. If the poison was very strong or fast-acting I had no hope of getting her to the Healer in time.

"I can delay it!" she panted as we stumbled into the kitchen. "I think."

I slammed the door shut behind us just as the hall carpet caught fire. Lurid light danced through the kitchen windows, they'd surely burst any moment. Callia showed me the ring bolt set in the kitchen floor. I sheathed my knife, grabbed the bolt with both hands and heaved even as I set my Shadow tearing at the spells on the hatch. They died with gratifying speed and the wood groaned as I dragged it open.

Dim sunlight reflected up off the water below. The sea was more than my own height's distance below the floor. How deep? No time to do anything but risk it. I helped her sit on the edge.

"Let me go first, then I'll catch you." I swung myself down, hung by my hands from the edge, and dropped, praying there wouldn't be anything sharp in the dark water.

My heels plunged through the surface and hit sand when I was waist deep. I caught my balance and beckoned Callia to me. She dropped through just as the kitchen windows exploded above. I managed to keep her head above water.

"I'll carry you," I told her as the floor over our heads began to smoke. Her face was a rictus as she gritted her teeth and closed her eyes. Both hands clutched at her wound with glowing yellow fingers; the poison must be painful but she didn't cry out.

I slogged toward the shore while I shielded us by sending my Shadow to plaster the planks overhead. It couldn't quell the flames but it would at least hide her from Zurtos. The wet sand and moving waves alternately tried to snag my feet and push me over. I got past the fire and under the bridge hoping we might hide a little longer. I'd barely put the burning house behind us when a powerful current started to move the sea. The water was still almost waist deep here and the damned current nearly dragged us out from under the bridge. I held onto her and hooked one leg around a piling. Barnacles bit through my hose and my skin as the swirling flood dragged at us.

Then the ocean rose up and smacked the burning house. Sooty water gushed everywhere and for a moment I thought we'd both drown. I had to let her legs drop so I could grab the piling with an arm too, half crushing her against me as I fought the mad currents.

Finally the water settled back where it belonged. The house billowed steam and smoke.

Callia got her feet back under her, spit water and coughed. "Ayello's work," she pointed to the court mage we'd left on the beach. He was still busy drowning the fire, obviously afraid we were inside. Meanwhile his compatriot hurled spells at the sky.

Something smashed a hole in the bridge a few feet away from us. Splinters stung my arm and bounced off the back of my piling. I peered through the hole and caught a glimpse of Zurtos's carpet hovering a hundred feet or more above. He must be guessing where we were. He wasn't even fighting the Dalbai mage, just shedding the man's spells.

I hurled a Shadow at the bastard's carpet.

The range was long but even so I nearly got him. His carpet barely dodged aside and I heard his assassin shriek and saw the man's legs flounder off the fabric's edge.

Zurtos sent another smashing blow at the wood above our heads. By then I had wrapped it in my Shadow and simply ate the attack. The Court Mage, confused, stopped attacking Zurtos and wasted a spell on my Shadow as well. That left him distracted when the carpet sped away.

I scooped Callia up and staggered through the waves to the beach. A couple troopers were still shooting useless arrows into the sky but others rushed into the water and helped us to shore. I shrugged off an attempt to take her from my arms until the priestess arrived and began to heal her wound.

"Set her on the sand," the woman ordered me. "Hold her head up, don't let her lie down."

I knelt and propped Callia into a sitting-up position against me. The priestess was knowledgeable and fast, she muttered and her aura glowed bright as she worked. Callia stared up at my face from a few fingerwidths away. Her eyes were a beautiful deep brown. I could have gotten lost in them if she hadn't been in such pain. All I could do was hold her in anguished sympathy. My mind lashed me for being tricked by Zurtos.

The agonized lines in her face gradually smoothed out. Her grip on my hand relaxed from terrified to simply needing comfort. She nestled against my chest, vulnerable as a little girl.

Time moved very slowly on that sandy beach.

At last the priestess broke into a pleased smile and withdrew her aura. "Done!" It was the best word I'd heard in a year.

"Do you think you can ride a horse?" I asked Callia.

"Slowly," she nodded. "Will you help me? I don't think I can mount by myself."

I picked her up. She wasn't light, but no great burden either as I lifted her into her saddle. Two of her men held her while I mounted my own horse, then we all rode carefully back to the Daleray Palace with me on Callia's right and the Priestess on her left.

~ ~ ~

Chapter 37: Daleray – Zurtos; Kirin

Ninety-fourth day of Summer

The carpet wobbled dangerously as Zurtos drove it along one of the sinuous channels branching into the vast marshland. The mage couldn't spare the attention needed to fix it in flight, not while also maintaining a concealment spell. He was relieved to find the tiny shack they'd rented on an islet in the marsh completely deserted. Wonder of wonders, the little boat they'd rented was still there too.

"Pack everything in the boat. We move to Beliat's ship immediately," Zurtos ordered, fuming.

I had her! I'd have killed her three times over, if only that thrice-cursed Shadowmage hadn't interfered!

His slave bowed and quickly loaded their possessions into two bags. Zurtos repaired the carpet's spells and then rolled it up and stowed it in the boat. Jos hoisted the bags in and tied them in place too, then the wiry slave looked apprehensively around the empty islet. He cleared his throat and dared a question.

"Master? Do you think they've traced us to this hiding place, Master?" He peered left and right as if expecting phalanxes of City Constables to appear right out of the reeds.

Zurtos shook his head; he already had watch spells set out and ready. "Not yet, but they'll be trying, may the Twelve-Horned God curse them with pox and boils! We can't wait for the moon tide tonight. We must be out of this trap of a harbor before sunset."

Jos obediently took up the pole while his master sat on the bags. They pushed off and the slave sent the little boat gliding through the channels. Zurtos cast a disguise spell over both of them, just in case, though they were dressed in unremarkable Dalbai clothing. He kept a poisoned dart at hand and a constriction spell at the ready, just in case he had to deal with trouble.

Unlikely, he knew, seething inside. *The Dalbais are very clever but not the most decisive. So long as we move fast, we'll probably escape.* He blew a pinch of kruff over the water to placate his god, and prayed he had moved fast *enough.*

Channels led to channels and a few scattered punts became crowds of boats at the riverside. Nobody paid attention to them. Nonetheless he held his vigilance until they drew up next to Beliat's *Falcon* and hastily loaded everything aboard.

"Cast off," Zurtos told the Klinto captain tightly.

Beliat had the mother-wit to ask no questions. He called in the two of his sailors lounging on the dock and put all five of his men to work. In scant minutes *Falcon* had left the dock behind and they were making their way downriver toward the Rock.

The Klinto cast a skeptical eye at Zurtos between watching the river-traffic.

"You don't have the air of a happy man," he remarked.

Zurtos growled in his throat.

"So." Beliat nodded, his pointed Klinto ears hidden under a hat. "I take it we leave a living princess behind us. What next?"

"The seed I planted with our traitor has had time to put out roots into fertile ground. We go to see what might have grown." Zurtos's teeth flashed in the sun. "It's time to move this game to where the odds will be in our favor. At sea."

Beliat nodded again, turned his attention back to the river. He had both jib sails set and the little sloop skated lively over the churning river. The Rock loomed ahead and the free sea beyond it.

~ ~ ~

Dismayed servants had taken charge of Callia. When her mother arrived she had questioned me and everyone else, then sighed in relief and went to sit with her daughter.

I excused myself and practically ran to the fortress atop the Rock. I'd met the commander earlier, he recognized and welcomed me. I managed minimal courtesy, told him what had happened, reassured him that his princess was unharmed and would recover, and begged him to take me to the parapet overlooking the river.

The man was no fool. He immediately led the way, asking no questions until we reached the grim basalt rampart. Huge catapults crouched there manned by twelve-man crews, and mages stood ready to send messages to the picket galleys that endlessly patrolled off the river mouth.

"You have magesight, my Lord Ambassador?" The commander asked me in an elaborately casual voice. He must have heard every rumor about me that had made it to Dalbai.

"Yes. I'm hoping . . ." I leaned over the wall. It had no crenellations, archers firing from up here were safe from return fire. Neither was it very thick. I could see most of the river for miles upstream and down, save the stretch at the very foot of the Rock itself. I could hope Zurtos wouldn't be nervy enough to pass so close. It was late afternoon and the tide hadn't yet turned. The big ships would be waiting for it so that they didn't have to fight the turbulent currents at the river mouth. Maybe the smaller ships would wait too?

I craned my neck and swept my gaze up and down the river below. Then I silently cursed my luck. There were at least a dozen smaller ships in motion. I called my Shadow into my eyes and began to study them one by one.

Two fishing boats headed out, neither with enough magic on board to matter. A sloop glowed with guard spells and I wasted precious seconds examining it before I realized it was sailing the wrong way. A couple shiny blue-painted ketches worked their way towards the sea and each boasted the glows of significant mages on their decks. Both men were working the winds to keep their crafts safe from the turbulence, and neither man was Zurtos. An older ketch wallowed along in their wakes, heavily loaded, but with only a modest glow below deck. I decided the spell was cargo and its flavor was all wrong for Zurtos, and sought the next. And the next. And the next. I was looking half a mile up the river now and straining my eyes. I stopped to wait for more ships, glanced back at the fortress commander –

And from the corner of my eye saw a sloop scoot out from under the shadow of the Rock, breast the turbulence and sail out into the ocean. She had two jib sails set and as I watched a big gaff sail rose and filled. On her deck a familiar mage glowed in my eyes. He was already beyond the distance that I could throw my Shadow.

"Salim take it!" I swore and pointed. "Commander, that's the mage who just tried to murder Princess Callia! I recognize his aura!"

It took precious minutes to explain, to get him to see the right ship, to persuade him that he should order it seized. Minutes in which Zurtos's sloop dodged both galleys and raced out into the bay. One of the fortress mages tried to throw a tracer spell on it but Zurtos broke that. The nearer galley received the commander's message construct and tried to pursue. That was useless, the sloop was built for speed and quickly lost her. Nothing available in the anchorage was big enough to fight the enemy and fast enough to catch them, or even ready to sail.

I pounded my fists on the stone in frustration. Then I went to tell Queen Sephora that her daughter's attempted assassin had just escaped.

~ ~ ~

It was late that night when I finally gave up trying to sleep and crawled back out of the luxurious bed. A breeze through my suite's open window offered welcome coolness. I leaned on the high sill and stared out over the Palace's night-dark rooftops to the sea. Calm had already passed out of sight overhead. Madness sank toward the horizon, drawing a ghostly path across the waters.

Queen Sephora had heard me out in Callia's room. Just being invited in there made me nervous. Is there anything more frightening than a princess's bedroom?

Callia lay wrapped in a big blanket and curled up on her bed. Her mother sat beside her. I bowed deeply and recited my news, my legs apart, my back spear-straight, and my hands clasped behind me. I almost wished Queen Sephora would blame me for losing Zurtos, but she didn't. Instead she thanked me for saving her daughter.

"My duty, Your Majesty," I croaked, embarrassed and glad of the damn codpiece on my tights. My eyes had wandered to Callia's face, still shadowed by recent pain and sleepy with exhaustion. Such a perfect face . . . perfect everything. She smiled a wan smile of thanks at me as well and I must have blushed red as a beetroot. There was no reason in the world that I should find that smile intensely arousing.

I had managed to excuse myself and scamper away. Dinner was a tormented meal in the small dining room, where Palace officials came to eat magnificent food that none of us tasted. Several of them got up the nerve to thank me too, after which they wanted to hear my version of what had happened. I escaped into the garden as soon as I decently could and wore myself out striding up and down the grid of paths at a speed greater than a walk and less than a run. Tonight's entertainment had been cancelled but nobody else sought a quiet walk. Or maybe nobody dared disturb me.

Now I leaned on my room's windowsill and gazed unseeing over stone and waves. There was no Terrell in my mind to bury me in his own desire, and still the memory of Callia's touch was wine and song. As it had been for my brother. But these were my sensations now.

I . . . crave my brother's betrothed.

I want her.

The strength of it shook me. Somewhere outside a nightingale trilled achingly sweet notes. I hurt from crotch to scalp.

No! This must be some leftover from him. These can't be my feelings. Damnit, I need to – I wish – Holy Haroun on a crutch!

I made myself breathe deep, five breaths, ten, twenty, and during each one I fought my traitor loins for control. At last I went to my dresser, poured water into the bowl and dunked my face. Holding my breath for whole minutes finally helped me win through to a fragile calm. I shook my head and mopped my face with a luxurious towel.

This is just some passing fancy, I told myself. *It's just triggered by me letting Terrell use my senses. It'll go away.*

I'll get over it.

I will!

Madness sank into the ocean and winked out. I saluted the dark night with a rude gesture and went back to bed, all the while telling myself, *These aren't really my feelings at all.*

And knew, somewhere deep inside, that I lied.

Cast of Characters

DiUmbra Family

(Note – Umbra was a city on the coastal plain that was drowned thousands of years ago when the sea rose. The family traces its lineage to there, and the right to use the noble-male 'Di' prefix derives from that ancient connection.)

Kirin Sule DiUmbra – Age 25, adopted son of Pieter Ille DiUmbra (deceased), husband of Maia Sule DiUmbra (deceased), father of Grigor Sule DiUmbra (missing); real name Ryghar DuRillin DiGwythlo, twin brother of Terrell (elder by two minutes). After Maia's death he stopped using Sule as his middle name.

Sevan Sule DiUmbra (Sevan the Younger) – Age 26, older brother of Maia Sule DiUmbra & Attir Sule DiUmbra, son of Sevan Sule (nee Ille) DiUmbra & Carmella Sule DiUmbra (nee Sabior). Kirin DiUmbra's brother-in-law. Married to Carlai, one daughter, two boys.

Carlai Sule DiUmbra – Age 25, wife of Sevan the Younger and mother of Marli, sister-in-law of Kirin DiUmbra.

Marli Sule DiUmbra – Age 7, daughter of Sevan the Younger and Carlai, niece to Kirin..

Sevan Sule (nee Ille) DiUmbra (Sevan the Elder) – Age 50, father of Sevan the Younger, Maia, and Attir; son of Grigor Ille DiUmbra (a/k/a Grandfather) & Milli Ille DiUmbra (nee Bidorian) (a/k/a Grandmother), husband of Carmella, older brother of Pieter (and a sister who is not named in these stories).

Gerghar Sorle (nee Sule) DiUmbra (Uncle Ger) – Age 49, eldest son of the younger brother of Grigor Ille (nee Sorle) DiUmbra, father of 3 sons (Habbir, Mellar, Berrin) and 2 daughters (one married, not a part of this story). Married to Silla Sorle DiUmbra (nee Nunes).

Attir Sule DiUmbra – Age 24, younger brother of Maia Sule DiUmbra & Sevan Sule DiUmbra, son of Sevan Sule (nee Ille) DiUmbra & Carmella Sule DiUmbra (nee Sabior). Kirin DiUmbra's brother-in-law.

Habbir Sorle DiUmbra – Age 23, eldest son of Uncle Ger and Aunt Silla, cousin to Kirin DiUmbra.

Other Silbaris

Sir Penghar DuVerhys DiLione (Pen) - Age 25, Baron, bodyguard to Prince Terrell.

Irreneetha – a magic sword inhabited by an angel. Also the name of the angel.

Prince Terrell DuRillin DiGwythlo – Age 25, Prince (King) of Silbar, son of Emperor Brion ob Gwythford and Queen-Empress Shyrill DuRillin DiGwythlo (nee DiSilbari), twin brother of Ryghar DuRillin DiGwythlo (a/k/a Kirin DiUmbra).

Ymera – Age 250+?, Baroness and Madam of the Red Street.

Gellir DuTallisen DiMaratini – Age 26, Royal Secretary to Prince Terrell.

Urhys Snowdon – Age 40, Royal Exchequer (Treasurer) of the Silbari Treasury.

Aytin D'Ivor Cervisi – Age 60, Archmage of Silbar and chairman of the Aretzo Council of Colors.

Admiral DiRovigo – Age 68, Flag Admiral of the Silbari Navy.

Dona Seraphina DuVigo Abnellambra – Age 70, Dona and Hectissima of the Temple Hierarchy, Healer and Confessor to Prince Terrell.

Hainin – Age 19, personal secretary to his grandmother Dona Seraphina DuVigo Abnellambra.

Dona Celestina Marate DiBelluno – Age 50, Superior of the Holy Mission.

Dona Fenecia Crasset Demorian – Age 71, Hierarch of the Faith.

Dona Meltha D'Ivor DiMun – Age 24, personal secretary to the Hierarch.

Dona Seelie DuVigo D'Isernia – Age 28, Priestess in the Silbari Temple Hierarchy, granddaughter of Dona Seraphina DuVigo Abnellambra, Healer for *the Queen of the Seas.*

Captain Witt Raisch D'Auson – Age 42, Captain of *The Queen of the Seas.*

Captain Morgin D'Ille Velis – Age 47, Captain of the Silbari Navy ship *Waverunner.*

Burlen Crasset DiMosil (Mage White) – Age 38, a member of the Council of Colors that rules the Aretzo Mageguild, also senior Ship's Mage for *Waverunner* and then *the Queen of the Seas.*

Rellir – Age 44, secondary Ship's Mage for *Waverunner* and then *the Queen of the Seas.*

Arlein – Age 48, tertiary Ship's Mage for *Waverunner* and then *the Queen of the Seas.*

Pallir D'Ibarra Viettar – Age 28, Lieutenant and commander of the Marines aboard *Waverunner* and then *the Queen of the Seas.*

Aymis – Age 45, Helmsman for *Waverunner* and then *the Queen of the Seas.*

Sains – Age 37, Bosun for *Waverunner* and then *the Queen of the Seas.*

Cassaret – Age 45, First Mate for *Waverunner* and then *the Queen of the Seas.*

DiPoer – Age 40, Second Mate for *Waverunner* and then *the Queen of the Seas.*

Dona Millente – Age 51, Priestess for *Waverunner.*

Lieutenant Connir Crebinet – Age 29, commander of Marines for *Waverunner.*

Sargent Collimi – Age 56, Sargent of Silbari Marines on *the Queen of the Seas.*

Fantillin – Age 65, Mayordomo and senior servant of the Royal Household in the Aretzo Palace.

Mage Blue – Age 66, Chairman of the Council of Colors (Aretzo Mage Guild governing body).

Mage Orange – Age 65, Member of the Council of Colors (Aretzo Mage Guild governing body).

Mage Red – Age 62, Member of the Council of Colors (Aretzo Mage Guild governing body).

Mage Black – Age 56, Member of the Council of Colors (Aretzo Mage Guild governing body).

Dalbai People

Princess Callia Abn Serziza – Age 19, third child and second daughter of Queen Sephora of Dalbai, betrothed to Prince Terrell.

Dona Catalona DuVigo Abnell– Age 38, missionary priestess of Silbar assigned to teach language to Princess Callia.

Princess Gadet– Age 34, Aunt to Callia, sister to Callia's father, wife of Count Yare.

Count Yare Abn Harren– Age 38, Dalbai noble and Uncle to Princess Callia.

Queen Sephora Abn Serziza – Age 46, ruling Queen of Dalbai, mother of Alliet and Callia.

Princess Alliet Abn Serziza – Age 22, second child and eldest daughter of Queen Sephora of Dalbai, heir to the Dalbai Throne.

Junia – Age 22, servant to Princess Callia.

Sharme – Age 40, servant to Princess Callia.

Aber Peng – Age 24, Dalbai Royal Guardsman.

Dal Morengal – Age 27, Dalbai Royal Guardsman.

Benor – Age 25, Dalbai Royal Guardsman.

Girr – Age 26, Dalbai Royal Guardsman.

Other Characters

Dameon Zurtos – Age 38, mage and agent of the foreign
    power Xiphree.

Jos – Age 46, assassin and slave to Zurtos.

Beliat – Age 34, Captain in the Klinto Navy, captain of the
    sloop *Falcon*.

King Revallix of Xiphree – Age 26, last survivor of the
    Xiphree Royal House

www.ingramcontent.com/pod-product-compliance
Lightning Source LLC
Chambersburg PA
CBHW022139010726
47493CB00002B/264